Joan[...] [...]er in
1994[...]anna
has gained a worldwide following with her cutting-edge
romantic suspense and Texas family series, such as Sons
of Troy Lee[...] and Big "D" Dads. Joanna currently
resides in a small community north of Houston, Texas,
with her husband. You may write Joanna at PO Box 852,
Montgomery, TX 77356, USA or connect with her at
www.joannawayne.com.

USA TODAY bestselling author **Barb Han** lives in north
Texas with her very own hero-worthy husband, three
beautiful children, a spunky golden retriever/standard
poodle mix and too many books in her to-read pile. In
her downtime, she plays video games and spends much
of her time on or around a basketball court. She loves
interacting with readers and is grateful for their support.
You can reach her at www.barbhan.com.

Also by Joanna Wayne

Riding Shotgun
Quick-Draw Cowboy
Fearless Gunfighter
Dropping the Hammer
Trumped Up Charges
Unrepentant Cowboy
Hard Ride to Dry Gulch
Midnight Rider
Showdown at Shadow Junction
Ambush at Dry Gulch

Also by Barb Han

Sudden Setup
Stockyard Snatching
Delivering Justice
One Tough Texan
Texas-Sized Trouble
Texas Witness
Texas Showdown
Texas Prey
Texas Takedown
Texas Hunt

Discover more at millsandboon.co.uk

DROPPING
THE HAMMER

JOANNA WAYNE

SUDDEN SETUP

BARB HAN

MILLS & BOON

First Published in Great Britain 2018
by Mills & Boon, an imprint of HarperCollins*Publishers*
1 London Bridge Street, London, SE1 9GF

Dropping The Hammer © 2018 Jo Ann Vest
Sudden Setup © 2018 Barb Han

ISBN: 978-0-263-26568-2

39-0418

MIX
Paper from
responsible sources
FSC™ C007454

This book is produced from independently certified FSC™ paper to ensure responsible forest management.

For more information visit: www.harpercollins.co.uk/green

Printed and bound in Spain

DROPPING THE HAMMER

JOANNA WAYNE

To the people in southeast Texas who not only survived Hurricane Harvey but showed amazing gusto in pitching in to help friends and absolute strangers who suffered devastating losses. And to the people around the state, country and the world who supported the relief efforts with their time, money and prayers. Your spirit of love and caring will never be forgotten.

Prologue

Death screamed, echoing shrilly through Rachel Maxwell's brain as Roy Sales's large, meaty hands tightened around her throat. His powerful body was stretched on top of hers, pinning her to her bed.

Her chest burned. She couldn't breathe. She was losing consciousness as fear clawed at her insides, tearing her apart bit by bloody bit. Even as life slipped away, her heart persisted, throbbing erratically.

"Don't worry, sweet Rachel. I won't let you die if you do what I say."

His maniacal laugh crawled inside her as his grip on her throat slowly eased. She coughed, choking as oxygen fought its way back into her lungs.

"Bucking against me is futile, sweetheart. I'll never let you go. You belong to me. You always will. You know you want it that way."

"Let me go," she pleaded, her voice dry and scratchy, little more than a whisper. "Please, let me go."

"That's the way, baby. Keep begging."

She closed her eyes tight so that she didn't have to see the evil that darkened his eyes. Pleading wouldn't help. He was heartless, devoid of compassion, his deranged soul as black as the depths of the deepest cave.

She writhed and twisted beneath him, finally getting her right arm free. She fisted her hand and swung wildly.

Blunt pain met her knuckles. There was a crash. She cried out in pain as blood splattered her face and dripped through her fingers.

She managed a scream. Loud. Shrill.

Her body stiffened and she kicked wildly, her feet tangling in the sheets as she escaped his grasping hands. Still screaming, she jerked into wakefulness—not to the sound of her cries, but to her cell phone's alarm.

Rachel gulped scratchy clumps of air. It was only a nightmare. She was in her own apartment. Alone. Safe.

She fumbled to turn off the alarm. Her phone was wet. Her hands were damp and clammy, but with water, not the blood she'd imagined in the clutches of the terrifying nightmare.

She'd evidently knocked over the glass of water she'd left on the bedside table. The dizziness and cold, hard terror began to subside as she dried her phone on the corner of the sheet.

She stretched her feet out in front of her, staring at the shadows that crawled across the wall in the faint glow of sunrise. She was safe and yet the horror of being kidnapped and held in captivity by the psychopath persisted along with anxiety attacks and sudden bouts of panic.

Something as routine as a strange man walking too close behind her in downtown Houston in broad daylight could set her off. Or a man approaching in the office parking lot. Or even the creepy feeling that someone was watching her when she got out of her car at night.

She had to get her act together and move past her own trauma. But even fully awake and in the safety of her own bedroom, she could feel killing fingers at her throat, choking the life from her.

She could sense danger deep in her soul.

Chapter One

Three months later

"Good morning, Miss Maxwell."

The firm's receptionist smiled as Rachel walked through the double glass doors of their fifteenth-floor office.

"You're here early this morning, Carrie," Rachel said.

"Yes, but it may be the first time I've ever arrived before you. Sometimes I think you sleep here."

"I've been tempted."

"Mr. Fitch Sr. beat you in this morning, too. He said to have you stop by his office when you arrived."

"Did he say why?"

"No, but I got the idea it's important."

Everything was important to Eric Fitch Sr. He had a controlling hand over everything that went on in this firm.

Rachel stopped by her office, shrugged out of her light gray overcoat and put it and her handbag away before heading to Eric's office.

His door was ajar. She tapped on it and he stood and motioned her inside.

"Carrie said you needed to see me?"

"Yes. It's going to be a very busy and hopefully productive day. If you have any appointments that aren't urgent, you'll need to cancel them."

"Sounds serious. What's up?"

"We have a potential very high-profile case I'd like to discuss with you."

Rachel couldn't imagine why he wanted to discuss that with her. She took the chair that faced his desk. He sat down again and leaned back in his oversize leather chair.

"Who's the defendant?" she asked.

"Hayden Covey. I suppose you've heard that he was arrested last night."

"It was breaking news on my phone alerts this morning." She was certain almost everyone in the state had heard by now.

Hayden was a student at University of Texas who'd allegedly brutally murdered his girlfriend days after she'd broken up with him.

He was also the only son of a popular and very influential state senator married to an extremely rich heiress.

The victim was Louann Black, nineteen years old, also a student at the university. Though not as wealthy and influential as the Coveys, her family was well-known in the Austin music circuit.

Hayden had written several songs for big-name performers and frequently performed around town himself in popular music venues.

This would likely be the trial of the decade in Texas.

"Do you think Hayden is innocent?" Rachel asked.

"He claims to be and I know his parents believe him."

"Most parents do, though the evidence against him looks extremely damaging."

"But not ironclad," Eric said. "A top-notch defense attorney could win the case."

"Then coming to you was a good decision," Rachel said. "Few would argue that you're not the top defense attorney in the South."

"But maybe not the best man to defend Hayden. I'll be honest with you, Rachel. Senator Covey and I have been close friends since our law school days at UT. I've known Hayden since he was born. He's a great kid."

"He's twenty," Rachel reminded him. "Not exactly a kid."

"That's true. He's turned into a fine young man with a great life and a pro football career in front of him. He's one of the top college running backs in the country and he's only a junior."

"Even great athletes commit crimes."

"Yes, but he's never been in trouble except for one unfortunate arrest last year for roughing up another student after an altercation at a bar near the university. Several witnesses said the victim was at fault."

According to the media over the last few days, those witnesses were Hayden's friends and the *roughing up* was a vicious attack that sent an unsuspecting underclassman to the hospital with a broken jaw and a serious concussion from repeated kicks to the head.

That was nothing compared to the brutality of the attack that killed his former girlfriend.

"Considering how my friendship with the senator

might negatively influence the jury, I'm not sure I'm the best one to officially lead Hayden's defense."

"Good point," she agreed, though she was certain he'd be a strong behind-the-scenes force in the case no matter who was the lead attorney of record.

"Luckily, the firm has several top-notch criminal defense attorneys," she noted.

"Yes, which makes this a tough decision. But I talked with my son and Edward last evening. We all three believe that you're the best choice for the job."

She stared at him, stunned by his words. "You mean as lead attorney?"

"Yes, though you'll have full backing from the firm and all the assistance you require. But you'll deliver the opening and closing statements and handle the press."

She'd worked her butt off for an opportunity like this ever since she started with the firm right after law school. But she was certain her performance had fallen off over the last few months. She tried harder than ever, but she had trouble concentrating and dealing with the never-ending panic attacks.

"Why me?" she asked.

"I've discussed it with my partners. We all agree that you have exactly the qualities needed for this trial. You're not only capable and thorough, you read the jury as well as or better than any attorney with the firm. You proved that time and time again."

"I've never headed up a high-profile like this."

"No, but you've demonstrated that you know your way around a courtroom. You won't be intimidated by a judge or daunted by the best the district attorney can hurl at you."

A year ago that might have been the case. Now she wasn't convinced she could navigate through all the brutal murder evidence and still stay on her game.

She'd only been a team member on the case they'd just tried and won, but even looking at the photos of a young female victim attacked in an elevator at her workplace had brought on an increase in Rachel's nightmares and a heightened anxiety level.

Her career had been her life, but it seemed to be turning on her. She definitely couldn't handle a murder case unless she was totally convinced of the defendant's innocence. "I appreciate the confidence, but—"

"I know it will be your biggest challenge to date," Fitch interrupted. "We think you're ready for it."

She stared into space as she let his statement sink in. What-ifs stormed her mind. What if she wasn't up to it? What if she wasn't convinced of Hayden Covey's innocence? What if she had a meltdown in front of the jury? If that happened in a case this high profile, it would be the end of her career.

Eric stood, walked to the front of his desk and stared down at her, his gaze intent, intimidating. "This case is very important to me and to the firm, Rachel. We've stood beside you and supported you in every way we could since your unfortunate incident. Now I'm asking for you to deliver. Don't let me down."

Don't let him down.

The tone and stance made it clear his words were a warning. This was more than an offer. It was a demand.

"I understand," she said.

"Good. Then I've made myself clear."

"Perfectly clear. When do I meet the defendant?" she asked, though she hadn't officially agreed to take the assignment. Ordinarily, the firm granted attorneys that privilege. This time that didn't appear to be the case.

"Hayden and his parents will be here this morning at ten," Fitch said. "I'll also sit in on that first meeting."

"I expected that you would. Is that all for now?"

"Yes, except that I should warn you that Hayden's mother, Claire, is in a distraught state. I hope you can give her full confidence in the defense we'll provide for her son."

"I'll do as much as I honestly can." Honestly was the key word in Rachel's mind.

Eric Fitch Sr. had gotten what he wanted. He stood, then smiled and nodded, acknowledging his win.

Rachel was getting the career boost she'd worked so hard for, the opportunity to make a name for herself and vastly improve her chance of being named at least a junior partner one day soon.

So why did she feel the almost overwhelming desire to tell Eric Fitch he could take this job and shove it?

Chapter Two

Luke Dawkins nudged his worn Stetson back on his head and took a long, hard look at the rusting metal gate. Arrowhead Hills Ranch was carved into the weathered wooden sign along with two imprints of arrowheads.

The last time he'd laid eyes on that gate, he'd seen it through the rearview mirror of the beat-up red pickup truck that he'd bought with money he'd earned working at the local feed and tack shop. That had been eleven years ago, when he was eighteen.

The rickety ranch gate seemed the same. Luke wasn't. *You Can't Go Home Again.* Thomas Wolfe had known his stuff. The home might not change. The person who'd left would.

A few years of bouncing from job to job followed by eight years in the military had turned Luke into a man, yet he still dreaded returning to the place he'd once called home.

A small Texas Hill Country town with a lot more cows than people, more barbwire than roads and some of the best ranch land in the state.

All Luke had against the town or the ranch could be

summed up in two words. Alfred Dawkins. Stubborn. Controlling. Bitter. Downright ornery.

The poor excuse for a father wouldn't like having Luke home again any more than Luke wanted to be here.

Neither of them had a lot of choice in the matter.

The old defiant angers festered in Luke's gut as he climbed out of his new double-cab pickup truck and stepped around a mud hole.

His boots scooted across the cattle gap as he un-latched and opened the gate before getting back into his truck and driving through it the way he'd done hundreds of times as a rebellious teenager.

He paused and took in the sights and sounds before he closed the gate behind him. A barking dog, though it wouldn't be Ace, the golden retriever he'd raised from a pup. Ace had died from a rattlesnake bite when he jumped between Luke and the striking snake.

Luke had been fourteen then. His dad had scorned him for shedding a few tears. Nothing new. Luke had never measured up in his dad's mind. Just one of the many reasons Luke had never looked back once he left Arrowhead Hills Ranch.

A crow scolded Luke from high in the branches of a nearby live oak. A horse neighed.

Luke looked to the left and spotted a couple of chest-nut mares giving him the once-over. So his dad still kept horses. Good to know.

It had been years since Luke was in the saddle. His consecutive tours in the Middle East hadn't allowed much time for revisiting the cowboy lifestyle.

It was shirtsleeve weather, warm for late January,

but a bracing breeze rustled the tall yellow strands of grass and the leaves in a persimmon tree that hugged the fence.

Luke closed the gate, climbed back into his truck and drove toward the old house. He had no idea what to expect or what kind of health his father had been in before he suffered the stroke that had led to his being placed in a rehab facility.

Significantly weakened on the left side of his body now and with difficulty putting his thoughts into coherent sentences, he was unable to take care of himself, much less the ranch.

Not that Luke had originally gotten that information firsthand. It was Esther Kavanaugh, a longtime neighbor who'd been his mother's best friend before her death, who'd called with the SOS. Luke had followed up with Alfred's doctor and the rehab center.

So here he was, back in Winding Creek.

The brown roof appeared as he rounded a curve in the dirt ranch road. Trees hid the rest of the clapboard house until he was closer.

It looked smaller than he remembered it. A bungalow with two bedrooms, two baths, a family den, a large kitchen downstairs and an upstairs dormer with another bedroom and bath that had been his hideaway.

Luke parked in a gravel drive in front of the carport that covered what he assumed was his dad's scratched and dented Chevy pickup truck. Alfred had always been a Chevy man and always hard on the finish of the vehicle. He'd never let bushes or shrubs get in the way of his getting where he wanted to go on the ranch.

The wide, covered porch that his mother had always filled with huge clay pots of colorful blooms was bare except for one old pottery planter full of dirt and dead flowers, a weathered wooden rocker and what looked to be a fairly new porch swing that dangled from the ceiling by only one chain.

Luke's mother's once prized flower beds that had bordered the porch were choked with weeds. The paint on the house was faded and peeling. A dark brown shutter on one of the windows hung askew.

Luke climbed out of the truck and took the cracked concrete walk from the driveway to the porch steps. A sense of foreboding rattled his mood. Stepping back into the house with its bittersweet memories of his mother would have been depressing in an ideal situation. This was far from ideal.

He had no idea what Alfred or the neighbors expected of him. He didn't mind the work, but it wasn't as if he had any authority to make decisions about the ranch. More than likely his father hadn't even named him in the will even though Luke had no siblings.

The door was unlocked. Luke swung it open, but before he could step inside, he heard approaching hoofbeats. He turned as the horseman rode into view, pulled on the reins and stopped in the shade a few yards from the porch.

The black mare snorted and tossed her head as the rider climbed from the saddle and looped the reins around a low-lying branch of a scraggly ash tree.

The rider acknowledged Luke with a smile and a nod. Luke tipped his Stetson.

"You must be Luke," the cowboy said as he approached the porch steps. "Esther Kavanaugh said you'd be here sometime this weekend. She wasn't sure when, so I was just coming by to see if you made it yet."

"Yep. Luke Dawkins. Just drove up. Haven't even made it inside." He met the guy on the edge of the porch and offered his hand.

"Buck Stalling," the guy said. "I'm a wrangler for Pierce Lawrence over at the Double K Ranch. He sends me over here twice a day to take care of the horses."

"Is Pierce running the ranch for Esther Kavanaugh now?" Luke asked.

"He owns it. Mrs. Kavanaugh sold it to him a few months back."

"Interesting. She didn't mention that she'd moved when I talked to her."

"She didn't move. She lives right there in the big house like she always has, close to her beloved chickens and garden."

"Does Pierce live there, too?"

"He did before he built himself, his pregnant wife, Grace, and his young daughter a house of their own no more than a good stone's throw away from Esther. Right nice setup."

"Sounds like a good deal for all of them. I just didn't realize Pierce was back in Winding Creek."

"Then you know Pierce," Buck said. "I'm surprised he never mentioned knowing you."

"No reason he should. Last time I saw him we were in high school, and he moved away before we graduated."

"Yeah. Tough on him and his brothers losing their

parents so early. Lucky for them that the Kavanaughs took them in until their uncle moved them to Kansas."

Tough on anyone that young to lose a parent. No one knew that any better than Luke.

"If you're taking care of the horses, who's looking after the critters?" Luke asked.

"Dudley Miles assigned a couple of his cowboys to help out with the herd until Alfred is functioning enough to hire on some new hands. That's how it is in Winding Creek. Neighbors take care of neighbors."

"Certainly seems that way," Luke agreed.

"I'm real sorry about your father's stroke," Buck said. "I didn't really know him very well, but all the same I sure feel bad for him and you."

"I appreciate that."

"I heard a dog barking when I came up. Is that Alfred's dog?"

"Nope. You probably heard Marley. He belongs to one of the cowboys who's working the critters. He brings him with him some days."

"That's a nice-looking horse you're riding," Luke said.

"Yep. Wish Lucky was mine. She's one hell of a cow pony."

"How many horses does Albert have?"

"Eight quarter horses that he keeps in his new fancy horse barn. Those are his pride and joy. Gonna be tough on your dad if he can't ride anymore."

"Hopefully that won't be the case."

"He also has three other cow ponies and one good cutter. They have stalls at the back of the old barn when they're not loose in the pasture."

"What's the size of the cattle herd?"

"I don't have the exact numbers, but I s'pect your dad has a hundred or so Black Angus and damn near that many Santa Gertrudis. That's just an estimate. Numbers change, of course, depending on when he takes the beef to market and how many calves are born in the spring."

"That sounds like a lot of work for a man who's almost seventy to manage," Luke said.

"He always kept a few hired hands around until he got mad about something and ran them off. He had two hired hands when he had the stroke. They weren't from around here. Just showed up from somewhere in Oklahoma around Thanksgiving looking for work. They disappeared when Albert had his stroke and wasn't around to pay them."

Luke couldn't really blame them for that. He couldn't imagine Albert had done anything to deserve a lot of loyalty from them.

He and Buck talked for a few minutes more, long enough to convince Luke that the ranch was not as neglected as the house.

He waited until Buck rode away before stepping inside. Déjà vu hit with a wallop. Memories, both bad and good, came crashing down on him.

It got worse when he reached the kitchen. He leaned against the counter and would have sworn he could smell frying chicken. His mother's shiny black hair would dance about her shoulders as she cooked and she'd be humming the latest hit from the pop chart. Her lips would shimmer with a bright shade of lipstick.

Before everything had gone bad. So many, many years ago.

Luke shut down the recollections before the bittersweet turned to just plain bitter. It was after three in the afternoon, and darkness set in early in January.

From all accounts, his father was being well cared for and might even be asleep for the night before Luke could make the drive to San Antonio, where he was recovering. A visit with him could wait until tomorrow.

Luke would spend the last of the daylight hours checking out the ranch by horseback.

Suddenly he found himself downright eager to get back in the saddle again. Or maybe he was just glad of an excuse to avoid seeing Alfred for one more day.

Chapter Three

Rachel shrugged out of her navy blue blazer and draped it over the arm of the comfortable wing chair before taking a seat in her psychologist's office. Her first visits to Dr. Stephen Lindquist's had been awkward and strained and had always ended with her in tears.

That had been in late September, during the first weeks after she'd been rescued by her sister, Sydney, and Sydney's now husband, Tucker Lawrence. Rachel had been a total wreck then, the panic attacks hitting with excessive regularity and crippling ferocity.

Work was impossible. Sleep deprivation was taking its toll.

Not atypical with her degree of post-traumatic stress, Dr. Lindquist had assured her. His skill and easy manner had quickly won her over, yet she wasn't making the kind of progress she'd hoped for.

She couldn't bring herself to talk about her experience in captivity. Couldn't deal with the fact that if her sister and Tucker had come moments later she would have been burned alive.

Talking or thinking about it brought it all back to life.

Dr. Lindquist settled in his rustic-brown leather chair. "Good to see you, Rachel."

"Thanks for fitting me in on a Friday afternoon with such short notice," she said.

"You sounded a bit panicky on the phone."

"I was. I am." She clasped her hands in her lap. "I had a major meltdown at work this morning." Her voice cracked. She wrapped her arms around her chest as if that could calm her shattered nerves.

"Take a few deep breaths," Dr. Lindquist suggested. "There's no rush. You're my last appointment for the day. You have me as long as you need me."

"Thanks, but you may be sorry you offered that."

"I won't be. Is it the nightmares again?"

"No, though I still have them from time to time. It's just that every time I seem to be getting in control of my fears, something happens to send me back into the self-destruction spiral."

"You're dealing with a lot. A little backsliding is to be expected. We've talked about that."

"I know. But this is more than a little backsliding. I may have blown my career."

The doctor crossed an ankle over his knee. "Why don't you tell me what happened from the beginning?"

"I suppose you've heard that Senator Covey's son, Hayden, has been arrested."

"No way to miss it. The murder of his ex-girlfriend is dominating the news. I'm sure the senator and his wife are devastated."

"And desperate. I didn't know it until this morning, but the senator is a good friend of my boss, Eric Fitch Sr."

"Guess that means your firm will be defending Hayden."

"It looks that way. I was offered the chance to be the lead attorney in charge of his defense."

"How do you feel about that?"

"Troubled. Confused. Anxious." Her muscles tightened and she felt a nagging ache at her right temple.

"It's the kind of high-profile case that can make or break a defense attorney," she continued, "the kind of opportunity I've been waiting for. The kind I thought I was ready for."

"And now you're not sure. What changed your mind?"

"Doubts that I can handle the job. Thoughts that I don't want to handle the job."

He leaned in closer. "Go on."

"Senator and Mrs. Covey brought their son into the office this morning for a preliminary interview. As I shook hands with Hayden, I stared into the cold, barren intensity of his predatory eyes and an icy shiver ran though me. In that second, it was as if I knew that he was capable of murder.

"No evidence had been presented. It was nothing Hayden had said or done. I just looked into his eyes and saw Roy Sales."

"What did you do?"

"I mumbled something about feeling ill, which I was, and then stood and staggered out of the meeting."

Rachel covered her eyes with her hands, fighting back salty tears of frustration. Her life had changed forever. Now the past was destroying her career with no relief in sight.

"If it turns out Hayden Covey is guilty of the brutal murder of his former girlfriend, I'd say your assessment of him is right on target," the doctor said.

"Which doesn't excuse my unprofessional behavior."

"Have you talked to your boss about the incident?"

"Not yet. I think he was with the Coveys the rest of the morning, but I'm sure it's just a matter of time until he confronts me about my reaction. I'll be lucky if I'm not fired. My boss put me to the test and I failed miserably."

"*Failure* is a strong word."

"And not one I'm used to," she admitted. "But nothing is what I'm used to anymore and I'm tired of having my friends and coworkers feel sorry for me instead of seeing me as an equal."

"I'm sure most of them mean well," Dr. Lindquist said.

"I know, but it's not the way I want to live."

"Maybe it's time you changed your life. Go somewhere where everyone doesn't know about your past."

"You're starting to sound like my sister, Dr. Lindquist, and I get her advice for free."

"What kind of advice does she give you?"

"Stop putting so much pressure on myself. She thinks I should quit the firm and spend some time finding myself again—away from the world of defending people accused of violent crimes."

"How do you feel about that?"

"You know, Doctor, sometimes I wish you'd just give

me answers instead of trying to lead me to work my way through the impossible maze."

An unexpected smile touched the doctor's lips. "Sometimes I wish I could, too. Unfortunately, that's not the way this works. The real answers must come from you.

"So, back to the question. How do you feel about Sydney's suggestion that you take a less stressful job for a while, maybe a change of scenery, as well?"

"It feels like I'd be giving up. It feels like I would have lost and Roy Sales has won."

"Any other considerations?"

As usual, she had the feeling Dr. Lindquist was seeing right through her. "There are times I long to walk away from it all," she admitted reluctantly. "But working for a prominent law firm was the dream that got me through law school. So much time and work have been invested into that dream. I can't just throw that away."

"Sometimes dreams change."

"Or they can be changed for you."

"Have you considered other career options?"

"Not exactly, but I have a friend who specializes in working with charitable organizations—handles lawsuits and tax issues for them and works with people who wish to set up foundations or donate money in their wills. She loves it. Says she always feels like she's on the right side."

"That has a lot of plusses?" the doctor said.

"Then is just walking away from my job what you think I should do?"

"It's what you think you should do that matters, Rachel. I don't see that as giving up. Sometimes changing life paths is the most difficult decision of all."

"I never looked at it that way."

"You're a tough, smart woman with good instincts. You'll make the right decision for you. It just takes time."

"You have more confidence in me than I do in myself."

"You'll get there. I am puzzled, though, why Eric Sr. didn't just take the lead on this case himself."

"He's concerned his friendship with the senator might bias the jury against him. And he claims that I'd be more effective at convincing the jury of Hayden's innocence."

"Because of your own past? Your opinion of Hayden Covey would likely count for a lot, considering what you've been through."

She thought painstakingly about Dr. Lindquist's comment and then cringed as the truth about Eric's more likely motives took root. He didn't think she was the most capable defense attorney at the firm.

He was using her, putting his faith in the jurors pitying her and believing she'd never defend Hayden unless she fully believed in his innocence.

Her insides twisted. She had no proof of the theory, but it made sense. How had she not seen that before?

By the time the session with Dr. Lindquist was finished and she reached her car, her decision had been made.

If she hurried, she could catch the most senior partner before he left the office.

She couldn't go on being a victim forever. She had to fight back.

Chapter Four

A light rain dotted her windshield as Rachel exited the multilevel parking garage at her firm and started toward home. Her emotions still on a roller coaster, the ringing of her phone startled her.

She checked the caller ID on the hands-free display. Her sister, Sydney. She took the call, though she'd hoped not to share her big announcement with her sister until she'd gotten used to it herself.

"Good evening, Sydney. How's the world inside the FBI this Friday night?"

"Urgent and crisis-filled, as usual, though I plan not to think about that his weekend. I'm only a few miles from Winding Creek now. I'll be there for dinner with Esther and the rest of the family. When are you arriving?"

When was she arriving? Oh, God. "This is the weekend of Grace's baby shower, isn't it?"

"Don't tell me you forgot, Rachel."

"Okay. I won't tell you. When is the shower?"

"Tomorrow afternoon at three. It's at Dani's Delights. Dani is closing the bakery early for the party. It's a really big deal. Half the women in town are coming. Everybody loves Grace."

"Me included," Rachel said, "but…"

"She'll be very disappointed if you're not here. Besides, you and I haven't gotten together since Christmas. I'm really looking forward to seeing you."

"Yeah. I'd like to see you, too," she admitted, suddenly realizing just how much. "I'll start out early in the morning. I'm far too tired to make that drive tonight."

"Super, though I was hoping you'd taken the afternoon off and were coming in tonight so we could have one of our all-talk and no-sleep slumber parties the way we used to."

"You mean back before you had a gorgeous husband to keep you entertained at night?"

"Right. But he's competing in a rodeo in Longview tonight and tomorrow morning, so he won't make it here until late tomorrow afternoon. The good news is we're both taking Monday and Tuesday off."

"So I'm second choice?"

"Yep. But I just checked the radar and it shows a line of thundershowers moving into the area over the next few hours, so it's just as well you're not driving this way now."

"I do hate driving in the rain."

"You did forget, though. I mean, there's nothing going on there that made you have second thoughts about coming?"

Sydney never took things at face value. It was all that FBI training, Rachel expected. But her insight hit too close to home far too often.

"What are you intimating, my crime-fighting sister?"

"Just wondering if it's the thought of returning to Winding Creek that's really bothering you."

"No," she lied. "I'm fine with Winding Creek."

"Then promise you're not going to make some new excuse to get out of coming tomorrow so you can stay home and work. You need a break."

Yes, she did. She hadn't intended to just blurt out her news, but there was no real reason to keep it a secret.

"I know you're sitting down, since you're driving," Rachel said, "but prepare yourself for a shock."

"You've met a man?"

"Gads. That's the last thing I need."

"A matter of opinion. Then what is it?"

"I will no longer be overworking. As of about thirty minutes ago, I don't have a job or a career. I did make off with a few company pens, though, as I stormed out of the building."

"You got fired?"

"No. I beat old Fitch to it. I quit."

"You're joking."

"Nope. In fact, I may be as shocked as you that I quit, but it felt right. Still does. But also a bit scary."

"I can't wait to hear all the details. But let me just say, I'm in favor of the decision. And you haven't lost a career permanently. You're still a dynamite attorney. You'll land on your feet somewhere where they don't expect you to give up sleep permanently in exchange for billable hours."

"I hope you're right. We'll talk more when I get there."

"Now I really can't wait to see you. Actually, the

whole family will be thrilled to see you again. Esther asks about you every time we talk."

Esther was a jewel. So were all three of the Lawrence brothers and their families who had come home to Winding Creek and to Esther Kavanaugh.

The only problem was that the warm and loving family members were Sydney's in-laws—not Rachel's.

"Don't mention my quitting my job to anyone else just yet."

"I'll have to tell Tucker. We talk about everything, but I'll tell him to keep it under his hat."

Rachel's new life was off and running—ready or not.

RACHEL KEPT HER eyes on the passing scenery, watching for the gate to the Double K Ranch. All things considered, she was feeling surprisingly upbeat, or at least several notches above gloom.

Perhaps the reality that she was unemployed for the first time since she'd graduated from law school hadn't fully sunk in. Or maybe Sydney was right about her needing a mental, emotional and physical break from the stress that Fitch, Fitch and Baumer provided.

The sun claimed dominance over a few cumulus clouds. Michael Bublé was crooning on her car's radio. And she was actually going to spend two full days with her sister instead of driving back home on Sunday morning to a crush of paperwork.

She basically had nothing on her plate in the foreseeable future except freedom and possibly a few hours doing wrap-up at the office. She'd offered two weeks' notice. A shocked and irritated Eric Fitch Sr. had said that wasn't necessary.

All he needed was a verbal agreement that she would answer any questions that might arise concerning cases she'd been involved with. Eric Fitch Jr. had come by while she was collecting her personal belongings and tried to talk her into staying, assuring her he'd cleared the offer with his dad.

He'd offered a raise. She'd been tempted, but not enough to stay.

Lost in her thoughts again, she almost missed the Double K's metal gate and had to throw on her brakes to keep from passing it by. She made the turn too fast, skidding across a wet patch of grass that bordered the ranch road.

She slowed and stopped at the closed and latched gate. Esther had talked about putting in an automatic gate opener to save herself having to get out in the weather. Obviously that was still on her to-do list. Neither weather nor much else slowed down Esther Kavanaugh.

Rachel switched the gear to Park but kept the motor running. She'd opened the door and was about to climb from behind the wheel when she was startled by the clattering engine noise of another vehicle.

She checked the rearview mirror. An old, mud-encrusted pickup truck had made the turn and had followed her to the gate. The male driver stopped mere inches behind her, blocking her between his front bumper and the closed gate.

She jerked her door closed and pushed the lock but-

ton. Her heart pounded against the walls of her chest.
Her lungs burned. Her stomach churned sickeningly.

The driver got out of his truck and started toward
her. She switched the gear to Drive and poised her foot
on the accelerator. If he so much as touched her car, she
would ram through the gate, knocking it from its hinges.
She wouldn't stop until she reached Esther's house.

As the man neared, he smiled and tipped his gray
Stetson. Nothing about him looked dangerous. His smile
was anything but threatening. Telling herself that only
barely eased her surge of apprehension.

She clutched the steering wheel so tight her knuckles turned white.

The cowboy sauntered past her locked door, walked
to the front of her car and unlatched the gate. He was
opening the door for her. She took a deep breath and
let her fingers relax their hold on the steering wheel.

The gate swung open and the cowboy motioned her
through—an extremely good-looking cowboy, though
she hadn't noticed that before. She lowered her window
and waved as she drove past him.

Her pulse was back to near normal by the time she
reached the rambling ranch house. The sight of Esther's
house had a further calming effect on her.

Colorful pillows adorned the wide porch swing.
Painted rocking chairs were pulled up to a round table
topped with a pot of colorful pansies. A clump of sweet
alyssum huddled next to the steps. Winter jasmine
climbed the railings on the north end of the porch.

Rachel parked in the gravel drive on the far side of

the house, a recent addition that kept visitors from dodging mud holes on mornings such as this.

Once more, the cowboy parked behind her. This time she waited for him to get out of the truck. The unwarranted panic attack had passed.

"Thanks for handling the gate chores," she said.

"My pleasure." He pointed to his worn Western boots. "Those high-heeled fancy boots you're wearing don't look like they'd take too well to mud. These goat-ropers are made for chunking through whatever they face."

"Goat-roper?"

"Just a term. I don't really rope goats in them—not that I couldn't."

"I'll bet."

He extended his hand. "Luke Dawkins. The prodigal son of Alfred Dawkins, returning to Winding Creek for duty."

She slid her hand into his much larger one. An unexpected wave of awareness zinged through her. That frightened her almost as much as her initial reaction to him had. "Rachel Maxwell. I'm Sydney Lawrence's sister, just visiting—no duty."

She waited for the look of pity that frequently followed the act of telling anyone her name. There was none. Evidently he didn't know of her past. The chances were slim to none she could keep it that way.

They started up the wide wooden steps to the porch together. Their arms brushed. Her first impulse was to pull away from him. She didn't.

Before she had time to ring the bell, the door opened

and Sydney appeared, with Esther a step behind. "You made it," Esther said.

Sidney spotted Luke and looked shocked. "And you bought a guest."

"Not intentionally," Luke said. "I'm just a stray who followed her home. Luke Dawkins."

"A prodigal son," Rachel offered to fill a sudden, awkward silence on Sydney's part.

"Well, of course you are," Esther said, pushing to the front. "You haven't changed a bit, Luke, except for that facial hair. Just threw me off that you arrived with our Rachel."

"What can I say? When a beautiful woman shows up, I don't argue with fate."

"You're in your dad's truck," Esther said, leaning over to look past them. "Hope that's not all you have to get around in. To hear Alfred tell it, it only runs half the time."

"I was afraid it wouldn't make it here," Luke admitted. "But I have my own truck back at the ranch, so if this one makes it back home, I'll park it and leave it until I can get it tuned up."

Luke touched a hand to the small of Rachel's back as they stepped inside.

Once again, her nerves zinged.

It couldn't get any crazier than this.

Chapter Five

Luke's ego took a blow. He was definitely the odd man out where the two sisters were concerned. They were both talking at once, the topics changing as fast as if this were a game-show lightning round. He didn't even try to keep up.

Within ten minutes Sydney and Rachel excused themselves to go wrap gifts for an afternoon baby shower. Luke watched Rachel walk away. She was hot as a bonfire and there was no gold band on her ring finger.

If he were planning to stick around awhile, he'd hit on her big-time, though she was probably miles out of his league. But as soon as he figured out what to do about his father and the Arrowhead Hills Ranch, he was out of here.

Unless Alfred kicked him out sooner.

"It's good to have you here in my house again after so many years," Esther said once they were alone. "You've grown into a fine-looking young man. Your mother would have been mighty proud of you."

"Thanks. Being here reminds me of her."

"She was a very special woman, one of the best

friends I've had in my life, even though she was a couple of decades younger and had four times the energy I did. I miss her to this day, but it's probably not the best time for going all syrupy. I know you're here to talk about Alfred's problems."

"I am," he agreed. "I still don't know much more than what you told me on the phone. The rehab center is not big on giving out information other than what's on his chart. Assisted shower at eight. Occupational therapy scheduled for one. That and other equally unhelpful info."

"Did you talk to the medical supervisor where he's staying or the doctor who cared for him in the hospital?"

"I've talked to both with equally worthless results. The doctor quoted some medical jargon to describe the stroke and possible causes but didn't give me anything definite on the prognosis. He insisted there was no way to be certain at this point if or how long Alfred would need permanent care. I'm supposed to meet with the medical supervisor this afternoon."

"You're driving to San Antonio today?"

"Yep. I need to see his condition for myself and at least let him know I'm here for him—if he cares."

"I visited him again Wednesday," Esther said. "He's throwing a fit to go home, but he can't get around well enough to take care of himself. He definitely can't handle cooking chores or bathing and shaving."

"Then you think he'll need someone with him twenty-four hours a day?"

"At least at first, and I predict he'll go through the

ceiling if you suggest he go anywhere when he leaves the rehab facility except back to the ranch."

"A ranch he can't take care of on his own. He'll have to hire someone to manage everything, and unless he's changed a lot in eleven years, he's not good at delegating authority." Luke couldn't see any way this was going to turn out well.

"I have a fresh pot of coffee in the kitchen," Esther said. "Will you have a cup with me?"

"Sure." He needed a beer more, but it was still morning and he had a visit with Alfred staring him in the face, so he'd stick with the caffeine.

He followed her to the kitchen.

"Cream or sugar?"

"Just black, thanks."

She filled two mugs and set them on the small table in the kitchen breakfast nook. He held her chair and then took a seat across from her.

Esther sipped her brew. "I've probably depressed you enough, but do you have any other questions that I might be able to answer?"

"How was Alfred's health before the stroke?"

"He was slowing down a bit, only sixty-nine, but looked older than he was. Not much meat on his bones. Comes from living alone, and you know how that Texas sun turns your skin to leather if you don't slather on sunscreen every day."

"But he still supervised the running of the ranch and rode his horses."

"Yes, indeed. From what I heard, he'd hardly let anyone else touch his quarter horses. Rumor was he loved them like they were his babies."

Too bad he hadn't felt that way about Luke or his mother.

Esther stared into her cup. "I guess the doctor told you the stroke affected his memory. I reckon it's getting better, though.

"The first time Grace and I drove down to visit him, he had no idea who we were. Went into a rant. Accused us of trying to steal things from his room."

"Now, that sounds like the father I remember."

"I think this was more than attitude. Before I left he was calling Grace and me by name, as if it just suddenly came to him who the heck we were. He settled down after that."

"I ran into Buck Stallings when I arrived at the ranch yesterday. He told me Dad's hired hands disappeared when my father had the stroke and wasn't around to pay them."

"They quit, all right. Just up and rode off without bothering to tell anybody. Pierce thinks they probably made off with enough equipment to make up for any wages they lost."

"Sounds like Alfred owes Pierce and Dudley Miles a great deal for stepping in and taking care of his livestock and horses."

"They aren't expecting any thanks. People around these parts take care of their neighbors when they see a need even if the neighbor is as ornery as Alfred. My Charlie would have been the first one to the rescue if he was still living."

"I'm sure he would. I'm sorry about your loss."

"I appreciate that. You know, I keep thinking I'll miss him less as days go by, but it doesn't work that way. Spend almost half a century of your life with a person and he's as much a part of you as breathing."

Luke's longest relationship to date had lasted just over three months. He couldn't even imagine that many years with the same woman, but he nodded like he got it.

Esther worried the handle of her coffee mug and then took another sip. "You think it's over, but life goes on. Blessings, too." A smile touched her lips and glinted in her eyes. "Never had a family of my own. Now I'm overrun with kids and grandkids that I couldn't love more if they were flesh and blood."

"You seem happy."

"If I felt any better, I'd drop my harp plumb through the clouds." She pushed her cup away. "And here I go rambling on about my good fortune with you here to talk about your poor father."

"I was just thinking that if Dad didn't recognize you, it's definitely not likely he'll recognize me."

"No way of knowing. How long has it been since you were last here in Winding Creek?"

"Going on twelve years."

"But you've surely talked since then?"

"I call at Christmas and Father's Day when I'm somewhere I can. The conversations are strained, awkward and short. We didn't talk a lot more when we lived together unless he was barking orders."

Esther reached across the table and laid a blue-veined and wrinkled hand on his. "I know you two have had a rocky relationship and it's mostly his doing. But he needs you, Luke. You're the only family he's got, and let's face it, he's better at making enemies than friends."

Dread ground in the pit of Luke's stomach. He'd arrived at Esther's this morning holding out a little hope that things weren't as bad as he feared. Now he figured they were worse and there was no easy fix in sight.

"Guess I'd better get going if I'm going to see Dad before I talk to the medical supervisor. I have a few more chores I want to get done at the ranch before I leave."

He finished off the rest of his coffee, stood and carried his cup to the sink.

Esther followed him. "I'll be gone to Grace's baby shower this afternoon, but I'll be home tonight or after church tomorrow if you want to discuss what comes next with Alfred or just blow off a little frustration."

"I may take you up on that, and I appreciate all you and the other neighbors have done."

"Even better, why don't you join us for dinner tonight, Luke? It's a night off from kitchen duties for the women, since we're throwing the baby shower for Pierce's wife, Grace, but Pierce and Riley are grilling."

"Riley Lawrence?"

"Yes. Pierce, Riley and Tucker Lawrence. I figured you'd remember them."

"I remember that you and Charlie took them in for nearly a year after their parents were killed in the car crash."

Luke had been envious of the brothers, had wished the Kavanaughs had taken him in after his mother died instead of leaving him to take the brunt of his dad's verbal abuse and mean disposition.

Luke twirled the strong black brew in his mug and then sipped. "Sounds like a family reunion."

"I guess it is, of sorts, except that two of the Lawrence brothers are happily married and living in Winding Creek now. Tucker and Sydney have an apartment in Dallas, but with his rodeoing and Sydney's work as an FBI agent, I think they call this home as much as anywhere else."

"Whatever works."

"That's what I say, too," Esther agreed. "Come to dinner tonight and the guys can catch you up on all their news."

"I'd love to see them if you're sure I won't be intruding."

"There's always room for one more at my old dining room table. How about you, Luke? Are you married?"

"Nope. Never even came close and plan to keep it that way."

She smiled and he could swear he saw a conspiratorial gleam in her eye.

"Seems like I remember Pierce, Riley and Tucker saying that exact same thing not too long ago."

He stood to go. "Stay here," he said. "I can let myself out."

"We'll be looking for you tonight. Come hungry."

"I'm always hungry."

When he reached the short hallway, he heard voices and recognized Rachel's at once. An unexpected surge of pleasure overrode some of the anxiety about dealing with his father.

A decent meal and a visit with the Lawrence brothers would be nice, but it was the thought of seeing Rachel again that really cranked up his anticipation.

SYDNEY LAWRENCE LOOKED up from the fingernail she was applying a mending touch of red polish to as Rachel swept into the room. "Holy Smoly, do you look hot!"

Rachel did a quick twirl in the full-skirted, jewel-toned dress and then struck a sexy pose. "Is it too dressy for an afternoon party?"

"It's perfect. I love the cutout at the neck."

"Not too much cleavage?"

"Heavens, no. Barely a hint. Love those strappy heels, too."

"It was either this or one of the depressing navy or gray suits I wear to work. Oops. I *used* to wear to work."

"I have to say you're taking your newly unemployed status well. I was afraid you'd be in the dumps and not even show."

"I'm not sure the full reality of my situation has hit me yet."

"Or maybe it has and that's why you're glowing."

"No. That's the new blush I picked up at Macy's last week. Dusty Fire. Guaranteed to set me apart from the crowd."

"From the way hunky Luke Dawkins was looking at you today, I'd say it's surpassing promised expectations."

"He was just being nice and making conversation."

"Really? Because it sure seemed like there was a sizzle between you two when I met you at the door."

"Don't even go there. My life is too screwed up right now to even notice a man."

But Sydney knew she had noticed. The rosy color creeping into her cheeks right now was proof of that. A casual flirtation might do Rachel good, but Sydney doubted she was emotionally ready for anything more.

Rachel sat on the edge of the bed amid the wrapped packages. "Is Esther going to ride into town with us?" she asked, no doubt ready to direct the conversation away from Luke.

"No, Pierce is going to drive Grace and Esther to the bakery and he'll pick up Dani's daughter, Constance, and bring her back here to play with his daughter, Jaci, while we party."

"Dad in charge. Everything around here really is a family affair," Rachel said.

"I know and I love it. Do you still want to keep the fact that you quit your job a secret from the rest of the family?"

"For now. This is Grace's special weekend. I don't want it to turn into a whine party for me."

"I haven't even had a chance to tell Tucker yet."

"When are you expecting him?"

"He called a few minutes ago. He's about an hour out, so he'll be at the ranch by the time we get back from the party."

"And then you'll forget the rest of us exist."

"True." Which was exactly why she should tackle the bad news she had for Rachel now.

She couldn't bring herself to do it. This was the most relaxed she'd seen Rachel since she'd lived through hell. She couldn't bring herself to spoil the moment. Tomorrow would be soon enough to drag her back into the Roy Sales hell.

ODDS WERE AGAINST Rachel feeling at home at a baby shower in Winding Creek. Everyone in town knew of her terrifying past.

The saving grace was that since they knew the intimate details, no one ever mentioned it to her.

There would be no endless questions the way there often were when she met someone new. No staring at her as if the experience made her less human now. No more expressions of pity that made Rachel feel worse instead of better about herself.

She and Sydney grabbed the gifts from the back of Sydney's car and joined the stream of chatting and laughing local women pouring into Dani's Delights.

Rachel set the wrapped baby carrier on the floor next to a long table that was already overflowing with presents. A squeal captured her attention just as Dani and Riley Lawrence's eleven-year-old newly adopted daughter threw her arms around Rachel's waist.

"Yay. You came. You can go riding with us tomorrow. We have two new horses. And I'm learning to be a barrel rider. I can show you."

Words spilled out of Constance's mouth so fast, Rachel could barely follow her train of thought. Constance's excitement was contagious, exactly what Rachel needed to keep her in the here and now. "I'm staying all day tomorrow and I brought my riding clothes. And I definitely want a barrel riding exhibition."

"I'm pretty good. One day I want to be in the rodeo like Uncle Tucker."

"Now, that sounds exciting. When you are, I'll be in the stands cheering for you."

"Yes, but my parents say I still have to study hard at school even if horses don't care if I know about geography and math. I hate math, especially word problems."

Dani appeared at her daughter's side, opened her arms and welcomed Rachel with a warm hug. "I'm so glad you could make it. By the way, you look terrific. I need to absorb some of your fashion savvy."

"You're the most popular woman in town in your chocolate-and flour-smeared white apron. If I were you, I wouldn't change a thing."

They laughed and then all attention turned to the front door as the guest of honor arrived, accompanied by Esther, Pierce and his daughter, Jaci.

The baby bump was no longer just a bump. Grace was due in a matter of weeks and, with her petite frame, she looked to be all baby.

Nonetheless, she was as beautiful as ever and Pierce helped her to the chair situated beneath a colorful balloon arch as if she was the most fragile and cherished treasure on earth.

Someone pushed a crystal flute of sparkling champagne into Rachel's hand. The bell around the door dinged as another group of laughing ladies entered. The party had begun and surprisingly the celebratory spirit overtook even Rachel.

Grace sounded positively joyous and yet she'd once lived in a hellish nightmare, too. Rachel wondered if she'd ever find the kind of happiness Grace enjoyed.

Could she let herself?

LUKE DAWKINS DROVE the forty-five minutes to the rehab center on the outskirts of San Antonio where his dad was receiving his care. He arrived at approximately half past two for a three o'clock appointment with the medical supervisor.

The L-shaped building was redbrick, set in a parklike setting with several bare-branched oak trees and a few pines shading benches and small, gurgling fountains.

Not the worst of places to be housed if you needed care, but definitely not the wide-open spaces of Arrowhead Hills.

There was a covered drop-off area at the front door. A sign directed him to a visitor parking lot in the rear. A couple of dozen cars and trucks and two vans emblazoned with the name of the center were parked near the back entrance.

Luke climbed out of his truck and locked it before sauntering up the narrow walk to the back door. He hesitated before opening the door, gearing himself to deal with whatever came next.

His father had been fifty-eight when Luke cut out. A big man, over six feet tall, muscles developed from a lifetime of hard work. Rigid. Hardheaded. His way or the highway.

But Luke himself had changed a lot in eleven years and not just physically. He was less impulsive, more prone to think before acting. Maybe time or aging and the stroke had mellowed Alfred.

He stopped at the nurses' station at the end of a short hallway. One nurse was at her computer. Another was on the phone. What he guessed was an aide pushed a patient in a wheelchair down the hall as Luke waited for one of the nurses to acknowledge him.

The man in the wheelchair waved and smiled—a dead giveaway it wasn't Alfred.

Nurse number two, a middle-aged brunette with short hair and extremely red lipstick, hung up her phone and asked if she could help him. Her name tag said she was an RN named Louise.

"I'm Alfred Dawkins's son. I have an appointment."

Louise clapped her hands together softly as a smile lit up her face. "You must be Luke. We've been hoping a family member would show up."

"I came as soon as I could and I was assured he was not in critical condition."

"He's fine, but he's a handful to deal with. I'm sure he'll be much easier to handle now that you're here."

"I wouldn't count on that. I also have an appointment with Carolyn Schultz."

"Great. I know she's looking forward to discussing Alfred's progress with you. She's not here yet, but your father is in his room, probably watching TV. I'm sure you're anxious to see him."

Anxious, but not eager. But he could think of no legitimate excuse to put the visit off.

"Alfred is in Room 109, just around the corner. Now,

don't get upset if he doesn't recognize you at once. He sometimes gets confused when he has visitors."

"I understand."

"Other times he's clued in and recognizes visitors right away. Either way, he's slow at getting his words out."

"I'll keep my expectations low." That should be easy enough.

He followed the nurse to Alfred's room. She entered before him. Alfred was propped up in a hospital bed, wearing a blue shirt only half-buttoned with food stains down the front. He looked frail and years older than Luke remembered him.

He felt a jolt to his gut. The man in the hospital bed was not the father he remembered.

Louise walked over and stood next to Alfred's bed. "You have a visitor," she announced in a cheery voice.

Alfred grunted and pulled up his sheet before looking at Luke. For the first few seconds, there was nothing in his facial expression to indicate he recognized Luke. Then his thin lips all but disappeared in a scowl.

Louise stood back so that Luke could step in closer. "Do you know who this is?" she asked.

"Hell, yes. But he's...too soon. I'm not...not dead yet."

That was the father he remembered.

Welcome home, Luke Dawkins.

Chapter Six

Luke's emotions had run the gauntlet over the past few hours. His nerves had skidded along for the maddening ride from concern to fuming to disgruntled exasperation. By the time he stopped behind a row of three pickup trucks at the Kavanaugh house, he was slowly inching toward reason.

His dad hadn't sent for him and clearly didn't want him around. The easiest and likely the smartest thing Luke could do right now was clear out. Let his dad hire someone to run his own damn ranch any way he liked or let it go to weed and empty pastures if that was the way hardheaded Alfred Dawkins wanted it.

But Luke had never looked for the easy way out or shirked responsibility—which left him stuck neck-deep in the dilemma of where to go from here.

He struggled to rein in his conflicting emotions as he reached Esther's wide front porch. He put his hand on the doorbell but didn't push.

Coming here was a mistake. There was no way he'd be decent dinner company tonight. Besides, judging from the trucks parked out front, he was likely late.

Before he could cut and run, the door opened and Rachel Maxwell greeted him with a melodic hello that softened the edges of his lousy mood like magic.

Her voice wasn't the half of it. She'd been a knockout this morning in her jeans and cotton shirt. All fancied up, she was luscious.

It wasn't the dress so much as the way she wore it. The soft fabric hugged her perfect breasts and then tightened at her tiny waist before billowing out over her shapely hips.

The skirt stopped a few inches above the knees, highlighting her dynamite calves and the straps on a pair of nosebleed heels that wrapped around her slender ankles.

When she smiled and looked at him with those gold-specked, dusky eyes, he turned away to keep from melting. He had to pull his gaze away from her before he could speak.

"I didn't know we were playing dress-up. I'd have come with my boots shined and my jeans creased," he said, determined to keep the tone light.

She laughed and motioned him inside. "You'll fit in perfectly. Normally I'd be in jeans myself, but I decided to go for the girly look at Grace's baby shower this afternoon."

"You aced it."

"Thank you, I guess."

"Is this the Grace who's married to Pierce Lawrence?"

"Yes. Have you met her?"

"Haven't had the pleasure."

"You'll love her, guaranteed. She went home to rest awhile, but she'll be back for dinner."

"Then I must be too early. I'm not crashing," he teased. "I was actually invited by Esther, but she didn't mention a time."

"The guys are doing the cooking chores tonight You can never tie them down to a time. They tend to grill for hours."

"Ranchers need their beef and plenty of it," Luke said.

"So it seems. I'm a city girl myself. Sushi and a salad are my usual Saturday night splurge."

"I'm going to pretend I didn't hear you say that."

"Does that mean you're a cowboy, too?"

"I am this week."

"There must be a story there."

"Not one you'd want to hear before dinner—or after, either, for that matter."

"Now you've really piqued my curiosity. Do you know all three of the Lawrence brothers?"

"We went to school together many years ago."

"Pierce and Riley are in the backyard slaving over the hot charcoal. They may put you to work if you venture that way, but I'm sure they'd love to see you again and say hello."

"Sounds like a good idea."

"Then follow me."

The view was almost as spectacular from the rear. Hard to imagine he could feel anything sensual after the visit he'd had with his father, but maybe it was his survival instincts kicking in. Or perhaps the fact that he hadn't been with a woman in more months than he could count on his fingers and toes.

More likely it was simply that she was a natural temptress.

They walked through the house, onto the covered back porch and down the few steps to the yard. Mouth-watering odors spilled from a huge barrel-shaped grill.

They walked closer and watched as Riley basted a slab of ribs with one hand. The fingers of the other hand were wrapped around a beer.

Pierce stepped over to greet them. "Glad you could make it, Luke. Esther said she twisted your arm to accept her dinner invitation."

"Actually, she just said 'food' and I jumped at the chance."

"As you can see, we have enough meat here to clog the arteries of a dozen more guys," Riley said.

"Don't bet on it. My arteries haven't seen a Texas meal like this in recent memory."

Pierce turned to Riley. "You remember Luke Dawkins, don't you?"

"I do." Riley set his beer down on the worktable and extended a hand to Luke. "It's been a while."

"Yes, it has. A lot of water under the bridge since those high school days."

"I remember you had a mean fastball," Pierce said. "Best southpaw to ever come out of the Hill Country, the newspapers used to brag. Did you ever go pro?"

"No. I knocked around in the Northwest for a few months and then joined the marines. Got to see the world—well, at least the stony cliffs of Afghanistan from an Apache helicopter."

"I'd like to hear about that one day," Pierce said.

"It was interesting," Luke admitted. "But get me started and you've wasted an evening."

"Sorry about your father," Riley said. "Have you seen him yet?"

"Today."

"How'd that go?" Pierce asked.

"It could have been worse. He could have shot me. Luckily he wasn't toting."

"Sounds like the stroke didn't affect his disposition," Riley joked.

"Not for the better," Luke said. "And that is a subject best discussed when we don't want to lose our appetites. What can I do to help with dinner? I'm great at opening cans or poking meat with a fork."

"Thanks for the offer, but we've got it covered," Pierce said. "I would suggest you and Rachel take a walk and get out of this smoke, except if she were to fall in those shoes, the height could cause major injuries."

Rachel's hands flew to her hips, but the sparkle in her eyes proved it was a show of fake indignation. "You don't like my shoes?"

"I love your shoes," Pierce said, "just not for walking."

"Walking is overrated," Riley said. "Beer, on the other hand…"

He reached into a cooler and pulled out two bottles of an amber brew. He opened them both and handed one to Rachel and one to Luke. "Now, you two find a less smoky spot and get better acquainted while I try to keep Pierce from burning his brisket."

"Don't you worry about my brisket, bro. You just take care of your ribs."

"I think that's our cue to get out of the way of the cooks," Rachel said. "Esther is resting from the day's activities, and I don't want to venture into what Sydney and Tucker might be doing after spending two weeks apart. But I'm pretty sure I can make it as far as the front porch in these shoes."

"I'll drink to that." Luke clinked his bottle with Rachel's. It was the best invitation he'd had in years.

THE LAST RAYS of the setting sun were shooting golden streaks across the sky as Luke and Rachel settled on the porch swing. The afternoon had been unusually warm for January, but a breeze stirred now and the temperatures were dropping.

Rachel shivered and wrapped her arms around her chest.

Without a word, Luke shrugged out of his denim jacket and cloaked it around her shoulders. His hands brushed her neck as he did, creating a startling tingle. There was no reasonable explanation for the way his nearness affected her.

"Now you'll be cold," she said. "I can step inside and get a wrap."

"What do you think I am, a wimp? Besides, the jacket looks far better on you. Adds a certain Texas flair to those daring shoes."

They both laughed and she realized that she actually felt at ease with him. That, paired with quitting her job, was probably a sign she was totally losing it.

Luke used his foot to move the swing in a slow, rhythmic motion. "Great family you have, Rachel Maxwell."

"They're not exactly my family, but they make me feel as if I am. I always feel at home here."

"I get that. As a kid, I loved coming here with my mother. There were always cookies and laughter and lots of times Charlie would play catcher while I worked on my fastball."

"Charlie must have been very special. Esther talks about him with such love. So do all the Lawrences."

"This family has grown significantly since my mother was alive. I need a crash course on who goes with whom."

"It's not that difficult. Pierce is married to Grace, who is pregnant and due in a few weeks. You can't confuse her with anyone else. Jaci is Pierce's six-year-old daughter from a previous marriage, but he has custody while her mother is in Cuba with her new husband."

"Got it. And I know Tucker is married to your sister, Sydney, whom I met earlier."

"Right. And Riley is married to Dani, whom you haven't met as yet. She is a fabulous pastry chef and owns Dani's Delights, a bakery and coffee shop on Main Street in Winding Creek."

"Do they have children?"

"They have just completed the adoption process for Dani's orphaned niece, Constance. Constance is only eleven, but she adores Tucker and loves the rodeo. If you stay in town long enough, she'll insist on demonstrating her barrel riding skills for you."

"How did Tucker and Sydney meet?"

And this was where the fun began. Rachel's chest tightened. She sipped her beer as she considered her answer.

"Sydney was in Winding Creek working an investigation and Tucker was here visiting Esther and his brothers. They met and that was it. Bells ringing, birds singing, butterflies fluttering. Just like in the movies."

"Then you believe in love at first sight?"

"For them. Not for everyone." She shifted in the swing, turning toward Luke. His rugged masculinity was daunting, yet enticing.

She'd never been particularly fond of facial hair, but his was incredibly sexy. Close-trimmed, little more than a five-o'clock shadow. She imagined how the trendy strip of hair above his mouth would tickle if they were to kiss.

Which they weren't going to do.

"Tell me about yourself, Luke Dawkins," she said, determined to change the subject before they entered forbidden territory.

"Not a lot to tell," Luke said.

"You said you're only a cowboy this week? Does that mean you're not a die-hard rancher like Pierce, Riley and Tucker?"

"I thought I might be at one time. That life didn't happen for me, so I took another path."

"And became a marine?"

"Eventually. That's a lifestyle all its own, though the guys in my squad did nickname me Maverick."

"It could be the saunter," Rachel said. "You authentic

Texas cowboys have that down to a fine art. And you still have a bit of that Texas drawl."

"Is that a bad thing?"

"Apparently not where women are concerned. Cowboys are the in thing these days. Just check out the covers of the romance novels on the shelves in your favorite bookstore."

"I'll make it a point to do that," he said, exaggerating his drawl for emphasis.

"How long have you been a civilian again?"

"Only three months."

"Has it been hard adjusting to your new life?"

"Much more difficult than I expected. Who knew it would be so hard to find a satisfactory replacement for combat?"

"Have you?"

"No, but I can tell you what doesn't work for me. Sitting at a desk all day. Bureaucracy and all the red tape that holds it together. Politics—at any level."

"So now you've come back to your roots."

"Not by choice. My dad had a stroke and I'm the only family he has, not that we have much of a relationship."

"Why is that?"

"He kicked me out of the house when I was eighteen and has pretty much cut me out of his life since then. That tends to cause a few bad feelings."

"I can see where it might."

"Enough about me and my charmed life. Tell me about you, or let me guess. A supermodel. Live in New York City. No dogs. One very demanding cat. Fight off the constant stream of wealthy, handsome admirers with the heels of your stilettos. Your admirers, not the cat's."

"Close. I live in Houston. Alone. No cats. No dogs. Not even a goldfish. No admirers. And this is my only pair of stilettos. They cost a small fortune, so I wouldn't dare risk breaking the heel in a fight. Basically, I'm your average dud."

"I'm not buying that. I see you more as a woman of mystery who possesses a multitude of intriguing secrets."

"No secrets. No mystery. The truth is my life is in a bit of chaos at the minute and I've escaped to Winding Creek for the weekend to put my concerns completely out of my mind."

"It's not some man who's caused the problem, is it? If it is, I can beat him up for you. Ooh-rah, and all that."

"There are no men in my life at present, at least none whose boots I'd let rest beneath my bed. What about you?"

"I fall in love every week or two."

"Really?"

"No. Got engaged once. She jilted me while I was in Afghanistan dodging IEDs."

"What a traitor. Want me to beat her up?"

"Would you?"

"Not in this dress. Bloodstains are too hard to remove."

He leaned back and stretched his legs in front of him. The denim of his jeans rubbed against her bare legs. Her breath caught.

Usually that was a warning sign of an all-too-frequent panic attack. But it wasn't anxiety that caused the tingly sensation deep inside her tonight.

She was so not ready for this with Luke or any other man. "I should probably go and see if I can help in the kitchen," she said.

"Why do I get the feeling you're trying to get rid of me?"

"You're welcome in the kitchen."

"Thanks, but I guess I'll go out back with the guys and trade in my empty beer bottle for a full one."

"Good idea."

They both stood.

He tipped his hat. "Nice chatting with you, Rachel Maxwell. I still think there's a mystery that I need to get to the bottom of."

And that was it. He walked away while she was fighting the effect he was having on her. She couldn't even guess what Dr. Lindquist would think about this.

RACHEL DIDN'T MAKE it to the kitchen. She ran into her sister in the hallway.

"Do you have a few minutes, Rachel?"

One look and she could tell this would not be good. She should have known things were going too well. "What's wrong?"

"I had the TV on while Tucker was grabbing a shower. I caught the beginning of the evening news. You were the lead story."

"What now, or dare I ask?" Rachel said.

"Tucker's getting dressed. Let's talk in your bedroom." She followed Rachel and closed the door behind them.

"Hit me with it," Rachel said, not bothering to hide her frustration.

"You did tell me that you officially resigned from Fitch, Fitch and Bauman, didn't you?"

"Yes. I can't imagine that made the news."

"You're right. There was no mention of resignation. The announcement was that you, Rachel Maxwell, are going to lead the firm's dream team representing Hayden Covey in his murder trial."

Rachel threw up her hands in total exasperation. "I can't believe this. It's beyond ludicrous."

"Supposedly this is straight from the mouth of Hayden's mother."

Rachel dropped to the bed. "Mrs. Covey may have given the information to the reporter, but this is all Eric Fitch's doing. He no doubt told Senator and Claire Covey that my past would influence the jury. He used me as a bargaining chip to get this case and he hasn't bothered to let Mrs. Covey know I'm no longer in his game plan."

"I don't see how letting the lie go public will help him."

"No, but he has a plan to either get me back or convince the Coveys that he can win Hayden's case without me. I guarantee you that. Now I'm wondering if he was lying about being such great friends with the senator. If he was, he shouldn't have needed me to seal the deal."

"It's all backfired on him now," Sydney said. "How

did he think this would possibly work out to his advantage?"

"I don't know, but I'm about to find out." Rachel walked over to the table and picked up her cell phone.

"Do you want me to leave you alone?" Sydney asked.

"Unless you want to be here for the fireworks."

"I think I'll wait for the recap."

Sydney let herself out the door.

Before Rachel could make her call, the phone rang. Eric Fitch. Obviously, he'd seen the same evening news as Sydney had.

"Hello, Mr. Fitch. I'm assuming you have a valid explanation for Mrs. Covey announcing that I'm defending her son."

"Don't try to turn this into some conspiracy, Rachel. You were upset yesterday. So was I, but I'm sure we can get past this. You're too valuable to the firm for us to lose you."

"That wasn't what you said yesterday."

"I'm saying it now, and my son spoke for me yesterday when he told you how much we value you. I'm sure we can work something out. It would be a terrible mistake for you to resign just as we were about to make you a junior partner."

She dropped back to the edge of the bed. This was not playing fair.

"Come in on Monday and we'll talk terms on your promotion."

"I'm out of town and don't plan to be back in Houston before Tuesday at the earliest."

"Then we'll plan to talk then. In the meantime, don't give any statements to the press."

"That's the only promise I'm making."

"Of course. We'll talk. In the meantime, let's keep the business dealings out of the press."

"Perhaps you should tell Claire Covey that."

"I'll handle that."

Rachel was certain he would, in a way that would ensure that Claire Covey didn't take her money and high-profile case to another firm.

She cut the conversation off and went to find Sydney to give her the lowdown.

If she went back, she'd be the youngest junior partner at the firm. Everything she'd worked so hard for was practically in her grasp.

And yet her heart had never felt so heavy.

Chapter Seven

The ribs and brisket had been delicious. So had the baked potatoes, the field peas, the green salad and Dani's fabulous red velvet cupcakes left over from the afternoon's baby shower.

The food had been devoured and the kitchen cleaned a couple of hours ago. Luke lingered with some of the others at the large dining room table, talking and laughing the way he'd always imagined normal families did.

Mostly he was captivated by Rachel, who seemed to be actively avoiding any interaction with him. Actually, she'd hardly talked to anyone since dinner. Sydney had tried several times to pull her sister into the conversation. Her attempts had elicited no more than a word or two.

Rachel seemed lost in a world of her own, most likely the chaotic one she'd mentioned earlier. She definitely hadn't gone to her happy place.

Esther and the two youngsters had taken their leave to find a quieter spot for a game of *Sorry*. The guys were still going strong, though the events of the day were catching up with Luke.

"The bull had it in for me," Tucker said, talking with his hands as much as his mouth. "It was personal. I knew it. The bull knew it. Everybody around the chutes knew it. No way was he going to give me the eight seconds I needed to win one of the most gorgeous silver belt buckles I'd ever seen."

"And you need another belt buckle so badly," Riley quipped. "Just to let you know, I'm kind of siding with the bull this time. No one ever gives him a buckle."

"What happened?" Dani asked, ignoring the brothers' good-natured ribbing.

"Not a dadburn thing. The bull got his revenge the easy way, ignored me completely. I pulled every trick I knew, and that contrary beast acted like he was out on a Sunday stroll.

"I could have stayed on it for half an hour and barely worked up a sweat."

"I take it that's a bad thing," Rachel said, finally joining in the conversation.

"I ended up with a paltry sixty-three points when I needed to be in the high eighties to take home the buckle."

"That doesn't seem fair," Dani said. "You did your part. It was the bull who goofed off."

"It's the luck of the draw," Tucker explained. "All random. You get the bull they give you, but you seldom get one that doesn't give you a decent fight. Rodeo bulls are raised to give the rider all he can handle."

"Still seems like you got ripped off," Dani said. "Can you make an official complaint?"

"Yes, and unlike the official complaints he makes to me, they take note," Sydney teased.

"Thankfully, I was allowed a second attempt on a different bull, since Torture II didn't give me a fighting chance."

"Torture II?" Riley laughed and slapped a hand on his knee. "I love it."

"You would."

"Then what happened?" Grace asked.

"I took home the silver buckle."

The men jokingly booed. The women clapped, even Rachel. Maybe he was reading too much into her mood. She might just be tired.

Grace stood, stretched and patted her stomach. "I hate to leave such good company, but I not only eat for two these days, I sleep for two, as well. Today was a perfect day and I can't thank you all enough for my shower, but I'm truly exhausted."

"I'll get Jaci," Pierce said, "though she'll complain that I'm messing up her fun."

"Why not just let her go home with us and spend the night?" Dani asked. "That way Grace and baby can sleep in tomorrow."

"I like it," Grace said. "And Jaci will love it. Do you have something she can sleep in?"

"It will be a little large, but she can wear one of Constance's T-shirts."

"Are we still on for the Sunday morning family trail ride?" Sydney asked.

"Sure, as long as you and Tucker are up for it," Pierce said. "Weather is supposed to be perfect in the morning, midfifties and clear. Nice day to take the Canyon Trail. Besides, I have everything ready for a cowboy breakfast when we reach the top."

"And I have a little special addition from Dani's Delights," Dani said.

"If it's your cinnamon rolls, count me in," Sydney chimed in. "Those are worth losing a little sleep over. For that matter, anything from your bakery is worth getting up early for."

"We'll drop Jaci off at your house in the morning, Grace, so she can change into her riding clothes," Dani said. "Pierce can take over from there."

"Sounds like a plan," Pierce said. "Why don't you join us, Luke? I know you're probably busy checking out the ranch, but we head out just after sunrise and are usually back here before ten. That will leave the rest of the day for whatever you've got planned."

Luke considered the offer. He'd love the opportunity to go riding with Rachel. But on the off chance that he'd had said or done something to upset her and put her in her edgy mood, he wasn't sure he should accept.

"I think the operative word here is family," Luke said. "I've horned in on your dinner tonight. I don't want to wear out my welcome my second day back in Winding Creek."

"It's a trail ride. The more the merrier," Riley said.

"Everyone might not feel that way," Luke cautioned. He turned to Rachel and waited for her to meet his questioning gaze.

She did but hesitated before nodding. "Of course

you should come. Sunrise over the canyon shouldn't be missed."

Not the most resounding invitation he'd ever received, but he'd take it. He was looking for a way in, not out.

"I'll be here," he said. "Shall I trailer over my own mount? Arrowhead Hills seems to be well stocked with quarter horses."

"No need to go to the trouble unless you want to. We've got you covered," Riley said, "with horse and saddle. You can ride Torture III. You get Tucker's belt buckle if you stay on till breakfast."

Luke joined in the laughter.

Grace and Pierce went to tell their daughter goodnight before heading to Pierce's truck for the very short ride to their cabin.

"I think I'll call it a night, as well," Rachel said. "It's been a long day. I'll see you all in the morning."

"Do you need to borrow some boots for the ride?" Luke teased.

"No, these will be fine." Rachel uncrossed her legs, showing off a gorgeous calf, then added a smile that knocked him for a wallop yet again. Her power over him appeared to be headed toward the danger zone despite the total lack of effort on her part.

"If you're going to be spending a lot of time on a ranch, you need some cowgirl boots."

"I'll keep that in mind—if I ever make a ranch my home."

Luke stood. "I'm out of here, too. But I gotta say, dinner was awesome."

"I thought it was good myself," Pierce said. "Even if we don't measure up to Esther's cooking."

"No one does," Sydney said.

"But Esther can't shoot like you, my sexy FBI bride," Tucker said as he stooped to give his wife a peck on the lips.

Rachel stepped closer to Luke. "I still have your jacket. I'll get it for you and meet you at the door."

"Sounds like a plan."

Luke reached the door just as Pierce was driving away. He stepped over to the porch railing, leaning his backside against it while he waited for Rachel. He wondered if this moment they'd have alone was by design or just happenstance.

Rachel joined him a minute later. She'd slipped out of her heels and into a pair of fluffy blue slippers. She held out his jacket and he crossed the porch to take it.

"Congratulations, Luke Dawkins. You not only survived but you hung right in there with the boisterous Lawrence brothers when they were in rare form. I'm impressed."

"Me, too. Never thought I'd say this, but it feels good to be back in Winding Creek—at least for tonight." That was mostly due to Rachel and would still likely change when dear old Dad was released from rehab and back on the ranch.

Luke refused to let that bother him while standing this close to Rachel. Moonlight streaked her luxuriant curls. Only a touch of lipstick remained on her full, tantalizing lips.

"You were awfully quiet tonight," he said. "The effect of the chaos you mentioned earlier?"

"Yes, but I'm working on shedding it from my life."

"It might help to talk about it with someone who's not family."

A stupid comment. Unlike his, her family was great. Why would she need a virtual stranger to confide in?

She pushed loose locks of hair behind her right ear and looked upward as if counting the stars that seemed close enough to touch.

"How much do you know about me?" she asked.

"Is this a trick question?"

"Not completely."

He reached across and took her small hand in his, half expecting her to pull away. When she didn't, a crazy protective urge swept through him. Only what or whom did she need protection from?

"I know you're gorgeous and you smell like lilacs." He trailed his fingers up her arm until they tangled into the delectable curls that fell past her shoulders. "What else should I know about you, Rachel?"

"Nothing that you won't find out for yourself soon enough."

Her words sounded like a pronouncement of lurking doom. A sense of hopeless dread chilled him as she backed against the front door and rested one hand on the knob. "I should go in now. We'll be up at dawn tomorrow."

"Then I guess this is good-night."

He tried to walk away. He honestly tried, but she looked so tempting. So irresistible.

He slid a thumb beneath her chin and nudged until she met his gaze. When she didn't turn away, his lips touched hers, brushing them like a feather, little more than a suggestion of a kiss. Even that was enough to send him reeling.

Rachel slipped her arms around his neck and kissed him back. Not shy or reluctant, but a bold, hungry kiss that set him on fire. He swayed against her, drunk on the thrill of lips on his, their tongues tangling, their breaths mingling.

Seconds later, she pulled away and placed an open hand against his chest, gently pushing him away. He was crazy with wanting her and was certain she could feel the pounding of his heart.

"See you tomorrow," she whispered as she opened the door and slipped back inside the house.

Tomorrow couldn't come too soon.

DAWN WAS LIGHTENING the sky before Rachel gave up on the tossing and turning and any chance of sound sleep. Her life was spinning out of control at a dizzying pace.

Two days ago, she'd had a career. She'd known what she would be doing from day to day. Admittedly, she'd still been struggling to move past the torture Roy Sales had put her through, but she was making progress.

Two days ago, she wasn't making headlines, another major detriment to defending Hayden. The terrors she was trying so hard to escape would be front and center.

People would stare. People would ask questions. Gossip magazines would feed on her trauma again.

Two days ago she hadn't met Luke Dawkins. Her

stomach hadn't fluttered at his incidental touch. There had been no heated zings of attraction when a rugged, hard-bodied stranger spoke her name or met her gaze.

A kiss hadn't rocked her with desire and left her aching for more. She put her fingertips to her lips, and a craving for his mouth on hers burned inside her.

This was absolutely crazy.

She kicked off the covers, crawled out of bed, padded to the window and opened the blinds. The crescent moon floated behind a gray cloud. The universe held steady, day following night, season following season, the earth remaining on its axis century after century.

She didn't expect that kind of order in her life, but neither could she continue to let the demonic Roy Sales pull the strings and control her reactions.

She had to fight to get what she wanted—once she decided what that was. She'd spend the next two or maybe three days here in Winding Creek trying to figure it all out. Then she'd drive back to Houston and face Eric Fitch Sr. straight on.

There were no decisions to make about Luke Dawkins. Once he learned of her past, he'd see her through different eyes. And he'd definitely learn about her past, since she was making news again. He'd pity her, and then he'd move on.

Who could blame him? Her emotional baggage was killing her.

RACHEL, SYDNEY AND DANI were sipping coffee from disposable cups and watching Jaci and Constance raced around the corral while the guys saddled the morning's mounts.

The first sun rays were chasing away the moon from what was now a cloudless sky. The air was brisk. The breeze was gentle. Exactly the kind of morning she'd have ordered for a trail ride.

Except that Luke had not shown.

This was just the eye-opener she needed to realize last night's kiss didn't mean anything. Nor should it. God knew she had more on her plate than she could handle. Luke had overwhelming problems of his own.

Nonetheless, she couldn't stop herself from turning every few seconds to look over her shoulder for his truck approaching the horse barn.

Pierce sauntered over and joined in the children's game of chase. He caught Jaci, swooping her into his arms and then balancing her atop his shoulders.

"Time to climb into the saddle," he said. "Dreamer's getting impatient."

Riley stepped out of the horse barn, leading another horse that was saddled and tossing its head as if eager to be ridden. "Beauty's ready, too, Constance. I think she's more excited about getting some exercise than you are."

"Jaci and Constance are amazing kids," Sydney said. "Precocious and outgoing and both so sweet. I may have to start thinking about starting a family myself one of these days."

That got Rachel's full attention. "That's the first time I've heard you say that."

"Don't go buying any diapers. I'm not ready yet,"

Sydney said. "I'm still having too much fun fighting crime, but one day."

"I would have said the same thing until Constance fell into my life," Dani said. "Now I can't imagine life without her."

"They sit in the saddle like experienced horse-women," Rachel said.

"Pierce and Riley both take up a lot of time with them, teaching them the basics about horses, including how to treat the animals. I swear I think Constance would much rather spend her time with horses than her school friends."

Tucker led a chestnut and a sorrel mare out of the barn, also saddled, bridled and ready to go. "Time to ride, ladies. This is Moonbeam, Rachel," he said, giving the chestnut a nose rub.

"She's beautiful."

"She's gentle and responds well even to a slight tug on the reins. She'll give you a great ride."

"Just listen to my gorgeous bull-riding hubby," Sydney said. "The way he talks about the Double K horses, you'd think he spent his time with horses instead of mean bulls."

"I told you I'm a man of many talents," Tucker teased.

"And so modest."

"Shouldn't we wait for Luke?" Dani asked.

"I had a call from him a few minutes ago," Pierce said as he fit the riding helmet on his young daughter. "He was out riding the fence line at dawn and came across a break in the fence from a fallen mulberry branch. He's fixing it before the cows head for greener pastures that might not belong to him."

"He'll be sorry he missed the cinnamon rolls," Riley said.

"And riding with all these beautiful women," Tucker added.

"He must agree with you," Pierce said. "He's still going to try to make it, but he said if he wasn't here when we got ready to start out, we should leave without him."

Rachel felt a tinge of relief. At least he wasn't avoiding her intentionally after she'd kissed him so ravenously last night—unless the break in the fence was just an excuse. Either way, she wouldn't have to face his questioning, pitying eyes if he'd already heard about the kidnapping

She walked over to get acquainted with Moonbeam. Her experience with horses was not as extensive as the rest of the riding party's, but she had ridden some in college. Half her friends' families either owned a ranch or knew someone who did. That was Texas.

She heard the hum of the truck's engine just as they started their procession. Her mood improved dramatically.

"You guys go ahead," Riley called from the rear of the line. "Luke and I will catch up with you."

Rachel was just getting comfortable in the saddle when Luke slowed his horse and fell in beside her.

She glanced his way, and her heart skipped a couple of beats. There should have been a law against any man being that heart-stoppingly sexy.

He tipped his gray Stetson. A few locks of his hair fell over his forehead. The jagged angles and planes of his face were made more rugged by the dark whiskers on his chin. His denim jacket was open, revealing a black T-shirt that emphasized his hard body.

She took a deep breath and waited for her pulse to return to normal. "Glad you could join us," she said.

"Pleasure is all mine."

"Did you get your fence fixed?"

"Patched. It needs more extensive work like everything else around Arrowhead Hills except the horse barn. Dad's quarter horses live like kings. The other outbuildings are practically caving in. But enough about my troubles."

He pointed to the left. "Check out that view."

She did. They'd been climbing steadily since they left the horse barn. Grassy hillsides stretched out behind them, the rambling ranch house no longer visible.

"It's magnificent," she said.

At that moment, a tall, antlered buck and two does stepped out from the tree line a few yards ahead of them. She pulled the reins, slowing Moonbeam to a full stop. The deer remained still, staring back at her until a fluffy-tailed rabbit scurried past them.

The buck turned and raced back into the woods with the does at his heels.

"I forgot about all the wildlife in this part of Texas and how peaceful it is on the open range," Luke said. "No traffic jams. Clean air. The smell of the earth."

"The rural lifestyle does have a lot to offer," she

agreed. "I should get to the Double K a lot more often than I do, but there never seems to be enough time."

"Which is exactly why you should spend more time here," Luke said. "That and the fact that Esther has a way of making everyone feel so welcome."

"She definitely does that."

Pierce dropped back to join them. "Having a problem?"

"Nope," Luke said. "Just stopped a moment to soak in the atmosphere."

"The scenery keeps getting better until we reach the canyon view," Pierce said. "Then it's phenomenal. We'll stop for breakfast there. Esther is bringing the food and supplies in the truck."

"I'm sure I'll be famished by then," Luke said. "And full as a tick when we head back."

They started along the trail again. Luke and Pierce immediately got into a conversation about cattle feed, hay and barn repairs.

Rachel left them behind and caught up with Sydney.

"I noticed you and Luke were riding together for a while," Rachel's sister commented.

"Only for a few minutes."

"So, what do you think of him other than the fact that he'd blow the top off any hunk-o-meter?"

"I hadn't noticed that."

"Really? When did you lose your eyesight?"

"Just kidding," Rachel confessed. "He's sexy. I'll give him that. And interesting."

"Then his attention isn't making you nervous."

"No, though strange men usually do. I suspect it has something to do with being here with all of you."

"I think that it's a good sign you're moving on."

"I hope you're right. It's been four months."

But moving on to what? It was peaceful here, but the real world was waiting to ambush her at the next turn.

ESTHER WAS WAITING for them at a flat, grassy spot with a nice view of Creek Canyon while still far enough away from the edge that Constance and Jaci weren't in danger of tumbling down the rocky decline. Neither of them ever slowed down.

In the Big Bend area of Texas, Creek Canyon would be considered more gulch than canyon, but it was impressive for the Hill Country.

Luke was familiar with the canyon from before, only he'd seen it from the other side on land that belonged to one of his baseball teammates. It was a favorite spot for going snake hunting, an activity they'd somehow thought fun back in the day.

Rachel didn't wait for his assistance but dismounted on her own and walked the horse over to a scrubby cluster of Texas walnut trees. She handed the reins to Pierce, who was already securing his and Jaci's mounts to a low branch.

There was no water for the horses, but they'd stopped at two streams on the way up, where the horses had drunk their fill.

The tailgate of Esther's four-wheel-drive pickup truck was down, making a nice serving area for the thermoses of coffee and hot chocolate that were waiting for them. Within minutes everyone had a steaming mug in hand or at least within easy reach.

The women started unpacking and arranging the food from two huge picnic baskets. Luke went with Riley to gather wood for a stone fire pit that had clearly seen its share of use.

Once they had the fire going, Pierce filled a black cast-iron skillet with a spicy egg and chorizo mixture, and the marvelous odors filled the air. If Luke hadn't already been starving, the smells alone would have had him drooling.

Nothing like cooking real food in the outdoors. It beat those tasteless MREs he'd choked down in the Afghanistan wilderness by a county mile.

Everything seemed under control, so he stepped back from the fire and checked out the scenery. His gaze got no further than Rachel. She might be a city girl at heart, but she looked completely at home in this setting.

She was natural beauty. If she had on any makeup at all, he couldn't tell, and yet she was stunning.

"My sister-in-law is always an attention grabber," Tucker said, startling him.

Luke had been so lost in his appreciation of Rachel's beauty, he hadn't seen or heard Tucker approach from behind. No use to deny he'd been ogling. "She is striking."

"My wife thinks there's some chemistry firing between you and Rachel."

"I can't speak for Rachel, but I admit I find her fascinating. Is that a problem?"

"It could be."

"She's not married, is she?"

"No, and ordinarily I'd be the first to say she's tough enough to take care of herself. But she's had a traumatic few months—none of it her doing. I just wouldn't want to see her get hurt. That's all."

"I barely know her. I'm not planning to push myself on her, so you can relax if that's what you're worried about. Did Sydney ask you to talk to me?"

"No way. She thinks you and Rachel might be good for each other. I just figured it wouldn't hurt to mention that she's awfully vulnerable."

"I appreciate that. Is there more I should know?"

"Probably, but I'll leave that to Rachel. If I were you, I wouldn't push for more than she wants to say."

"I won't. Thanks for the update."

There it was again, innuendos that seemed to slide around straight facts. Luke usually liked a good mystery, but not this time. Mainly because he sensed it was troubling Rachel.

Tucker went back to the fire to relieve Pierce and take over the job of warming the tortillas in a black iron skillet.

Rachel was helping Esther set out plates of sliced avocados, jalapeños and pico de gallo. Luke started to walk over and join them, but quickly reconsidered as a new idea came to mind.

He walked away from the group, pulled his phone from his pocket and did a Google search on Rachel Maxwell. Her image quickly stared back at him as well as a full page of offerings.

He started reading, his rage building with each sentence.

Rachel Maxwell had every reason to be vulnerable. She'd been through hell.

Chapter Eight

Roy Sales was walking by the TV in the community room when he heard the announcer say his name. He stopped and stared at his picture on the screen.

"Rachel Maxwell, one of the victims of the Lone Star Snatcher, will defend Hayden Covey against murder charges."

Damn. Had he heard that right?

"Shut up," Roy yelled at the old man who sat a few feet from him, chanting gibberish so loud Roy could barely hear what the pretty blonde TV announcer was saying.

Rachel's picture flashed on the screen. That was her, all right. She looked exactly as she had that first day he saw her—before he'd beaten the hell out of her and left her so bruised and bloody he could barely recognize her.

He strained to hear what the reporter was saying. The smart-mouthed attendants controlled the volume on the TV the way they controlled everything else in this stinking place.

He caught enough of the morning report to get the gist of the breaking news. His blood boiled. How dare she defend that rich son of a bitch after the way she'd talked about *him* after his arrest?

Rachel's words bellowed inside his head. *"Mentally unhinged." "A monster." "Crazy." "Psychopath."*

She was the reason he was locked up in this loony bin. But he had news for her. This wasn't over. He was smarter than every doctor in this horrible place.

He didn't swallow those mind-numbing pills they gave him every morning. He only played the game.

He'd be out of here soon. He had a plan. And then he'd get to finally watch Rachel Maxwell die.

Slow. Tortured. Begging for mercy as she gasped for her last breaths. He'd be every bit as evil as the monster she'd made him out to be.

"You just watch, Mommy. You'll be so proud of me."

Chapter Nine

As much as Rachel had enjoyed the first half of the trail ride, she was glad to get back to the horse barn. She had recognized the change in Luke even before they left the canyon.

He had come and sat down beside her while she finished her taco, but the conversation was strained. More telling was the fact that he didn't ride near her on the way back down the trail.

She'd seen him looking at something on his phone. Possibly another breaking news item. She and Hayden would take over the news cycle for a few days.

If they'd mentioned her, they would have talked about her abduction by Roy Sales. It was her horrifying claim to fame.

Before Rachel could dismount, Luke showed up and offered a hand to help her. "Ready to cool your saddle?"

"If that means am I ready to dismount, the answer is yes."

"That's what it means. Need some help?"

"No, thanks. I've got it."

Still holding the reins, she took hold of the saddle

horn and threw her right foot back over the saddle. Moonbeam knew the procedure well, standing still until both of Rachel's feet were on solid ground.

She stretched, brushed off her tired bottom and then ran her fingers through Moonbeam's long, thick mane.

"How was your ride?" Luke asked.

"Enjoyable. What about you?"

"Great, and just what I needed to get me back in the fun part of the cowboy groove. So glad you and the rest of your crew invited me to intrude on your family fun."

He was trying to keep things light. Rachel would give him that, but she still sensed a difference in him.

He reached for the reins. "I'll take care of Moonbeam for you and see that she's put away properly."

"Thanks."

She started to walk away. Luke reached for her wrist with his left hand and held her back. "Any way we can talk privately after the horses are taken care of?"

She shrugged. "That's not necessary."

"I didn't mean to suggest that it was, but if you'd rather not, I understand."

Because he felt the need to say something about what he'd learned, yet had to protect her tender feelings. Perhaps the worst was that there was some truth to the way her emotions could crater without warning.

"How did you find out?" she asked.

"I looked you up on the internet," he said, obviously knowing what she was referring to. "It's not exactly a secret."

"I know. I'm infamous. If you'd been in the country,

especially in Texas, you'd already know all the gory details."

"I don't need the gory details. I just have one question."

"That's a shocker. Most people have a hundred."

"Where is Roy Sales now? Please tell me he's in prison."

"No. It's been just over four months, but unfortunately, he hasn't been deemed mentally competent to stand trial yet. He's being cared for in a maximum-security forensic mental hospital between here and Houston. It's supposedly state-of-the-art in treatment options."

"Probably a good place for him. Look, I know you're here to visit with your family this weekend, but it would be great if you had some time to fit me into your schedule."

"I smell like horseflesh."

"Nothing wrong with that. But it doesn't have to be now and I promise this has zero to do with the kidnapping, if that's what you're concerned about."

"Then what is it you want to talk about?"

"Us."

"There is no us, Luke. We just met. I live in Houston. You have a father with health concerns to take care of in Winding Creek."

"Correct me if I'm wrong, but I kind of got the idea we have a little attraction going here."

"The kiss. I can explain that. Well, actually, I can't, but we shouldn't try to make more of that than it was. I think I got carried away in the moment."

"Why not check it out and see where it goes? I'm not necessarily talking sex. Talk is good. A beer or two. A long walk. Dinner in town or dancing at the roadhouse. I guess that's still going strong."

He made this sound so natural, but nothing in her life had been natural since Sales had held her in captivity. Seeing where this could go might be dangerous. She should just send him away.

Yet she couldn't deny how desperately she wanted to see him again.

"I'd invite you to Arrowhead Hills for lunch," Luke said, "but I think the whole house needs to be fumigated or at the very least scrubbed with bleach and a generous application of elbow grease. I don't know if my dad's eyesight is failing and he can't see the built-up crud and mildew or if he's so used to it he doesn't notice or possibly care."

"Scrubbing away crud and grime. Cleansing. Physical activity that requires no brain cells. Call me crazy," Rachel said, "but I find that extremely alluring today."

"I wouldn't think a highfalutin attorney like you ever stooped to such mundane tasks."

"I'll have you know there is nothing highfalutin about me, though it has been many a moon since I've gotten on my hands and knees to scrub a floor."

"Sounds intriguing," he teased. "Forget the cleaning, but I am serious about wanting to spend some time with you this afternoon."

"I can't make any promises until I see what Sydney has planned. I get to see my sister so seldom, but I still have to share her with her bull-rider hubby. I can give you a call later."

"Whenever you can get away is fine. Just give me

enough warning to grab a shower. I'll likely be checking out the livestock. Dad's record keeping is like deciphering a secret code."

"Ugh. Does Esther have your phone number?"

"Yes, and so does Pierce. He's going to give me a cram course on modern ranching one afternoon this week. I'd write the number down for you, but I don't have a pen on me."

Moonbeam tossed her head and pawed the dirt.

"That's horse talk for 'I've had enough of this,'" Luke said. He tipped his hat and grinned. "I'll be waiting for your call."

Amazing how he could start her heart spinning with just a smile.

He thought her talk of scrubbing was facetious, but something physically demanding might be exactly what she needed. At least she'd be doing something useful.

But she had to admit that getting rid of grease and grime would be the weirdest first date ever.

Except this wouldn't be a date. They couldn't take this too far, but it was possible they could be friends.

SYDNEY HAD STOPPED to wait on Rachel about halfway down the worn path from the horse barn to the big house. Rachel hurried to catch up.

"You look flushed," Sydney said.

"Too much wind and sun."

"Nice try. I think it's the Luke Dawkins effect."

"I have no idea what you're talking about."

"You know exactly what I'm talking about. The way you two look at each other could ignite a five-alarm fire."

"We're practically strangers."

"That has nothing to do with chemistry."

"There is no place in my life for chemistry."

Sydney linked her arm with Rachel's. "Maybe, but there's nothing wrong with enjoying the company of a hunk like Luke who also happens to be a nice man."

"How do you know that?"

"He's a former marine, with a couple of medals for bravery, according to Esther. He's giving up his life temporarily to take care of an unhealthy father who basically disowned him when he was just a teenager. Esther likes him and she's a great judge of character."

"You have this all figured out, Sydney, which means you're spending too much time worrying about me."

"Not worried. Encouraging. Just because you spend time with a man doesn't mean you have to hop in bed with him—although I'm not knocking that, either. But I'll leave it up to you to know when the time is right."

"Thank you for that vote of confidence." Not that she was sure she was worthy. "You know, you and Dr. Lindquist think alike on so many things. You would have made a great psychologist."

"Or perhaps he should have become an FBI agent. I wish your psych was here right now."

"To encourage me to jump Luke's bones?"

"No." Her tone became strained. "But he'd do a better job of sharing more bad news than I will."

Rachel's spirits plunged. "What now?"

"It's nothing horrible—or urgent. It's—"

"Don't bother sugarcoating it," Rachel interrupted.

"Okay. I got a call last Wednesday from Dr. Leonard Kincaid."

Rachel's stomach knotted. "What's wrong with your health?"

"Nothing. Dr. Kincaid is Roy Sales's psychiatrist."

A shudder ripped thought Rachel. "They didn't release him. Please tell me they didn't say he was unfit to stand trial and just set him free."

"No. He's still in the maximum-security facility. You're safe. That I'm sure of, one of the perks you get from having a sister with the FBI."

"Then why would Sales's doctor call you?"

"He was trying to get in touch with you, but since you changed your cell phone to a secure number to avoid the constant harassment of the media, he couldn't reach you."

"And I want to keep it that way. Apparently you didn't give Dr. Kincaid my number."

"No, but I told him I'd give you a message."

"Which is?"

"All he would say is that it's important he talk to you. He wouldn't give me any of the pertinent reasons why. He claimed doctor/patient privilege."

"You're an FBI agent. I thought you were cleared for everything, even doctor/patient privilege."

"It doesn't work quite that way. Anyway, he wanted me to tell you that he'd very much like to talk to you, preferably in person."

"In person, like in my going to the facility where Roy Sales is being treated? That's not going to happen."

"He said he'll travel to you."

"That makes zero sense. Everything I could tell him about Sales is well documented."

Rachel stopped walking as they approached the house. "I know you've had time to think about this and I trust your judgment. Can you think of any good reason I should get involved with Sales or his psychiatrist?"

"There is one positive side to at least talking to him."

"Which is?"

"The sooner Roy Sales faces trial, the sooner you can put all this totally behind you. If you have any insight—even information you don't think is important that could make that happen faster—it might be worth talking to Kincaid."

"Then you think I should call him?"

"It's not my decision, Rachel. I only want what's best for you, but if you do agree to seeing him, I'd like to be with you."

"As a sister or as an FBI agent?"

"Both, but mostly as a sister who doesn't want to see Roy Sales put you though any more torment."

"This just seems so bizarre," Rachel said. "Did the doctor say if he's talked to the other kidnapping victims?"

"I asked. He said he hadn't and didn't judge it to be useful at this point."

Rachel kicked at a small stone that was in her path and sent it flying toward Esther's front porch. "So this is personal between Roy Sales and me? Something Kincaid thinks I know that the other victims don't?"

"I got that impression, but it could be that he thinks

your experience as a criminal defense attorney might make you a more valuable source of information."

"That's possible, I guess."

"You don't have to decide this minute, especially with all that's going on with your career. Take your time. Think about it. And remember, you can always tell him no. You aren't required to help Roy Sales in any way."

"The only help I'd give is to make certain he's never free to torture and murder again."

"That's what we all want."

"I'll think about calling Dr. Kincaid, but right now I'm not leaning that way. If he called you on Wednesday, why are you just now mentioning it to me?"

"I wanted to tell you in person, but then you were dealing with the job situation and I didn't want to lay more problems on you the minute I saw you."

"Which granted me a short reprieve," Rachel said. "A day or two to adjust to one problem before the next punches me in the gut. That's about average."

"You don't have to deal with this now or ever."

But she'd be thinking about it, and just hearing Sales's name cast a shadow over her world.

She had a nauseating suspicion that Roy Sales was orchestrating all this, trying to pull her back into his sphere of evil for his own sick pleasure.

His madness was real, but that didn't mean he wasn't smart enough to manipulate a whole team of psychiatrists.

Too bad she couldn't just scrub every memory of him from her life. But there was no cleanser that strong in all the world.

BY TWO IN the afternoon, life at the Double K Ranch had settled into a quiet, sleepy Sunday afternoon bliss. Esther was stretched out on the couch watching a Lifetime movie. Sydney and Tucker were taking advantage of the unseasonably warm weather to attend a winter festival in a neighboring town.

They'd invited Rachel to go with them, but she had enough sense to know it was private time together they were looking for. With their careers taking them in different directions, they cherished the time they had together.

Sydney truly loved working with the FBI. She thrived on the excitement and even the danger, the same way Tucker couldn't imagine life without the rodeo.

Indications were the lifestyle worked for them. Rachel envied them that.

She'd thought she'd found her niche in life, and now she wasn't even sure she wanted to take the firm's very generous promotion offer. Her priorities seemed to be shifting by the hour.

She was tempted to call Luke Dawkins, but what was the point? Roy Sales wasn't physically strangling her the way he did in her recurring nightmares, but he was emotionally strangling her.

Luke was interested in getting to know her better, and that would lead to the attraction building. How could she trust herself in a romantic entanglement with her life in a tailspin? She had nothing to offer but trouble. She liked him too much to add her burdens to his.

Weakening in her resolve not to call him, she walked back to the guest bedroom and grabbed her purse and her keys. She didn't bother to change from the denim cutoffs and loose-fitting T-shirt she'd changed into after lunch. She had to get out of here.

Her phone rang as she was pulling into a parking spot on Main Street. She answered as she climbed out of the car and started walking. "Hello."

"Hi, Rachel. Glad I caught you."

"Luke." Her pulse quickened at the sound of his voice. This was quickly swelling out of hand. "I'm sorry I didn't call."

"Me, too. That's why I called you. How about I pick you up and we take a drive, give me the opportunity to see how the area's changed since I moved away?"

"What happened to our scrubbing hoedown?"

"Believe me, this mess is more than you want to tackle. I don't even know where to begin."

"In the kitchen, of course. Kitchens always have more grease and grime than any other area."

"You're serious, aren't you?"

"I am. My brain is exhausted, but my muscles are atrophying."

"In that case, I'll pick you up as soon as I make a run to the store for some supplies."

"I'm already in town. I'll stop off at the market, pick up the supplies and drive to your place. And don't worry, I won't charge you the full price for my billable hours."

"I should have known there was a catch."

"Well, you are dealing with an attorney."

He gave her easy-to-follow directions. She turned to start back to the car, but then stopped and looked around her. Two youngsters holding doubled-dipped cones of chocolate ice cream walked past her, the melted treat dripping from their mouths and hands.

Their youthful parents followed close behind, laughing and chatting and holding hands like lovers.

Small-town Texas. Friendly. Safe.

Until that facade had been shattered by a psychopath who'd chosen his victims from this very street. Familiar fear crawled inside her like a hairy spider. She stopped walking and looked around as the apprehension swelled.

No place was ever completely safe.

She walked a few feet and then stopped to stare into the Christmas shop. Even in January, miniature villages, their roofs topped with fake snow, filled the display windows. A little girl walked up and stopped next to her, her nose pressed against the glass, no doubt already dreaming of Christmas.

Rachel took deep breaths until the unwanted flare of tenseness eased. Then she quickly walked to her car and drove the short distance to the market.

She stocked up on cleansers, protective gloves and some fruit, chips and salsa in case she needed some calorie fortification for the tasks at hand. Having no idea what kind of munchie Luke liked, she picked up some peanuts and a couple of packs of cheese crackers and cookies.

The last stop on the way to checkout was the beer aisle. She figured she couldn't go wrong with that.

Once she checked out, she made a phone call to Sydney to let her know she would be spending the afternoon with Luke Dawkins. There was no answer. She left a message.

Minutes later, she was on her way to Arrowhead Hills.

Still a bit uneasy, she tried to soothe her mind. How much trouble could she possibly get into scrubbing floors with Luke Dawkins?

Chapter Ten

Luke stuck his head into the oven for one last check. "Spotless as new and ready for inspection," he announced. "My guess is for the first time in years. I could almost swear there was part of a pizza I warmed up eleven years ago still stuck to the top shelf."

"Gross." Rachel walked over and checked it out. "I'm impressed. I'd actually eat something cooked in there now."

"And mess up my clean oven? No way," he protested. "We're not turning on that oven for anything."

"Not even for pizza?"

"There might be some exceptions."

He leaned his backside against the counter—which was also spotless—and watched Rachel as she went back to returning foods to the dust-and crumb-free pantry.

"Now that we've thrown away everything that was out-of-date, you'll have to restock," she said.

"Yes, ma'am. Another day. It's gotta be Miller time by now."

"Don't tell me a little housework is harder than being in the marines."

"Only difference is you're holding me hostage with a broom instead of enemy fire."

She returned the last item to the top shelf of the pantry and surveyed the finished product.

Luke walked behind her and put his arms around her waist. "Do you have any idea how sexy you look right now?"

"I suppose you're about to tell me you're turned on by the fragrance of bleach."

"Is that what that is?" He sniffed behind her ear. "I thought it was awfully pungent for perfume."

He was telling the truth about her being sexy and so damn easy to be around. But she was right about one thing. Now that he knew, he couldn't help thinking about what that monster had put her through.

He'd love to meet that guy in a dark alley with only their fists between them. Fat chance he'd get that opportunity, but it riled him to think the guy wasn't tried and sentenced to life in prison. There was no doubt the guy was evil, but he wondered just how crazy he really was.

Rachel was vulnerable like Tucker had warned him. She'd have to be after what she'd been through. But she was also tough and smart. And energetic.

"Wonder Woman in denim," he said.

She straightened a can of peas and then closed the panty door. "Are you summoning a superpower to rescue you from the slave driver attorney?"

"I was talking about you. You are amazing. Up at sunrise to go horseback riding. Sun's setting and you're still going, gung ho, unlike the poor cowboy trying to keep up with you." He nibbled her ear.

She stepped out of his arms. "This isn't work. It's therapy, and you can't let your father return to this. When will he be coming home?"

"I don't know. I have an appointment with his doctor tomorrow. I'll stop by and see Dad after that. After the greeting he gave me yesterday, I'm not sure he wants to come home if I'm here."

"It can't be that bad."

"Wait till you meet him. Which is a great idea now that I think about it. Why don't you ride into town with me tomorrow? One look at you and he'll forget I'm even around."

"How old is he?"

"Sixty-nine, but he's not dead. He'll notice you."

Luke opened the refrigerator and took out two cold beers. He opened them both and handed one to her.

She sipped and then turned slowly, pointing out their day's accomplishments as she did. "Appliances shiny clean. Countertops and sink sparkling and hygienic. Cabinets organized. Kitchen window washed, ceiling fan blades dusted. Woodwork and floors thoroughly scrubbed."

"I couldn't have done it without you. Actually, I probably wouldn't have attempted it without you. How about we take our beers and go sit outside?" Luke suggested. "My muscles ache. I think I'm allergic to all this cleanness."

"You'll forget that once you get my bill."

"Now you're scaring me—unless, of course, you want to work it out in trade."

"I'm not even going there."

RACHEL WAS TIRED to the bone, but even that didn't prevent her from reacting to every look and touch from Luke. She'd practically gone into orbit when he nibbled her ear.

Working barefoot and shirtless, his jeans riding a few inches below his waist and his muscles flexing, had further certified his hunk status.

That was just the start of what excited her about him. There was no pretense with him. Great sense of humor. Virile and masculine to the core but without any of the machismo that would have made her uncomfortable.

Still she felt guarded, afraid that if she ever let her full fears seep out, they'd explode and spill all over her like a deadly poison.

Luke was beside her, his hand on the small of her back, protective and possessive, as they walked through the house and onto the porch. The sun was low in the sky, but the humidity and temperature still made it feel like a summer day. The cold beer felt good in her hand. She suspected a cool shower would feel even better after all the work they'd put in this afternoon.

She brushed a few wisps of hair from her face, pushed them behind her ears and headed for the old porch rocker.

She started to sit down and then squealed and jumped backward as a large scorpion dropped from the arm of the chair and fell onto the seat.

Luke flew into action, knocking the scorpion out of the chair. The despicable arachnid fell onto the porch and took off in her direction, its stinger curved and ready to strike.

She dashed for the edge of the porch and climbed onto the railing, holding her feet in the air and almost toppling over the back, butt first.

"Kill it," she screamed. "Don't let it get away."

Thinking quickly, he didn't stamp it with his bare feet but grabbed a heavy pot of dead flowers and crashed it on top of the scorpion. The pot broke into a thousand pieces.

The scorpion wiggled like a creature from *The Walking Dead* before finally lying unmoving in the grave of sunbaked dirt and pottery shrapnel.

Luke broke into laughter.

"There is nothing funny about scorpions," she scolded.

"No, but can I see that rail-riding stunt again? You may be ready for bronc riding."

She planted her feet back on the porch. "Very funny. And here I was about to claim you as my hero."

"In that case, scorpions are nothing. Wait until you see my finesse with a rattlesnake."

"No demonstration needed. I'll take your word on that."

She walked to the busted pot, stooped and started picking up the larger pieces of broken pottery. She kept a wary lookout for any other bug that might be hiding in the chunks of dried earth.

"Just pile the pieces on the step," Luke said after the two of them had gathered the larger pieces. "I'll get a trash bag."

She did and then she spotted a hose that was hooked up to a faucet on the side of the porch. Exactly what she needed to wash the dirt off the porch before it got tracked back inside and ended up on her freshly scrubbed kitchen floor.

She turned on the hose and adjusted the nozzle to a jet spray. The powerful flow made quick work of getting rid of the dirt and tiny pieces of pottery.

Now that she was at it, she decided to wash off the rest of the porch and the old rocking chair that might have any number of creepy, crawly things hiding beneath the weathered slats.

She didn't hear or see the front door open and wasn't aware Luke had rejoined her as she turned to aim the spray at the chairs.

He yelped.

She turned to see him wiping water from his face and eyes with both hands. His hair was dripping wet. So were his jeans.

She aimed the spray into the yard. "Oops. Sorry."

"Oops?" Luke yelled. "Too late for 'oops' and 'sorry.' That was an act of war." He started toward her.

She backed up, sprayed him again and then dropped the hose and ran. He picked up the hose and aimed the spray at her. In minutes, they were both soaking wet.

By the time Luke dropped the hose, he was laughing hysterically. She started laughing, too. Hard. Uncontrollable. She laughed so hard that tears started running down her face.

Laughed the way she hadn't laughed in months and maybe longer.

Then, as if someone had slapped her across the face,

the tears became bitter and the laughter became chok-ing sobs. Tremors shook her body.

Luke ran to her, alarm firing in his eyes. "What's wrong? Are you hurt? Or angry?"

"No," she murmured through the painful sobs. "I don't know what's wrong with me. I don't know why I'm crying."

She expected him to back away fast from the crazy woman having a meltdown over too much fun. Instead he picked her up and cradled her in his arms as he car-ried her inside the house. "Cry if you need to, baby. Cry all you want. I'm here for you and I'm not going anywhere."

He settled in on the brown leather sofa, still holding her in his strong arms.

"I never used to lose it like this," she whispered through the sobs and the knot in her throat. "I'm sorry. I'm so sorry."

"You've done nothing to apologize for, Rachel. Your emotions are raw and have every reason to be, but maybe it's time you stop trying to be so strong. Maybe it's time you stop holding all the hurt and fears inside and just let them pour out."

"I think maybe it is," she admitted. More impor-tant, for the first time since the abduction, she thought maybe she could.

Chapter Eleven

"I can't remember the last time I ate canned chicken noodle soup," Rachel said.

Luke wiped his mouth with a paper napkin. "Me, either. It's better than I remember or else the mess hall food set a really low bar for tasty."

"Good that it's edible, since it's basically the only food option available now that the expired choices have been eliminated."

"Yeah. I guess I should buy some staples, like you said. I can't expect Esther and the Lawrence brothers to feed me all the time, though it's worked well so far."

"Wait until you try Esther's award-winning peach cobbler and homemade ice cream. If you can keep from going back for seconds, you have no taste buds."

Rachel tugged a bit on the soft cotton blanket she was wearing sarong-style, conscious every second that she was naked beneath it.

She'd been trembling when Luke carried her inside, chilly after the bout with the hose, but mostly emotionally shaken.

He'd insisted she get out of her wet clothes. He'd

given her the blanket and pointed her to the bathroom. While she'd showered under a refreshing spray, he'd thrown her jeans, shirt and undies in the wash.

Her hair was still wet when she'd met him back in the kitchen, once again wrapped in her cotton blanket. A box of tissue rested on the corner of the table. Obviously, Luke was prepared for the next meltdown.

He'd changed out of his wet jeans and was wearing clean ones and a sky blue pullover. But still no shoes. Inexplicably, his bare feet made the scene cozier, made him seem more familiar, like a friend she'd known for years instead of a stranger she was considering spilling her guts to.

She spooned up another mouthful of warm soup, but this time it didn't soothe. As she swallowed, the sickening image of Roy Sales stamped itself into her brain.

"We can talk whenever you're ready," Luke said, likely fearing from her facial expression that she was on the verge of another flood of tears.

"Not that I'm pressing," Luke added, "but if you keep things bottled up inside you too long, they have a way of eating you alive."

"I've found that out the hard way," she admitted. "I don't know where to start."

"How about the beginning?"

"You do have a way of cutting to the chase, Luke Dawkins."

"I'm a simple man."

That, she wasn't buying, but she trusted him and that was what mattered now. "I left my house on Friday, the eighth of September. We'd just won a difficult case that should have ended days before. I'd already booked a spa resort in Austin for some much-needed R and R."

"Were you traveling alone?"

"Yes. I often do, or at least I did. I haven't traveled anywhere except here to see Sydney since then. I spent that Friday night in the small town of La Grange and then, on the recommendation of the owner of the B and B, I drove to the quaint western town of Winding Creek on Saturday morning."

"Was that your first time in Winding Creek?"

"Yes, at that point neither Sydney nor I had ever met Esther Kavanaugh or the Lawrence brothers. I stopped at Dani's Delight for coffee and a pastry, so luckily I met Dani that day. As it turned out, she was an important lead to Sydney's finding me."

"Thank goodness you stopped in for coffee."

"Right. When I left the bakery, there were still several more hours of daylight, so I took the meandering scenic drive back to the interstate."

The interstate she'd never reached.

"A few miles out of town, a cowboy pulled up beside me in his pickup truck and started motioning and hollering at me to pull over."

"Was he alone?"

"Yes. I lowered my window but couldn't understand what he was saying. I considered pulling over, but something about the situation made me uncomfortable, especially since my car was running fine."

"Were there other cars around?"

"No. I'd passed other cars since leaving Winding

Creek, but there were no vehicles in sight then. No houses. Nothing but barbwire, pastures and cattle."

The pressure began to build inside her. Tears burned at the back of her eyes. She gritted her teeth and kept talking.

"I decided to keep driving until I reached the highway and a service station where I could safely check things out. I slammed my foot down on the accelerator and drove as fast as I dared on the curving road."

"But he kept coming?"

"Stayed right on my tail. I was afraid he was going to try to force me off the road. Then I heard what sounded like an explosion. I checked the rearview mirror and saw sparks and smoke."

"Gunshots?"

"No." Her voice was barely a whisper. Her insides quivered. She forced the words to keep coming. It was the first time since she'd given the police the information that she'd retold the events in such detail.

"I assumed my gas tank had exploded. I panicked, pulled to the shoulder and jumped from the car."

"Which is exactly what the low-life son of a bitch was counting on."

"Yes. It was the same strategy he'd used with the others, though no one knew that at the time. When I looked up, Sales was running toward me.

"I felt his fists hammer my face. That was the last thing I remembered until I woke up in a dark, dank room with my eyes swollen almost closed and my body covered in bruises."

Luke muttered a few curses. "Sorry, but it's too damn

bad you weren't carrying a .45. That's the only straight talking a bastard like that understands."

"I wouldn't have known how to use it."

"It's time you learn, though hopefully you'll never encounter a psychopath like Sales again. I'm sorry for interrupting you," Luke said. "Go on. I'll keep quiet, but I am serious about your learning to shoot."

"The rest is a nightmare," she said. "Are you sure you want to hear it?"

"I'm sure *I* can handle it. You're the one being faced with the horrors again. How are you holding up?"

"I'm good." Not true, but she'd gotten this far. There was no reason not to get it all out now.

"When I came to, I was lying on a thin pallet on a hard floor. I was in such pain I could barely move and had no clue where I was, only that there was a good chance the monster who'd attacked me was nearby.

"The room was windowless and the only light came from a strip of illumination creeping in from beneath a closed door. I was sure the door would be locked, but I had to try it, so I scooted stomach-down across the floor.

"All for nothing. The door was locked. I was the monster's prisoner. I had never been so afraid in my life. I hope to never be again."

Luke stretched his arms across the table and reached for Rachel's hands. She pulled away, stood and started to pace the kitchen. She had to get through this on her own. Leaning on his strength would steal the courage she needed.

Her thoughts rambled, her fears mingling with her words as they spilled from her mouth without filter.

Sales's maniacal laughter. The cold, dead cruelty in his eyes. The periods of hunger and thirst and the knowledge that she'd lost all control. The unending fear and the paralysis that hit when she heard his footsteps outside the door.

The constant prayers that Sydney would find her before it was too late.

Rachel stopped pacing and stared out the window into the darkness as the blistering mental scars burst into malignant abscesses all over again.

"I wasn't the only one held captive in that hellhole," she said. "There were three others, though I never saw them until the night we were rescued.

"That was the night Roy realized his horrid abduction game was coming to an end. He set fire to the compound and attempted to burn all of us alive. I can't smell smoke or see a fire without reliving that night. I'm not sure I ever will."

She finally got up the nerve to face Luke again. His lips were a thin line, his face jagged angles, his jaw protruded.

"The Lone Star Snatcher." Luke spit the infamous title like a curse. "That's how the internet article referred to him."

"That's what the FBI termed him," Rachel explained. "I didn't know any of that until after my rescue. I just thought of him as the monster."

"More fitting, if there were a word to describe a devil in the body of a man."

"He is evil incarnate," Rachel said. "I'm sure he hasn't changed. How could he after the beastly crimes he's committed? He murdered a runaway teenage girl who'd been living on the streets of San Antonio. He killed Esther's husband, Charlie, in cold blood—in his own barn. She found him with a bullet through his head."

"Charlie? He murdered Charlie Kavanaugh? I didn't know."

"Only because you were halfway around the world in a news vacuum. That's another long story, another unthinkable crime Sales committed with no remorse. Sydney could better fill you in on that information."

Rachel squeezed her eyes tight to hold back the salty tears that were pushing for release. "Two weeks in captivity have torn me apart. Charlie Kavanagh is dead and Esther will suffer from that grief every day for as long as she lives."

Rachel buried her face in her hands as tears began to rain down her cheeks. Reliving the horror hadn't helped. How could she have believed it would?

She heard the scrape of Luke's chair and the slap of his bare feet on the kitchen floor as he walked over and stopped behind her. His hands clasped her shoulders and then pulled her around to face him.

"You are one of the bravest people I've ever met, Rachel, and believe me, that's saying a lot." He dabbed at her tears with a tissue.

"No. I'm not brave at all. I'm stuck in this nauseating time warp of nerves and fear. The horror of Roy Sales won't let go."

"It will. It just takes time." He reached for more tissues and put a wad of them to her nose. "Blow."

She did, then sniffled and tried to stop shaking.

Luke pulled her into his arms and she let her head rest on his broad shoulder. "I'm sorry," she murmured.

"Don't be. You can cry on my shoulder all night if that's what it takes to make you feel safe. I'll be here as long as you need me."

"Thanks, Lu—"

Her words were lost in the touch of his lips on hers. Her mind screamed this was the wrong time, the wrong place. Her body ignored the warnings.

She needed his touch, needed his strength. Needed him.

The kiss consumed her, taking her breath away. His fingers tangled in her hair as he pulled her closer.

She splayed her hands across his back, loving the feel of his bare flesh and the strong cords of his muscles.

He moaned her name.

Her insides became molten.

And then all on its own, the cotton loops worked free and the blanket dropped and pooled at her feet.

Chapter Twelve

Luke stared at Rachel, his body rock hard, his breath ragged.

Her arms fell to her sides. She didn't reach for the blanket but just stood there inches away from him. The same need that rocketed through him was mirrored in her beautiful, dusky eyes.

The urge to take her right here and now was savage. On the table, on the floor, against the wall. He ached to touch her perfect breasts, to suck the nipples that stood at attention like bullets.

He fisted his hands to keep from running them down the smooth flesh of her belly to find the sweet heat hidden beneath the triangle of dark hair.

He'd never wanted a woman more.

Yet his brain was yelling no. She'd just bared her soul to him. She was vulnerable. Making love might be fantastic for him, but she might wake up tomorrow with deep regrets.

Somehow he found the strength to look away. He stooped, picked up the blanket and wrapped her in it again. "Why does this feel like I'm rewrapping the best gift I've ever received?"

"Why are you?" she asked.

The truth hit hard. It was because he didn't want to be the guy who'd just happened to be there when she faced all her fears and weaknesses head-on. He didn't want to be a one-night stand remembered with remorse. Not with Rachel.

Her phone rang, saving him from having to put feelings he didn't fully understand himself into words.

She walked over to the table and picked up her phone. "It's Sydney."

"Better take it," he said. "She's probably worried that you're still scrubbing floors."

She took the call and he reluctantly went to get her clothes from the dryer.

"HI, SYDNEY."

"Hi, yourself, and where are you?"

"At Luke Dalton's place. I left you a message."

"Hours ago. Are you okay?"

"I'm great."

"Did you have dinner?"

"I did." Canned soup while wearing a blanket. That would take a lot more explaining than Rachel cared to share.

"At the risk of being the nosy younger sister, when are you coming home?"

"That's not nosy. I'll be leaving here within the next half hour."

"I'll see you then. Can't wait to hear about your afternoon."

"Now you're being nosy?"

"Sister's privilege."

They had always shared a lot with each other. This time Rachel would keep a few intimate details to herself. Like how wildly her heart had beat when she stood naked in front of Luke. Like how much she'd wanted him to claim her like some morally unencumbered Neanderthal.

Only he wasn't like that. He was a decent guy, a caring cowboy who'd turned away when she'd stood before him naked.

Luke returned as she finished the call and broke the connection. Her clean and dry clothes were draped over his arm.

"You'd best change into these," he said. "If that blanket were to fall again, I make no promises of controlling my urges or my sanity."

"It's getting a bit warm anyway," she said, "and I need to be going."

"I'll drive you home," he said.

"That's not necessary."

"It is," he assured her. "No cowboy worth his spurs would let a beautiful woman drive herself home on these old ranch roads after dark."

"I'd only have to come back in the morning for my car."

"Not if you go with me to visit my dad in San Antonio. I'd pick you up whatever time you say."

"You don't need me for that."

"Probably not, but I'd really enjoy your company. I would like your feedback on what the doctor says about Dad's prognosis. And if the weather holds, we could follow the unpleasantness with a margarita and a stroll along the River Walk."

"Your invitation just gained a lot more appeal, Luke Dawkins."

"I can add more exciting options, if you're interested," he teased.

She started to take her clothes back to the bedroom to change but stopped at the door. "Just tell me one thing, Luke. Why didn't you make a move on me tonight when the sexual tension was going through the roof?"

"For the record, not touching you was one of the hardest things I've ever done in my life, and that includes combat. But I know how difficult it was for you to open up about Roy Sales. I didn't want to confuse the emotional lines between lover and confidant."

"So you were protecting me?"

"Yes, but that wasn't the whole of it. When we make love for the first time, and believe me, I'm counting on that happening, I want you to have nothing on your mind but me."

Any doubt of how hard she was falling for Luke vanished. "Then all you're asking for is perfection?"

"Damn straight."

"Have a seat and Dr. Riche will see you in a few minutes."

Luke and Rachel did as the nurse instructed. Rachel sat on the end of a deep blue sofa. He moved a health magazine out of the way and sat down next to her.

The drive from Winding Creek to the doctor's office had been slightly awkward, his attempts at casual conversation falling flat. The sensual sizzle from last night was still there but lurking beneath the surface in the bright light of day.

He still had no idea where he'd gotten the power to control his libido when that blanket hit the floor. It made him weak just thinking about it.

The attraction was out in the open now, but did he dare act on it? She was struggling with fears he couldn't fully understand. He suspected no one could unless they'd faced what she had.

The last thing he wanted to do was hurt her.

And there was Alfred, a father who needed but clearly did not want Luke's help. A father who was a stranger by choice. A man who had always lived life on his terms and who'd suddenly lost the ability to function without assistance.

Even if everything was in their favor, Luke couldn't imagine a lasting relationship developing between Rachel and him. She was a high-powered attorney in Houston. He was an ex-marine still trying to find where he fit in life as a civilian.

"Are you sure you want me to go in to see the doctor with you?" she asked. "I can wait here if you'd like more privacy."

"You may as well hear the worst—or the best—from Dr. Riche. Otherwise I'll have to repeat it all later when I beg for your input as to how I'm supposed to handle this."

"You do know my input is pretty much worthless. I know nothing about health care and my only legal expertise is dealing with alleged criminals. Even that is suspect now."

"Why do you say that?"

"It's a long and complicated story."

Everything with her seemed to be, which made her all the more intriguing. "As I said before, you are a very mysterious woman."

"More like a beleaguered woman. I'll explain later. Alfred's problems get top billing now."

As if on cue, a nurse opened a door on the far side of the room and called his name. "Ready or not, here we come," he muttered to no one in particular.

Rachel slipped her hand in his and squeezed. His spirits lifted. For what it was worth, it was nice having her on his side.

They were ushered into a small office with almost a dozen framed diplomas and other honors and acknowledgments hanging behind a large, neat desk. The man behind the desk looked to be in his midfifties, thin, with a receding hairline.

"I'm Dr. Riche," he said, extending a hand.

Luke shook it. "Luke Dawkins, and this is Rachel Maxwell."

The doctor shook Rachel's hand, as well. "Are you a relative of Alfred's, too?"

"No."

"She's a friend of mine," Luke explained quickly, "and an attorney, so feel free to speak honestly in front of her. Hopefully she'll guide me through any legal minefields we might run into in getting my dad the appropriate care."

"That could be useful before this is all over," the doctor affirmed, "though I won't be involved in that. My advice will strictly be medical except if you need medical information to support getting power of attorney. We have a lot to cover, so we might as well sit down and dive right in."

"That works for me," Luke said. "Just don't hit me with a lot of medical terms I won't understand. I'm a basic fact kind of guy."

To his credit, the doctor did keep the professional terminology to a minimum, repeating what he'd told Luke on the phone the first time they talked about the type and possible causes of the stroke. He utilized an illustrated chart on his wall to further explain Alfred's atrial fibrillation and the possibilities for treating it.

"As I explained on the phone, your father's stroke was relatively mild and he should improve with the proper therapy, though he may not regain everything he's lost."

"What would that therapy entail?"

"He'll need to continue with the physical therapy to address the weakness on the left side of his body. In the meantime, he'll require a walker or a cane to help with balance and will continue to need a wheelchair for longer distances and uneven surfaces."

"Is he using a wheelchair now? He wasn't in one when I saw him Saturday."

"He refuses to use one most of the time, so someone must be with him anytime he walks more than a few feet. He is a very stubborn man."

"That I know. What else does he need in the way of therapy?"

"An occupational therapist can help with using eating utensils, bathing, opening jars and bottles, making himself a sandwich and other daily living skills. And he'll need a speech therapist, though some of his problems with finding the right word are closely related to his memory loss. We'll have to wait and see if that improves."

"Sounds like he could be in rehab for months."

"That won't be necessary. The social worker can help you set it up so that Alfred can get his therapy at home. But he will need someone with him. It could be months before he's capable of functioning totally on his own."

"Months?"

"Yes, but if all goes well, he'll be making progress during that time. The alternative to at-home care would be to put him in a long-term-care facility until he can function more independently."

"You mean like a nursing home?"

"Yes. There are facilities with differing levels of care so that a patient can move from one level to another as required."

"I'd have to hog-tie him to get him into one of those," Luke said, thinking out loud.

The doctor smiled. "And lock him in to keep him there."

"How long are we talking about before he can live on the ranch by himself with a minimum of help?"

"I'll be completely honest with you, Mr. Dawkins. I don't know how much of the ranch work your father was doing before the stroke, but he may never be able to do all the physical activities needed to fully run his ranch."

Luke felt as if he'd been slammed into a brick wall. Ranching was his father's life, more important than family had ever been to him.

Luke had resented that fact growing up. Now he couldn't help pitying his father.

"Alfred can go home with you as early as next week, or you can start making arrangements to put him in a long-term-care facility."

The walls began to close in around Luke. Letting Luke or anyone else take over Arrowhead Hills Ranch would finish what the stroke had started. It would completely destroy his father.

"I can't make that decision today," Luke said. "I'm not sure my father would consider letting me live at the ranch. We didn't part on good terms. Our only contact in years has been short phone calls initiated by me."

"That does complicate matters," Dr. Riche said. "Perhaps the social worker can help you sort out some of that. And luckily you have Rachel to help you with the legal issues, such as power of attorney for medical and financial issues."

Yeah. Just what Rachel needed. His problems heaped on top of hers.

He listened to the rest of what the doctor had to say, but his mind was on Rachel instead of Alfred. He had no choice but to back out of her life while he dealt with the hell that had been dropped in his hands.

Alfred Dawkins had once again ruined his life.

RACHEL PICKED UP her pace to keep up with Luke as he practically ran across the parking lot and back to his truck. As upset as he was, he still stopped and opened her door for her. "Forgive my running off and leaving you back there. Guess I was trying to escape the inescapable."

"Been there," she said.

"I know. And now I feel like a rat for pulling you into my dilemma—not that it comes close to matching what you've been through."

"Maybe we shouldn't go and see Alfred just yet," she said as Luke started the engine and exited the parking garage. "You could probably use some time to look at the situation from different angles."

"Great idea," Luke agreed. "Another eleven years would help."

"I was thinking more like an hour or two."

"Lawyers are so rational. Are you hungry?"

"Not yet, and if your stomach is as tight as the way you're clutching the steering wheel, I doubt it would welcome food."

"No, but I could use a drink. It's almost noon. How about a margarita along the River Walk?"

"An excellent idea."

Traffic wasn't heavy and in less than a half hour, they'd driven to the center of the city, parked at one of the major hotels and made their way to the bustling waterway.

Visiting the River Walk always seemed like stepping into a new world to Rachel. Colorful umbrellas covered the waterside tables of a steady stream of restaurants.

Bright blooms in colorful pots were profuse even in

January. Decorated boats filled with smiling people enjoying the view floated down the shallow river.

And music with a delightful Latin beat wafted through the air. It was the perfect place to spend a carefree January day, the blustery wind blocked by the city's skyscrapers, the noon sun making it seem more like spring than winter.

Unfortunately, this was anything but a carefree day for either of them. Rachel suspected that much of what Luke was feeling was heartache. Admittedly he'd never been close to his father, and now it might be too late to ever really know him.

Luke would have to dig deep to pull all that out and deal with it. She had no idea how to help him with that, especially with her own life in such a muddled and worrisome state.

They walked for a good ten minutes, stopping once to enjoy the music of a sidewalk mariachi band before finally checking out a less busy outdoor café attached to a hotel farther down the river. It was quieter here. Good for talking if he felt like it.

"How do those margaritas look to you?" he asked.

"Cool and refreshing."

It was the first time they'd spoken since leaving the parked car.

The hostess led them to a small table near the far side of the grouping of outdoor tables. They'd just ordered their drinks when Rachel's phone rang.

She checked the caller ID. It was Eric Fitch Sr. She killed the call.

"An unwanted admirer?" Luke teased.

"An unwanted ex-boss."

"Have you changed jobs recently?"

"You might say that."

"There you go with the mysterious explanations again."

The waitress returned with their drinks. She set them down, but instead of walking away she stared at Rachel. "You look just like the defense attorney whose picture was on television earlier. You know, the one who's defending Senator Covey's son."

"Do I? Sorry. Not my claim to fame," Rachel quipped.

"Good. That guy's guilty, sure as I'm standing here. That's how it is with those rich bastards. They think they can do anything they want and get away with it. It even has a name now. Affluenza or something like that."

"If he's guilty, hopefully he won't get away with it," Rachel said.

"He killed her, all right. He's evil. I've got a sense about these things, and soon as I saw him on television, I could see the evil in him."

An icy chill stitched itself around Rachel's heart. She turned away. Her breathing became difficult. An unconscionable reaction, considering she was getting this from a waitress who'd never met Hayden in person.

"Enjoy your drinks," the waitress said, oblivious to the anxiety churning inside Rachel. "No hurry. I'll take your food order when you're ready."

Rachel bit her bottom lip hard, needing the physical pain to override the panic attack.

Luke stretched his arms across the table and rested his hands on top of hers. "Your hands are cold as ice."

"I know. Give me a minute. I'll be okay." Her voice trembled.

"Don't let what the waitress said get to you. I can see how it would remind you of Roy Sales, but it doesn't mean anything."

"I know." Rachel gulped in a deep breath and exhaled slowly. "I'm the defense attorney the waitress was talking about," she admitted. "I saw that same evil in Hayden's eyes and I was only a few feet away from him."

"You're defending Hayden Covey?"

"That's to be determined at this point. I resigned from Fitch, Fitch and Bauman on Friday afternoon to avoid having to defend him. Eric Fitch Sr. is not used to being told no."

"Where do things stand now?"

"Somewhere between decayed and rotten. I thought my resignation had been accepted. Then Saturday night Senator Covey's wife was on the news announcing that Rachel Maxwell, who had been kidnapped and held hostage by the Lone Star Snatcher, was going to defend her son."

"She said all that, did she?"

"According to Sydney. I didn't hear it."

"Playing on the jury's sympathies even before the trial begins."

"You catch on fast."

"Gotta read the enemy if you want to stay alive."

"More marine rules?" she asked.

"Yep, and I'm alive. Proof it's a good rule. What are you going to do now?"

"Either go to the office and accept the sizable raise and offer of being named a junior partner Eric Fitch Sr. is blackmailing me with or call him and tell him what he can do with his offer. Essentially that equals wasting all the hard work I've put in for years and giving up my dream of one day being a partner with one of the most prestigious law firms in the state."

"You're dealing with all that today and yet you're here with me? Either you're a glutton for punishment or I'm one of the luckiest men around."

"You weren't feeling too lucky a few minutes ago," she reminded him.

"Everything is relative. Which way are you leaning?"

"It changes by the minute. My plan is to drive to Houston and see if some great revelation comes to me when I'm standing at the large glass double doors of Fitch, Fitch and Bauman."

"I'm going with you," he announced.

"You have Alfred to deal with."

"He's not going anywhere tomorrow. Neither is the ranch and I'm hiring help."

"That's fast."

"The wranglers were working for Adam McElroy before he sold off half his horses this past summer. Pierce highly recommends them, and that's good enough for me."

"For a man who claims to be a temporary cowboy, you are sure getting into the Western swing of things."

"It's growing on me. But I didn't mean to change the subject. Back to you."

"There is more," she admitted reluctantly. And no real reason not to spill it all now that she was on a roll. She sipped her drink, appreciating the cold, tart liquid as it slid down her dry throat. "Dr. Kincaid has been calling my sister, Sydney, to get in touch with me."

"You lost me already. Who's Dr. Kincaid?"

"The lead psychiatrist in charge of Roy Sales's treatment."

"Why in hell would he call you?"

"Who knows? I'm guessing he thinks I know something that would help him pull Roy from his mental quagmire."

"Talk about gall. You don't owe him anything and you sure don't owe Roy Sales anything. Are you going to return his call?"

"Yes."

She didn't know that was her answer until it shot from her mouth. As much as she hated the thought of any involvement with Roy Sales, she needed to move on. Spending time these past three days with Luke had convinced her of that.

She hadn't died at Sales's torturous hand and she wouldn't let him win now. If she stayed trapped in the past, she'd lose the opportunity to truly live.

As crazy as she was about Luke, she knew he might not be her forever guy, but he'd awakened feelings inside her that she'd never expected to feel again.

Men like Luke wouldn't come along every day, but at least she knew they existed now.

"I doubt I have anything to say that would help Dr. Kincaid get Sales fit to stand trial any sooner," she explained, "but it's worth a chance."

She took a sip of her margarita and then took her phone from her handbag.

"You're going to call him right now?"

"Yes, before I change my mind." She punched in the doctor's phone number. Apparently it went to his private cell phone, since he took the call.

They barely got past the awkward small talk before he hurled the zinger.

"It's important that I observe Roy Sales interacting with you—in person."

Chapter Thirteen

Luke would have loved to hear Dr. Kincaid's side of the conversation, but he had to make do with Rachel's words and visible reactions. That was enough to know that the outcome of this call would not be good.

As if on cue, dark clouds began to roll in, hiding the sun and dropping the temperature a few degrees. Patrons at the tables around them finished their lunches quickly, paid their tabs and wandered off before they got caught in a storm.

The forecast was for a cold front to move in tonight, ushered in by heavy rain. This looked more like an afternoon thundershower. Unexpected changes in the weather were typical for this part of Texas.

But they should probably move on themselves to be on the safe side. Not that he'd hate getting caught in the rain with Rachel.

For that matter, doing anything with Rachel from scrubbing floors to having a water fight beat anything he'd done with anyone in recent memory.

It had been years since a woman affected him like this—if ever. He knew he was falling too fast and too hard, but logic had nothing to do with this. He'd lain awake for hours last night thinking of how she was messing with his mind and libido.

It was hard to be around her without touching her. Impossible to touch her and not want more. And kissing her literally left him aching to make love with her.

All in due time. When she was ready. When she wanted him the way he wanted her. God help him if that didn't come soon.

She finally broke the phone connection. "That was lovely," she said, her voice dripping satire.

"I got the feeling it might be. From what I heard it sounded like he wants you to come and talk to him in person."

"For starters. Then he wants me to talk to Roy Sales."

Luke muttered a few curses under his breath. "Surely you didn't agree to that."

"Not yet, but he's leaving an appointment open for me tomorrow morning in case I decide to cooperate."

"What does he expect to accomplish by putting you through that hell?"

"He thinks that Sales is either genuinely obsessed with me or else trying to play mind games with the doctor. He insists that it's all part of deciding if Sales is sane enough to stand trial."

"The psycho was so obsessed with you he tortured and tried to kill you."

"Yes, but either Roy doesn't remember or understand my captivity the way it was in actuality or he is manipulating the sessions. From what I know about him, I'd go with the latter."

"Exactly how does Sales remember it?"

"That I was with him willingly, that we shared an ethereal bond. Without a doubt he's mentally unbalanced, yet I'm convinced he was sane enough that he knew exactly what he was doing when he kidnapped me and the others. Sane enough that he knew to keep us hidden away and under lock and key."

"And that's sane enough to stand trial," Luke added.

"I definitely agree, and if my spending a few minutes with the monster can make that happen, it will be worth the emotional strain on me. I need this to be over once and for all."

"Then you plan to keep the appointment?"

"Unless I change my mind between now and tomorrow. I can stop at the mental facility on my way to Houston. It's not far out of the way."

"Sweetheart, you are piling it higher and higher on your plate. Are you sure you're up to this?"

"No. But I'm sure I need to do whatever it takes to get my life back. I don't expect to ever forget what Roy Sales put me through. I don't expect the nightmares to stop completely or to never have another panic attack."

She shoved her phone back in her purse and stood. "Talking about it with you was a breakthrough, but only a start. I have to keep pushing out the darkness so the light can come in."

"I have plenty of muscle power, courtesy of the marines. If you need any help pushing, count me in—for whatever you need."

"Then let's get started. No more talk of Roy Sales today. I want to think about music and flowers and the beautiful costumed girls who were dancing on the last boat that passed by. I want to think about walking in a field of clover and horseback riding across endless pastures and along bubbling creeks."

Luke walked over and tugged her up into his arms. "Anything else you want?"

"You. I want you, Luke Dawkins."

The first drops of rain began to pelt the umbrellas and the ledge, splashing raindrops on their heads and shoulders. Luke took her hand and they made a run for the restaurant door.

By the time they reached it, water was dripping from Rachel's hair and onto her forehead. He wiped it away with the palm of his hand.

The inside dining area was a few steps up a wide staircase and opened into a small but elegant boutique hotel.

"Would you like a table for two?" the hostess asked.

"Not just yet," Luke answered. "Give me a minute, Rachel. I'll be right back."

His heart hammered against his chest as he walked away. One should always give a lady what she wanted.

RACHEL LOOKED UP as Luke sauntered back across the room. He smiled and literally took her breath away. No man should look that good.

He handed her a hotel key.

"What is this?"

"Room service. We can dry off and eat comfortably."

"You rented a room for…"

She stopped midsentence as the gesture sank in

slowly. She'd come on to him, said she wanted him. He'd taken her at her word and rented a room.

They were going to be alone. With a bed and crisp white sheets.

If that wasn't what she wanted, she'd best say so now.

Her pulse raced. She looked up, met his gaze and melted into it. She felt no fear or hesitancy. This was Luke Dawkins. A real man. A protector. A hero.

"I love room service," she whispered.

"Are you sure?"

"Never been surer in my life."

By the time they reached the room, she felt light-headed, the margarita and the anticipation both hitting her at once.

She stared at the bed, not afraid, but the moment was still awkward—until Luke wrapped her in his arms and covered her mouth in long, wet kisses that left her hungering for more.

He picked her up and carried her to the bed, shoved the coverlet out of the way and laid her between the soft cotton sheets. Luke pulled off her black booties and then kicked out of his boots and socks.

Standing next to the bed, he yanked his knit shirt over his head and dropped it onto a chair. His bronzed skin practically glowed in the dim light, the dark hairs on his chest all but hypnotizing as they narrowed into a V and disappeared into his jeans.

Desire swelled inside her, heating her insides and dancing along her nerves as he unzipped his jeans. He wiggled out of them. They fell to the floor. He kicked them away, leaving his clothes scattered around the room.

Even that was a turn-on.

He crawled into bed and stretched out beside her. His fingers fumbled with the buttons on her blouse. Her impulse was to help him, to hasten the moment his hands found her bare breasts and pebbled nipples. But she didn't want to miss one second of the foreplay for their first time together.

When they were both finally naked, his exploring fingers and sweet kisses trailed over her body.

She reached between them and took his erection in her hand.

"Now," she whispered. "I don't think I can wait another second."

"I don't want to hurt you, baby. You tell me if anything is too much and I'll pull back, I promise. I'd die before I hurt you."

Tears filled her eyes. Her body trembled with love. "You could never hurt me, Luke."

And he didn't. They came together in a rush of passion and pleasure that rocked her whole body.

When they got around to room service, it was perfect, too. They fed each other loaded nachos and washed the hot, spicy peppers down with another margarita.

"Perfection?" she asked when it was time to get dressed again.

"I'm not sure. I'll let you know after we try it a few thousand more times."

GOING FROM MIDDAY in heaven to an afternoon with his dad was as anticlimactic as one could get. But they'd driven here to see Alfred and his doctor, so he might as well get to the second part of his agenda.

It was four forty when Luke walked down the long hallway to Alfred's room. Rachel had excused herself to go to the ladies' room and to call Sydney. The sisters were close.

Luke couldn't see how anything good could come from Rachel's seeing Roy Sales again. If Sydney agreed with him, maybe she could talk some sense into Rachel.

Alfred's door was open. Luke tapped and then walked in. Alfred was in his hospital bed, the head raised until he was practically in a sitting position. The TV was on, but the volume was turned too low to make out what was being said.

Luke took off his slightly damp Stetson and tossed it onto an empty chair near the single narrow window.

"You look comfortable," he said. "How are you feeling?"

Alfred looked at him and then went back to staring at a rerun of *Home Improvement* on the muted TV.

Luke approached the foot of the bed. "Do you know who I am?"

"Yep."

"That's good. Did you have a good day?"

"Nope."

"We got some rain," Luke offered.

"Who's taking care—" Alfred hesitated, coughing before he finished the sentence "—care of the horses?"

"Your horses are in good hands. Pierce Lawrence is seeing to that. He's helping me find wranglers and cowpunchers."

"Pierce."

"Yes. He said to tell you all is well at Arrowhead Hills."

"Good man."

"He is that."

Another tap on the open door. Luke turned and motioned Rachel to join them.

She smiled and walked over to stand next to Alfred. "Good afternoon, Mr. Dawkins."

A confused look settled on Alfred's face. "I took my...pills already. You a new...nurse?"

"I'm glad you took your meds. I'm not a nurse. I'm Rachel, a friend of Luke's."

"Humph."

"Luke talks about you all the time," she continued. "I'm so glad to finally meet you."

Alfred went back to staring at the TV.

"Don't let Luke sell my horses," he muttered, the rhythm of his words uneven. Apparently he was talking to Rachel, though he didn't look at her.

"Luke would never do that," Rachel answered. "He's taking good care of them. I visited your ranch. It's very nice."

"House is a mess."

"Not anymore," Luke said. "Rachel gave it a good cleaning."

"Luke helped," Rachel said.

"You like horses?"

"I do."

"Know how to ride?"

"I don't ride often, but I can stay in the saddle."

"I gotta go home. Horses need me."

"You have to get well first," Luke reminded him.

Alfred tried to push himself up on his elbows. His left elbow collapsed under him. Frustration deepened the wrinkles around his eyes and mouth.

Luke got a sick feeling deep in his gut. Alfred wasn't just ornery. He was also scared. Life as he knew it had been stolen by events he had no control over.

They might not have much of a father/son relationship, but Luke couldn't bear seeing him like this.

"Gotta get home," Alfred said again. "Horses need me."

"They do," Luke agreed. And Alfred desperately needed them. The decision Luke had expected to wrestle with for days had just made itself.

"I'm taking you home in a few days, Dad. I'll get everything ready and then I'll take you home. That's a promise."

Alfred turned away, but not before Luke saw the tears in his eyes.

"Your mama won't be there," Alfred said, his voice catching in a gruff sob.

Luke had no idea where that had come from, but his eyes grew moist, as well. Life took some bizarre turns.

Rachel walked over to Luke and squeezed his hand.

"I didn't know I had it in me," Luke muttered.

"I did."

The room grew silent until an aide entered with Alfred's dinner. Luke and Rachel introduced themselves.

"Does he always eat in his room?" Luke asked. "You must have a cafeteria of sorts."

"We have a great cafeteria. Alfred goes down for breakfast and lunch but insists he have dinner in his room. Don't you, Alfred?"

"Too much talking."

Luke wasn't sure if that meant it was difficult for him to talk and it wasn't worth the effort by the end of the day or that he'd had enough of people in general by then. Luke suspected it was a little of both.

When the aide left, Rachel handed Alfred the wet cloth to wash his hands and then opened his carton of milk, stuck the straw into it and arranged his tray so that he could get to everything easily.

Alfred smiled appreciatively. No doubt he liked Rachel. But then, who wouldn't?

"We should go and let you eat while it's hot," Luke said.

"Not…" He hesitated. "Never hot," Alfred complained as he shoved a spoonful of mashed potatoes into his mouth.

A bit spilled from his mouth and landed on his shirt. He didn't seem to notice.

Rachel wiped the blob of food from his shirt with a napkin and spread his napkin under his chin to catch any additional mishaps.

They were practically out the door when Alfred's angry yell got their instant intention.

"Murderer."

"What did you say?" Luke asked.

"Murderer." He pointed his spoon at the TV.

Luke checked it out. The five o'clock news had come

on and the Breaking News warning was splashed across the screen with the picture of Hayden Covey just below it.

Rachel grabbed the remote and turned up the volume.

The judge had set Hayden Covey's bail at one million dollars.

Luke let out a low whistle. "That's a lot of cash for a schoolboy."

"He's twenty. That's not a schoolboy in the legal system. A million dollars is not out of line for someone arrested for murder."

"Guess it doesn't matter in his case," Luke said. "His father will come up with it. How does that affect your resignation?"

"If Eric has already replaced me with the attorney who arranged for bail, then I'm definitely in the market for a new job."

Which wouldn't be bad in Luke's mind, but he wasn't counting that a done deal yet.

RACHEL'S MIND WAS whirling as Luke pulled in behind Sydney's car. For four months, she'd felt trapped in a time warp, trying to block everything to do with Roy Sales from her mind, only to be faced with her fears at every turn.

She'd passed some kind of milestone in a few days, pulled her abduction and captivity from the dark crevices of her mind and exposed them to the stark light of reality. Now she was about to face Roy Sales straight on. Weirdly, she felt more emboldened than afraid.

Luke killed the engine and reached for her hand.

"Are you sure I can't persuade you to go home with me tonight?"

"No, but you get points for making it hard to say good-night. Thanks for a memorable day."

"No reason we can't top that off with an even more memorable night."

"That is the most tempting offer of my life, but seriously, I need to spend some time with Sydney. I'd like her input on meeting with Sales and Eric Fitch. And you have a ranch to run now that you've officially made the decision to stay at Arrowhead Hills. At least, I think that's what you meant when you promised to take your dad home."

"I did, though it may turn out to be the biggest mistake of my life."

"It was the right thing to do."

"Keep telling me that when I start to rip my hair out and run around wildly in circles."

"I will. I'm sure Esther has some leftovers from dinner if you're hungry."

"No. I'm good. Pierce said Esther had him deliver a food basket to the ranch today. He claims it's enough food to last me till spring."

"When did you talk to Pierce?"

"While you were drying your hair back at the hotel. I had high hopes then for not making it back to the ranch tonight. To be honest, I had hopes for not making it back for days."

"I don't think a good cowboy would ever shirk his job to mess around," she teased..

"You've got a lot to learn about cowboys. Afternoon delight with a beautiful woman trumps wrangling every time."

He let go of her hand and opened the door.

"You don't have to walk me to the door," she said.

"I know, but I have to kiss you good-night properly, or better yet, improperly."

He rounded the truck quickly and opened her door.

"Are you sure you want to drive me to Houston tomorrow? You really do have a lot of work to do. And they're forecasting storms for tonight and early morning."

"The work will get done with or without me. Buck Stallings is going to give the new wranglers a trial run for the rest of the week. Dudley Miles says he can spare even more cowpunchers if I need them. Barring the unexpected, January is a relatively quiet time in the ranching business."

"It might be storming."

"Then we'll leave a little later. Call me when you're ready to leave. No way am I letting you face Roy Sales alone."

He pulled her into his arms. The kiss was improper enough that she was weak-kneed and dizzy with desire by the time she made it to the porch.

Sydney met her at the door, a worried look on her face.

"What's wrong?" Rachel asked.

"You have company."

"Who?"

"Claire Covey. She's bordering on hysterical and says it's urgent that she talk to you."

Chapter Fourteen

Rachel stepped into the small office at the end of the hall that Esther used for clipping and organizing coupons and for keeping up with the church and community organizations she enjoyed so much. It consisted of a desk, an office chair, a bookcase and a comfortable accent chair near the one narrow window.

Claire was waiting, standing near the desk. She wasn't hysterical at the moment, but her eyes were red and swollen and a pile of tissues lying on the desk beside her were ripped to shreds.

Except for the red and swollen eyes, Claire was an attractive woman, likely somewhere in her early forties. Her short blond hair was cut into a stylish pageboy.

Her slacks and sweater were classic but had that designer edge to them that shouted money. The handbag on the floor beside her chair was Gucci.

"I'm Rachel Maxwell. How can I help you?"

"I know who you are. I know all about you and what you've been through. I don't know how you endured it."

"It was difficult, but I'm sure that's not what brought you here tonight."

"I need your help. The police are pinning a murder on my son. He's innocent, but that doesn't matter to them. They won't listen to reason. All they want is to send him to prison."

Claire burst into tears and buried her face in her hands as sobs shook her body.

Rachel gave her a minute to regain a semblance of composure. She could understand Claire's fears. She was a mother who loved her son. "Do you believe Hayden is innocent?"

"I know he's innocent. He would never hurt anyone. Never. The girl was after him, calling him all hours of the night, and then he'd see her out with other guys."

Blaming the victim was a common counter, but it seldom led anywhere. "You should probably be discussing this with your attorney."

"That was supposed to be you," Claire said. "Eric Fitch promised us it would be you. The jury will believe you if you tell them he's innocent. You'd never defend a monster. Not after what you've been through."

"The jury would be right," Rachel agreed. "I'd never defend an accused murderer unless I was convinced he was innocent. But defending a case involves a lot more than just connecting with the jury."

"Eric said you were an extremely talented defense attorney, the best chance of Hayden being acquitted."

"Eric may have exaggerated that a bit. Exactly when did Eric tell you that I wouldn't be handling your case?"

"This afternoon. He called about two and said you'd left the firm for personal reasons, but I'm begging you, please don't turn your back on Hayden. Don't let them ruin his life. Don't let them take my son."

Her words cracked into sobs.

Rachel wondered if Eric had changed his mind about wanting her back or if he was just covering the odds. Was he trying to make sure that he didn't lose the Coveys as clients if Rachel didn't come back?

"Who arranged the bail?" Rachel asked.

"Eric. He wants to be the lead attorney," Claire explained.

"Eric does have a lot of influence in this state. It's doubtful anyone else could have done that so quickly if at all," Rachel said, giving him his due.

"I don't care about his influence. I don't care about my husband's reputation. I don't care about anything except my boy I'll get on my knees if it will help. I'll pay you any amount of money you want. Just please save my boy."

Claire's pain seemed to cut right into Rachel's heart. Like all mothers, she was no doubt prejudiced, but that didn't mean she was wrong. Rachel had judged Hayden on one look, but that might have been colored by her own fears.

"Just talk to Hayden," Claire begged. "You'll see he could never have killed anyone. You'll see the goodness in him. I know you will."

It was hard to say no to that simple request.

"I'll meet with him. That's all I can promise. Even if I decide to take Hayden's case, I may not be doing it in conjunction with Eric's firm."

"I don't care."

"But there could be legal and ethical issues that apply to my taking a case from Fitch, Fitch and Bauman so soon after my resignation."

"It's my son's future that's at stake," Claire begged. "What could be unethical about that?"

"Does your husband agree with you on moving the case from the law firm?"

"He'll do what I say."

If she took Hayden's case, her plate wouldn't just be piled high as Luke said. It would spill over and pool at her feet like acid rain. "When do you expect Hayden to be released on bail?"

"Hopefully tomorrow, but Eric said it could take days."

"I'm driving to Houston in the morning and I'll likely be there until Wednesday afternoon. If Hayden is released before that, give me a call and we can set up an appointment for me to meet with Hayden. The meeting will likely not be at Fitch's law firm."

"I'll bring him wherever you say—whenever you want."

"Good. We can decide that later."

Tears filled Claire's eyes again. She sniffled and grabbed a new tissue. "You can't imagine what this means to me."

Rachel could imagine, but she couldn't let this decision be ruled by emotions. Murder was not a game of hearts. "I hope I can help, Claire. I sincerely hope I can deliver what you're asking, but remember, all I'm agreeing to now is a meeting with Hayden. We'll see where it goes from there."

When Claire stood to go, she trembled, and for a second Rachel thought she might pass out. Rachel extended an arm for support and Claire leaned against her, her head resting on Rachel's shoulder.

Rachel hoped beyond hope that Hayden was the young man his mother believed him to be. But deep down in Rachel's soul, she had the grievous feeling that he wasn't.

RACHEL HAD SHOWERED and changed into a pair of pink flannel pajamas by the time Sydney joined her in her bedroom. Sydney was dressed in jeans and a sapphire-colored sweater.

"Sorry to be so late, but I was painting Esther's toenails for her. She thinks shop pedicures are a waste of money. Besides, I thought you might need some time to regroup after Claire Covey left."

"I don't know that it helped."

"Want to start from the top with Claire Covey?"

Rachel fed her the details.

"Eric Fitch is going explode when he hears you lured the highest-profile case of the decade."

"I didn't lure."

"You'll never convince him of that."

"Does that mean you think I shouldn't take the Covey case?"

"No. It means I hate to miss the blowup when he gets what he deserves for trying to manipulate and then blackmail you."

"It wasn't quite that bad."

"It is from my point of view. Do you think you'll run into legal hassles?"

"My contract was renewed a little over a year ago. A friend from law school specializes in contract law. She reviewed the contract and I'm certain she didn't let me sign anything overly constrictive at that point in my career."

"I guess the legalese would matter. I mean, if it says you can't start your own firm and lure away his clients, that wouldn't cut it in this case, would it? You're not opening your own firm and you didn't lure her from him. Claire Covey came to you."

"True to a point. The most pressing question may come down to, do I really want to defend a young man I just gave up a prosperous career position over so that I didn't have to defend him?"

"That's a tongue twister," Sydney said. "But you didn't actually resign because Eric asked you to take a case you didn't want."

"True. I resigned because I was being used. At the time, money and promotions had nothing to do with my decision."

"Do you want to defend Hayden Covey?" Sydney asked.

"Not unless I can believe in his innocence. The murder was brutal. I get sick just reading about it."

"I'll see what I can find out about the crime, though the FBI is not involved. I checked."

"Anything would help."

"I wish I could hang around with you for a few more days and keep up with your continuing saga, but I have to cut my minivacation even shorter. I'm needed in Wisconsin asap for an important investigation. All hush-hush."

"Okay, now I'll worry about you instead of me."

"Please don't. I've got the FBI behind me, and it doesn't get any safer than that."

Rachel wasn't convinced that was always true. "Not to try to outdo you, but I have other news, as well. I'm seeing Dr. Kincaid and Roy Sales tomorrow."

"I don't like the sound of this," Sydney lamented. "I can understand talking to the doctor, but why Roy Sales? I wouldn't have told you the doctor called if I'd known he was going to ask that of you."

"Sure you would have. You're a stickler for the truth and we always level with each other. Besides, if it helps get Sales to trial, it will be worth it."

"Not necessarily. At any rate, if things get too harried in Houston, you can always come to Winding Creek for a rest. Esther would love to have you. So would the rest of the family."

"Actually, I'll be staying in Houston only one night."

"Really? Does this have anything to do with Luke Dawkins?"

"He's driving me to Houston. He wants to be there when I talk to Roy Sales. He thinks I may need a little moral support for that and for my talk with Eric if I decide to meet with him."

"That's generous of him and probably a good idea."

"He's a genuine guy."

"I don't doubt that. I just worry that with all that's

going on in your life right now, is this the best time to fall into a serious relationship?"

"Is there ever a good time to fall into a relationship?"

"Some might be better than others."

"Was it the right time when you met Tucker? His best bull-rider friend had just been killed in competition. You were trying to find and rescue me from a monster."

"Point made. Tucker and I didn't find love. It found us. We were just smart enough to listen to our hearts."

"I'm just taking this one day as at a time," Rachel said, "but I like him and I like being with him. That feels really good right now."

More than good and she more than liked him. And she couldn't wait to make love with him again. That part she wouldn't share with Sydney.

"Don't worry about me, Sydney. I'm not fully healed. I may never be, but I'm making progress. You and Tucker saved my life. I'm planning to make the most of it, and right now that includes Luke."

"Got it. Just keep me posted—about Sales and Hayden Covey. And what you decide about your job."

"I will, but I'm definitely leaning toward leaving the firm."

"Take that job and shove it. I'm with you all the way. There's more to life than work. Try it. You might like it."

"You're a fine one to talk, but I may just do that."

"I'm really glad we had this time together," Sydney said.

"Me, too. Luke and I didn't set a time to leave in the morning, but I doubt I'll be leaving before you get up."

"Unfortunately, I'm leaving—" Sydney glanced at

her watch "—in about thirty minutes. I have to catch
an early flight to Kansas and Tucker wasn't ready to
say goodbye, so we booked a hotel near the airport for
the night. He'll see me off and head out a day early for
his next competition."

"Then I guess this is goodbye." Rachel pulled Sydney into a hug. "Stay safe," she whispered.

"That's the plan. You be careful and call me if you
need to talk about anything. And forget what I said
about your relationship with Luke. If he makes you
happy, that's all that matters. I love you, sis."

"I love you, too."

And the good part was they always would.

ROY SALES WATCHED as Eddie cracked his knuckles and
then stuck his index finger into his water glass like it
was a straw.

"Get your finger out of your water," Doug the crank
complained. "You've got no manners."

"Don't need them in this place," Eddie said. "I'm
leaving here any day now. My son's got a yacht down
in the Gulf. He wants me to come live with him."

"Sure he does," Roy said. "I'll come down and visit
you."

"You wouldn't like it. My boy Rick don't allow no
drinking or smoking. He don't even cuss."

"Then why go there?" Doug asked. "You might as
well go to jail."

"Jail's for jerks," Eddie said.

Roy smiled. Any other time, Doug and Eddie would

be getting on his nerves so bad he'd have gone back to his room and read another paperback Western.

He never thought he'd say it, but he missed working for Dudley Miles. Work was hard sometimes, but he had a lot of freedom and a house of his own.

He wouldn't be going back to Dudley's, but he wouldn't be leaving Texas just yet. He had one little detail left over from his life here to take care of.

Killing Rachel Maxwell wasn't just for fun. It was necessary if he was going to even the score. A real man had to even the score.

Doug Crank was going on and on now about the fact that they didn't ever get a decent steak. That was the damn truth, but it wouldn't matter much longer to Roy.

He'd played the game like a championship boxer going for the knockout punch. He'd figured out fast who could help him and how to make sure they would.

The pawns were all in place. It was only a matter of time. Maybe tomorrow. By next week, for sure.

First he'd take care of business and then he'd get his steak.

He looked up and saw Dr. Kincaid walking toward him. Something must be up. Kincaid never came around this late in the day.

"Good evening," the doc said, approaching the group of three.

"You working overtime?" Eddie asked.

"No, I'm here to talk to Roy. Would you two mind giving us a few minutes alone?"

"We can go to my room," Roy said, not that it was much of a room, but it was still nicer than any bunkhouse he'd ever slept in. He had a nice bed with clean chairs and a soft pillow. There was even a chest and a small desk. The chair wasn't so much, but it was good enough.

The doc followed him to his room. Roy sat on the edge of the bed and the doc took the chair. "I'm not in trouble, am I? That yelling fight at lunch wasn't my fault."

"You're not in trouble. In fact, I have a surprise for you."

Roy didn't bite. He just waited to see what the doc had to say.

"You're having a visitor tomorrow."

That was a shocker. The only visitors he'd had since he'd been here were unfriendly reporters and his jerk of an attorney, and they weren't allowed in often.

"Aren't you going to ask who?" Kincaid asked.

"I figure you're going to tell me or you wouldn't be here."

"You're right. Rachel Maxwell is stopping by tomorrow."

Roy swallowed hard. That was the last person he'd expected. "What does she want?"

"I asked her to come."

Roy should have known this wasn't Rachel's idea.

"You're always telling me how the two of you bonded. I figured you'd enjoy seeing her."

"Yeah, well, you never know about women. She wanted to run away with me, but she lied about that to the police and she'll probably lie about it again."

"Maybe she won't. Anyway, I thought I'd prepare

you for her visit so you wouldn't be too surprised when she shows up."

"Are you going to be with us in the room when we talk?"

"Do you want me to be?"

"Suit yourself."

"We'll talk about those arrangements tomorrow with Rachel."

The doc blabbered on a few minutes and then left.

Roy kicked off his shoes and stretched out on the bed. Rachel Maxwell was coming here. She probably felt bad about all those lies she told about him. He wasn't that bad. She'd wanted him to come around and always wanted him to stay longer. But then when he had his back against the wall, she'd turned on him.

She'd left him no choice but to leave her to burn to death in the fire.

He tried to remember what she looked like the day he first saw her in downtown Winding Creek. All that hair catching the sun and shining like gold. Great eyes. He'd never seen eyes as beautiful as hers.

He hadn't wanted to hurt her so bad, but she kept fighting him.

He didn't want to kill her now, but she'd betrayed him. In the end, she'd treated him like a monster, the way the others had.

"What should I do, Mommy?"

"Wait and see. We just have to wait and see."

Chapter Fifteen

Light rain pattered on the roof as Rachel fell into a troubled sleep. She woke to a blazing streak of lightning that lit up her bedroom like a flashing neon sign. A thunderous bolt of thunder that shook the windows followed a second later.

It was pitch-dark outside until the next light show created an eerie shadow dance on her wall.

Rachel shivered and reached for the extra quilt on the foot of the bed. Evidently the promised cold front had arrived with the storm. From short sleeves to jackets in a matter of hours and then back to shorts again within days. That was Texas weather.

She'd just snuggled under the extra covers again when she got a whiff of coffee. The storm must have wakened Esther, too, though she was always up with the rooster's first crow. She claimed the big, noisy bird that Grace swore had it in for her was the only alarm clock she could always count on.

Esther loved her chickens. The fresh eggs were just a bonus.

Rachel reached for her phone and checked the time.

Ten after five. She looked a second time to be sure she'd seen that right.

Seven hours straight of sound sleep and she might still be asleep if not for the storm. She hadn't slept that long since…

Since Roy Sales with his tortured brand of misery had forced himself into her life.

And now she'd agreed to interact with him again. Agreed to stare into his cold, heartless eyes and get another glimpse of his dark soul. She had a growing fear that she might live to regret this.

Rachel swallowed hard, kicked off the covers and slid her feet to the soft rug as the nauseating memories began to haunt her mind yet again. Only this time, she wouldn't give in to the terror.

Luke had been the catalyst who helped her bring everything into the open. They were friends and lovers, but she wasn't so naive that she was convinced what they had would last forever. She didn't need a promise of forever.

What they shared was enough for now.

Rachel padded to the window in her bare feet and opened the blinds. Rain pelted the windows, the water falling in sheets. Hopefully the storm would pass before they had to leave for Houston. It wouldn't be safe driving in this. Sydney and Tucker had been smart to leave the night before.

Wide-awake, she grabbed a robe and gave in to the lure of the smell of coffee. She heard male voices. Surely Luke hadn't shown up this early and in the peak of the storm.

When she reached the kitchen, she saw that it was Pierce and a young man she didn't recognize, both in their work clothes as if this was just another ranching day.

Pierce turned toward her and tipped his steaming coffee mug. "Good morning, Rachel. Hope we didn't wake you."

"The storm beat you to it. Is something wrong? Are Jaci and Grace okay?"

"They're fine, though Grace didn't sleep much last night. Between the storm, going to the bathroom and trying to find some way to get comfortable, she tossed half the night."

Esther poured another mug of coffee and handed it to Rachel. "I don't know if you've met Buck Stallings," she said, nodding toward the other man in the room.

"I've heard his name from Luke," she said, "but no, I haven't met him."

"Buck's only the hardest working wrangler in the county," Pierce said. "And the closest thing I've ever seen to what I'd call a real horse whisperer."

"Don't buy that tall tale," Buck said. "Most of what I know I've learned from Pierce over the last year."

Esther shook her head. "Don't neither one of you seem to have the sense God gave a goose this morning. No good reason I can see for you two to get out in this weather. It's not like the cows need you to bring them a slicker."

"Horses are likely riled," Buck said. "A soft voice, a couple of pats and some fresh hay to chew on will settle them down a bit."

"You'll be back for a hot breakfast, won't you?" Esther asked. "I'm thinking fried chicken and waffles."

"You do know how to tempt a guy, but I can't make any promises," Pierce said. "It all depends on what we run into. I've got a few pastures I need to check. Drainage is improved, but it hasn't been tested like this."

"You need hot food," she mumbled, obviously reluctant to give up the argument. He and Buck were already pulling on their jackets.

"I'm hoping Grace went back to sleep for another hour or so. If I'm not back by seven, can one of you give Grace a call just to make sure she's okay and see if she needs any help getting Jaci up and ready for school? Not that I expect you to get out in the storm, but call me if you think she needs me and I'll get back her on the double."

"Of course we will," Esther said. "Would have done that even if you hadn't asked. I don't care if the doctor did say she had another two weeks to go. That son of yours is about to kick himself into the world."

"I know Grace hopes you're right. You two stay warm and dry." Pierce gave Esther a peck on the check and he and Buck headed toward the back door.

Esther went after them and pushed a large thermos of hot coffee into Pierce's hand. "Be careful," she said.

"Always. And like I said, if you think for a minute Grace needs me, call."

"You bet your best past pair of spurs I will."

"I can't believe they're going out in this weather," Rachel said when the door shut behind them.

"It's the ranching life," Esther said. "Living with

my Charlie for fifty-two years, I learned that the live-stock comes first. You get used to it, honey. Fact is, I wouldn't have changed it for life in a golden tower. I sure wouldn't change it for city life where you're lucky to even know your neighbors.

"Not that I'm faulting your life, Rachel. The world needs good lawyers, too. It just wouldn't be the life for me."

"There are days I'm not sure it's the life for me."

This was one of those days, but Rachel was doubt-ful she'd fit into this life, either.

Another bolt of lightning sizzled across the sky. This time the thunder was so loud the house felt like a giant was shaking it.

Rachel wondered if Luke was out in the storm, checking on livestock this morning. If so he was no doubt regretting that he'd offered—no, insisted—to drive her to Houston today. Like Esther said, livestock comes first.

Rachel's life was in Houston. Luke's was here, at least for the time being. She couldn't imagine the two lifestyles meshing.

Only, unless she and Eric Fitch Sr. came to an agree-ment, she didn't exactly have a lifestyle or a career.

And work was the only life she knew.

AN HOUR LATER, the sky had grown lighter and the thunder rumbled in the distance instead of shaking the house. The rain was still falling steadily, with bursts of monsoon-level intensity. If this kept up, she might have to delay her trip to Houston until tomorrow.

Rachel bypassed the dark gray suit she had planned to wear and instead chose a pair of chocolate-colored slacks and a wine-colored sweater.

She pulled on a pair of brown, flat-heeled leather boots that had previously encountered mud puddles and proven their survival skills. She'd need to pick up additional clothing at her apartment if she planned to stay in Winding Creek through the following weekend.

Any longer than that would definitely be taking advantage of Esther's hospitality.

Rachel found Esther in the kitchen, shelling pecans into a small bowl that was already half-full. "There's a fresh pot of coffee," Esther said.

"Thanks. Have you heard from Grace?"

"No, but I'm sure she's up. This is the worst gully washer we've had in years. I do remember one June, though, when I thought we were going to wash plumb away. Charlie joked he was building an ark and swatting the mosquitoes before it started floating so he wouldn't be saving them."

Rachel poured herself a cup of coffee. "Hopefully we won't reach ark stage this time, but I do like his mosquito extermination program."

There was a loud banging at the back door followed by the sound of stamping feet.

"About time Pierce got back here," Esther said. She dropped the cracked pecan in the basket.

But when the door opened, it was Luke, not Pierce, who was standing there. The gray slicker he was wearing pooled on the mat. His boots were caked in mud despite the stamping.

Esther grabbed the nearest dish towel and rushed to the door. "Sakes alive, Luke, you look like you fell into Winding Creek and stayed for a fish dinner."

"Feel like it, too," he agreed. "Never mind the towel. I'm too big a mess to come in."

"Of course you can come in. That's what mops are for."

"I can just stay a minute." He stepped inside and onto the indoor mat.

"Is something wrong?" Rachel asked.

"I got a call from Pierce. He says there's been a mudslide out near the gorge. It took part of the fence line with it."

Esther covered her mouth with both hands as if holding in an exclamation. "Are the cattle okay?"

"Most of them. Some of the young cows have gotten tangled in the downed barbwire or stuck in the mud. Three or four have slid partway into the gorge. Pierce and Buck have their hands full, so I came to help."

"Did they call Riley?" Esther asked.

"Riley's on his way. He's bringing his own four-wheeler, since there's no way to get a truck to that area without getting it stuck. Pierce says there's another four-wheeler in the barn."

"There is," Esther said. "The key's in it. There should be some ropes in there, as well."

"I brought some with me. Pierce just wanted me to let you know what's going on so you didn't worry when he doesn't show up for breakfast. And he wants someone to let Grace know what's going on. He said try not to upset her."

"I'll get you a thermos of coffee to take with you and a few tea cakes. You guys will need something to warm your insides and give you energy."

Rachel walked over to the door while Esther prepared the treats.

"I'm sorry about this," Luke said. "I'm not sure how long this is going to take, but I don't want you going to Houston without me."

"Don't worry about me. I'll be fine," she assured him.

"That's not the answer I'm looking for. I don't want you facing that sick son of a bitch alone. Promise me you aren't making that trip without me or I'm not leaving here."

He was worried and protective. And caring. Her heart caved. "I promise, Luke. Now go, cowboy. You have cows to rescue." He kissed her hard on the mouth. Possessive, as if they belonged to each other.

Esther handed him the thermos and a plastic tote full of disposable cups and the cake-like sugar cookies as he left. Into the storm and the frosty temperatures.

Pierce needed him and he was eager to help. There was little room for doubt now. The odds were good that he was a rancher at heart.

And that she was too crazy about him for words.

"No use to cook breakfast for the men," Esther said. "It will be lunchtime or later before we see them again."

"Do you really think it will take that long?"

"I s'pect it will. Not fretting about it. Livestock and the land. That's a rancher's lifeblood. I can't tell you how many plans of mine got canceled over the years because of an animal emergency."

"You must have gotten annoyed with that on occasion."

"Would've been a big, fat waste of time if I did. Besides, I knew my Charlie loved me. Deep down, I was proud of how responsible he was. Made me feel safe."

Safe.

That was how Luke made Rachel feel. Safe. She'd forgotten how it felt until Luke had come along.

"I can whip up some bacon and eggs for the two of us in no time or I can make us a nice peach cobbler from the summer fruit I froze. Some folks don't like cobbler for breakfast, but I say if it's good, time of day don't matter."

"Please don't go to that trouble for me. Toast is fine, especially topped off with some of your homemade fig preserves."

"That sounds mighty good to me, too, along with a tall glass of milk."

Rachel put two slices of artisan bread from Dani's bakery in the toaster and set the table while Esther got out the preserves, butter and milk.

"It sure was nice having Tucker and Sydney here this weekend," Esther said as they sat down across from each other in the breakfast nook. "Having you here, too, made it extraspecial."

"I hope I'm not wearing out my welcome."

"Don't you ever worry about that. Does an old woman good not to wander around a big house like this all alone every night. Not that I don't have plenty of family, but there's always room for one more if they're nice as you."

"Thank you."

"What do you think of the Dawkins boy?"

Rachel didn't think of Luke as a boy, but Esther had her own way of saying things. "He's very nice."

"He was a good kid, too. Me and his mama were best friends before she died. She was a good twenty years younger than me, but we just hit it off right from the day we met."

"How old was Luke when she died?"

"A couple of years older than Jaci is now, around eight, I suspect. Luke was her heart from the day he was born. He was all that mattered to her. Broke her heart when she walked away and left him behind."

"Why did she leave him?"

"She didn't leave him. She left Alfred. I think he was a good man deep down, but he was controlling and ornery."

"Alfred must have been a lot older than her."

"He was, but he was a good-looking man with a lot going for him. He adored her and she loved him at first."

"What happened?" Rachel asked.

"He was jealous and that brought out the worst in him. He didn't want her to leave the house and got too crotchety to bear. She was like a butterfly, flitting around, bringing beauty and light to everything and everyone she touched."

"Everyone except Alfred?"

"I reckon he was so afraid of losing her that he eventually ran her off. Before she got settled and came back for Luke, she got killed in a head-on collision."

Esther picked up the napkin and dabbed her eyes. "I swear I can't think of that day without getting all weepy."

That explained why Luke felt the way he did about his dad. He probably blamed him for losing his mother. Yet he'd come home to take care of his father when Alfred needed him.

Luke Dawkins was an amazing man.

RACHEL TOOK ADVANTAGE of a slowdown in the rain to make the ten-minute drive to Pierce and Grace's cabin. The old blacktop ranch road gave way to a long, curving gravel drive for the last fifty yards. Driving was slick and water flowed like a river along the eastern edge of the road.

There was no garage, but Pierce and his brothers had built a covered carport that provided a dry, mud-free path to the back door. Rachel parked, walked to the door and knocked. The damp, cold air chilled her to the bone. Her black waterproof trench coat would have felt good, but it was back in Houston.

Jaci opened the door and did a twirl to show off her new yellow-flowered raincoat with matching yellow boots. Even the opened umbrella matched.

"You look like you're going out dancing in the rain."

"I wanted to, but Mommy won't let me. Like, what's the point of having a new raincoat if I can't get out in the rain?"

She twirled again as if that would make her point.

"You don't want to get those boots all wet, do you?" Rachel asked.

"Well, a girl's gotta do what a girl's gotta do. That's what my cousin Constance says."

"But you, young lady, have to do what Mommy and Daddy say," Grace reminded her. "And we say it's much too cold and wet to be jumping into mud puddles, especially before school."

Jaci's hands went to her hips, but then she quickly went back to regaling them with her dance routine.

Grace fell back into one of the kitchen chairs. She looked pale and frail.

"How are you feeling?" Rachel asked.

"Tired. I'm at that stage in the pregnancy where a good night's sleep would be more exciting than winning the lottery."

"That's tired," Rachel agreed. And it showed in Grace's face and the stoop to her shoulders. Her ready smile was nowhere to be seen.

"Have you had breakfast?" Rachel asked.

"I ate a few bites of yogurt, but I have no appetite this morning."

That didn't sound like a good thing to Rachel, but she wasn't going to push food on Grace when she didn't feel like eating. "What about Jaci? Has she had breakfast?"

"I had a peanut butter sandwich and it was yummy," Jaci said, jumping into the conversation.

"It's what she wanted," Grace said, "and I didn't have the energy to argue with her. I figure peanut butter and jelly is as good for her as those sugary cereals she likes so much."

"Sounds healthy enough to me," Rachel agreed.

She was far more worried about Grace's health. If you'd asked Rachel yesterday, she would have sworn the one thing consuming her thoughts this morning would have been the impending meeting with Roy Sales.

Now she was seriously worried about Grace, and cows and the men taking care of them. She was also concerned that she was becoming so involved in this life that she really didn't want to go to Houston today without Luke.

"Perhaps you should call your obstetrician," Rachel said, "just to be on the safe side. You don't want to come down with a virus this close to your due date."

"I will if I don't feel better soon, but I think I'm just tired. One decent night's sleep would work miracles."

"My little brother is growing in Mommy's tummy," Jaci said. "That's why she's getting so fat." Jaci put down her umbrella and patted Grace's stomach. "I'll be a big sister."

"That is very exciting," Rachel said. "Would you like me to drive you to the gate to wait on your school bus?"

"Yes. Can she, Mommy?"

"Absolutely, but the bus won't be here for about twenty more minutes. Why don't you go and practice this week's new words until it's time to go?"

"I don't need practice. I already know them all. But I could go work on my coloring. Art is my favorite subject."

She skipped off, leaving Rachel and Grace alone.

"You're going to have your hands full with Jaci and the baby. Are you ready for it?"

"To tell you the truth, it scares me to death. Jaci and I have bonded so beautifully and I don't want to lose any of that. Still, I know the baby is going to require a lot of my time. Pierce keeps trying to reassure me, but I worry that Jaci will feel left out."

"You'll have a lot of help," Rachel said. "This family seems to stick together in everything."

"You're right about that. It would be supernice if you lived closer. You may need a lot more time unwinding on the back of a horse if you're really going to represent Hayden Covey."

"So you heard about that?"

"Everyone has. It was on the news all day yesterday. The family just doesn't want you to think they're butting into your business, so they won't ask about it until you mention it."

"The news media have jumped the gun. The decision hasn't been made as to whether or not I'll defend him."

Grace started to get out of the chair but winced in pain and grabbed her side.

Rachel panicked. "Was that a labor pain?"

"I don't think so. I was just at the doctor's yesterday. He said it would likely be at least another week, maybe two."

"Is that the first pain like that you've had?"

"The second," Grade admitted. "I had one when I first got out of bed this morning."

"I know next to nothing about labor pains," Rachel admitted, "but I think you should call your doctor or at least call Esther."

"I will if…"

Grace stopped talking and stood perfectly still as water began to run down her legs and pool around her feet. "I think my water just broke."

"Call your doctor." This time Rachel ordered instead of suggesting. "I'm calling Esther and she can call Pierce."

Esther was at the door only a minute or two after Grace got off the phone with her doctor's nurse.

"They want me to come in now," Grace said.

"I can drive you," Rachel said.

"That's what Pierce suggested, as well," Esther said. "He'll meet you there as fast as he can get back here and scrape off some of the mud."

"Can you drive Jaci to the school bus stop?" Grace asked Esther.

"Of course I can."

Minutes later, Grace and Rachel were in the car driving to the hospital. Grace was having her baby.

Roy Sales and even Eric Fitch would just have to wait. The biggest drama of life couldn't.

Chapter Sixteen

Luke arrived at Esther's house to pick up Rachel before eight o'clock on Wednesday morning. Every muscle in his body ached from the hours they'd spent saving a few cows yesterday.

But it was a sunny fifty-two degrees this morning and he and Rachel were off to Houston with a stop along the way to visit a man he'd be happy to see dead.

He'd been up since dawn working his own ranch. He could have used a few more hours of sleep, but other than that, he had no complaints. In fact, he wasn't sure when he'd been happier.

Esther opened the door and invited him in. "Glad to see you're still kicking," she said.

"I spent years in the marines. A day of hard work isn't going to slow me down."

"Good, because you were definitely christened into the life of a Texas rancher yesterday. Pierce couldn't brag enough about you last night."

"All I heard was Pierce's crowing about his new son."

"Charlie. They named him Charlie. I'm tickled

pink. I figure my Charlie is wearing the biggest smile in heaven today."

"Pierce was smiling pretty good himself last night when I stopped by the hospital."

"He was mighty happy," Esther agreed. "And Grace looked positively angelic holding her new son in her arms. Come on back to the kitchen. I'll get you some coffee. Rachel will be out in a minute."

"Sounds good." He'd hoped she'd back off the idea of having a face-to-face visit with Roy Sales, but she'd made it clear last night it was still on.

Esther poured and then handed him a mug of black coffee. "There's cream in the fridge if you want it and sugar in that chicken cup on the counter."

"No, thanks. I like it strong and black." He took a sip. "This fits the bill perfectly."

"Rachel said you're planning to bring Alfred home soon and that you'll stay on awhile if it works out."

"That's the plan."

"That's a really nice thing to do," Esther said. "I know you and your dad have had some real differences, but he was always proud of you."

"If he was, he hid it well."

"You know, I've got something I've been saving for you a long time. Alfred told me to see that you got it when he died. I figure he came close enough to dying that you should have it. Wait here. I'll get it."

Rachel arrived before Esther got back. As always, just seeing her made his insides melt. He kissed her and felt a longing that went far deeper than mere sexual desire.

"Good morning, cowboy," she said. "Or did all that work yesterday change your mind about adopting the lifestyle?"

"I'm still in. My muscles are protesting."

The truth was he'd envied Pierce his lifestyle yesterday. Not just the ranch but his life. He'd never seen a man who fit so well in his own skin.

He and Grace were a team and so in love with each other and their growing family. They seemed to have it all. Luke could get used to a life like that.

Esther rejoined them in the kitchen. She held out a sealed letter-size envelope to Luke. "I can't say if this is good or bad, but Alfred wanted you to have it. I'm just making the delivery a little soon."

He took the envelope but didn't open it. "How long have you had it?"

"I'm not sure. A year or two after you left home."

In that case, there was no reason to stop everything and read it now. He had more important things on his mind, like being with Rachel when she paid a visit to her recent and frightening past.

It wasn't how he'd have chosen to spend the day, but Rachel thought it was necessary and who was he to argue that she was wrong?

The important thing was moving on. She deserved to feel safe and live her life to the fullest—which wouldn't necessarily include him.

DR. KINCAID ARRIVED at work early to check on his patients, especially Roy Sales. Sales had become so aggrcssivc ycstcrday aftcr hcaring that Rachel Maxwell wasn't coming that the staff had to sedate him.

Kincaid wanted plenty of time to prepare him for her visit today. The longer he worked with Roy, the more uncertain he became of his true mental and emotional condition. There were days he was convinced that Sales would never be fit to face a trial.

Other days, he was certain that Roy Sales knew what he was doing and that he was running the show exactly as he planned.

Hopefully, watching him interact with the victim he continuously talked about in sessions would give Kincaid some much-needed insight.

Kincaid's office phone rang just as he was leaving to head toward Sales's floor.

"Di. Kincaid. I'm so glad you're in early."

He could hear the alarm in the director's voice. "What's wrong?"

"One of your patients was missing at the early morning medicine round. We're checking every nook and cranny, but he hasn't been located."

"Which patient?" Kincaid held his breath as he waited for the answer, though he was certain he already knew who it would be.

"Roy Sales. It would be impossible for him to get past the guard for his floor even if he got past the first two checkpoints. We've never had a patient escape from this facility."

"Did the night nurse report any problems?"

"No. According to the charts, his last bed check was at three fifteen. He was present and accounted for."

"I'm on my way." He prayed they wouldn't find that Sales had committed suicide—or worse.

He didn't even want to go there in his mind. He did know that if Roy Sales wasn't found soon, Rachel Maxwell would have to be warned.

LUKE AND RACHEL were about an hour away from the facility where Sales was being held when Rachel got a phone call from Sydney.

They'd talked on the phone yesterday, but those conversations had centered on Grace's giving birth. It was an exciting time and Rachel had felt as if she was right in the middle of the beautiful miracle.

"Hello, Sydney."

Sydney skipped the greeting. "Where are you?"

"On my way to Houston."

"Is Luke with you?"

"Yes, he's driving. We're in his truck."

"Good. Put the phone on Speaker. He needs to hear this, too."

She did. "What's wrong?"

"Are you still planning to stop and see Roy Sales?"

"Yes, but we're still at least an hour away."

"You have a change of plans. Don't go anywhere near that place."

"What's happened?" Luke asked, his voice tense.

"Roy Sales is missing."

"Missing. Are you saying he's escaped?" Luke asked.

"All they're saying at this point is that he's unaccounted for. He could well be still inside the facility.

It's maximum security. No one has ever escaped from there before."

Rachel's heart began to pound against the walls of her chest. Her chest constricted painfully. She couldn't breathe. An all-too-familiar anxiety attack was setting in. Only this time with good reason.

"I hate to have to tell you this," Sydney said, "but you need to know. I don't think it's a good idea to go to your apartment."

"My apartment." She barely had the breath to get two words from her mouth.

"I think you should turn around and go back to Winding Creek."

"I can't go back to Winding Creek and put everyone there in danger."

"I'll take care of Rachel," Luke said, answering for her as she tried to catch her breath. "I'll be with her every second. Count on it."

"No. You don't know what you're up against," Rachel said.

"I'm a marine. I've been up against the worst that can come at you. And I'm armed with a license to carry."

"Be careful," Sydney warned. "Like I said, it's doubtful he's truly escaped, but we can't be sure of that. I'll get you updated information as soon as I hear."

"I'm counting on that," Luke said.

"Take care of my sister."

"I'll guard her with my life."

"I love you, Rachel," Sydney said. Rachel was shaking so hard she couldn't respond.

Luke pulled the car into a crowded truck stop parking area. He killed the motor and reached across the seat and took her hand. "It's okay, baby. I've got your back. I'll be right here. You're safe. I promise you, I'll keep you safe."

Her breathing slowly returned to normal. It took moments longer for the shaking to stop and her pulse to approach normal.

"He's coming for me," she whispered, her voice shaky. "Deep in my heart, I always knew this wasn't over. It won't be over until one of us is dead."

"If anyone ends up dead, it won't be you.

"Do you still want to go to your apartment?"

"It's where I live. Just drop me off there and you can go. It's dangerous to be around me."

"Cut that crazy talk out now. I'm not going anywhere without you. We can get your things and then you're going home with me. That's settled."

"You should run like the wind to get as far away from me as you can."

"It's too late for that, sweetheart. I'm in this for as long as you'll have me."

He kissed away any further protests.

But this time he couldn't kiss the fear away.

LUKE STARED AT the endless line of unmoving cars in front of him. "Is I-10 always a parking lot?"

"During high traffic times for the commuters, but not at this time of the day. There must be a wreck ahead."

"In every lane?"

"They usually try to keep a lane or two open for rubberneckers."

Luke knew she was trying hard not to succumb to the memories and resurfacing fears. As strong-willed as she was, he hated to think what her captivity had been like for it to have such a powerful effect on her.

"Traffic is a mess, but then, millions of people call the Houston metropolis home."

"I'll never be one of them."

The stupidity of that remark was obvious the second the words cleared his mouth. This was her home and he had no right to knock it.

"I'm sure Houston has a lot to offer. Professional football, baseball, basketball and the largest indoor rodeo in the country, or so I've heard."

"It also has theater, a great symphony and world-class museums. The sad part is I spent so much time working I seldom took advantage of any of it. Fitch, Fitch and Bauman was my life."

"Did the firm require it?"

"When I first started, wrapping up billable hours was the measuring by which the newly hired were judged. But even after that, I had a humongous need to outwork everyone else. I demanded far too much of myself."

"That sounds like a sure path to burnout."

"I was probably headed for that. I was reminded yesterday of how isolated I'd become from friends and family and from the drama of day-to-day life. The truth is I can't remember not being driven."

"Maybe you need someone around to remind you to smell the roses or kick the ball—something like that."

She smiled. "Or someone to soak me with the water hose every now and then?"

"Or treat you to room service."

"That will work equally well. Thanks for helping me through the anxiety attack. Hearing that Sales has possibly escaped sucked me right back into the trauma. I'm still partially there."

"That's not a sign of weakness. It's a sign you're normal."

The traffic began to inch forward. A half mile farther and they reached the cause of the delay. Two cop cars, one tow truck loaded with a severely damaged compact car and one pickup on the shoulder that had survived the incident with barely a dent.

"The good news is we're practically at my apartment," Rachel said. "Take the next exit and then turn right at the light."

Rachel was silent the rest of the way except for giving directions. His mind went back to Sales. Luke had hoped to hear from Sydney by now that he'd been found and returned to his supposedly secure area.

They made a couple more turns before Rachel had him pull into a large parking garage. She pushed her remote, and the doors opened.

They took the elevator to her floor. One look inside the apartment and he was beyond impressed. "I feel like I'm taking a tour of the rich and famous. Did you inherit your fortune or do attorneys actually get paid this well?"

"No inheritance, and it's not as expensive as it looks. It's also safe and extremely convenient. That means a lot when you work in the city."

The place was spotlessly clean, not a throw pillow, a cushion or a knickknack out of order. The room smelled of vanilla, likely from the scented candles in stunning containers placed about the room.

"It's hard to believe that the woman who lives here was actually scrubbing my kitchen three nights ago."

"Sydney always says I got the family neat-freak gene." Rachel kicked off her shoes. "Make yourself at home. There's wine in the bar just off the kitchen and whiskey and some vodka, I think. No beer. Sorry about that."

"Whiskey always works. What can I get you?"

"Nothing yet."

Luke decided to check out the bedroom first. It didn't look like a place to kick off cowboy boots, but it did have a king-size bed.

Unless they got good news from Sydney, this would not be the night to try it out appropriately, but at least he could sleep beside her and hold her in his arms.

For all the lavish amenities, he'd rather be back at Arrowhead Hills. But only if Rachel was there with him. He had no intention of letting her out of his sight until Roy Sales was found and locked away again.

RACHEL JUMPED WHEN her phone rang, and then dashed across the living room to retrieve it. Her heart sank when she saw the caller was Claire Covey.

"Hayden's here," Claire said. "He's home." Her voice rang with joy. "I know you mentioned a possible meeting on Wednesday. We can meet you anytime today."

"I know what I said, but unfortunately this isn't a good day for me."

"I'm begging you to meet with us if only for a few

minutes. I can meet you anywhere in Houston and any time you say. I'll just feel so much better about everything once you get to talk to Hayden one-on-one."

Claire was clearly overcome with optimism and the excitement of having her son out of jail. It was difficult to put her off.

"He knows things the police aren't saying." Claire insisted.

"What kind of things?"

"That information will be better coming from him. He's innocent. After you talk to him you'll realize that. Please. He's so scared. He needs to know someone besides his father and me are on his side."

"You do understand that this will only be an interview," Rachel said. "I can't make a commitment this soon for a variety of reasons."

"He didn't kill Louann Black. What other reasons could possibly matter?"

"I have to trust him to level with me. This isn't a game. I can't accept lies or omissions from him. And he may not feel comfortable working with me."

"He'll tell the truth. He has nothing to hide."

It could be that Hayden Covey was as innocent as his mother claimed. Or he could be a brutal killer who deserved to pay for his crime.

Rachel still couldn't rule out the chance that the evil she had sensed in him might have been only a reflection of the way she felt about Roy Sales. "Okay, I'm in downtown Houston," Rachel said, giving in to Claire's pleas. "I can see him now if that works for you."

"We can be there in thirty minutes. Just give me an address."

Rachel gave her the directions.

Take two on Hayden Covey. Innocent or a psycho. Hopefully Rachel would make the right call.

Chapter Seventeen

Rachel sat across from Hayden Covey in the small office connected to her dining area. Luke and Claire were on the balcony that overlooked the pool, ensuring Rachel and Hayden absolute privacy.

Claire hadn't wanted it that way. Rachel had insisted.

Rachel didn't feel the immediate evil vibes she had sensed on Friday. They would be starting fresh. "Tell me about yourself, Hayden."

"I thought this was supposed to be about the way the police are trying to railroad me just because they don't like my dad."

"We'll get to that later. First I'd just like to get to know you better."

"I'm a running back for University of Texas. I was mentioned for the Heisman this year. I didn't get nominated, but some people think if I stay on the top of my game next year, I'll be a shoo-in."

"Obviously football is very important to you."

"Yeah, well, I like it, and I'm good at it."

"What else are you good at?"

"Most every type of sports. Dad says I'm a born athlete. I'm disciplined. Never miss a practice, hardly ever miss a game. I play hurt."

"What are your interests besides sports?"

"Mostly just hanging out with the guys on the team."

"What do you do when you hang out?"

"You know. Guy stuff."

"Do you date much?"

"Some."

"Tell me about Louann Black."

He started to squirm. "It's nothing like the police are saying, I can promise you that."

"What's it like?"

"We dated for a few months. We had some good times. It was never anything serious."

"Did Louann want it to be serious?"

"No. She was a party girl. Drank too much. Always wanting me to buy drugs for her. It got old."

"But you didn't break up with her?"

"I was getting around to it. She heard about it and dumped me first. No big deal."

Not until Louann was murdered.

"You must have been shocked to hear that she'd been killed."

"I was, but I was nowhere around her the night it happened. I hadn't seen her for days. I've got people who'll swear to that."

He had people, but he also had money, and people could be bought.

Their interview lasted for two hours, in which time Hayden changed the story about his relationship with Louann at least three times. That was never a good sign, but sometimes defendants just said what they thought you wanted to hear, especially when they were scared.

Hayden was clearly scared. Rachel wasn't convinced he was innocent, but it was early in the process. She had a lot of research to do on him, Louann and the police report before she could make a studied decision.

She had a good detective friend in Homicide who might shed a bit more light on the subject. As soon as Claire and Hayden left, she'd give Matt a call.

Right now she just wanted to get the news that Roy Sales was back in his supposedly secure facility.

IT WAS TEN minutes before ten and Rachel had already showered and slipped into a pale blue satin nightshirt when Sydney finally called.

Rachel answered on the first ring and pressed Speaker so Luke could hear what was said. "Tell me you're calling with good news."

"I'd love to, but the facility administrator is still trying to sell the idea that Sales is hiding out somewhere inside the building. He's convinced Sales couldn't breach every safeguard they have in place."

"Only because he doesn't know Roy Sales the way I do."

"I'm starting to have my doubts, as well. I wish they'd call in the FBI so I could be official instead of relying on back channels—legally, of course. Did you decide to spend the night in Houston?"

"Yes. Luke and I are in my apartment. I haven't made any decisions about what I'll do tomorrow but we're definitely staying here tonight."

"I don't think you should be anyplace alone until Sales is located."

"I'm not going anywhere without her," Luke promised.

"So don't worry about me," Rachel said to assure her sister. "I'm protected by a genuine hero-status former member of the US Marines."

"That does ease my mind a bit. I'll give you a call in the morning or before if I hear something. You do the same."

"I will. I just keep wondering if my not showing up to see Sales yesterday instigated any of this."

"Don't go getting the idea that any of this is your fault."

"It was just a thought." A very disturbing thought that she was having trouble shaking.

Rachel was still pondering that possibility long after the call from Sydney was finished. She walked over and sat on the bed beside Luke. She couldn't miss seeing the weapon on the table beside the bed.

"You look worried." He slipped an arm around her waist. "Are you afraid that I might not be a match for Roy Sales?"

She thought about it before she answered, "The memories are so sickening that they pull me back into the fear without warning. But no. I'm never afraid when I'm with you."

"In that case, let's get some sleep. After the way this week has started, there's no telling what tomorrow will bring. Besides, this will be our first night to sleep together."

He pulled down the top sheet and crawled into bed.

Rachel hesitated. "I feel safe with you, but I'm not sure I can re-create the magic of Monday's afternoon delight. I couldn't do the night or us justice."

"I'm not expecting you to."

She crawled in beside him. He rolled over to face her and trailed a finger along her lips. "We never talked about it," he said, "and we don't have to talk about it now, but when I picture that monster touching you, abusing you, defiling you, the rage roars inside me."

"He defiled me in many ways, but not sexually," she said, understanding what he was thinking even if he couldn't bring himself to say the words. "He touched me inappropriately a few times, but only on my breasts and thighs.

"It was never about sex with him, though he threatened it. It was all about control and pleasing his dead mother, who'd once abused him. That seemed to be the root of his madness, but his evil seemed to come from hell itself."

"I'd love to come face-to-face with the slimy bastard. I'd wring his neck with my bare hands."

They snuggled together, his chest to her back, his muscular thigh sliding in between her legs, his breath falling on the nape of her neck.

Her world was falling apart, and yet it never seemed more together than when she was in Luke Dawkins's arms.

RACHEL WOKE TO the first light of day sliding through her blinds. She'd slept so soundly it took a moment to realizc where she was. She rolled over, reached out for Luke and felt a wave of disappointment that he wasn't there.

She went to the bathroom and splashed her face with cold water. In spite of not knowing Sale's whereabouts, it was the best night's sleep she'd had since the abduction.

She found Luke in the kitchen, staring at the blinking light on her one-server coffee maker.

"I was going to brew coffee and bring you a cup in bed, but the blinking bluc light refuses to let me."

"Here, let me do it."

A minute later she handed him his cup.

"I'd cook breakfast, but your fridge is empty except for butter, ketchup and a few other condiments. Your pantry isn't much better."

"I don't do a lot of cooking. I usually pick up a bagel on the way to work, and that holds me until lunch."

"Don't let Esther hear you say that. She'll force-feed you bacon until you oink."

"If I could cook as well as Esther, I'd change my eating habits."

"What is our plan for today?" Luke asked.

"I know you need to get back to the ranch and perhaps check on Alfred."

"I can spare another day if you have things to take care of here—like talking to Eric Fitch Sr. or seeing Hayden Covey again."

"I need to find out more details of Louann Black's murder bcforc I sec Hayden or his mother. And I need to decide what I'm going to do about that before I discuss a future with the firm."

"Have you considered other options for a career?"

"A few."

Her phone rang and she raced back to the bedroom to get it.

It was Dr. Kincaid. She whispered a prayer that this was good news.

Chapter Eighteen

"Good morning, Dr. Kincaid."

"Is this Rachel Maxwell?"

"Yes, and I do hope you have some good news."

"I wish that were the case. Unfortunately, I fear just the opposite."

"Then Roy Sales has escaped the facility?"

"We don't have positive proof of that, but the buildings and grounds have been thoroughly searched and there's no sign of him."

"I was afraid of that from the beginning. I appreciate you giving me the heads-up."

"There's another reason I called. I don't know what the law authorities are going to tell you, but I've worked with Sales for months now. He's obsessed with you and convinced you betrayed him."

"That is a really warped way of looking at things after what he put me through."

"In my judgment, he's a really sick man. I have a strong suspicion that he's going to try to kill you. Whether it's to satisfy him or his mother, I can't be sure. But I do think your life is at risk until he's found and taken back into custody."

"Have you told anyone else this?"

"I've told the administration and I just talked to your sister, Sydney. I'm sure she'll have advice for keeping you safe. Follow it."

"I will. I do have one question. Do you think my not showing up to visit him as planned triggered this?"

"It may have had something to do with the timing, but he didn't just conceive of an escape plan one day and execute it the next. Not from this facility. This had to be something he was working on for months, probably ever since he's been here."

"Thanks again for calling," she said, "but I have to go. I have another call coming through now. I'm sure it's Sydney."

"Good. If you have any other questions, feel free to call me."

"I will." She went straight to Sydney's call.

Sydney repeated what she'd heard from Dr. Kincaid before switching to her own take on everything.

"Don't panic," Sydney cautioned. "I'm sure every law enforcement officer in the state—from local to the Texas Rangers—is looking for the Lone Star Snatcher."

"What do you suggest I do?"

"Hire a bodyguard. I'll fax you a list of reliable sources in your area. Enlist them for 24/7 service and then follow their orders. Or just let me know where you'll be and I can take care of everything."

"I have a bodyguard."

"Doesn't he have a ranch to run and a father to take care of?"

"He does." Expecting more from him was unreasonable. "Send me the list. I'll hire bodyguard protection."

She was just starting to get a grip on life again. She would not let Sales snatch that away.

"I DON'T LIKE IT," Luke said. "I respect your sister's judgment, but this time I think she's wrong."

"You don't have to stay here with me, Luke. Drive back to the ranch. I can find a way to get my car from Esther's house later."

"What is it you don't understand about I'm not leaving here without you. Besides, going back to Winding Creek and staying with me makes a lot more sense."

"You have a ranch to run."

"To hell with the ranch."

"You don't mean that, and I can't let you spend your every second looking out for me."

"If you don't go back to Winding Creek with me, then I'm not going back, so you're not doing me any favors."

"Did you get your stubbornness from Alfred?"

"Insults won't change my mind."

And the truth was she didn't want to change his mind. She wanted to go back to Arrowhead Hills. She wanted to sleep in Luke's arms every night and have coffee with him every morning. She might even learn to make pancakes or fry eggs.

"I'll go back with you to Winding Creek under one condition."

"Name it," Luke said.

"I hire a protection service not only for me but for Esther's ranch, as well."

"Does Roy Sales know Esther?"

"He killed her husband."

"Point made."

"If you want bodyguards, we'll have bodyguards, but you'll be at Arrowhead Hills, not in Houston."

"You've got yourself a deal."

She had only one stop to make before they left Houston.

THE POLICE PRECINCT was hopping, but Matt managed to find a few minutes for Rachel. They were usually working for opposites sides and purposes, but they had a mutual respect for each other.

As far as Rachel was concerned, he was the best homicide detective in the city. She'd have loved to include Luke in their discussion but was afraid Matt would hold something back with him in the room.

Matt wouldn't give her any information that hadn't already been released to the public, but she'd pick up a lot from how he said it.

Matt grabbed an armload of files off a metal folding chair and piled them on his already cluttered desk.

"Have a seat."

She did.

He propped his backside on the corner of his desk. "I'd like to say 'Good to see you,' but 'Are you nuts?' has a more appropriate ring to it."

"Any particular reason?"

"It's all over the news that you're defending a murdering piece of… You get the picture."

"I take it you're convinced Hayden is guilty."

"Without a doubt. Have you seen the police report?"

"Not yet. I'm not officially on the case yet in spite of what you hear on the news."

"Then I take it you haven't seen the crime scene pictures, either?"

"No."

"They're as brutal as I've ever seen. Lots of slashing. Enough blood to fill a barrel."

"Hayden claims he's innocent," Rachel said.

"He isn't. We've got enough evidence to bury him, and he knows it. He's counting on his parents to save him. And now I guess he's counting on you, too."

"I haven't seen a lot of motive for murder, as yet," Rachel said. "There's lots of hearsay but nothing solid."

"Believe me, you'll hear it at the trial. He's guilty. But he's smart, hard to trip up when you're talking to him. You think you've seen evil? You've never seen it the way you're gonna face it in Hayden Covey. He's guilty and he's going down. Represent him, and you will, too."

"I'll keep that in mind."

"By the way, I heard about Roy Sales breaking out of the psychiatric hospital, or at least disappearing. That's another one who should have gone directly to death row. Not worth the air he's breathing."

"I couldn't agree more."

"He won't stay on the loose long. Every cop in the state is dying to arrest the Lone Star Snatcher."

"That's what I hear," Rachel said.

"In the meantime, stay safe. I can't imagine him wanting to get anywhere near you and your FBI sister, but you never can tell what a lunatic will do."

"I'll be careful. And thanks."

"Yeah. Take what I told you about Hayden as gospel. I'm not bluffing. I'm dead serious this time."

She stood and he walked her to the door, picking up a file and handing it to her as she left.

"A little bedtime entertainment—if you're looking for nightmares. By the way, you didn't get this from me, even though it's not confidential since it's already been leaked. It's just too brutal for the media to show. It's already making the rounds on the internet, though."

Fortunately, Rachel didn't wait until bedtime to open the file. She didn't even wait for Luke to back out of his parking space.

She took one look at the gory crime scene shot inside the file and gagged, struggling not to throw up.

Luke killed the engine. "What's wrong?"

She handed him the picture.

He didn't hold back the curses that expressed his feelings. She would have been shocked if he did.

"If there's a chance Hayden Covey is guilty of that, I don't want you around him unless I'm there with you." Hayden Covey might be innocent, but whoever murdered Louann Black needed to be convicted. That kind of evil wasn't just bone deep. It went to the deepest pits of the soul. Roy Sales had taught her that.

If she had any doubts of Hayden's innocence, she would never be able to defend him.

Rachel took out her phone and made a call to Claire Covey. "Some things have come up and I need to see your son as soon as possible."

"He's not here right now. He's with friends and I'm not sure when he'll be back. Will tomorrow afternoon work?"

"I'll be back in Winding Creek by then."

"I can get him there. Where shall we meet you?"

"I'd like to see him by himself this time."

"Fine. I'll get a hotel room and we'll stay in Winding Creek as long as you need us. I can't rest until I know you're on our side."

"Then I'll see you tomorrow at two."

Rachel gave her directions to the ranch. She was leaning strongly toward turning down the case, but she'd give Hayden one more chance to convince her he was innocent.

She studied the picture again and then tossed it into the back seat.

LUKE AND PIERCE took their mugs of hot coffee and a couple of Esther's famous oatmeal cookies to Pierce's front porch. Rachel, last seen cradling baby Charlie in her arms and crooning baby talk to him, had stayed inside with Esther and Grace.

"There have been some new developments with Roy Sales," Luke said. "He's missing from the maximum-security facility where he was being held."

"I heard about it from Sheriff Cavazos and from Sydney and Tucker. It's also being reported all over the internet. I'm sure it will make the evening news. Can't keep something like that quiet."

"They managed to keep it quiet for a day," Luke said. "I guess you also know that Sydney has handled the hiring of protection services for both our ranches."

"Sydney called and told me she's hired protection for the ranch and that will include my house and Esther's and bodyguards for Esther and Grace. I told her it was a waste of money. I have the manpower to protect my own ranch. Every one of us can drop the hammer and hit the target faster than you can sneeze."

"What did she say?" Luke asked.

"She had Tucker call me. He convinced me it would be much easier to give in to Sydney and Rachel on this than to argue with them. Hopefully we're talking about only a few days before they recapture Sales."

"Is Esther going along with this?"

"Surprisingly, yes. She's staying with us a few days anyway to help Grace out with Charlie. She thinks it will be a hoot to have a bodyguard help her feed the chickens and gather eggs."

"We need a video of that. Is Grace okay with having a personal bodyguard?"

"She says I'm all the bodyguard she needs, but she's willing to put up with it. I think she's secretly glad to have it. She's faced enough terror in her own life. And Jaci is staying with Riley and Dani a few days so she won't be frightened by strangers with guns hanging around the house."

"When are you expecting your strangers with guns?" Luke asked.

"Five o'clock."

"Same here."

"There's plenty of room for Rachel at our place if she wants to stay here," Pierce offered.

"She's staying with me," Luke assured him.

"I kind of figured that. It's fine with me, by the way. I know she's in good hands."

IT WAS FOUR O'CLOCK when Rachel and Luke finished putting away the groceries they'd bought at the local grocery. The pantry was officially full. So was the refrigerator.

Luke knew it wasn't official or lasting, but it felt as if he and Rachel were setting up house together. He liked the feeling. He'd like it even better with her sleeping in his bed tonight.

Rachel stood at the open door of the refrigerator, staring at the full shelves. "Do you like beef stew?"

"Doesn't everybody?"

"I think I'll call Esther and ask her for her recipe. I'm sure hers will be delicious. And how hard can stew be?"

"You don't have to go to that much trouble. I can grill some steaks."

"I think we need stew. It's comfort food, and after the last few days, I could use a lot of comfort."

He started to remind her they had an hour before the cavalry arrived and that time could be better spent. He figured that might be pushing things. He didn't want her to think this was all about sex for him, especially with all she was dealing with.

Luke grabbed a cold beer and his jacket and walked

out to the porch while Rachel got started on her stew project.

The letter Esther had given him was folded and in the back pocket of his jeans. He pulled it out, looked at the envelope for a few minutes and finally broke the seal.

He settled on the top porch step and finished his beer before he started to read.

Son,

If you're reading this, I'm dead, but there's things I need to say. I'm not the man I wanted to be. Not the man I needed to be. If I were, things might have turned out differently for all of us.

I'm not blaming this on anyone, but I was raised by Grandpa Hank. You never met him, but he was one of the meanest scoundrels in the county. I tried hard not to be like him. I didn't do so good at that.

I never showed it right, but I loved your mother more than anything in the world. I love you, too. I never said it, but I'm proud of you.

All I got to leave you is Arrowhead Hills Ranch. I own it free and clear. If you don't want it, sell it and take the money. You deserve the life you want. Would like it if you make sure the horses get good homes when you sell them.

My will is in my safe-deposit box up at the bank on Main Street with everything else that's worth saving.

I got lots of regrets and I'm not even dying yet. I figure when I do, won't nobody shed a tear.

Can't blame them. Don't be a fool like me. Find
a woman you can love and show her how much
every day of your life.
Alfred P. Dawkins.
PS, I should have come and watched you play
ball that day.

Luke blinked hard to hold back the tears as he folded
the letter and slipped it back in his pocket.

It didn't change everything, but it was the best look
he'd ever gotten into his dad's mind. The first time Alfred had ever told him he loved him or was proud of
him.

THIS PART OF the parking lot at a small neighborhood
grocery store was nearly empty as the elderly woman
opened the back seat of her car and deposited her handbag and a shopping bag.

Roy waited until she was settling behind the wheel
before he approached her car from behind. She closed
her door and started the engine. He jumped from behind her car and dived into the back seat where she'd
put the packages.

"What do you want?" Her voice trembled.

"A ride."

"Who are you?"

"Your worst nightmare." Roy pulled the sharp carv-
ing knife from his boot holster and flashed it for her
to see.

She screamed.

He fit his hand around the back of her neck. "Shut

up now or I'll cut out your tongue. Do exactly as I say and you won't get hurt. Leave the engine running and get out of the car. Call the cops and I'll come back and kill you."

He took his hands from the woman's neck. She jumped from the car, started to run, then slipped and fell. The back of her head hit the concrete, and blood splattered everywhere.

Roy gunned the engine and sped away. He'd hide out until it was full dark and then he'd take the back roads to Winding Creek. He'd wasted too much time already, only to learn that she'd quit her job. No luck at her apartment, either. No sign of movement and no lights had come on at dark.

He wouldn't take the risk of getting past the apartment's security only to break into an empty apartment.

He figured his next best hope of finding her was at the Double K Ranch. Esther Kavanaugh wouldn't have hesitated to take her in. Hopefully he'd find Rachel and Esther alone in the sprawling ranch house.

Roy loved the way the news kept saying he couldn't possibly have escaped the infamous barred asylum. They'd underestimated him. Everyone always did.

He laid the knife on the seat beside him and ran his index finger along the razor-sharp edge. The crazy thing was he hadn't even had to use it to escape. The meanest guard in the place had worked it all out for him.

The guard had sent him through the gates in the back of a truck carrying medical waste that no one ever wanted to look in or to touch.

Roy wasn't afraid. He was in his own bag with only a few air holes to let him breathe.

It was all in the way you played the game.

All Roy had had to do was promise to kill someone for the hated guard. He might even keep the promise.

But first he'd take care of Rachel Maxwell. People who betrayed you must pay.

Mommy would be proud of him.

Chapter Nineteen

Luke took one bite of the stew, and his tongue caught fire. He forced himself to swallow. "Wow!"

"Do you like it?"

"Love it. It's a little spicy and maybe a tad too much salt, but that's the way I love it."

Rachel dipped her spoon into her bowl and took a bite. She didn't swallow, but ran to the sink to spit it out. "It's horrible. How could you say you loved it?"

"I'm tactful?"

"I followed the recipe except that Esther doesn't have real measurements. She says pinch of this, tad of that, a handful of this, a dozen peppers."

"A dozen peppers. What kind of peppers?"

"Jalapeños."

"She told you to use a dozen jalapeños?"

"Yes, but I didn't have that many, so I added the two jars of sliced ones we bought at the store."

"That explains the fire."

Rachel checked the recipe. "Oops. There is a tiny little hyphen between the one and the two. Don't know how I missed that. I thought twelve sounded like a lot."

"I'm sure if you hadn't misread the recipe the stew would have been delicious."

"I guess I'd best not offer any to the hired protection."

"Not if you want them to save you. Tell you what, I'll make us a BLT sandwich. The guys seem to have all they need except a bathroom in that fancy van of theirs."

"They assured me they didn't need a thing," Rachel said. "But a BLT sounds good to me. I actually can fry bacon and I'm a whiz at slicing tomatoes."

"But how are you at toasting bread?"

"You're just plain making fun of me now."

He walked over, wrapped his arms around her waist and nibbled on her earlobe. "I would never do that. So how about you start frying and slicing and I'll go lay a fire in the fireplace? Might as well add a romantic touch to our gourmet meal."

"You do realize there will be a shortage of privacy," Rachel said. "You never know when one of the guards will need a bathroom break."

"Yes, but I have something I want to talk to you about and it's still a little muddy to take a walk in your cute little suede booties. You'll have to get a pair of real cowboy boots if you're going to make it on the ranch."

A stupid comment. He'd had to practically force her to come home with him this time and she was in danger. He'd had no indication from her she was interested in leaving her lush Houston apartment for the boondocks.

"You sound serious," Rachel said. "Is this about Roy Sales?"

"No."

"Then start the fire."

RACHEL'S JAW CLENCHED as she started frying the bacon. Her stomach churned. It was her typical first reaction at anything to do with a fire.

She was with Luke. She could do this.

By the time they were cuddled in front of the fire and munching on their sandwiches, her impulsive fears had dissolved. Luke kept the talk pleasant with no mention of Roy or the security personnel standing guard over the house and immediate surrounding area.

When they'd finished eating, he walked over and stoked the fire. Before sitting down, he took a folded letter from his back pocket and handed it to her. "Esther gave me this Tuesday. She was supposed to give it to me when Alfred died, though I'm not sure why he was so confident she'd outlive him or exactly why she decided to give it to me now, but she did."

"It must be personal," Rachel said. "Are you sure you want me to read it?"

"I'm sure."

She unfolded the letter and started to read. Tears filled her eyes before she reached the end.

"He told you a lot in a few words," Rachel said. "A lifetime of regrets."

"So it seems."

"The two of you must have always had a strained relationship."

Luke sat back down beside her. "We never really had a relationship of any kind. I don't remember having one meaningful conversation with him. Nothing except complaints about whatever I tried to do. I finally started doing things that angered him on purpose."

"Your mother must have felt the same heartbreak you did."

"I blamed Alfred for her death. He drove her away. She died before the two of us could have a life that offered more than endless putdowns."

"And yet he sounds sincere when he says he loved you both. That must touch you."

"It does. I'm not sure what our chances are of ever having anything that approaches a father/son relationship, but maybe there's a chance for us to live together in some sort of harmony. At least I'm willing to try."

She squeezed his hand as a tear rolled down her cheek. "What game was he talking about that he missed? It has clearly lain heavy on his mind for all these years."

"My high school baseball team was playing in the state championship. I was to be the pitcher and several major league scouts were going to be there to watch me pitch. It was the biggest day in my life to that point, one that could have affected the rest of my life."

"Why didn't he go?"

"He was doing the spring roundup and branding that day. The plans were made before we knew we were going to state. He'd hired the extras he needed. When I told him I wouldn't be around to help, he exploded. The ranch was everything to him and he thought it should be to me, too. He told me if I went to the game, I didn't need to come home."

"And you didn't?"

"I didn't."

"What about your chance to play professional baseball?"

"I blew it. I didn't even graduate, just drove up to Austin after the game and joined the marines.

"It was a long time before I even admitted to myself that I wasn't only furious. Finally admitting to myself that he cared nothing about me and would rather I be out of his life devastated me."

"Of course it did. You were only eighteen. That game was the biggest thing in your life."

"Crazy thing is, now that I'm back here on the ranch, I realize I never hated ranching. It's likely in my blood as much as it is in his. I was just tired of life the way it was."

"So much hurt," Rachel said. "So much misunderstanding. So many years lost."

Luke put an arm around her shoulder and pulled her close.

At least Luke knew what he wanted to do with his life now. She didn't, but she was having serious doubts about ever going back to criminal defense.

It was a worthy profession. It saved many innocent people from being punished for crimes they didn't commit. It forced the courts to present solid evidence and then hope for the jury to make sound decisions.

Sometimes they failed. Most of the time they didn't.

It just wasn't the life for her, at least not now. Maybe it never would be, but she had plenty of time to make up her mind.

She couldn't wait where Hayden Covey was concerned. It wasn't fair to him or his parents. Right or wrong, she was not convinced of his innocence. Eric Fitch Sr. would represent him far better than she could.

She'd call Claire Covey tonight.

Now all she had to worry about was a madman who wanted her dead.

RACHEL'S PHONE RANG in the wee hours of the morning, waking her from a sound sleep. She sat up in bed and grabbed her phone. "Hello."

"This is Sheriff Cavazos. I'm calling about Roy Sales."

Chapter Twenty

Rachel's heart pounded.

"What about Roy Sales?"

Luke sat up in bed beside her, his hand on her back.

"He's dead," Cavazos said.

She couldn't have heard that right. Sales didn't die. He tortured and ruined lives. He murdered. "Are you sure?"

"I pulled the trigger that sent the bullet through his brains myself."

"Sales is dead," she whispered to Luke. "I'm switching the call to Speaker so Luke can listen in," she told Cavazos.

If she'd had any hope that people in Winding Creek didn't know she was sleeping with Luke, she'd just blown that.

"How did it happen?" she asked.

"Good law enforcement. I knew you had those high-dollar guards over at Pierce's cabin, so I had deputies watching the main gate and the back gate at the Double K Ranch. I figured if Sales came to Winding Creek looking for revenge, he'd show up at Esther's spread first."

"Really?" That surprised Luke. "From what Sales's psychiatrist said, we figured his first strike would be against Rachel."

"Exactly. We think he tried her apartment first and must have found out she wasn't there."

"How do you know that?" Rachel asked.

"A man fitting Sales's description carjacked a woman in a parking lot a few blocks from your apartment. She was found bleeding from a head wound and with a concussion. Sales's style of brutality, though she says she fell as he drove away in her car.

"She still managed to ID him for the officer who showed up to investigate," Cavazos continued. "The report was all over law enforcement wires. He ditched the car about thirty miles from Winding Creek."

"So he ditched one car, picked up another and headed to Esther's place," Luke surmised.

"Yep," Cavazos said. "It was common knowledge Rachel and her sister spent some time at the Double K Ranch with Esther after Sales was first arrested."

Rachel took a deep breath and exhaled slowly. "I'm having a hard time getting my head around the fact that Roy Sales is really dead."

"I understand that after what he put you through. But it was going to happen sooner or later," Cavazos said. "I'm just glad it happened before he hurt or killed someone else. Too much evil stewing around in his sick mind."

"I don't see how anyone could argue with that," Luke said.

"I s'pect you'd have enjoyed dropping the hammer

on him yourself, Luke. Probably better I beat you to it. Less paperwork and headaches for you."

"No doubt," Luke agreed.

"I'm heading over to Pierce's house now," Cavazos said. "I figure I'd best let them all know what took place at their back gate this morning. I could use some hot coffee, and one of Esther's breakfasts would taste mighty good this morning, too. It's been a long night."

"I'm sure you'll get breakfast," Rachel said, "along with many thanks. I'm still practically speechless, so I know I'm not doing an adequate job of thanking you myself."

"That goes for me, as well," Luke said. "I plan to be moving to Winding Creek permanently. If there's ever anything I can help you with, all it takes is a call."

"Careful what you offer," Cavazos said. "Never know when I might need to deputize a former medaled marine. Even a small, friendly town like Winding Creek gets hit by trouble every now and then."

"A little too often for me," Rachel said.

"Yes, but you can let those high-priced gun-toting gorillas off your dime. You've got nothing to worry about now. We'll talk more soon."

Cavazos made it sound like a done deal. She knew the trauma of her time in captivity wouldn't disappear in an instant. But for the first time she was confident that she'd move past it.

She cuddled back in Luke's arms. But not to sleep.

They made love until the sun shot its first golden rays over the horizon. Time enough to release the bodyguards that she hoped never to need again.

HAYDEN COVEY WAS watching from a well-hidden spot when he saw a white van carrying two men drive down the hard dirt ranch road and approach the Arrowhead Hills Ranch gate. The passenger who got out to unlatch the gate did not look like your typical Texas cowboy.

He was missing the familiar Western hat but was wearing a pair of stylish aviator sunglasses. He wore a black long-sleeved T-shirt over jeans that looked like they'd never seen a horse or even a lot of wear, for that matter. A large semiautomatic pistol was holstered at his waist.

Looked like a security guard to Hayden.

The lawyer babe must really be running scared if she was hiring protection. Guess her own cowboy, the guy called Luke something or other, wasn't tough enough to keep her safe from the crazy guy who was after her.

Not that it mattered to Hayden. He wouldn't be dealing with Luke. He liked things one-on-one with the odds always in his favor. He'd teach that bitch to give him the runaround and then turn against him.

He was getting enough crap from the homicide detectives. He wasn't about to take it from her. Besides, he'd never even be suspected of killing her. She already had a genuine nutcase killer after her.

He put his earphones back in his ears and let the banging background bass get him even more stirred up. He'd been driving most of the night. He needed to stay awake a few more hours.

He drove to the gate, got out and swung it open before getting back into a stolen car and barreling over the cattle gap.

A stolen car that would never be traced back to Hayden.

Chapter Twenty-One

Rachel pulled the sheets from the bed in Alfred's room. The thin drapes needed laundering, as well. Better yet, they should be trashed. She'd see what kind of replacement she could find in town or online.

In her mind, the best homecoming for Alfred would be a house that was spotlessly clean from floor to ceiling. Luke had his own ideas about what Alfred needed on the functional side.

He'd just left to go talk to one of the wranglers about some special feed they needed for the quarter horses. He was driving into town then to pick up the feed and some safety support rails and grab bars to install in the bathroom and anywhere else Alfred might need them.

There was plenty of work to do, but Rachel couldn't keep from humming as she added the sheets and some detergent to the washing machine.

There was really no reason she was still here now that she was out of danger. No reason except that she was unemployed and had no reason to rush back to Houston. The main reason she was still here was Luke, not that she expected what they had going for them was permanent. He'd never mentioned forever, and things were too unsettled for either of them right now to make firm plans for the future.

The front door creaked open as she started the washer.

"Back so soon?" she called. "What did you forget?"

The footsteps grew louder. There was no answer. She walked back to the kitchen. Hayden Covey was standing there, a black briefcase in his right hand.

His clothes were rumpled, as if he'd slept in his car. He looked around as if sizing up the place.

"I wasn't expecting you this morning," she said. "Didn't your mother give you my message?"

"You mean that message where you said to hell with me, you had your own problems?"

"I'm sure you know that's not what I said. I explained everything to your mother. I know she was upset, but I thought she understood that I was not in a good place to represent you. Eric Fitch Sr. will do a much better job."

"She understood, all right. We both understand. You've already decided I'm guilty." He placed his briefcase on the kitchen table, unlatching but not opening it.

Rachel met his gaze and was instantly struck with that same aura of evil she'd first felt at the law firm. Anxiety dried her lips and made her hands clammy.

"I decided to do some explaining myself," Hayden said.

"What do you want to explain?"

"How it was with me and Louann. Louann was no innocent young coed. She liked sex and she liked it dirty. Handcuffs, whips, hot candle wax. You know what I'm talking about.?"

Cold sweat broke out on Rachel's forehead and between her breasts. Her stomach churned.

"I'm not complaining," Hayden said. "I gave her all the pain she wanted, but that wasn't good enough. She found someone else, a nice guy, she said, who treated her like a lady. She didn't want to see me anymore."

She forced a semi-calm to her voice. "That must have upset you."

"Not much. Louann wasn't that great in bed. Wasn't that pretty, either. What pissed me off was the way she started spreading all kinds of lies about me around campus. Saying I was a control freak, that I was a psycho with a temper."

"If those were lies, I can see why they made you angry." She was playing along with him now. If he kept this up, he just might confess.

"I don't need that trash talk about me. I'm the star of the football team. I'm pro football material."

Rachel eased backward, closer to the counter that held the knife block—just in case this turned really ugly. "Is that why you killed her?"

"I warned her. She didn't listen. But you should have heard how she screamed when I made that first slash with the jagged-edged hunting knife. Guess she didn't want to be gutted."

Rachel reached for the longest, sharpest knife. She yanked it from the block and pointed it at Hayden. "Get out. Get out now."

"Or you'll do what, kill me? I don't think so."

But he turned and started walking away. Her heart was in her throat. Her insides were tied into knots. Despite the fear, she knew she'd kill him if she had to, but she didn't want to.

In a split second, he turned back toward her, grabbed something from his briefcase and tackled her to the floor.

He straddled her, pinning her wrists to the floor, rendering her knife useless. She tried to force him off her, but he was incredibly strong. She screamed, praying one of the hands would be near enough to hear her.

No one came.

Hayden released one wrist. She slammed a fist into his face and then tried to jam her fingers into his eyes. She was fighting for her life. For her future. For the chance to be with Luke Dawkins.

That was when she saw the ropes dangling from Hayden's hand. The briefcase was open. Apparently he'd stored his ropes and who knew what else in there.

He slammed a fist into her stomach. She doubled over in pain. He rolled her to her stomach like a rag doll while she was struggling to breathe.

She felt a yank and her wrists being bound behind her back. Her skin burned as the rope tightened.

"You'll never get away with this, Hayden Covey. Attacking me is like hammering another nail in your own coffin. You'll never escape jail now."

"That's not exactly true. They can't tie me to this. I have an alibi. I'm with my football friends. They'll back me, same as always. Besides, you have a madman after you. It will just look like he found you."

"Roy Sales is dead."

"Shut up, you lying bitch."

"I'm not lying. He was killed a few hours ago by the sheriff."

"I don't believe you. I did my homework. I'm setting you on fire, just the way he would have. You could say I'm just helping him out."

Rachel rolled and twisted, fighting to break free as he tied the rough-hewn rope around her ankles. After that he tied the rope to the leg of the heavy wooden table with her fighting him all the way.

He flipped her over, forcing her to watch as he slowly and methodically took a jar from his briefcase. He opened it and poured a ring of gasoline around her. "Are you ready for some fun, lawyer babe?"

Fear engulfed her. He hadn't even lit a match, but she could already smell the smoke and feel the flames.

She was in hell all over again, but this time Roy Sales was not the ruling demon.

LUKE WAS FIVE miles down the road but still bothered by the fact that his gate had been left open. Cowboys always closed the gate behind them. It was drilled into their minds from the time they were big enough to hop out of the truck and open the gate.

His hired hands had all arrived after the security team left. Who else was on his ranch and why?

He called Rachel. No answer.

Roy Sales was dead. There was no reason to expect that someone else would cause trouble. It likely had something to do with Roy Sales and the evil embedded in him, but Luke couldn't just blow off the open gate.

He had this unwavering hunch that something might be wrong.

He made a U-turn on the narrow road and headed back toward the ranch.

He tried calling Rachel again.

Still no answer. He put the pedal to the metal and practically flew the rest of the way home.

The house looked just as he'd left it. He jumped from his truck and raced up the steps. The front door was ajar even though the temperature was still in the low forties this morning.

The front of the house was empty. He walked back to the kitchen and into hell.

Hayden Covey was standing over Rachel, taunting her with a large, unlit fireplace match, so absorbed in what he was doing that he apparently hadn't heard Luke come in.

Luke pulled his pistol. "Drop that match or I will splatter your brains all over the wall."

Hayden turned toward Luke and went white. The hand that was holding the match began to shake.

Luke expected Hayden to beg for his life. Instead he lit the match. His whole body began to tremble. He was running scared, but he held Rachel's life in his hands.

Luke had been on more dangerous missions in the marines than he could bear to remember. He'd never been truly afraid, never been this scared in all his life.

If Hayden pulled the trigger, the match would still fall into the gasoline. Luke would have seconds to save her from the burst of flames.

He could do it. He'd have to do it.

He cocked his gun.

Hayden heard it and turned. He jumped up and made a run for the back door, tossing the lit match behind him.

Luke dived into the gasoline in a split second, extinguishing the match before it ignited the fuel and set them all on fire.

Hayden slipped in the liquid. He fell forward, his head bouncing off the edge of the table, knocking him out cold.

Wary, Luke held the gun on him with one hand and pulled a knife from his pocket with the other. He cut the ropes from Rachel's wrists and ankles and the one that bound her to the kitchen table.

"Are you hurt?" Luke asked.

"No. I don't think so unless my heart beats itself out of my chest."

Luke wrapped an arm around her and pulled her close, the gun in his right hand still pointed at Hayden.

Luke tried to speak. There were so many things he wanted to say, but he couldn't get them out. So he did the next best thing. He held Rachel like he'd never let her go.

She lifted her head from Luke's shoulder. "Is Hayden dead?"

"Nope," Luke said. "He's breathing, but he hadn't intended for you to be."

"He definitely meant to kill me. He confessed to murdering Louann before he spread the gasoline."

"Thank God. He left the gate open."

"What?"

"I'll fill you in later," he said. "I think we should call the sheriff now. Our patient is starting to squirm."

"I'll make the call," she said.

Reluctantly, Luke finally let her go. He'd almost lost her. He couldn't imagine a horror worse than that.

The sheriff and two deputies were there in under fifteen minutes. One of the deputies left in an ambulance with Hayden.

By the time the sheriff and his other deputy had done their bit and left, Luke had finally decided what he had to do before he lost his courage.

His dad had never found the right words and he'd admittedly regretted that all his life. Luke wasn't taking that chance, but he didn't know what he'd do if Rachel's answer was no.

He opened his arms and Rachel stepped inside them. "I love you, Rachel. It's probably not the right time or place, but I gotta ask or go crazy. Would you ever consider marrying a cowboy?"

"Absolutely not. Unless that cowboy is you."

"You almost gave me a heart attack."

"The answer is yes. I'll marry you, Luke Dawkins. I love you with all my heart. I don't know how it happened so fast. I only know that it did."

He kissed her, and the promise of forever didn't frighten her at all.

She'd best go shopping for some Western boots. She was home to stay.

* * * * *

SUDDEN SETUP

BARB HAN

Many thanks to Allison Lyons, the absolute best editor. My enduring gratitude to Jill Marsal, the absolute best agent. I'm privileged to work with both of you and count my blessings every day.

Brandon, Jacob and Tori, nothing in my life would make sense without the three of you. Your smiles bring joy and light to every day. Bitty Bug—our fairy-light chats are the highlight of every evening.

Babe, how lucky am I? You make me laugh, lift me up when I cry and cheer me on every single day. If I could be granted one wish, it would be that every person could have this kind of love. I can only imagine how much better the world would be for it. I love you.

Chapter One

Whoever said mistakes don't define a person didn't have a clue. Holden Crawford stood over the petite woman curled in his bed, figuring that helping her would cost him dearly. He shook his head at his own stupidity. She'd already been in and out of sleep for a day and a half, and he was beginning to worry that she'd taken a harder knock to the head than he initially assessed. As soon as she woke and he made sure she was all right, he'd drive her close to the sheriff's office. Then he'd disappear. Again.

Holden had recognized Ella Butler immediately when he saw her hiking. She was the daughter of the wealthiest man in Cattle Barge, Texas—a man who was helping Holden out while he needed a hand and a protected place to stay off the grid.

His daughter was trouble times ten. His best bet would be to leave her in the cabin with a few supplies and take off before anyone connected the dots that he'd been there. And yet, abandoning her while she was so vulnerable wasn't something he could do. Even someone as hardened as him couldn't walk away like this.

Holden ignored the annoying voice in his head that tried to convince him sticking around might be an option. His duffel was already packed and sitting next to the door.

He'd told himself that staring at the wavy-haired beauty as she hiked along Devil's Lid was for survival reasons and not because those long, silky legs of hers were highlighted perfectly in pale pink running shorts. He'd needed to see if she would detour to the cabin on the outskirts of her father's property where he stayed and expose his hiding spot. Hell, it had been his sanctuary.

Out of nowhere, her head had snapped to one side and then she'd lost her footing. She'd free-fallen a good ten feet before hitting the hard clay soil. She'd rolled another twenty before meeting an equally rough landing at the bottom of the gulch.

It had been no accident.

At that point, Holden had had two choices: help or walk away. Tracking the responsible party hadn't been a serious consideration, although Holden didn't doubt his own skills. It was more important to make sure she was safe first. But there was a problem with helping her.

Ella Butler was news.

If it hadn't been ninety-five degrees at eight o'clock in the morning, he would've cleaned her wound and then left her with a couple of water bottles for when she woke. August weather was too unforgiving to leave her stranded and the gash on her head was serious. Holden had had no choice but to bring her back to the cabin.

To complicate matters, she'd blinked up at him. He

had to know if she remembered him when she woke because if she could give his description to law enforcement, the real trouble would begin.

Holden walked another circle around the room.

Questions ate at him. First of which, what kind of fool hiked alone in one of the most remote and barren places of the Butler property? There were all kinds of dangerous creatures out there, and he should know because he'd found a scorpion in his boot yesterday morning and had crossed paths with a coral snake by lunch. He recalled the childhood saying he'd been taught to tell the difference between a coral and a harmless snake with similar markings: *red on yellow, kill a fellow; red on black, venom lack.* This part of the country had no shortage of venomous creatures.

There were other concerns about leaving her alone. Did she know there was no ready water supply? He'd had to hike for miles to locate a decent place to dig to find the lifesaving liquid when he first arrived. Making the trek had become part of his daily routine after morning push-ups and was the reason he'd seen her in the first place. His daily schedule had been the dividing line between life and death for Ella Butler.

Holden had kept an eye on her to ensure that she didn't get too close to his camp. The place sat on the westernmost boundary of the Butler property referred to as Tierra del Fuego, meaning *land of fire* in Spanish.

If he was being completely honest, he'd admit to being intrigued by Ella. He'd chalked it up to too many days without female companionship and his dread at realizing the time had come to move on from Cattle Barge.

He'd spent a little more than two years on the run. Two years of not speaking to another person. Two years of eating every meal by himself without anyone to share his life with. And yet in a strange way, Holden had felt alone his entire life.

Scouting a new location was a lot of work, but his diligence had kept him alive so far. He'd been on the move twenty-five consecutive months, never pausing for more than a pair of weeks in one spot. This was the longest he'd stayed in one place, and his instincts had told him that it was time to go even before he'd witnessed the assault.

The problem was that he liked Cattle Barge. Holden felt an unexplainable connection to the land. He'd let his emotions win over logic in staying on too long. He'd erred by not listening to his instincts. And there'd be a price to pay for that lapse in judgment, he thought as he looked down at her.

ELLA'S EYES BURNED as harsh light and a sharp pain in that spot right in the center of her forehead, like a brain freeze, nailed her. She blinked a few times, trying to clear the blur. The outline of a very large man looming over her came into focus, causing very real fear to surge through her. Ella tried to force herself awake but darkness pulled. Her mind screamed to get up and run. Her limbs couldn't comply and so no matter how hard she fought against it, her eyes closed and she gave in to sleep.

It was dark by the time Ella woke again. She vaguely remembered being helped outside to go to the bathroom once, or maybe it was twice, but then she might've dreamed the whole episode.

Glancing around, she tried to get her bearings. Her head pounded as she strained to figure out where she was. The bed was hard but comfortable. There was a blanket draped over her. It was clean and soft.

Instincts kicked in and she felt around to make sure she had clothes on. Movement sent shards of pain needling through her skin. A flicker of relief washed over her when she realized her shirt and shorts were on. The respite was short-lived. Her eyes were beginning to adjust to the darkness when she saw the silhouette of a man folded forward in a chair in the corner. Based on his steady breathing, she surmised that he was asleep.

Ella couldn't make out his face from across the room but a warning buzz shot through her at the sheer size of him. Questions raced through her mind but she couldn't bring one into focus. Exhaustion kicked in again and it felt like she'd run a marathon in the August Texas heat. All she could do was close her eyes and rest. So she did.

"What time is it?" Ella asked, unsure how long she'd dozed. She'd been awake for a few minutes, assessing whether or not it was safe to talk. The sun was up. Her thoughts had been engaged in a battle of good versus evil, debating the intentions of the stranger in the room. Eventually, logic won out. If this man had wanted to hurt her, he could've done so already. Still, she'd walk a fine line with him and make sure she didn't provoke him.

"You're asking the wrong question," the strong male voice said—a voice that sent electric chills up her back.

"What should I be asking then?" She tried to push up to sit but her arms were too weak. The male figure made no move to help her.

"It's Thursday." He turned his back to her in a surprising show of trust and picked up whatever was on his plate. He popped something into his mouth. It must be what smelled so amazing. Her stomach growled despite being convinced that she wasn't hungry.

She scanned the room for anything she could use as a weapon while he wasn't watching. Her vision was improving even though looking around still made her eyes hurt. She glanced at the door, hoping to find a baseball bat or something she could use if push came to shove. There had to be one around there somewhere, her head would argue because it felt like one had been used to crack it open.

The room was sparse. There was the makeshift bed in the corner that she was presently resting on. A very uncomfortable-looking lawn chair—the one he'd slept on last night—was pushed up to a table, which was nothing more than a piece of drift board propped up by stick legs tied off by rope. Either this guy was a survivalist or a former Boy Scout. She couldn't decide which one.

Ella remembered that the stranger had slept hunched forward on that chair made of lightweight aluminum and cheap material. Only a gentleman would give up his bed…right?

Embarrassment heated her cheeks as she recalled

him helping her outside to use the bathroom. If he'd wanted to take advantage of her, he'd had plenty of opportunity. And yet he wasn't being welcoming.

The plate the stranger ate from was some kind of metal, like she'd used for camping with her brothers and sister when they were old enough to set up a tent in the backyard. It had come in an outdoorsman kit, she remembered.

She performed a mental calculation that took longer than it should have and made her brain pound against her skull. "I've been out for two days?"

"In and out," the stranger said. She didn't recognize his voice at all and she knew she would remember such a deep baritone if she'd heard it before. There was an intense but calming quality and it sent a trill of awareness through her, which was totally inappropriate and unwelcomed. She chalked her reaction up to hitting her head too hard.

"I'm sorry, have we met before?" she asked, hoping to place him. Her mind was fuzzy and she was having a hard time processing information.

"No."

"Then can I ask who you are?" Ella racked her brain trying to figure out who he could be.

"No." There was finality to his tone that sent a different kind of shiver down her spine, an icy chill that said he was a man with secrets.

The thought of being alone with a person who wouldn't identify himself made Ella want to curl into a ball to protect herself. Her father was one of the richest men in Cattle Barge, Texas, and her life had turned upside down after being given the news of his death a few days ago. When she really thought about it, this man could be after her father's money. She was still fuzzy as to why she was here in the first place, and no matter how hard she tried she couldn't come up with a good explanation. She'd lost more than the last two days because she didn't even remember why she'd gone hiking in the first place.

And then it hit her. Had she been abducted?

"Good luck if you're trying to get ransom for me from my brothers," she said. "My father was killed and all of our money is tied up right now."

"I'm not interested," he said, his voice a low rumble. He froze.

If it wasn't ransom money he was after…then what?

Ella didn't want to go there with the physical thing. Besides, there was something strange in his voice when she'd mentioned that her father had been killed. He'd stopped what he was doing, too.

"I should go." She tried to force herself up on weak arms.

"That's not a good idea."

Icy fingers gripped her spine at his response.

"I'm perfectly capable of getting up and walking out of here and you can't stop me," she said with more indignation than she'd intended. It was the latent Irishwoman in her. Her mother had had the bright red hair to match, or so Ella had been told. Dear Mother had disappeared when Ella was too young to remember her and had never looked back. Ella took after her father with his honey-wheat locks and blue eyes. She had the stubbornness to match. She was also astute, and it didn't take a rocket scientist to realize the stranger was hiding from something or someone. And now she was alone in a cabin with him.

She had no plans to let her guard down.

"You need to hydrate. You wouldn't make it a mile in this heat in your present condition," he said.

"Do you live here?" she asked. He seemed to know the area pretty darn well and he was right. She wouldn't last long in the August heat without provisions.

All he did was grunt in response.

Ella looked around, trying to find clues as to who the mystery man could be. The place was tidy. There was no dust on the floor. Her gaze slid to the door where a makeshift broom was positioned. It had been made from hay that had been tied together at the base of a tree limb. Whoever this mystery man was, he'd set up shop with the intention of sticking around awhile. He had survival skills, too. Her mind immediately headed down a negative path... Who would want to be alone on the most remote area of her father's land? *A man who has something to hide*, a little voice answered. He could be a doomsday prepper, bank robber or—gasp— serial killer.

Her gaze darted around in an effort to find evidence as to which one he was.

To the other side of the doorway sat a duffel bag that had been zipped closed. She fought against her worst fears that there were torture instruments in there.

The stranger turned around and she could barely make out his features for all the facial hair. His build was football player big and he had to weigh in at well over two hundred pounds. He was pure muscle and his size was intimidating. That thought sent a trill of awareness skittering across her skin. Under different circumstances, she could appreciate the athletic grace with which he moved. Ella's five-foot-five-inch frame was no match for this guy. Working the ranch kept her strong and in shape but she was small by comparison.

The lawn chair scraped against the hardwood flooring, drawing her attention.

"You didn't tell me your name," she said.

Another grunt came in response as the large figure moved toward the bed. Ella scrambled backward—pain shooting through her with every movement—until her back was against the wall. She fisted her hands, ready to swing if he gave her any indication that his intentions had changed.

There was something in his hand as he moved toward her, the light to his back. His sheer size blocked out the sun rays coming from the window and bathed her in darkness. Her body was ironing board rigid.

"Be still. And relax. I'm not going to hurt you," he said, and he looked offended as his features came into focus.

"If that's true, why won't you tell me your name?" she asked, not ready to trust him.

"You're better off not knowing." His side was turned to her and his face was partially hidden. He didn't make eye contact. Up close, she could see that he would be quite attractive if he cleaned up that beard or shaved it off altogether. More than attractive, actually, she thought as her stomach did an inappropriate little flip when he turned and she could really see into his eyes.

The man was clearly hiding something and an attraction was so out of the question that she had to choke back a laugh. Her emotions were all over the map. How hard had she hit her head?

"I'll be the judge of that," she said, seeing how far she could push her luck.

The layer of blankets dipped where he sat.

Her heart pounded in her chest and it felt like there was glue in her mouth for how dry her tongue was. Her entire body was strung tight.

"Let me see that gash on your forehead," he said in his deep baritone. It had an amaretto-over-vanilla-ice-cream feeling and had that same warming effect on her insides. This close, she could see that he had deep-set, serious eyes that were the lightest, most pure shade of blue that she'd ever seen. A square jaw was covered by that dark beard. He had thick, curly hair the shade of a dark cup of coffee.

"What happened to me?" She inched toward him, not ready to give much more.

"I'm a man of my word. I already told you that I wouldn't hurt you and I won't. So move a little faster, will you." He sounded frustrated and impatient.

"Well, excuse me if I don't jump into the arms of a complete stranger when he beckons," she snapped back. Talking made her skull hurt. Could her brain be in actual pain? Speaking of which, now that blood was returning to her limbs, her entire body was screaming at her.

A smirk lifted the corner of the stranger's mouth. He quickly reeled it in.

"I have two pain relievers in my hand if you'll sit up and take them," he said, holding out his flat palm.

Okay, so he wasn't lying about the twin tablets. But who knew if they were OTC or not.

"What are those?" she asked.

"Ibuprofen," he stated. His tone was about as flat as stale beer.

She stared at them like they were bombs about to detonate.

"There's a bottle of water on the floor," he said, leaning toward her.

She let out a yelp that caused his entire face to frown.

"I've already said that I won't hurt you. I brought pain relievers and a wet napkin to clean some of the dried blood from your forehead so I can get a look at your injury. I didn't do it before because I didn't want you to wake with a stranger standing over you." He shot her a look of aggravation.

That actually made a lot of sense and was considerate when she really thought about it. She wasn't exactly ready to relax because he could still be a weirdo, and she was too weak to put up much of a fight. Besides, what was with the secrets? Sharing his name would go a long way toward winning her trust. Instead, he acted like a criminal. If he wasn't one, he needed to come clean.

"I'd apologize personally if I knew your name," she said, matching his level of irritation. He wasn't the only one who could be frustrated.

"What were you doing out here all alone?" the stranger asked.

"I don't know," she responded. If he wouldn't give out any information, neither would she.

He shot her a look that cut right through her.

"I was hiking. I must've lost my footing and hit my head," Ella said, pressing her fingertips to her temples. "It's all still a little fuzzy."

Brooding pale blue eyes examined her and she saw the dark circles cradling them. Whoever this guy was, he had a lot on his mind. There was something else there, too, but she didn't want to analyze it because it made awareness electrify her nerve endings. It also made her aware that if she'd been asleep for two days she must look like a train wreck and have breath that could wilt a flower.

Blue Eyes dabbed the wet cloth on her forehead above her right temple. She winced.

He muttered a curse and pulled his hand back. "That hurt. I'm sorry."

"It's okay." Why was she reassuring him? Reason took over, reminding her that he seemed intent on helping her. She was in a vulnerable state and while she couldn't exactly trust him, she also had no reason to think he had plans to hurt her.

He gave her an apologetic look.

"Best as I can remember, I was hiking pretty far out on the trail. Most of how I ended up here is fuzzy. Am I allowed to ask what you were doing out there?" Ella flinched again when the cold, wet cloth touched her skin.

"No more questions," Blue Eyes said. He made a move to stand.

Ella caught his elbow.

"Please don't leave. My father was killed and that's the last thing I remember. I have no idea what happened or how I got here. I'm not trying to be a jerk, but I've just been told that I've been out of it for two days. I have a gash on my head that I don't even know how it got there, and I'm so thirsty I could suck a cactus dry, and despite that, I really need to go to the bathroom," Ella said, letting all the words gush out at once like a geyser whose time to erupt had come.

"Can you manage on your own?" He motioned toward the door and there was a storm brewing behind those blue eyes at the mention of her father.

"I believe so," she said.

"Toothbrush and toothpaste are on the sink. Bathroom's outside." He turned and walked out.

Chapter Two

Holden needed air. He lifted his face to the sun. The Texas heat beat down on his exposed skin, warming him. Maverick Mike was dead?

For a split second Holden feared that he could be the reason, that the men who were after him had somehow connected him to his father's friend. But that was impossible.

This was a wake-up call. Helping Ella had been a knee-jerk reaction and Holden could feel himself sliding down a slippery slope with nothing solid to grab hold of. He owed her father for offering him a place to stay when Holden was at a low point, and that was the reason he'd told himself that he stepped in with Ella. Speaking of her father, the news still hadn't quite absorbed. Holden rubbed his chin through the overgrown scruff. How could Butler be gone?

The door opened and Ella froze as soon as she saw him standing there.

"I'll give you privacy," he mumbled. Someone needed to toss him a lifeline because the woman stirred feelings he hadn't allowed in longer than he could remember—feelings he never wanted to experience again. Then there was the obvious fact that he couldn't afford those feelings. They'd have him wanting to stick around and protect Ella Butler while they figured out who wanted to kill her. Holden reminded himself that he'd done his part. He'd kept her alive.

"Why did you help me? You could've walked away. Left me there. No one would've known any different." She positioned her hands on either side of the doorjamb.

"No, I couldn't have." He made a move toward the door to indicate that he was done talking. She didn't flinch.

"Sure you could. It would've been easy. My body would've been found eventually and no one would be the wiser that there was someone who could've saved my life." She stared at him for a long moment without saying another word. "Something tells me you know how to cover your tracks, so there must've been some reason."

"You're welcome for saving your life," he said, debating whether or not he should tell her everything. She needed to know that her fall had been no accident, but he'd keep the part about his connection to her father to himself. "Now that you're up and around, I'll drop you off in town tonight."

"And then what? You'll disappear?" Her gaze zeroed in.

She shouldn't care what happened to him because she needed to be concerned about herself.

"Don't worry about me," he said.

"Too late for that." She issued another pause while

staring at him. There was something about her cornflower blue eyes that he couldn't afford to notice. "I'd like to properly thank you for what you've done to save my life. Any chance I can convince you to come back to the main house with me?"

"Sweetheart, I've been taking care of myself for a long time. I really don't need—"

"Obviously, you need a place to stay." She glanced around as if for emphasis. "We're always looking for a good pair of hands around the ranch. It's clear to me that you'd make a good addition and we need more men like you."

"You ought to be careful who you go offering jobs to," he stated.

"I trust you."

"That's a mistake," he said plainly.

"No, it isn't. But even if it was, it wouldn't be my last." One of her balled fists was on her hip now. She had a lot of sass for someone in such a vulnerable position. He'd give her that.

This conversation was going nowhere so Holden did what he did best: went silent as he stared her down. She should be more afraid of him than she was acting. She had been earlier when she'd opened her eyes, and as much as he didn't like it at first, her reaction was for the best. What had he done to make her so comfortable now?

"You want coffee?" he finally asked, shaking his head. She was as stubborn as the stories he'd heard about her father.

"That would be amazing, actually," she said with a small smile.

"Then get out of my way."

She twisted her mouth in a frown at his sharp tone but stepped aside. He walked straight past her without making eye contact even though she stood there expectantly for minutes afterward. And then she slammed the door shut. Not only was Ella stubborn but she had a temper. The nuances of her personality were none of his business. Period.

Holden refocused on the facts. Ella Butler had been missing for two days. His position at the cabin had been compromised from the moment he'd witnessed the attack, and he could see now that it was a miracle no one had shown up. The situation was declining. Fast.

There'd be a search underway by now. The news that "Maverick" Mike Butler was killed would be enough to create a full-scale media circus in Cattle Barge. Add a missing heiress to the equation and Holden couldn't begin to wrap his mind around how out of control the coverage would be. He'd been so far off the grid that he'd missed all of it.

The news that her father had been murdered before an attempt had been made on her life sat in Holden's gut like he'd eaten a pack of nails. The media attention surrounding her disappearance—and that would be big news—must be the reason the person who'd chucked that rock at her hadn't returned. Holden had been watching out for the culprit.

She needed to know that the blow to her head wasn't an accident. He wasn't sure how she'd react, especially given the fact that she'd just lost her father. Normally, he'd suspect someone close to her, a family member. Money or greed would be motive for murder, and especially when considering the amount Maverick Mike had amassed. His fortune was legendary but so were his antics. He had a lot of enemies. Holden wanted to ask about the circumstances surrounding her father's death but decided against it for the time being. He shouldn't show too much interest in the Butler family. Once he settled into a new location far away from Cattle Barge, he could find out what had happened. Mike Butler's death would be all over the news, so it would be easy to find.

Holden glanced at his watch. Ella had been gone a full ten minutes. Should he check on her?

A thousand thoughts rolled through his head. Adjusting while in action had always been Holden's strong suit. He told himself this time would be no different. The door opened at about the time he'd made up his mind to mount his own search. She looked at him boldly.

"Coffee's getting cold," he snapped. She needed to be afraid. He set her cup on the table that he'd made by hand after he arrived last month. The cabin was the first place he'd bothered to put together anything that resembled furniture. His thinking had always been "get too attached to any one place and leaving would be that much more difficult."

His plans had really gone south in Texas—but then he was beginning to see why the place was so appealing with its wide-open skies and thousands of stars at night.

Ella moved to the table and picked up the tin mug.

She cradled it in her hands like it was made of pure gold when she sipped. A little sound of pleasure drew from her lips. "This is really good. How did you do this?"

"You haven't had any for too long. Muddy water would taste good to you right now." Holden kept the part that he liked giving her that small moment of happiness to himself.

"I promise the coffee's not this good at the main house." She paused and then her eyes brightened. "I don't know what I've been thinking. My brothers and sister are probably frantic with worry right now. There's no chance you have a working cell phone, is there?"

"No." He was completely off the grid. There was no way to track him using technology.

"I need to reach them and let them know that I'm okay. I know what I said earlier about our money being tied up, but if you're in some kind of trouble I can help." The determined set to her jaw said she meant it.

Holden shook his head. The less she knew about his circumstance, the better.

"I'm more concerned about you right now," he said. "Besides, you're news and that's bad for me."

"You're on the run from something." She had part of that right.

More like *someone*.

Her gaze penetrated deep into him. "You know who I am, don't you? You've always known."

He nodded.

"And you're not out to hurt me. So far, from what I can tell, you've been helping me," she continued.

"I want you to listen carefully to what I'm about to

say. What happened to you out there was no accident," he warned.

She gasped. "Not *you*…"

"No, it wasn't me. But someone did that—" he motioned toward the gash on her head "—on purpose."

He let the revelation sink in for a minute.

"It wasn't you and it wasn't an accident," she said so quietly that he had to strain to hear.

Holden handed her another cup filled with beans he'd warmed in the fire. "You're used to better food, but this is protein and it'll keep your stomach from growling."

Ella took the offering with trembling hands as his message seemed to be taking seed. "Who would want me dead?"

He didn't like that momentary lost look in her eyes.

"I'm telling you because you're going to want to be careful from now on. Take necessary precautions and don't wander off alone." Holden leaned his hip against the counter.

She took a bite of food and chewed.

"You said that your father was killed," he continued.

"Yes."

"You'll want to look at people who stand to gain from your death after his to start. Scrutinize those closest to you," he said, figuring with her money she could hire proper security who could keep her safe until the law found the man trying to kill her.

"I have no idea. I mean, I think what you're saying is that my brothers or sister might want me dead to get me out of the way or take my share of our inheritance, but I trust them with my life," she said.

"What happened to your father?" he asked. The look he shot her must've been interesting.

"He was shot twelve times while he slept naked in the spare bedroom attached to his office in the barn," she informed.

"No one heard anything?" he asked, thinking that someone had wanted to make a point. An act like that came across as anger motivated.

"The barn isn't near the main house. Dad liked to keep home and work separate," she said.

"Which is difficult, considering you do live your work when you own a ranch," Holden said. "Your family would know everyone's sleeping patterns and where your father would be on a given day."

"He spent a lot of nights in the barn. What makes you so sure it's one of them? Did you used to work in law enforcement?" She turned the tables.

"No." Holden had no plans to elaborate on his background. The less she knew, the better for both of them.

"We leave as soon as the sun goes down," he said, closing the bag to the coffee grinds.

ELLA REALIZED SHE'D been gripping the coffee mug so tightly that her knuckles were white. She reminded herself to breathe as she tried to absorb the reality that had become her life. Her brothers would not try to hurt her. For one, the Butler kids had had each other's backs since childhood after their mother had taken off and left them with their father. They'd had to. Their father wasn't exactly skilled in the parenting department. He'd loved them in his own way, Ella thought defensively. She'd always felt the need to protect her father. But he wasn't the problem this time.

Thinking made her brain cramp.

Ella eyed the stranger carefully. By nightfall, she'd be done with him. He'd be out of her life forever. She should be happy about that, and yet the thought tugged at her heart. Maybe it was because she'd lost so much already with her father's death. Or it could be her soft spot for lost causes. There'd been countless stray animals that she'd made space for in the barn only for her father to tell her they had to go. Usually, they were injured and she knew they'd never survive on their own. Her brothers or sister would come to her rescue and help her keep them hidden until she'd manage to nurse them back to health and then find a new home.

A few were worked into the menagerie of pets on the ranch. Oftentimes one of the hired hands would end up with a new pet to take home to his family. And many of the employees at Hereford Ranch covered for her to help with her causes. No one went against Maverick Mike's wishes directly, but everyone pitched in behind the scenes to help Ella.

Looking back, it was probably difficult for them to turn away such a persistent little girl. Ella had been told more than once that she had the campaigning abilities of a politician.

Her gaze drifted to the wounded person standing before her with no name. If anyone needed to find his way, it was the man across the room. She told herself that was the reason she felt an unexplainable draw toward the mystery man and it had nothing to do with the inappropriate surge of attraction she felt every time she glanced his way.

"What will you do once you drop me off? You can't stay here anymore, can you?" she asked.

"You need to worry about yourself. Use some of that money you have to hire extra security," he snapped.

Ella bristled.

His voice softened when he said, "You're in danger and you owe it to your father to be careful."

"Why do you care?" she asked.

"I don't," he said. "But you should."

A noise sounded outside and Blue Eyes dropped into a crouching position in half a second flat. The remarkable thing was that he made no noise with his movement, and that made her think he might have a military background.

His gaze locked onto hers and the look he shot her warned her to be quiet. She froze, fearing that whoever had tried to kill her was back. Would they have returned to verify that she was dead and then go hunting for her when they didn't find a body?

Her pulse raced.

With effort, she slid off the chair and made herself as small as she could on the floor. Movement hurt despite the couple of pain relievers he'd supplied earlier. Ella knew Blue Eyes had this under control. And it struck her as odd that she felt safe with the stranger.

Thinking about the attempt on her life made her realize that there could be others coming to town to get a piece of her father's will. Hadn't his attorney, Ed Staples, warned that there could be a lot of surprises forthcoming? Even though he couldn't possibly have meant this, Ella was beginning to fear that the actions of her father would haunt her and her siblings long after his death.

When the silence had stretched on for minutes, Blue Eyes moved to the window and checked outside. Without speaking a word, he slipped out the door.

Ella moved to the window to get a look for herself, watching as he moved stealthily. There was a certain grace about him.

Despite his untamed appearance, his muscles gave the impression he maintained a disciplined workout schedule. In fact, looking around the room, it was obvious that he liked things tidy. Something had made him want to drop out of civilization for a while. He couldn't be a doomsday prepper because he seemed to have on hand only what he needed for a couple of days. She wanted to offer him some type of reward for saving her life but he'd already refused work. What else could she do? Offer a reward?

Ella thought about her two brothers, Dade and Dalton, and sister, Cadence. She wasn't kidding before. They'd be frantic with worry about her by now. Even though her siblings had left town to escape the media circus in Cattle Barge, one of the employees would've contacted them about her disappearance. She'd been out of communication for two days...and with a total stranger. He could've done anything he'd wanted to her. A shiver raced through her. But he hadn't.

For that reason and a few others that she didn't want to overanalyze, Ella intended to figure out who this man was and why he was running.

Chapter Three

Blue Eyes walked back into the cabin, glanced around and then picked up his duffel bag. "Finish your coffee. We're leaving ahead of schedule."

"Everything okay outside?" Ella asked.

He didn't respond.

"Is someone out there?" Her heart rate jumped a few notches higher.

"Not now. There will be," he said and mumbled, "I should've gone a long time ago."

That statement implied he wouldn't have been around to help her and she didn't appreciate the sentiment. "Well, I, for one, am glad you outstayed your welcome. I wouldn't be alive otherwise."

She was getting indignant. She couldn't help herself. He wouldn't tell her anything about himself and she wasn't trying to take advantage of him or turn him in to the FBI. All she wanted to do was find a proper way to thank him. The guy was working her last nerve and her head still pounded.

"Why don't you come to work for me on the ranch?" she asked while watching him pull out bleach wipes from his bag. He wiped down the dishes before placing them inside the duffel. Now he really had her curiosity heightened.

"I already said that I don't need a job." For the irritated sound that came out of his mouth next, she would've thought she'd just asked him to scrub the toilet with his toothbrush.

Ella made a production of glancing around. "Are you being serious?"

He shot her a warning glance. It said to tread lightly. She ignored it.

"Because as far as I can tell, you very much need a paycheck. And a decent place to sleep." She waved her hand around.

"I had one until you came along and messed it up for me," he quickly countered.

"You can't be serious," she said.

"Try me."

"Is that a threat?" She planted her balled fist on her hip. It was probably the fact that she'd almost been killed that was giving her this new bravado. She didn't care. The guy had some explaining to do and he was squatting on her family's land.

"No. If you haven't figured it out already, I'm trying to help you," he said, opening up a knife and cutting the rope he'd used to hold together the table. The metal sparkled in the light. He wiped down each leg.

"Why won't you let me return the favor?" she asked.

Another frustrated noise tore from his throat. "You don't have anything I want."

That sounded personal. She tried not to take offense.

"I'd like to offer a financial reward. Surely, you could use some money."

He didn't look up but waved her off.

"At least tell me your name," she persisted. Why was he being so obstinate? Was it really that difficult to give her something? Granted, she was used to getting what she wanted and with enough persistence she was sure that she could wear this guy down, too. She didn't have the luxury of time and she wanted to send a proper thank-you or reward for his help.

"I've already told you that's not a good idea." He broke one of the legs in half and then tossed it into the fireplace.

"I disagree." She stood there, fist planted.

"You always this stubborn when you're wrong?" he asked, breaking the second leg and tossing it on top of the last.

"I'm usually right," she said. Ella glanced around. It wouldn't be dark outside for hours.

"Since you're feeling better, I'll take you to town. Go to the sheriff and tell him what happened. I'd appreciate it if you left me out of your statement. That's how you can thank me for saving you." Another broken table leg, more tinder for the fireplace.

"I thought we weren't leaving until the sun went down," she said, a moment of panic crushing her. Her father was gone. Nothing at the ranch would be the same without him. She hadn't even begun to deal with his murder. An attempt had been made on her life. Of course she would go to the sheriff but she wasn't quite ready to return to town and the unknown waiting there.

"Plans changed."

"You won't tell me why? I mean, I realize that we heard a noise but everything's okay now, right?" She was still trying to figure out why she was arguing for more time with the man who wouldn't even tell her his name. Logic be damned. Ella needed to know he was going to be all right. At least, that's what she tried to convince herself and not that there was something magnetic about this man that was completely foreign to her.

"Being seen anywhere near you is dangerous for me."

"What have you done wrong?" she asked, figuring she might as well go for it.

"Nothing that concerns you." He broke the final leg and tossed it into the fireplace. She might not understand his way of life but she appreciated his self-sufficiency.

"Then tell me what you're running from," she said in a last-ditch effort to get him to talk.

A moment of silence passed between them as they stared each other down.

Okay, he won. Ella wasn't in a position to bargain and this stranger seemed intent on keeping his secrets. He'd helped her and she was grateful.

"I probably haven't sounded like it so far, but I really do appreciate everything you've done for me," she said as she moved toward him, toward the door.

She paused before crossing over. For a second, time stopped and they just stood there, staring at each other. A sensual shiver goose bumped Ella's arms. The stranger had the most amazing eyes, piercing eyes. Eyes that she could stare into for days. As odd as it sounded even to her, the moment felt intimate.

The attraction she felt caught her completely off guard. Rugged mountain men had never been her type. It was probably the mystery surrounding him that held so much appeal and the fact that all her senses were on full alert.

Ella broke contact as she heard the *whop-whop-whop* of helicopter blades in the distance.

"Let's go," she said.

HOLDEN SAT AT the counter of the diner in neighboring Rio Suerte. Another couple of hours and he'd be out of Texas altogether. He'd dropped off Ella Butler two blocks from the sheriff's office. She could retrieve her Jeep near Devil's Lid once she gave her statement to law enforcement. Ella was smart enough to take it from there. He'd done his part, repaid his debt to Maverick Mike.

Time to move on, he thought with a heavy sigh. He hadn't thought about the murders he'd been accused of for two days while he was with Ella. The initials, HA, hadn't haunted him. He'd discovered them etched into the bottom of a chair leg at his father's place—the chair where his father had been tortured and killed.

Holden shook off the bad memory. He was no closer to figuring out what had happened then he'd been two years ago.

The restaurant was a typical off-the-highway food stop and seemed like the place frequented mostly by truck drivers. Holden had befriended more than his fair share while crossing the country, making his way to Texas. The diner was shaped like a train car. There was one row of booths behind him matched by a long counter with bar stools for single travelers. Two families were in the booths, no doubt stopping off for a quick meal while on a road trip.

There was only one truck driver in the building. Bathrooms were to Holden's left, near the end of the counter where the cash register was located. There was one cook in the kitchen and only one waitress on duty. The cook was significantly shorter than Holden, bald, with thick arms. He bench-pressed. The man was in his early fifties with a cook's belly. Holden dismissed him as a threat. He fell into the same category as the dads. One drove a minivan, the other a Suburban. Holden could tell they were from the suburbs based on their clothing—one was in jeans and a polo shirt, the other wore warm-ups and a T-shirt. They had that haggard look that came with long road trips with young kids.

The truck driver was substantial in size, mostly fat from spending his days seated. He looked strong, though. Holden could see his arms in the sleeveless flannel shirt he wore. The man couldn't be ignored as a threat. If Holden assigned levels, five being the highest, the dads were ones and the truck driver was a two and a half, maybe three.

There were exactly two exits in the building: the front door he'd come through and the one in the kitchen. Holden was used to memorizing every detail, looking for every possible escape route. Doing so had kept him alive. Was he really living?

Holden dismissed the thought as going too long without human companionship. His brief run-in with Ella Butler reminded him of everything he didn't have. He'd been alone for a very long time, focused on staying alive, staying one step ahead of the men who were after him. They were good. He was the best. And that was precisely the reason he was still breathing.

The waitress approached. Her metal-plated name tag read Deena.

"Make up your mind?" Deena asked, motioning toward the menu. She was in her late thirties and had early wrinkles around her eyes and mouth. Her neck was the biggest giveaway of her age.

"Chicken-fried steak with mashed potatoes and gravy, carrots. More coffee when you have a chance," he said.

She wrote down his order on the ticket with a smile, a nod and a wink. "Sam makes the best."

"I'm counting on it," Holden said, returning the smile. He excused himself to the restroom. He wanted to splash water on his face and wash his hands before he ate. He didn't sleep much while he'd been taking care of Ella.

As he stood in front of the bathroom mirror, he was shocked at the stranger looking back at him. Furry face. Dark circles under his eyes. His thoughts snapped to Ella Butler and her initial reaction to seeing him. No wonder she'd been so afraid when she'd first opened her eyes. Hell, he would be, too.

He pushed those unproductive thoughts aside.

Holden splashed cold water on his face before washing his hands. Maybe it was time to shave the overgrowth. He hardly recognized himself anymore, and he certainly looked more animal than man. It was easy to do while he'd been mostly living off the land. And yet his reflection had caught him off guard.

Walking out of the restroom, he scanned the room. The situation was the same. The threat potential was low. He reclaimed his bar stool and did his level best not to look at the TV mounted in the corner of the room. A cursory glance revealed the channel was set to local news.

Holden picked up his fresh cup of coffee, ignoring the screen. He didn't treat himself to a restaurant meal often. This was a delicacy he had every intention of enjoying.

And then he made the mistake of looking up.

There was a picture of the Butler ranch on the TV screen. The story was about an heiress's life being in danger. Holden gripped the cup and waited...

Another attempt had been made on Ella's life. A witness had seen a man trap a woman between two vehicles on a residential street one block from the sheriff's office. The woman managed to fight off her attacker before slipping around an SUV and disappearing between two houses as at least one shot was fired. The witness, who would only agree to speak anonymously, recognized Ella Butler but was too frightened to get close enough to get a description of the heiress's attacker. There was a lot of blood at the scene and a manhunt was underway for a gunman wearing a ski mask. He was considered dangerous and authorities cautioned people to keep a distance and call law enforcement immediately if he was spotted.

Holden could think of a few other things he'd like to do to the guy besides turn him in.

He released a string of curses under his breath. It was his fault for taking her to town in the first place. He'd left her there without transportation or a way to escape. Damn it. This was on him.

Anger roared through him along with an overdose of guilt.

He listened for any other news about Ella and sighed sharply when he learned she was missing and believed to be injured.

"I need my check," he said to Deena.

Chapter Four

Ella rolled onto her side, ignoring the pain shouting at her. She could feel her pulse pound in her thigh where she'd been shot and pain gripped her in between the temples. She was losing blood, which was not a good sign. At least she'd managed to fight off her attacker and run. She'd poked her fingers through the ski mask he wore and had managed to knock him off balance. Then she'd bolted. It had all happened so fast. The blast. The cold, wet feeling spreading through her thigh.

Who would want to hurt her?

The stranger's warning hadn't been an overreaction. Her life was in danger. She'd been in such a fog earlier that she hadn't even thought to ask any of the right questions. Could Blue Eyes have identified the rock thrower?

She crawled into the front landscaping of the modest home on Sixth Street, gasping. How long could she stay there unnoticed? A few minutes? Hours? The night?

It was getting late. She'd barely escaped the gunman. If only she'd been able to get a look at his face. And now she was hiding, on the run from someone determined to get her out of the way. She searched her mind for a name, anyone who would want her gone. Could this be related to her father's death? Or was the timing a coincidence?

Her father had enemies and plenty of people didn't like him, but it was as if he'd been made of Teflon and she could scarcely believe that someone had managed to get to him. Her heart fisted and grief shrouded her, weighing down her limbs. Her larger-than-life father was gone. She was hiding in someone's landscaping and she had nowhere to go.

A sob released before she had time to force it back. Tears brimmed but she couldn't allow herself to cry. Not now. Let that dam break and the flood might just leave a trail big enough for her attacker to find her. Start crying and she might not be able to stop.

A branch snapped. She glanced around, afraid to breathe in case the gunman was closing in on her.

Hope that the noise could've been the sheriff or one of his deputies—anyone who could help—fizzled when she saw the bobcat winding through the front landscaping. He was fairly small and definitely not a threat. But it reminded her that there would be others. Soon.

Ella needed a plan. Her thoughts shifted to the compelling stranger in her father's cabin. He was strong enough to defend her. She told herself that was the only reason he entered her thoughts and not because of something deeper, something like missing him. Missing a stranger sounded ridiculous, even to her. How much blood had she lost? She had to be delirious if she was thinking about Blue Eyes.

One thing was certain. If she surfaced in the open,

she'd be killed the second her chaser caught sight of her. The shotgun that had been fired at her shot real shells, as evidenced by the blood on the outside of her thigh where shrapnel had grazed her. Speaking of which, she needed to clean her wound before it got infected.

She couldn't go home. There was too much chaos going on since news of her father's murder broke and she'd be an open target.

She had no idea what the person targeting her wanted. Ransom? Revenge?

She and her siblings were close-knit. They'd had to be since it was generally up to the four of them to handle things at home. Their father had been tougher on the twins. She'd been protective of Dade and Dalton when they were young. They'd long since grown into men who could take care of themselves and everyone around them. Ella and the twins had always looked after their younger sister, Cadence.

Speaking of her siblings, she needed to warn them but had no way to contact them. Thankfully, they were tucked away, far out of town, having left immediately after news broke of their father's murder. They'd decided to get away from Cattle Barge until this whole mess blew over and life returned to normal, whatever that would be now that their father was gone. With his unconventional lifestyle, she and her siblings had feared people would come out of the woodwork to claim stakes in his vast fortune. Based on the traffic she'd seen coming into town and the resulting chaos, the others had been smart to leave. Someone had to stick around and make sure the ranch was still running, and Ella had convinced them it should be her.

But being in town was dangerous. So was the ranch. She didn't suspect any of the workers who'd been around for years. There were a few new hands. She couldn't rule out the team her father had put together even if she doubted he'd put anyone questionable to work on his ranch. He loved his family and was fiercely protective of them even if their relationships with him were highly individual and complicated. He'd never knowingly put them in jeopardy. *Knowingly* might be the key word. Could her father have put his trust in someone who'd duped him?

Her brain hurt. Her body ached. And some of her memories were patchy thanks to the blow she'd taken. At present, she was exhausted, hungry and bleeding. Her mind was going to places that she wouldn't normally consider. She knew exactly where she needed to go so she could take a step back and think this through but had no idea how to get there. Her Jeep was parked near Devil's Lid, which wasn't doing her a lot of good. Blue Eyes had ridden her into town on his motorcycle.

There was no way she could make it to the sheriff's office. The person who was after her could be watching. If she got anywhere near—

A hand clamped over her mouth. Ella gasped. She tried to bite but whoever was behind her was too fast at securing his grip—and it had to be a man. His hand was huge. He'd been stealthy, too. She hadn't heard a peep. Her pulse pounded and adrenaline caused her body to shake.

"Be quiet and I'll get you out of here," said the familiar voice—the voice that belonged to Blue Eyes. "Can you walk?"

Her pulse raced from fear mixed with another shot of adrenaline. She nodded and his other hand slipped around her. A second later, she was being helped to her feet.

"I'm shot," she said and could feel the physical impact of those words. No matter how much Blue Eyes tried to deny he cared about what happened to her, his body language belied his words when his muscles pulled taut with the news.

"How did you find me?" she asked as the initial shock began to wear off while they were on the move.

The motorcycle was parked at the end of a quiet street.

"I saw the news story about the attempt against your life," he responded without missing a beat. "I recognized this area as close to where I dropped you off and tracked you by the blood trail I found."

He made it sound easy but it couldn't have been. How had this stranger become so good at hunting down a person? She decided this wasn't the time to ask. By all accounts he was helping her…but he was so secretive before and it had her imagination churning against all logic. She didn't like the confusing feelings she had toward him.

"How do I know you're not going to hurt me?" she asked.

A frustrated-sounding grunt tore from his throat. "Seriously?"

Now all her defenses flared. "Yes. I'm a woman. I'm injured. Basic survival instincts kick in at some point. I have no idea who you are. I don't even know your name."

"If I wanted to hurt you, I would've already done it." That deep voice reverberated through her, sending a trill of awareness coursing through her. "We've already covered that."

Okay, she could concede that point.

"Who are you?"

"My name is Holden Crawford. Now that you've heard it, forget it as fast as you can. Knowing my name will only end up hurting you more," he said. "That's why I didn't tell you before now. It's not because I'm trying to hide something from you or don't trust you. I haven't had a real conversation with someone in more than two years. So I'm guessing by your reactions to me that I'm pretty bad at it. Can't say I was especially good with idle chitchat before, so…" He shrugged massive shoulders. "And the last person I really cared about ended up dead."

She gasped.

"Not telling you my name has been my way of trying to protect you," he continued. "Your father was good to me, offered to let me stay on his land, and I figured I owed him one for it. That's the reason I helped you and didn't walk away. I'm not that good of a person to stick around for pure reasons. It was a debt. One that has been paid."

"Sounds like you're a better man than you want to admit," she said.

"Me? Nah. I know exactly who I am, what I am, and it's not good for someone like you," he stated. "You're better off without me."

A frustrated grunt tore from her throat.

He turned to face her.

"I'm sorry about that." He glanced at her thigh and a trill of awareness blasted through her, which was unwelcomed. There was something primal and magnetic that pulled her in when she was near Blue Eyes. Sex appeal over standard good looks? "That was my fault, and I came back to make it right."

"You're on the run from something you didn't do."

"That's what I said." He held out a helmet and waited for her to make a decision.

"Maybe I can help you," she offered.

The look on his face said he doubted it.

"It's now or never, sweetheart. The choice is up to you. Go with me and I can't take you to the law."

Ella figured her options were pretty limited at the moment. She had no idea who was after her. Going to the sheriff was logical, but getting there safely wasn't guaranteed and the man who was after her would most likely expect her there. Striking out on her own wasn't even a consideration. She was injured and had none of the necessary skills to survive. Go back to the ranch and she couldn't be certain that she'd be safe.

"Let's go," she said, taking the offering. "And my name is Ella, so you can stop calling me sweetheart."

She slid onto the seat behind him. He took her hands and wrapped them around his chest.

"Hold on," he said, like there was another option.

Ella turned her head and pressed it against his strong back as wind whipped around her.

Adrenaline had long since faded by the time they reached the cabin and exhaustion made it difficult to lift her leg over the motorcycle. Holden helped her take off the helmet and then he secured it to the back of the seat, mumbling something about needing to get another one. Texas didn't require one by law, but most riders seemed smart enough to take the precaution.

Ella stared at his face. Beneath all that wild facial hair was an attractive and capable man, and she ignored what the revelation did to her stomach.

"Did you get a look at who did this to you?" he asked.

"No. He had on a ski mask and it was dark outside, so I couldn't get a good look at his face," she said.

A disgusted look crossed his features. "This is my fault. I shouldn't have left you there and especially not without a vehicle."

She leaned her weight on him as he put his arm around her waist, hoping she'd feel less vulnerable if she knew a little more about the stranger who was helping her. More electricity fizzed through her as he walked her inside the cabin, and the overwhelming feeling that she was safe for now settled over her.

"Sit still," he said as he retrieved a bottle of water and poured it over her thigh. "I have something that'll help with the cut on my bike."

He brought in medical supplies and attended to her wounded leg.

"Who are you *really*?" she asked, staring up at him.

"A man defined by his mistakes." He stepped back

but maintained eye contact, holding a second too long. The dark lines of his serious expression said he meant every word of that. Fire shot through her when she realized the implication of what he said.

"You think helping me was a mistake?" She scoffed. Anger had been building and she'd explode if she held it in any longer. "Well, then, I'm sure glad you went against your *superior* judgment or I'd be dead."

"Twice," he said through clenched teeth as he stood. His breath was a mix of mint and coffee. An infuriating part of her wanted to see what that tasted like. He raked his fingers through thick, wavy hair.

"Now that you've saved me again, why not just leave? My Jeep isn't far from here. I'll head north, away from the ranch, until I figure out who's doing this to me," she said with more anger than she'd intended.

He took a threatening step toward her, closing the gap between them even more, and this close she could almost sense what his skin would feel like pressed against hers as she stood.

Ella blew out a frustrated breath. She thought the same curse that he muttered when she said, "Mistakes aren't the only things that define a person."

Holden caught her gaze again and she felt the moment her anger turned to awareness. Awareness of his strong, masculine body so close to hers. Awareness of how much he turned her on even though she fought against it. Awareness of how good it would feel to have his hands on her, roaming her skin.

"Do tell," he said, and there was so much sexual undercurrent running between them.

"We're also defined by our choices," she said.

"Fine. This is one of mine." He dipped his head and kissed her.

His lips, pressed to hers, sent a current of need rippling through her and heat pooled inside her thighs. She'd never been *this* aroused *this* quickly in her life, but then a sexual current had been building between them since she'd first seen him.

He tensed, like he expected her to fight back, but all she could do was surrender to the out-of-control wildfire spreading through her. She stretched her fingers out and smoothed them across his chest as she parted her lips. His tongue dipped inside her mouth and she could feel the groan rumble from deep in his chest.

The realization she was having the same effect on him that he had on her was satisfying. A frustrating and intense sexual draw stronger than anything she'd ever experienced enveloped her. That strength of an emotion could be dangerous. Holden was dangerous.

Instead of pulling back, which would be the most sensible move, Ella wrapped her hands around his neck and deepened the kiss.

His arms looped her waist and he hauled her body against his. She could feel his heart pound inside his chest at a frantic pace. Her breasts strained against her bra as they pressed flush against his muscled chest.

How on earth was it possible to feel so much heat in one kiss?

Holden's strong, flat palm slipped inside her shirt and her nipples pebbled. He hesitated at the snap on her bra and then all of a sudden her breasts were freed. He released a guttural groan as he took one of her full breasts in his hand. He teased the nipple, rolling it between his thumb and forefinger, and her stomach fluttered.

He pulled back long enough to search her eyes. He seemed to need reassurance from her that all of this was okay.

Was it?

Ella didn't want to think. For once, she wanted to go with what her body craved…and right now, that was the blue-eyed stranger.

He pulled back. "See what I'm talking about?"

She studied him.

"I've needed to do that since you woke up the other day," he grumbled. "And it's a huge mistake."

He had that right, she thought, as anger flared through her.

"Don't worry. I'll make sure nothing like it ever happens again," she said.

Chapter Five

Ella could not, under any circumstances, allow Holden Crawford to affect her. She moved away from him and onto the makeshift bed, grateful that he'd left it intact. She needed…something—physical space, maybe—to clear her mind. What she wouldn't do for a strong cup of coffee right now.

"I need to get a message to my family and make sure they're okay. Whoever is doing this to me might also be targeting them," she said, needing to redirect her thoughts and gain control of her overwrought emotions. Her attraction to him could be explained in simple terms. She'd almost been killed. Twice. He'd saved her. Twice. The magnetic pull she felt was nothing more than primal urge.

Holden studied her for a long moment. He had that wrinkled-forehead expression that made her believe he wanted to speak his mind. He seemed to decide better of it.

"Where are the twins and your sister?" he asked.

Ella couldn't mask her surprise. She was going to have to get used to the fact that this stranger knew more about her than she did about him, reminding herself that he was one of her father's many acquaintances. But then, it seemed like everyone knew her father or at least believed they did. She also realized that for all his antics, her father wouldn't help someone who broke the law. Maverick Mike was many things, but he wouldn't harbor a criminal and especially not anywhere near his beloved family or ranch. Despite complicated relationships, family was everything to Maverick Mike. His property was a close second. Her father had loved his land and everything about Texas was sacred to the man. She'd inherited his zest for family, the ranch and her home state.

"I don't know exactly. They disappeared to get away from the media circus surrounding Dad's death and I didn't think to ask," she said. "We all have places we go when we need time away."

"Why did you stick around?" His gaze narrowed and his lips thinned.

"Someone had to stay in order to keep an eye on the business," she stated. "An operation as big as Hereford doesn't run itself."

He gave her a look of concession. "Your brothers didn't see it as their jobs?"

"As a matter of fact, they did," she said, a little indignant. "They wanted to stay but I convinced them that they should take some time away."

"Your arguing skills aren't in question but I'm still surprised they agreed," he said with a shake of his head.

"Well, they put up a good fight. But I managed to

convince them." That was putting it lightly. She'd almost had to physically force them off the property.

She looked at Holden, who seemed not to believe her.

"You may not realize it, but I can be pretty convincing when I need to be," she defended.

"On second thought, I shouldn't doubt that you know exactly how to get what you want," he said with a tone she decided to ignore rather than explore. Mostly because it sent more of those unwelcomed shivers up her arms.

"What about you?" she asked, realizing that he wasn't saying more than two words about himself.

He didn't answer.

Shocking.

"What's next?" she asked. Adrenaline must've worn off because she was starting to feel every ache and the pain was taking the fight out of her. Besides, the chemistry constantly sizzling between them was exhausting.

Holden paced. She waited.

"You make a choice," he finally said. There was so much frustration and warning in his voice.

"I can't go back to Hereford until I know who's trying to kill me," she stated. "I have no idea if this person has access to the main house, but he's made his intentions clear."

"It's best to assume he does, and especially after what happened to your father on the property. I can keep you safe while the sheriff investigates the attempts on your life. Or we can figure out a better way to get you to law enforcement."

She was shaking her head before he finished his sentence.

"If you accept my help that means going off the grid. You have to follow my rules and cut off all communication with everyone but me," he said, and the look in his eyes said he meant every word. "You already know what it's like to be around me. This is what you'll be stuck with until this...*issue* is resolved."

"I'm aware of your magnetic personality," she shot back. She was also aware that he was the only one who seemed capable of keeping her alive. He might not be one to talk much, but it was obvious that he knew how to hide and a piece of her—a piece she should probably ignore—felt safe when he was around.

"Good. Being angry with me will keep us both from making another mistake like the one we made earlier," he said, and his gaze dipped to her lips. He refocused on the patch of wall behind her head.

Did he have to keep reminding her?

"If I can't speak to anyone else, how will the sheriff know what's happened?" she asked.

"I'll arrange for you to give a statement, but it won't be in person," he said. "Then we'll disappear."

She could hire a security company to keep her safe, but there was no time. She needed protection *now*. And it was too risky to give up her location to anyone before she could thoroughly vet the agency's employees. This wasn't the time to chide herself for not thinking of having a security team ready to go sooner. She hadn't needed to consider it before now. Security on the ranch had always proved up to the task until her father...

Thinking about him caused tears to threaten.

Going to the ranch was out. Again, her father had been murdered at home, so someone had slipped past security. Either way, returning to Hereford might not prove good for her longevity.

Her father had trusted Holden Crawford. And that was saying a lot.

"I want your help," she stated. "There are reporters everywhere in Cattle Barge and apparently—" she blew out a frustrated breath "—I'm news. If I surface anywhere, then my face will be all over the internet, on live feeds, and that will lead whoever is after me to my location. I can't afford to be seen right now, and since you seem very good at staying under the radar, you're my best chance at staying alive."

His lips thinned and his gaze narrowed.

"I was afraid you'd say that," he ground out as he walked right past her and out the door.

HOLDEN STALKED OUTSIDE and paced. The room had felt confining, like he was strapped in a straitjacket. Being in the Texas night air always gave him perspective.

Maverick Mike was dead. He'd been killed in a manner that was meant to make a statement. Sure, the man knew how to have a good time. Holden's own father had always gotten a look of appreciation when he'd talked about his poker buddy from Texas. The annual secret game that had happened at Hereford every year was legendary but rarely spoken about. Holden was unclear as to how his father had been included, but he'd been making the trip since Holden could remember. Thinking of Pop brought a wave of anger to the surface. Holden should've been there to stop it. His fists clenched and that familiar sense of frustration bore down on him. Beating himself up over Pop's death again wouldn't change the past.

The door squeaked open behind him. He turned to look at Ella and his heart hammered against his ribs a little harder. The tension of the day was written in the worry lines bracketing her mouth, and Holden had an overwhelming urge to kiss her again. Self-control was normally second nature to him, so his reaction to her threw him off balance.

"Do you think the guys who are after me had anything to do with my father's death?" she asked, and he was grateful for the change in subject.

Was someone planning to systematically kill off the Butler family?

The question was worth considering.

But his noncommittal shrug had the effect of a raging fire in her eyes.

"I'm sorry about throwing my problems in your lap, but why volunteer for this since it's so obvious that it pains you so much to help me?" The spark in her eyes lit something else inside him that he couldn't allow. Holden couldn't go there to that place where he cared about someone again. Not when the two people closest to him were dead because of him.

"There's no need to be sorry," Holden said, unsure of what else he could say in this situation. He'd been away from people for too long and she wasn't making it easy to keep her at arm's length.

The breath she blew out could've put out candles lit across the entire Lone Star State.

Good. Maybe her anger would warn her to keep a safe distance from him.

"You may not realize what it's like for your father to be killed practically under your nose," she said.

Those words lit a fire inside him that no amount of reasoning could extinguish. He stalked toward her until her back was against the wood structure and her lips weren't five inches from his.

"Don't you ever mention my father again," he ground out. "Do you understand me?"

There should be a look of fear on her face because he could damn well be intimidating when he needed to be and he'd released only a tiny portion of what he was capable of. Most people would be shaking right now. Not her. Not Ella. Instead of flinching, her face was soft with compassion. Her arms were at her sides, her hands open.

He planted his palms to either side of her head and practically growled at her.

"I'm sorry for your loss," she said quietly as her cornflower blue eyes rose to meet his. Her honey-wheat hair fell around her shoulders in loose curls. And with that one look, he almost faltered.

Holden, dude, get a grip.

He pushed off the wall and took a couple of steps in the opposite direction. He needed to steer the conversation away from his problems and back to the danger at hand.

"Earlier you said that your father was shot and he

was na—" he shifted his gaze back toward her "—not wearing clothes."

"Yes, that's right."

"The sheriff most likely already made the connection that the murderer was making some kind of statement," he said and could see that her mind was clicking.

"Or seeking revenge," she said.

Holden nodded. "I see it like this. Someone wanted the whole world to know that they could access him at his home while he slept." He started pacing again. He could see out of the corner of his eye that she was nodding.

"Did he have a girlfriend?" he asked.

A harrumph noise tore from her throat. "Several, but he seemed to be getting serious with one, Andrea Caldwell."

"Did she know about the others?" he asked.

"Yes," she replied.

"Since a male attacked you, it's probably safe to rule her out," he said.

"Right after my father's murder the sheriff asked for a list of employees, family, friends who might've been there that night. We were putting it together when the room started spinning and my mouth felt dry. I had to get out, to go take a walk," she said. "He was gone by the time I got back."

Holden ignored the fact that he'd felt the same way a few minutes ago. *Almost ignored*, a little voice reminded—a voice he tamped down the second it made itself known. That her stress reaction was similar to his had registered. Fine. The knowledge would help him

memorize her habits and reactions, and that could mean
the difference between life and death at some point.
Holden filed away those facts with others he knew about
Ella. She was strong, independent and intelligent.

"Did you ever complete that list and turn it in?" he
asked.

"May, our housekeeper, was still working on it with
me," she said and then a different kind of emotion lit
behind her eyes—concern. "She's probably worried
sick after my disappearance and then the news story
about my attack. I need to contact her and let her know
that I'm okay."

And now Ella was pacing, too.

"Out of the question," he said.

"I wouldn't tell her where I am. Just that I'm safe,"
she defended.

"We don't take any unnecessary risks. The man who
tried to shoot you meant business and I won't—"

Her hand came up as if to stop him and her gaze
dramatically swept down across her thigh. "Save your
breath. I already know that."

Holden didn't want to look at those long legs of hers.

"She's looked after me since I was a baby. She's
like a mother to us. Please figure out a way to get a
message to her and let her know that I'm not lying in
a ditch somewhere because that's what she's thinking.
She's getting older and I can't stand the thought of her
worrying herself sick," she said with eyes that pleaded.

And it was working. He thought about Rose, the
friend of his father's who Holden had known all his
life. He hadn't been in contact with her since he'd been

on the run, and now he wondered how many sleepless nights she'd spent worrying about him.

Hell, he was beginning to see how Ella managed to get her way with people. It was a combination of her arguing skills, concern for others and passion. She gave the impression that she cared deeply about others and that was compelling. Those eyes didn't hurt either.

"No." He needed to see that she would listen to him even when she didn't agree. Not even Holden could keep someone alive who was determined to work against him.

She balked and her cheeks reddened with anger, but to her credit she didn't continue to argue her point.

"And don't get any ideas about going behind my back," he said, testing her further. "I'll know."

"How?" she blurted out.

"Trust me, I will," he stated.

Ella stalked past him again, wearing a path in the dirt.

"Fine," she said. "But when are you going to start actually trusting me?"

Chapter Six

Holden had no response. No one had ever been able to read him that well, and especially not someone who barely knew him. Never mind that he felt a deeper connection to Ella Butler than anyone he had ever known. He pushed it out of his mind and chalked it up to them being in similar situations.

Ella's hand came up. "I get it. This is real and you need to feel like you know me. I'm not going to betray you. In case you haven't already figured it out, I need you right now more than you need me. So I won't mess up and risk forcing you to walk away for your own safety's sake. I get what's on the line here for both of us."

Well, those words did a lot toward building a tentative bridge of trust.

"Whatever has you on the run has also caused you to stop believing that you can rely on people," she continued.

He begrudgingly nodded. She was intelligent and observant. He could use that to their advantage.

"Even if it means nothing to you right now, I give you my word that I'll do whatever you ask. Whoever is after me could also be targeting my brothers and sister. They're safely out of the public eye right now, and I'll do whatever it takes to protect them," she said with a defiant sparkle in her eyes.

"Family blood runs thick. I get it," he started.

"Do you really?" she asked. "Because I'm beginning to think that all you know is how to be alone."

He started to tell her that his personal life was none of her business but thought better of it. "What about you? Where is your boyfriend in all this because I need to know if someone else is going to interfere?"

"I don't have one," she admitted. Her cheeks flushed.

Relief washed over him and he chalked it up to the kiss, not wanting to admit how truly interested he'd been in her answer.

A thought struck him. She needed to see that he trusted her with information and he could give up a little. "My mother took off when I was little and I wouldn't know her if she walked past me. I don't have biological brothers or sisters. At least, none that I know of."

He had no plans to elaborate further.

"But I understand and appreciate your loyalty to yours." His comfort zone had been shattered twenty minutes ago, but she'd been painfully honest with him and he figured he owed her something in return. "And your loyalty to me until this mess is untangled is your best chance at staying alive."

"We're in agreement," she said.

Holden remembered her telling him that she'd been good at campaigning for what was important to her. He could hand it to her. She'd gotten more out of him in the little time he'd known her than any other human had gotten out of him in months. He wasn't much into sharing.

He could also admit to admiring her inner strength as much as he could appreciate that she was a beautiful woman. Okay, where'd that last part come from? *The heart*, that annoying little voice supplied. Time to shut it down and turn it off—whatever *it* was. Holden refused to think that he could have real feelings for her, for anyone, and especially not someone he barely knew. He didn't believe he could be that cruel to another person again. And he needed to get this conversation back on track and off this slippery slope of feelings.

"Earlier, you mentioned the list," he said. "Did any of the names stick out to you?"

"Not really." She blew out a breath and it was like a balloon deflating. "My father was well liked and just as well hated, I guess. Depends on which side of the fence you stand on. If he was your friend, there was no one better. If you crossed him, he would have nothing to do with you. He was dating a few women but he seemed keen on Andrea. I got the feeling that he was getting close to making a real commitment to her."

"Could she have gotten tired of waiting?" he asked.

"I suppose. But she's a good person. And, like you said, she couldn't be the one who attacked me." Her proud shoulders were starting to curl forward and dark circles had formed underneath her eyes. A good look at her said she was exhausted.

"Let's finish talking about this inside," he said and wasn't surprised she didn't put up a fight.

Ella accepted the arm he held out. Her grip was weakening, so he wrapped his arm around her waist to absorb her weight. It was probably a mistake for their bodies to be anywhere near this close to each other. Heat sizzled between them despite the amount of energy it took for her to walk.

"Thank you, by the way. Again. For saving my life," she said quietly.

"Not necessary," he said.

She gave him a look and he quickly added, "It's the least I can do for someone who needs a hand up. Our fathers knew each other and that's how I know yours. When I reached out, he didn't hesitate to help me. I owe him for that."

That seemed to ease her stress and she rewarded him with a warm smile. He helped her inside and to the bed in the corner. "I have a few supplies on my bike. I'll be right back."

She winced as she scooted her back against the wall in obvious pain.

Holden retrieved his pack from his motorcycle. He had several clean rolled-up T-shirts that he positioned as a pillow for Ella. The bed might be hard but she could at least put her head down on something soft. "This is a far cry from what you're used to on the ranch."

"If you really think that then you have no idea how I spent my childhood," she quipped, and he could see a flash of humor in her eyes. She quickly reeled in her smile but he liked the curve of her lips when she was happy, fleeting as it might've been.

"And how was that, exactly?" He went to work on

her leg, cleaning the area with wipes and dabbing the ointment generously. Being prepared for the possibility that he'd have to patch himself up at some point, he was grateful for the medical supplies he kept on hand. He used a patch of white gauze and medical tape to cover the wound.

"In a tent in the backyard," she said. "More bluebonnets than you could count in the spring and we'd come in with more bug bites than should be allowed. But we liked being outside and when we got old enough, Dad would let us build a fire." She shook her head before curling on her side. "May would be so furious with him that she'd sit up half the night in the screened-in porch watching over us. Dad sure didn't make her job easy."

"Sounds like a good way to live if you ask me," he said. But before they could get too far off course and mired in nostalgia he added, "I'm guessing security is lighter around the barn area of the property."

"Dad liked his privacy. He didn't want anyone, and that included his security team, too entangled in his personal affairs," she stated. "He liked to be able to come and go as he pleased without his extracurricular life part of our dinner conversation."

He could appreciate that a single man wouldn't want his children waking up to a stranger in the house. He also didn't need to say out loud that was a mistake that had cost her father gravely. He could see that she'd made that connection by the look in her eyes. "The person who did this to him wanted to make a statement with his death."

"I know that we ruled out a woman, but could it be?

Someone whose heart he broke?" she asked and her voice was almost hopeful.

"Maybe one of the others figured out he was about to cut them loose and decided to show him," he said without conviction.

"He wanted to create office space for me, my sister and twin brothers. He'd been dropping hints to me that he was at least thinking about retiring from the day-to-day operations of the ranch," she said.

"I can't see a man like Maverick Mike retiring from anything," Holden pointed out.

"True. I got the impression he had other plans. Maybe he was thinking of doing something different. Ever since he'd turned sixty-five he'd been acting strange."

"How so? Like midlife-crisis, go-out-and-buy-a-corvette strange?" he asked.

"Not really. My father never really denied himself cars or much of anything else he wanted. It was more like something was stirring. There was a new excitement in his tone that I hadn't heard in a few years." She shrugged. "At the time I thought it had something to do with Andrea. Maybe he was considering his legacy."

"I owe an apology for what I'm about to say, but from what my father said about yours, Maverick Mike didn't seem the type to wax altruistic. Don't get me wrong, he was a good man on many counts." Holden figured she was remembering her father how she might've wanted him to be instead of the man he was, flawed. He'd done the same with his own father, who also happened to be a good man. It was so easy to forget the imperfections of someone who was never coming back.

"I can see why outsiders would feel that way about him," she said. "But Dad had another side to him that even I rarely ever saw."

"A side that makes you think it's possible for a scorned woman to wiggle her way into his heart and then try to destroy him?" he asked.

"I learned a long time ago not to put people in boxes, Mr. Crawford," she said as she stared right at him.

He could concede that point. He'd seen himself in the mirror at the diner—the person he'd become—and yet she trusted him, his word. Despite what his appearance might've cautioned her. Having seen it for himself, he was shocked at the transformation. A shave didn't sound like the worst thing.

Maybe it was time to clean up.

"Morning will come early," he said after giving her a protein bar and finishing one off himself.

"Good night, Holden," Ella said before rolling onto her other side so her back was to him.

He shouldn't like the sound of his name on her tongue. Hell, he shouldn't be thinking about her tongue at all.

ELLA WOKE THE next morning thinking about what Holden Crawford had said to her last night. There were so many possibilities roaring through her head as she blinked her eyes open to find an empty room. She pushed up onto her elbows to get a better view and panic roared through her when she realized he was gone.

The makeshift pillow he'd placed underneath her head was still there. She forced herself to stand on shaky legs and ignored the pounding at that spot on her fore-head between her eyes. A little bit of rest was almost worse than no sleep. She moved to the door to check on his motorcycle. Relief washed over her when she saw it.

Holden Crawford. She liked the sound of his name.

There was a bottle of water on the kitchen counter and something bright yellow positioned next to it. She moved closer to get a good look—a toothbrush. Funny how little things mattered so much when everything was taken away. Being able to wash her face and brush her teeth, things she took for granted literally every day, suddenly felt like gifts from heaven. Ella brushed her teeth in the sink using water from the bottle and used one of the rolled-up shirts that she'd slept on as a wash rag. She doused it and washed her face. The cool liquid felt so good on her skin. Next, she poured water into her hair and then finger-combed it, figuring that was better than nothing.

The door opened and Holden walked in, balancing two tin mugs of what looked like coffee.

"It's strong," he said, holding out the offering.

"Good. I need it," she replied, taking the cup and wasting no time sipping. Seriously, this was heaven in a cup. "How do you do this? It's amazing."

"Let's just say I've had a lot of practice," he said with a look that seemed so lonely and yet so resigned at the same time.

"Why is it you have two cups?" she asked. "Being that you've been alone for a while."

He chuckled and it was a low rumble from deep in his chest. "I always have a backup for the important things. I never know how quickly I'll have to abandon a place. Plus, one's always clean and ready to go."

"Makes sense," she said after another sip of the fresh brew. "This is the best coffee I've ever had."

He produced another protein bar.

"In your condition, boiled mud would taste good." He laughed a low rumble from his chest and it sent goose bumps racing up her arms.

"I doubt it," she countered, taking the offering and finishing it in a few bites.

"There's something about coffee brewed over an open fire that makes it taste better," he conceded, rewarding her with a smile.

"Not better. Heavenly," she said, returning the friendly gesture. "I've been thinking about everything that's happened to me, my father."

"What did you come up with?" he asked.

"My father's murder seemed planned and, as you already said, like someone wasn't just making sure he was dead. He or she was making their frustration known."

Holden nodded, listening. For someone who, by his own admission, wasn't great at talking, he excelled at listening.

"My attacks seem just as calculated. And so we have to decide if these two could possibly be linked," she continued. "Maybe he planned my father's murder and now wants to get rid of his heirs, or doesn't feel the need to take extra precautions with me. Maybe this person is just interested in taking me out and possibly my siblings next. We don't know if the others have been targeted and won't until I make contact." She brought her hand up. "Which I won't do unless you say it's okay, and besides, I don't have a phone. But if we figure out who killed my father, then we might be led to the guy who's after me and possibly them. And I'm making myself sick with worry about what might happen next. What if they get hurt or worse because I didn't warn them? How could I live with myself?"

He waited until he seemed sure she was finished.

"I understand if you want to search for the person who killed your father," he said. "The sheriff is already on the case and could have an answer soon."

"I keep going back and forth in my mind, but there must be some link, right?"

He shot her a look that said he wasn't convinced. "I recommend focusing our energy on who's coming after you."

"I guess I'm not much good to my father's investigation if I'm dead," she conceded.

"Won't happen on my watch," he said, and she believed that he meant it. She wished for half of his confidence. "It'll be best if you call in your statement to the sheriff. He might offer to arrange witness protection and you should consider it. After all, you're a high-profile case and you're being targeted. The feds will most likely offer assistance."

"What about you?" she asked, a little stunned at the suggestion.

"I can't go near anyone in law enforcement," he said emphatically. "And I need you to leave it at that."

Ella stopped herself from asking why. "I won't ask

for details you're not willing to give. But I'm curious why you think law enforcement wouldn't help you, too."

"Simple. Because the evidence they have makes them believe I'm guilty of something I didn't do." He looked at her dead on.

She did her best not to flinch at his last words. "There's more to the story, though."

"Hell, yeah. But they think they've done their jobs. All I have to contradict the investigation is my word and the knowledge that I'm innocent," he said, and she figured that was more than he'd planned to say by the way he leaned forward and placed his elbows on his knees. That was a move reserved for people who felt exposed.

Ella took a sip of coffee, and it was pretty much a stall tactic so she could think hard about her next words. She didn't want to anger the man who was helping her or offend him. But she'd always been bad at holding her tongue. "You don't strike me as the kind of person who would just check out and give up so easily." He started to say something but she held out her hand, palm up. "Hold on. Before you get upset with me. Hear me out."

He nodded but she could tell there were a whole string of words backing up on the tip of his tongue. Lucky for her, he bit them back.

"You've put yourself in jeopardy twice to save me, and I'm someone you've never met." She made eyes at him. "Granted, you knew my father but he's gone. You didn't have to come back that second time. So as much as you want me to believe otherwise, you're not a bad person."

He opened his mouth to speak but she pointed her index finger at him.

"You're about to mention my father," she stated, already figuring out his next argument based on the look in his eyes.

Holden nodded this time, making a frustrated-looking gesture about being forced to hold his tongue.

"I know what you're thinking and it's not true. You already repaid the debt to him," she said. "You didn't have to come back even if you blamed yourself for dropping me off. You're a decent man no matter how much you blame yourself for whatever happened in the past. I understand why you refuse to go there with a stranger. You say it's because you're afraid for me, but it's so much more than that."

"Oh, yeah?" Holden crossed his massive arms over his chest. "Enlighten me."

"From my point of view, you're afraid to let anyone else in," she stated. She was finished so she steadied herself for his argument, bracing herself against the counter.

Except now, Holden Crawford really was mute.

Chapter Seven

"Since you know me so well, tell me, what's our next step?" Holden asked the woman who left him scratching his head. She was perceptive and thought she'd figured him out. She was wrong. Keeping her at a distance was more for her benefit than his. It was the best way to protect her and keep her safe.

Wasn't it? Or was there a shred of truth to her words?

"We find a way to tell the sheriff what happened last night," she stated, interrupting his thoughts. "In order to do that, we have to leave here. How's that for starters?"

"Obvious but decent," he responded.

"Okay, so where will we go? You've been successfully hiding in rural areas for a while, so I'm guessing you'll stick to what you know. We'll stay somewhere around here." She had a self-satisfied grin and just enough defiance in her eyes to rile him up.

"Sorry. No dice," he stated. "We leave Texas. That's a given. I have a contact in New Mexico who will put us up. I want to stay close and keep my ear to the ground for a few days but we need to stay on the move. We'll head south for an hour and then stop to make the call to the sheriff. Then we can retrace our steps and head west. If the sheriff is going to catch this person, his best chance is while the trail is still hot. If he hasn't made progress in a few days, a week, then we'll have to find a way to get answers ourselves. Interfere too soon and we might hamper his investigation."

"Is this New Mexico person you're referring to a woman by chance?" Ella asked, and there was a mix of emotion playing out behind her eyes that he couldn't quite pinpoint.

"As a matter of fact, yes. Why?" He couldn't wait to hear the answer to this.

She shrugged him off but he could've sworn that she'd bristled. "Curious."

And then it hit him. She was worried they were about to be on their way to see a woman he'd *spent* time with. "She's—"

"None of my business," Ella stated.

"A friend of my father's," he continued. It was important to him that she knew the truth for reasons he didn't want to analyze. "She was sixty-seven on her last birthday."

Ella's cheeks flushed and he forced himself not to think about how attractive it made her, how attractive she already was.

"Finish your coffee. We need to get on the road," he said, harsher than he'd intended.

An hour south, he stopped off at the first megaconvenience store and bought a cell phone with prepaid minutes before returning to Ella outside. "Using this will keep us under the radar. If the call is somehow tracked, which should be impossible, we'll take the precaution of tossing it away as soon as we're done. Do you know the numbers of your brothers or sister?"

"Without my cell?" Ella shifted her weight to her left foot and her gaze darted up and to the left. "How sad is it that I tap on a name when I want to call someone and don't remember phone numbers anymore?"

"What about the ranch?" he asked.

"That one I know. It hasn't changed since we had to memorize our phone number and address in elementary school," she stated. "Are you saying I can call home?"

Holden handed over the cell and nodded.

After punching in numbers and listening for someone to pick up, her face lit up.

"May, it's me, Ella." Her excitement was barely contained. The sparkle in her eyes matched.

Holden dropped his gaze to the ground and listened.

"I'm fine, but please don't tell anyone that I called other than my brothers and sister." She paused for a beat. "I promise that I'm okay. Do I have your word?" Another few seconds passed. "So you have heard from all three of them? And they're okay."

Ella looked at Holden, so he brought his gaze up to meet her gaze. She nodded and smiled. The relief in her expression detailed just how much she loved her siblings.

"The next time you talk to them, tell them to stay out of sight until the sheriff figures this out," she said into the phone. "And tell them I'll do the same." Another beat passed. "No, tell both of my brothers to stay put. I'm nowhere near the ranch and I won't be. I appreciate that they want to stop whoever's doing this but they can help me more if they stay out of the media and away from danger."

Good. She was giving the right direction.

"Tell them it won't matter because I'm not coming back until this is over," she stated, and there was conviction in her voice—conviction that would keep her brothers alive and she seemed to know it. "Just tell them that I love them both and I'm safe. No one can hurt me because they'll never find me."

Holden had every intention of making sure she kept that promise.

"I'm good," she continued, "and, more important, safe." She glanced up at Holden. "I'm in good hands, May. But that's all I can say right now."

May seemed to accept Ella's answers.

"I need to call the sheriff and give a statement now, so I have to go." Her face morphed and gave the saddest look Holden believed he'd ever seen. It caused his chest to clutch.

"I will," Ella promised. After a few more affirmations into the phone and an almost-tearful goodbye, Ella ended the call. She looked away and Holden gave her a little time to gather herself.

Missing a home like Hereford had to be hell. Holden and his father had moved around during his childhood. His father had served in the military and Holden had signed up the day after graduating from high school. There was no place that made him feel like Ella's Hereford.

Ella spun around and took in a breath. "Okay. I'm ready to call the sheriff now."

The conversation was brief. An all-too-familiar anger rumbled in Holden's chest as he listened to the details of Ella being ambushed and then hunted while she bled. He could hear the fear in her voice as she recounted the scene and her vulnerability made him want to put his hands on the man who was trying to kill her. His own past, the horror that his girlfriend, Karen, had endured, filled his chest with rage. The image of the crime scene flashed in his thoughts—an image that had replayed a thousand times in his nightmares for the past two years. Karen splayed across his bed in a pool of blood, her pajamas torn half off her body. The blade of his KA-BAR jammed through her heart.

"Holden," Ella's voice caught him off guard, breaking through his heavy thoughts.

"Yeah?" he responded, even though his clenched jaw had fought against movement. His hands were fisted at his sides and his muscles pulled taut.

She stood there, examining him, and her penetrating gaze threatened to crack through his walls.

"Are you okay?" she asked.

"I will be." He handed her the helmet and threw his leg over the bike. "Ready?"

BY THE TIME they reached Rose's place near the Texas border in Ruidoso, New Mexico, the desert air was cold and Ella shivered. Eight hours on the back of a motorcycle had seemed to take a toll on Ella, but she didn't complain.

He'd stopped off three times for bathroom breaks but had barely spoken to her. Talking about himself had dredged up memories. Remembering his pain was good because being around Ella made him want to forget, to move on. Karen was dead. His father was dead. Holden had been accused of the murders. Those were the only facts that mattered.

"Rose Naples is an artist who specializes in Southwest art," Holden said to Ella as he parked his motorcycle behind her rustic brown log cabin with a green tin roof. "She's lived here most of her life and she and my father went to elementary school together. They stayed in touch but very few people ever knew about her. She leads a quiet life. We'll have food and shelter."

"After eight hours on a bike, all I need is a hot shower and a soft bed," Ella said. She no doubt picked up on the change in him. Good. She needed to stay at arm's length. "I take that back—the bed doesn't even need to be soft."

He started toward the door and she put her hand on his arm. He ignored the fission of heat that was like a lightning bolt to his heart.

"She'll be safe, right?" she asked. "I mean, us being here won't put her in jeopardy, will it?"

"I wouldn't be here if I thought there was the slightest chance," was all he said as he linked their fingers. "It's best if we act like a couple. And to be safe, we can't stay long. A day or two should give us enough time to let the sheriff do his job or come up with a plan."

The word *couple* sat sourly on his lips. He thought about Karen. It had been two long years since she'd been killed, and that same old rage filled his chest when he thought about not being able to bring her killer to justice. Instead, the coward had framed Holden and gotten away with murder. Twice.

Holden picked up the blue cactus pot and located the spare key Rose kept there for him. The sun dipped below the horizon and his stomach reminded him that it had been a while since lunch.

No one should be able to track them to New Mexico. No matter how dire his situation had become, he'd avoided making contact with Rose. She was all he had left.

Best-case scenario, he and Ella could stay a few days. Worst-case, they would get a few hours and then divert to Big Bend National Park to camp out. It was August and he wasn't convinced that Ella would do well under extreme conditions and especially not with her injuries. She needed guaranteed access to clean water to keep the gashes on her head and her leg from becoming infected.

Holden listened at the door for any signs Rose was inside.

The pump action of a bullet being engaged in a shotgun chamber sounded.

"It's me, Rose. It's Holden."

The light flipped on and the door swung open.

Rose dropped the nose of the weapon and flew toward Holden. He caught her in time to give her a bear hug.

"Holden Crawford, you're alive." Shock widened her tearful green eyes. Droplets streamed down her cheeks even though her smile was wide. She was just as thin as he remembered, and her Southwest style of teal poncho, jeans tucked into boots and lots of turquoise jewelry was intact. "I didn't think I'd ever see you again."

"I couldn't risk getting in touch before now." His heart clutched as he noticed the deep worry lines in her face. "But I'm here and I'm okay."

"I'm so sorry about your father." She wiped tears as her gaze shifted from Holden to Ella.

She stepped back and focused on his companion. "I'm sorry. I promise I have better manners than this. I haven't seen this guy in two and a half years and thought I might never again."

"Rose, I'd like you to meet my girlfriend, Ella," he said. The word *girlfriend* sounded a little too right rolling off his tongue. He felt Ella's fingers tense and she radiated a genuine smile.

"I've heard so much about you," Ella said. "And normally I'd hug you but I don't want to offend you by my smell."

"It won't bother me," Rose quipped. "What happened to the two of you?"

"Lost my wallet camping and Ella came out with a pretty bad injury climbing," Holden said by way of excuse. Rose's narrowed gaze said she didn't buy any of it but she smiled anyway. "Can we bunk here for the night until I arrange a transfer of funds and find another place to stay?"

"Do you really have to ask?" Rose set a balled fist on her right hip and pursed her lips. He knew her well enough to know questions were mounting. And he knew her well enough to realize that she wouldn't ask until he gave her the green light.

"Thank you," Ella said, breaking the tension. "Could I trouble you to use your shower?"

"Of course, dear. Follow me," Rose said. She set her shotgun down and motioned for Ella to follow her. "I've got plenty of clean clothes if you need something fresh to borrow."

"I would love that, actually," Ella said.

The two disappeared down the hall and he poured himself a glass of water.

There were so many holes in Holden's plan to pretend he and Ella were in a relationship. He knew nothing about her and vice versa. The plan that he'd been living by to shut Ella out of his personal life was most likely about to backfire. Rose wasn't stupid and he wanted to tell her more. But Ella's secrets weren't his to share.

Rose returned a couple of minutes later and took a seat at the table in her eat-in kitchen.

Holden followed suit, taking the chair across from her at the round table.

"Where have you been?" She took his hand and squeezed.

"All over," he said.

"I know you didn't do it." She gave him a sincere look. "I've been following the story and there's no way you would've done that to Karen. I know you better than that and started to come forward, but before I could get on a plane I read about what they did to your father."

"I'm glad you stayed put and I appreciate your confidence in me." Gratitude filled Holden's chest.

"Sorry I couldn't attend your father's funeral," she said, twisting her hands. "I was sick about it but he wouldn't have wanted me to go and especially not after the way he was…"

She stopped as though she couldn't say the words.

"No, he wouldn't," Holden agreed. "For the record, that makes both of us."

"You couldn't be there either, could you?" She shook her head and her voice was filled with sadness. Like a heavy rain cloud before the first drop of rain spilled, he decided.

"Not because I didn't want to be," he said.

"Your father got a message to me after Karen was murdered. He said that I should tell you 1-9-6-4. I have no idea what it means. Do you? He also mentioned a place you used to fish but I can't remember where. Now it feels so important but at the time I had no idea."

He shook his head. The numbers didn't register as important or click any puzzle pieces together. "I'll have to think about it. Could be a year?"

"I thought about that, too. But why a year?" One of her brows spiked.

Rose picked up the saltshaker and rolled it in between her flat palms. Then Rose set it down and looked him straight in the eye. "Do you have any inkling why they were killed?"

"Other than to cover for someone who wanted Karen dead and set me up for murder? No," he admitted.

"He must've worried they'd come after him or he wouldn't have sent the message." She focused on the saltshaker. "Guess he thought he could handle them when they did."

"They got to him before I could," he said and then stood.

"Don't go," she said, and she must've realized how difficult it was for him to speak about the past.

He reclaimed his seat. Those same frustrations of getting nowhere with his own investigation enveloped him.

"Who's the girl?"

"My girlfriend." Could he share a little without endangering her?

"How'd the two of you meet?" Her gaze penetrated him.

"I didn't underestimate you, Rose. And you know I'd tell you anything that I could." The thought of defining his relationship with Ella or his need to help her spiked his blood pressure. "I was wrong to come here. We'll leave after she finishes in the shower."

"Maybe it was a mistake to come here because I can read you so well," she said. "I'm not concerned that you hurt Karen. I know that for the lie it is. But I know you, Holden, and there's something going on between you and Ella. You're not telling me every—"

"You're reading too much into it. She's a friend in trouble. Can we leave it at that?" Trying to continue the charade was going nowhere. Rose knew him too well. His father had brought him to New Mexico every summer. Sometimes they'd stay with Rose. Others they'd camp the entire time. But they always met her for a meal. The woman had watched Holden grow from a young child. It was Rose who had stepped in from afar when his own mother took off. He'd considered Rose a mother figure, if not his mother. And since she knew him so well, he needed to tread carefully when it came to Ella.

"All I'm saying is that I hope you can find a way to forgive yourself for the past—"

He started to argue but she waved him off.

"Two years wandering. Lost. Karen didn't deserve what happened to her, but neither did you. You didn't do anything wrong," she said, and an odd wave of relief washed over him. Strange that one person's opinion mattered so much to him. But it was Rose, and their relationship went way back.

"That means a lot coming from you," Holden said quietly. Was she right? Was he punishing himself by cutting himself off from the world?

"Promise me you'll try to forgive yourself, Holden," she continued.

"When I find the killer and bring him to justice."

She started to protest but he held up a hand.

"As far as she goes, can we leave it alone for now?" He nodded toward the hallway. "Keep up the charade for her sake?"

"My lips are sealed." She pretended to close a zipper over her mouth. "If and when you can talk about it without violating her trust, I'm here for you."

Holden thanked her again, drained his glass and poured another. "Any chance you have an extra razor in that guest bathroom of yours?"

A CLEAN BODY and fresh clothes borrowed from Rose did wonders for Ella's attitude. Holden had disappeared into the bathroom after redressing the bandages on her thigh and forehead. Rose was cooking up something that smelled amazing. Ella's stomach growled so loudly that her cheeks flushed with embarrassment. "Excuse me."

Rose turned and chuckled. She moved to the fridge and pulled out a container of what looked like home-made salsa. After, she poured tortilla chips into a bowl and set both down on the table in front of Ella. "This should help until the food's ready."

Ella immediately dug into the offering. It was good. So good. And nice to be in a safe place. "This is amazing. Thank you."

"I grow the cilantro fresh in pots out back," Rose said, looking pleased. "Makes all the difference in the world."

The older woman moved with grace, and her half dozen bracelets jangled in time with her fluid movements. Her all-white hair was pulled back in a neat ponytail. Turquoise earrings dangled from her ears. She embodied Southwest elegance at its best.

Ella was grateful that Rose seemed content to be together in the same room without the need for conversation. So much had gone on in the past few days that Ella could scarcely wrap her thoughts around it, and she was still trying to break through the fog. She dipped another chip in the homemade salsa, took a bite and savored the taste of the fresh tomatoes.

"Did you grow these, too?"

Rose nodded and smiled.

Ella thought about May. She grew her own garden

and said the same things with a similar look of pride. Ella's heart squeezed. She felt naked without her cell phone and she missed home more than she wanted to show. And so many questions loomed, keeping her away from everything she loved.

Why would someone come after her? So far, the others in her family were safe. Ed Staples, the family's lawyer, had promised May that he would help keep the ranch running while Ella was away. Ella had learned that during her phone call with May. He was a good man and close confidant to her father. She could trust him to hold up his end.

"I'll get you started eating." Rose interrupted Ella's thoughts. The older woman set a plate down in front of Ella and then motioned toward the chili peppers. "I wasn't sure which you liked, red or green, so there's both."

"That's perfect," Ella said, accepting the literally mouthwatering chalupa. She dug in immediately and the shredded chicken was tender beyond belief. The covering of homemade guacamole was smooth and creamy in her mouth. And she already knew the salsa on top was in a whole new class of Tex-Mex.

"It's Holden's favorite dish, chalupas." Rose went back to work, humming while she deep-fried what had to be his.

"He talks about your guacamole all the time," Ella offered, pretending she knew more about her "boyfriend" than she actually did.

"Really? He's been allergic to avocados since he was seven years old." Rose didn't turn around but her humming picked up.

Ella figured trying to save herself after that slip was futile, so she focused on her food. Her back was to the hallway, so she didn't see Holden when he first entered the room. She had a big bite in her mouth when she turned around and it took everything inside her not to spit it out. She covered her mouth as she finished chewing and swallowed. "Holden?"

He seemed almost embarrassed by her reaction.

"Sorry," she quickly added. "It's just… I've never seen…you look…" She could feel herself digging a hole as the right way to frame this conversation didn't hit her. What did strike her was how drop-dead gorgeous Holden Crawford was underneath all that untamed facial hair. She'd seen a hint of it before in his eyes—those bold blue irises. "Your face. You look…good."

"I thought you should finally see what you're getting yourself into," he said easily, and she realized that he was covering for her slip, her second mistake. There was a slight curve to his lips, not exactly a smile but a hint of one. He walked right over to her and kissed her on the forehead. The second his soft lips touched her skin, a thunderclap of need rocketed through her.

All she could do was look up at him, mute, with a dry throat. It suddenly felt like she'd licked a glue stick.

Holden had that strong square jaw that most women obsessed over, and she could admit that it looked damn good on him. She already knew he had a body made for athletics. He had stacked muscles that surfers, or anyone who wore very little clothing for their sport, would lust after. She had to force her gaze away from his lips. *Okay, come on.* This was getting a little ridiculous. It wasn't like Holden was the first attractive man Ella had ever seen. Of course, she'd never met one with his sex appeal and magnetism before. And she'd spent a few days with him already so she needed to pick her jaw up off the floor and get a grip.

Out of her peripheral she could see that Rose continued on with her work, ignoring the show of affection on display for her benefit, and for a split second she wondered if the woman was on to them.

Holden took a seat next to Ella, his right thigh touching hers, and the contact sent warmth to all kinds of places that didn't need to be aroused at the dinner table of such a kind stranger.

Ella needed to redirect her energy. She studied her chalupa as she dug into another bite.

"Do you grow your own chili peppers?" she asked Rose, and her voice came out a little strained.

"Is there any other way?" Rose quipped with a satisfied smirk.

"Your food is the best thing I've ever tasted aside from Holden's coffee," she said.

"Thank you." Rose had cleaned up the last of the dishes. "It's late, so I'll make up the guest room for you two."

Rose padded down the hall.

Right. Ella and Holden were supposed to be a couple and couples slept together. With his leg touching hers and the way he'd just looked at her, she almost believed the lie herself.

Ella finished up the food on her plate, surprised that she could eat a bite let alone empty the plate so quickly. "So, you're allergic to avocados?"

"No." He seemed confused at first but then he cracked another smile. "That what Rose told you?"

She nodded.

He shook his head. "She's a tricky one."

"A little too smart for her own good if you ask me," Ella said, feeling the burn in her cheeks. Or was that a simple reaction to the attractive man sitting next to her.

It didn't take long for Holden to finish the food on his plate, guacamole and all.

Rose reappeared in the hallway. "Leave the dishes. I'll take care of those."

Ella started to protest but Rose shut her down.

"Found a couple of unused toothbrushes in my cupboard. Leftovers from visits to the dentist over the years. I used to save them to use on trips but I haven't wanted to leave home in more years than I want to admit," the older woman continued.

"I can see why. You have a beautiful home," Ella said with true appreciation. The style of this place reflected that of its owner—elegant Southwest.

Holden stood, rinsed off their plates and linked his hand with Ella's as he led her down the hallway after Rose. She tried, rather unsuccessfully, to ignore the chemistry fizzing between them.

"I put fresh sheets on the bed, so you should be good," Rose said, stepping aside so they could enter the bedroom.

Ella wasn't sure what she'd been expecting to find. It was a bedroom after all.

But seeing one bed with turned-down sheets sent her pulse thundering.

Chapter Eight

"I can take the couch," Holden offered as soon as Rose disappeared down the hallway, figuring him and Ella alone in a bed might not be the best way to get a night of rest.

Ella stared at the bed for a thoughtful minute and then stepped inside the room. "It'll be best if we both get a good night's sleep and someone your size won't fit on the sofa. Plus, Rose will get the wrong idea about us being in a relationship. No reason to raise suspicion because that would be bad for her in the long run."

"I could always tell her we had a fight," he said, his gaze stopping on the base of Ella's throat where he could see her pulse pounding. And that wasn't helping matters for him one bit.

"It's okay," she said. "I trust you."

He hoped she wasn't making a mistake because he could tell she meant those words even though she'd said them so low he practically had to strain to hear.

She climbed into bed and turned onto her side, facing the opposite wall. She smelled like flowers and citrus, clean and like spring. Holden was already in trouble because he liked Ella Butler, and any kind of a relationship, no matter how short-lived it would be, was a slippery slope best avoided.

He pushed the covers aside and moved to the spot next to her. She rolled over and curled her body around his left side. Flat on his back, she nestled into the crook of his arm and rested her head on his chest.

Freezing up when a woman shared a bed with him was foreign to Holden, but then he'd never been in this circumstance before. In the past, a warm body beside him, hell, curled around him, meant two consenting adults who equally wanted to be there. Expectations were clear on both sides: great sex. This was not the same. The water was muddy with Ella. She wanted to be home, not there with him, but had to stay away in order to live.

Holden could hear her breathing and almost convinced himself that she was asleep until her eyes slowly opened and she looked up at him. That's all it took for him to do what he knew he shouldn't. He dipped his head down and claimed her mouth. Her lips parted and he delved his tongue inside, tasting her sweet honey. Her tongue teased him and she sucked on his bottom lip before gently biting. Need stirred from deep within. He wrapped his arms around her and hauled her tight against his chest. Her body fitted his, melding against him perfectly, and he could hear her breathing quicken.

Her hands were on his chest, her fingertips sliding along the ridges of muscles there. It would be so easy to let go with her…

Karen popped into his thoughts. Her lifeless body

lying in the bed they'd shared the night before, and his eyes shot open as he pushed up to his elbows. Ella was still partially tangled up with him so she repositioned, curling her legs around his midsection and balancing by digging her hands into his shoulders rather than spill off his lap.

"Not a good idea" was all he could manage to say.

Face-to-face, her minty toothpaste washed over him with every quick breath. She had that all-too-familiar hungry look in her eyes.

"Really, Holden?" she asked.

"This is getting out of hand," he said through ragged breaths. His body argued that a night of hot sex with Ella—and he was pretty damn certain it would rock his world—would be all he needed to get past his attraction to her and move on so he could focus on what was important: saving her life. And he could almost convince himself that once the mystery was gone, it would somehow become easier to be around her without so much sexual chemistry firing between them, distracting him. But that logic was as smart as pouring gasoline onto a forest fire and expecting to curb the flames. Laws of physics dictated a raging inferno.

"I'm confused," Ella said, and he could see the emotion in her eyes—eyes that were so expressive she was easy to read.

For lack of a real answer, he said, "So am I."

She crawled off his lap and curled onto her side again, hugging the edge of the bed. He mumbled another apology but she didn't respond. He repositioned onto his back and stared at the ceiling. He might be the dumbest man alive because not having sex with Ella wasn't exactly stopping him from thinking about the soft curve of her hips when they'd pressed against him. Nor did the intensity of their chemistry ease. Being with her was like sleeping with fireworks under the blanket.

Holden sighed harshly. If only he hadn't gone jogging at five that morning twenty-five months ago. Karen would be alive and so would his father.

By the time sunlight peeked through the blinds, he heard Rose padding down the hall toward the kitchen. Ella was still asleep based on her even breathing and he didn't want to wake her, so he peeled off the covers and slipped out of bed.

Rose was in the kitchen with a fresh pot of coffee brewing that he smelled from the bathroom where he stood at the sink brushing his teeth. His thoughts had bounced around last night. Most of them entailed how sweet Ella's silky skin felt against his body. The silhouette of her sweet round bottom had broken his concentration more than once. He dozed off in fits and starts because something was trying to break through. Something was bugging him. And he couldn't pinpoint what that something was. It was frustrating the hell out of him. He'd lost perspective and he needed to talk about it. He hoped a strong cup of coffee could clear his head.

"Morning," he said to Rose as he walked into the kitchen.

She nodded and caught his eye. "I haven't seen you this twisted up since you were in the eighth grade and that girl—what was her name? Tara—went off with your friend because she was convinced you didn't like her. And you did like her. But once you realized your friend did, too, you knew that you could never ask her out."

If only his problems could be that simple again, deciding between a hot girl and loyalty to his best friend. Holden had made the obvious choice—loyalty. But it had felt like a huge sacrifice at the time.

"I was awake chewing on something all night," he said. He could talk the basics of the case through without giving exact details or violating Ella's trust. "In a murder case, investigators always look to the people closest to the victim, to their inner circle, and work outward from there."

"True," she said, and she would know because her father had spent his entire life working for the Santa Fe Police Department. "Tell me more about this person's family. What are they like?"

"I couldn't say, personally. They seem to care for each other on the surface. There are twin brothers and a younger sister in this situation." He appreciated Rose going along with him without asking if they were talking about Ella.

"Does this have anything to do with what you're going through?" Rose studied him before taking a sip of coffee.

"No. This is different," he clarified. "There's no tie. This person's siblings seem to care. Both of her brothers had wanted to drop what they were doing and come to her but she'd convinced them that it would be too risky. They might lead the men targeting her right to her. Her sister shared a similar sentiment."

"So, let's rule out the immediate family," she said. "You've no doubt considered who stands to gain from her death."

"That's where things get complicated. Her father is wealthy. He was recently murdered and an attempt was made on her life almost immediately after," he said.

"She was the only one targeted out of four children?" A gray eyebrow hiked.

"The others left as soon as news of their father's death broke. She stayed to run the ranch," he supplied, holding back the fact that her father hadn't been gone for a whole week when she'd been attacked.

"All the siblings are out of town and that's not a convenient excuse?" she asked.

"I don't believe so."

"And that's where everything gets confusing, isn't it?" She picked up the spoon on the table and stirred her coffee absently. Rose always did that when she didn't have a good answer. There was so much comfort in knowing someone well enough to know their little quirks.

Holden had been away from civilization far too long. On balance, he had to consider if he was really living at all or just existing. Hiding. He raked a hand over his shaved chin, half expecting his beard to still be there and feeling nothing but exposed skin.

"Let's circle back then, to the actual attempt on the victim," Rose said. "What were the circumstances?"

"A rock was thrown at her head and she was left to die while hiking alone," he supplied.

Rose's eyes lit up. "That tells me whoever did this

wanted to make it look like an accident, so they have something to lose. It could be more than just status in the community."

"I thought that, too, until she was shot at on the way to the sheriff's office to give a statement a couple of days later," he said.

"Killer might've been expecting that. He goes back for the body where she was hiking. Doesn't find one, so he camps around the sheriff's office, figuring she might've gotten a good enough look at him to give a description," she said. "She shows and he figures he has to take her out. He's afraid to leave a possible witness."

"Good points." Holden reached for his beard again. Halfway there he realized he'd shaved and stopped as he held out his hand awkwardly in midair. "I suspect you're right and this person wants to keep his place in the community."

ELLA STRETCHED SORE muscles and pain rifled through her thigh. Her hand shot to the spot as she grimaced and blew out a breath. Contact was a bad idea even though all she touched was gauze and tape.

There'd most likely be some pain relievers in the kitchen and, more important, caffeine. More movement was going to hurt. *Time to suck it up, buttercup.*

Forcing herself to move her legs against all the resistance her body was giving seemed like the worst of bad ideas. Movement took every bit of effort inside her. Ella cursed under her breath and repeated the word a few more times as she pushed off the bed. Brushing her teeth was the first respite she had from the stabbing pain as she leaned her weight against the counter. Even her hip was sore. And all that screaming pain distracted her from the monster-sized headache raging between her temples.

After turning off the water, she heard the low hum of Holden's voice coming from the kitchen, and awareness trilled through her and her cheeks burned with embarrassment. She'd practically thrown herself at him last night and he'd stopped abruptly. She'd blame the entire episode on herself except that she'd seen that momentary flash of terror in his eyes that he tucked so masterfully behind that steel-jawed facade before rejecting her. She'd be angry with him for the rejection—and part of her was—but he'd said the last person he'd cared about ended up dead because of him, and she sensed that he couldn't go there with her and especially not under the circumstances.

He was right, though. Her life was complicated enough right now without adding to the confusion with a romantic entanglement with the man keeping her alive. Emotions were heightened. She needed to focus on being grateful to him and nothing more.

That's as far as she planned to allow her feelings for Holden Crawford to go.

Hopefully she'd be able to stick to her plan.

Chapter Nine

"We're leaving today. We'll pack up after breakfast," Holden said to Ella as she entered the kitchen. He barely glanced up.

"What's the rush?" Rose stood and moved toward the counter with the coffee maker. She looked to Ella when she said, "Have a seat. I'll get a cup for you."

Ella thanked her and sat next to Holden. The sexual chemistry between them zinged as intensely as ever and her stomach gave a little flip when her knee touched his thigh.

She must've also winced with movement when she sat because Holden stopped what he was doing and said, "You're in pain."

"A little," she admitted.

"I have something for that. I'll make something to eat first," Rose said, handing over a fresh mug. "Doc is always warning me about taking ibuprofen on an empty stomach."

"Thank you." Ella stared into the brown liquid before taking a sip. Anything to take the focus off how she felt whenever Holden was near and the assortment of aches and pains her body had racked up. She took a sip, enjoying the burn. "This is so good."

The breakfast burritos were equally wonderful.

"I have a few errands to run in town this morning," Rose said. "Can I pick up anything for you?"

Holden's gaze flicked up and held. "Do me a favor?"

She nodded. "Anything."

"Don't mention having houseguests." The concerned look on his face seemed to resonate with the older woman.

"Not a problem," she said before grabbing her keys off the counter and her purse off a hook positioned near the back door. "I'll only be a couple of hours. Will you be here when I return?"

"Yes," he said.

Relief washed over Ella as the older woman smiled and disappeared through the door. No way would she want to put Rose in danger but she had hoped they could stick around a few days. Being near her, in her calm presence, was comforting. Since Holden had already said they were leaving today, she sipped her coffee and tried not to think about having to get on the back of the motorcycle again.

"She'll be safe, right?" she asked Holden as he studied a laptop screen.

"As long as no one figures out we've been here, she will be," he said. "And I have every intention of ensuring that she is."

Shock reverberated through Ella as reality once again bore down on her. They were both on the run from dangerous men.

"Where do we go next?" she asked.

"That depends on how your leg's doing and how close the sheriff is to figuring this out." He didn't look up and she took it as a sign that he didn't want to talk.

The physical presence of him was difficult to ignore. He was big and imposing. *And sexy*, a little voice decided to add. It was an annoying little voice, like a fly at a picnic, buzzing around her face. She squashed that bug immediately. Holden Crawford was complicated. Danger practically radiated from his muscled biceps.

She drained her mug and pushed to standing, wincing as she tried to regain her balance, not yet steady on her feet.

"Don't do that," he said, rising to catch her. She had no intention of falling, pain or not.

"My leg is just sore. I need to walk it off," she defended, motioning toward her thigh.

"Mind if I take a look?" His gaze was on her now. The intensity of those honest blue eyes released a thousand butterflies in her stomach. Her throat felt like she'd downed a bottle of glue and her upper lip stuck to her top row of teeth when she managed a weak attempt at a smile. "Okay."

Ella took a seat again and showed him the injury.

Holden set up a few supplies, wipes and antibiotic ointment on the table next to her. She could've sworn he took in a sharp breath and muttered something that sounded like a swear word before he dropped to his knees in front of her.

She flexed her fingers when she thought about how deep the ridges in his shoulders were and how thick that dark hair of his was. Focusing her attention on the investigation would hopefully diffuse some of the sexual tension pinging thickly between them.

"We can't rule anyone out other than my siblings until we hear my father's will," she said.

"I have to consider everyone." His gaze was focused on the tape as he made a move to tear at one of the corners.

"So, what? The entire town is suspect? We'll never figure out who's responsible at this rate. We haven't ruled anyone out in your opinion, and I have no chance of going home anytime soon." She was frustrated and taking it out on him. In part because she needed to keep herself from thinking about doing other things to him. She clasped her hands and forced them on her lap. Thoughts of missing her father, of missing her family and of missing home struck a hole in her chest.

Holden tugged at the medical tape. A patch of skin pulled up along the tear line. As light as the touch might've been, she could've been hit by a bolt of lightning for the effect it had on her skin. A trail scorched from contact and her entire thigh warmed and zinged with awareness. Other places did, too, but she was determined not to think about those.

"Does this hurt?" His gaze flicked up to hers.

"That? No." There was so much going on inside her emotionally that the pain in her leg barely registered. She was having a difficult enough time fighting the barrage of tears threatening. Her thoughts were a jumbled mess spanning everything from his rejection to how much she wished life could go back to the way it was two weeks ago.

"Not the whole town, just people who would benefit from you disappearing." Holden went back to work.

"Like the people who work for us?" she asked.

"If they fit the bill. I was thinking more along the lines of projects you're involved in that impact other people." He dabbed antibiotic ointment along the gash, which looked like a crack in her skin.

"Ranch business impacts a lot of people, provides a lot of jobs directly and indirectly," she said.

"Any vendors who've been cut out of the pie recently?" He took scissors to a gauze pad, cutting it down to fit her wound.

"No. We've been doing business with most of our suppliers for years. Many are second- or third-generation owners." Thinking hurt. "We pay all our bills on time."

Ella must've made a face because he froze.

"Did that hurt?" He lifted the bandage slowly.

"No."

"I know you're upset and that's partly my fault. I let things get too far last night and I regret it," he started.

"Don't give me a speech about how there's nothing wrong with me. That you're just not attracted to my type," she quipped with more anger than she'd intended. "I'm sure you haven't been with a woman in a long time since you've been on the run."

His gaze locked onto hers.

"For your information, there've been plenty of women since I've been off the grid, just none that I could really care about. That doesn't happen often for me," he said, the intensity of his gaze washing over her like a rogue wave.

"Really? Maybe it's your magnetic personality," she bit out sarcastically, still fuming.

"Probably." He leaned back on his heels and placed his hands on his massive thighs, elbows out. "But the last person I cared about was killed by the men tracking me and I'm no closer to figuring out why now than I was two years ago. My father was also killed before I could get to him, which you already know but those thoughts keep rewinding inside my head."

His words sucked the wind out of her and all she could manage to say was, "Oh."

"So, yeah, I don't want to care about you and I'm frustrated because you're smart and beautiful with a body made for sinning on Sundays but none of that matters." His gaze was searing her skin as his eyes traveled her body. "Because if I allow myself to get soft enough to actually care what happens to you beyond blind loyalty to your father, you might end up dead, too. And I can't do that to another person. Not again. I wouldn't survive. There's enough blood on my hands."

"In case you haven't noticed, I don't need to worry about *your* men chasing after me. I seem to have attracted my own jerk intent on doing me harm all by my lonesome," Ella barked, ignoring the shivers racing up her arms with Holden this close. "I'm guessing someone wants to see my family suffer or has something to gain by targeting me after killing my father, but I have no idea what or who. So how's that for infuriating?"

"You should probably calm down," Holden said.

And that was like pouring gasoline on a fire. Ella pushed to her feet quickly.

"Because what? I'll raise my blood pressure? Have a heart attack?" She was really getting worked up now, like an out-of-control wildfire she couldn't douse, the flames roaring inside her. "In case you haven't noticed, I may not live to see tomorrow so I'll scream all I want."

Holden pushed up to his feet, too, and was standing inches away from her. She could see his chest rise and fall rapidly as his hands came up to cup her face.

"Because we'll make mistakes if we let emotions override rational thinking. It's best for Rose if no one knows we're here. I'm thinking about doing what's right for her, for you." There was something so calming about his physical presence. "Not kissing you is taking what little self-discipline I have left after last night, but I'm not doing it *because* I care about you. We'll figure out who's after you and I'll make sure the person responsible is locked away for a very long time or buried ten feet under. It'll be his choice. But, damn it, when this is over, I have every intention of walking away from you and never looking back."

His gaze had narrowed and his lips thinned.

Ella grabbed a fistful of his T-shirt, her knuckles meeting a wall of muscle.

"You may be able to stop yourself from kissing me but what will you do, Holden Crawford, when I kiss you?" she asked, locking onto his gaze. Her cheeks flushed against his hungry stare. And she might be baiting a bull, but she didn't care.

"It would be a mistake on your part," he said. His eyes had that dark, hungry look she'd seen moments before the first time he'd kissed her.

"What makes you say that?" she continued, knowing full well that she was enticing him.

"Because you don't have any idea what you're really asking for," he stated. And then he turned away from her and sat down at the laptop.

Neither frustration nor rejection would stop Ella at this point. She took the couple of steps toward Holden and straddled his thighs. He could ignore her once they were face-to-face.

"I'm a grown woman. You're a consenting adult male," she said, and she could see that he was considering her words.

He brought his hands up to grip her hips and her stomach quivered.

"Believe me, you don't want anything to do with me," he said before leaning forward to rest his forehead on hers. "It would be a mistake to think otherwise."

There was that word again. *Mistake.*

He seemed determined to avoid anything good that could happen between them. He couldn't let go of the past and she couldn't compete with a ghost. No amount of logic could change a man who was so strong willed.

Ella stood up.

"Mistakes don't define a person. Everybody makes those. It's part of how we learn. But choices do," she said before walking out of the room.

He could take it or leave it. Ella was done.

AN HOUR HAD passed and Holden still hadn't found the right words to say to Ella about whatever was happening between them. He felt it, too. The current running between them was strong and powerful. And just like a power cord in water, dangerous.

"Why do you really owe my father?" Ella asked as she entered the room.

The question caught Holden off guard.

"I already told you." He didn't look up, didn't need to. She was watching him and he could feel her glare roaming over him. Yeah, she was giving him the signal that would normally make him react differently, but he didn't go into anything deeper than a one-night fling without both parties being completely aware of what they were getting into. Ella Butler was in over her head and had no idea.

He hammered the keyboard.

"No, you didn't. All you said was that you owed him a favor. Why?" she pressed.

"Maybe you weren't listening before in the cabin," he started, but she cut him off with a strangled noise.

"Don't say he put a roof over your head so you wanted to return the favor," she said.

"I wasn't going to. He did a helluva lot more. He could've turned me in with one quick call to law enforcement. He didn't. He knew what he was getting into and he had every right to turn his back. He didn't. Helping me put him directly in danger. I don't know the man from Adam, personally. He and my father were friends. Maverick Mike said he owed my father one and I didn't ask a lot of questions, considering how short on options I was," he said, studying a section of map on the screen, searching for a safe place to camp for a day or two. Exhaustion poured over him and he—once again—fought against it. If he had his druthers, he'd still be at the cabin on the Butler property, the place that had felt like his first real home in longer than Holden could remember. Virginia had never really been the place where he saw himself setting down roots. Although Holden had lived there going on five years before his world had come crumbling down around him. And Karen? He still couldn't believe she was gone. It had all happened so fast.

"Do you ever directly answer a question?" she asked, and he could almost feel the heat oozing off her.

"Yes."

The silence in the room stretched on for longer than he should've allowed. He shook his head and went back to work, scouting locations from the map on the screen. Not any closer to finding an appropriate place to go than he had been an hour ago.

Ella's earlier words kept winding through his thoughts. Was he afraid to let anyone in? No matter how much he wanted to continue to refute them, he couldn't ignore the shred of truth. And he was getting tired of the war raging in his head trying to keep her away.

"I OWE YOU an apology. I'm going stir-crazy sitting around here. My mind is starting to think about all the things I need to do but I can't." Ella paced in the charming kitchen, wringing her hands together. Her chest squeezed thinking about how distant she felt from everything she'd ever known, everything familiar. Work was no doubt piling up. "I feel so disconnected. Normally, my cell is an extension of my hand

and I'm feeling panicked without it. My inbox is probably exploding. I guess there's no chance I can check email on that thing." She motioned toward the laptop.

"Your location can be traced back here based on the unique IP address if you access anything personal." Holden shook his head, twisting his lips in an apologetic look. "Nothing matters more to me than keeping you alive, finding out why you're being targeted and ensuring Rose's safety."

"I know we've discussed this before, but have you ruled out my father's killer trying to erase the family?" she asked.

"That's one possibility," he responded. "I'd like to explore a few others. Is anyone upset with you? Have you had any fallings-out with a friend?"

"None that I can think of," she stated. "But honestly, the days leading up to me going hiking are still a blur. I'd just found out about my father and this—" she motioned toward the covered gash on her forehead "—can't be helping."

"Was anyone jealous of you?" he asked.

"People like me overall, I think." She really thought about what he was saying. Could she have upset someone enough for a person to want her dead? The notion that someone she knew could be hunting her sent an icy chill down her spine. "I do a lot of work to give back to the community. I don't always agree with people's opinions and, sure, there are conflicts from time to time within pretty much all my charity work. Anytime you get ten or fifteen different people in the room there are going to be that many opposing views. We argue, debate and then eventually come to a resolution. Does everyone walk away happy? No. But what could possibly warrant this?" She heard her own voice rise defensively.

"It would be easier to pin down the responsible party if we could trace them to you instead of your father," he said.

"I don't know." Flustered, she paced.

"I'm not trying to upset you." He tried to reassure her.

"I know. And what you're saying makes sense," she said, wishing she could will her pounding pulse to calm down.

"What about your friends?" he asked.

"I have a few people who are close but between helping run the ranch and my work with organizations, I don't have a lot of time for happy hour." Hearing her life put in those terms sounded like a sad existence. She felt the need to add, "I spend most of my time with my family."

"You already said that you aren't seeing anyone special." His gaze intensified on the screen. "Are you dating around?"

"I can't see why that would be—"

"Before you get distraught with me I'm only asking to see if there could be a jealous guy in the mix," he added, and he still didn't look at her. "Someone who looks like you would attract a lot of interested men."

"I date a little." She shrugged. The compliment caused her cheeks to heat. "I love living on the ranch and Cattle Barge is home, but there aren't a lot of interesting men around. I grew up there and it's a small town so I dated around in high school and haven't looked back since college. Not a lot of new people move to town unless you count the men who work in the stable, and I would never date inside the ranch. It's bad business and someone would lose their job if things got awkward after."

The only truly good-looking person she'd seen in the past year was a new guy who'd moved to the outskirts of town and kept to himself. But she didn't mention him to Holden.

"And besides, I'm too busy with work and my charities to get out much," she defended. "I haven't been serious about anyone for a long time, and I've been thinking that I need to spend more time in Austin or San Antonio so I can meet someone."

Holden waited for her to finish. She was oversharing. Being nervous had her talking more than she should.

"I'm sure my life sounds awful to someone like you but—"

"Tell me more about your charity work." He leaned back in his chair and finally took his eyes off the screen.

One look from him caused her heart to flutter and she hadn't experienced that with anyone in too long.

"I pick projects that I'm passionate about, especially ones that need a helping hand," she responded, thankful for the redirection.

"What kind?" He folded his arms over a broad chest, and it was the most relaxed she'd seen him since they met.

"Mostly local stuff. Animal rights, various park cleanup and preservation initiatives, our local food bank and charities that serve the elderly in our community," she said.

"Sounds like a lot." His brows shot up.

"Does it?" She shrugged. "I don't know. I see something that needs to be done and I pitch in to help it along."

"The Butler name opens a lot of doors," he said, and she picked up on a hint of sarcasm.

"Yes, it does. If you expect me to be ashamed of it, you need to think again." Her shaky voice belied the confidence she was trying to project.

"I didn't mean anything by it. I'm sure it helps to have that name behind you," he said.

"It does. And I was born with a silver spoon in my mouth. There. Are you happy?" She went ahead and said it for him…for everyone who'd discounted her because her father had made a show out of giving her everything. Had it been too much? Yes. "If you think wearing nice clothes and being given lavish gifts makes you feel good about yourself or loved, you're wrong. A little girl needs to be held when she cries. Not handed an expensive doll and left alone in her room to sort through her emotions."

"So you're saying that giving a little girl everything she could possibly desire is a bad thing?" Holden asked. "Because if I had a daughter, I'd move heaven and earth to give her the world."

Her stomach gave a little flip at the thought of a newborn wrapped in a pink blanket in the burly man's arms. A thought struck her like a rogue wave…*their daughter*.

Before she tumbled into the surf with that one, she

made a couple of laps around the breakfast table. She stopped.

"How do I say this without sounding ungrateful?" She wished for the right words. "*Things* are nice. But there's so much more to bringing up a child than presents. All kids really need is love."

"Try filling a growing boy's stomach on that," he said.

"Everyone needs food. A child also needs to be comforted after waking from a nightmare. All the gifts in the world don't mean as much as hearing the words *I love you*." Ella hadn't planned to cry, so the stray tear rolling down her cheek caught her off guard. "I'm sorry. I know my father loved us in his own way. I didn't mean—"

"No, it's fine." Holden said. "Don't be embarrassed about telling me how you really feel. Believe it or not, I might've made the same mistakes as a father. All a man wants to do with a little girl is spoil her."

There was a quiet reassurance to his voice. A dangerous comfort under the circumstances. Ella couldn't afford to let her guard down around Holden and especially since he seemed too intent on keeping her at a distance, except in times like these when he was being her comfort while she was vulnerable.

And then he'd just push her away again.

Ella thought better of it this time.

"I'm tired," she said.

His brows drew together like he was confused.

"We're leaving later, right?" she asked.

"That's the plan." His gaze bounced from her to the screen and back.

Her sense of security with Holden was false. He hadn't opened up one bit. He'd been clear about one thing. She should keep her distance.

"Then I better get some more rest before we leave." She intended to listen this time even if her heart fought her on it.

"I'll think about what you said." Holden glanced up and it was like stepping into sunlight, being bathed in warmth.

"Great. Maybe you'll have this whole situation figured out by the time I open my eyes again." She managed a weak smile as she turned to leave.

"I'm not talking about that," he said. His voice was a low rumble in his chest. "What you said about choices earlier. You might have had a point."

She didn't dare turn around and let him get a good look at her face. She hadn't inherited her father's gift at poker. Her face was easy to read.

And she didn't want to be *this* attracted to Holden Crawford.

Chapter Ten

"It's time to go." Holden's voice was a whisper in Ella's ear. It took a second to register that she wasn't dreaming, and his soothing, deep baritone had her reaching for him. Until she realized she was awake.

"Okay." She pushed up to sitting, keenly aware of the strong male presence next to her on the bed. Thoughts like those were as unproductive as trying to grow grapevines in clay soil.

Ella tried to clear her thoughts. She'd dozed off after an exhausting afternoon. Exhausting because she'd basically done nothing but climb the walls all day and her exchange with Holden had her emotions all over the map.

There was no other choice but to be cooped up and she knew it. Still, she couldn't help but feel like a caged animal and her confusing feelings for Holden intensified everything. Beginning to feel better was almost a curse under the circumstances. She was well enough to move around but they had to keep a low profile or risk endangering Rose. There was no way Ella would knowingly put that sweet old woman in danger.

Every noise had had Ella feeling skittish. Constantly being on alert with no outlet for her energy had caused fatigue.

"I'll wait in the other hall," Holden said. And then she felt his weight leave the mattress. The heat in the room vanished with him.

Ella dressed using only the light from the moon sliding through the slats in the blinds. As much as she didn't want to leave *la hacienda*, putting Rose at risk by staying wasn't an option. And at least she would finally have something to do, a purpose, even if it was dangerous. She'd go stir-crazy if she stayed inside much longer.

Holden was waiting outside the door.

"Ready?" he asked as he took the duffel from her.

"I think so," she said. "Any chance we can wake her and tell her goodbye?"

Ella didn't have to ask to know that Holden had wiped the place clean. The smell of bleach permeated the air.

Her eyes widened at the sound of a motorized vehicle outside. Holden muttered a curse. "Stay right here unless I tell you to come out."

He dropped to the ground and instructed her to do the same. Pain shot up her right thigh at the quick movement. She swallowed her gasp, making no sound as she hit all fours and scooted behind a cabinet.

The kitchen door opened and closed so fast and so quietly it barely registered. Ella was reminded how little she knew about the man who was helping her. Why was he so adept at moving stealthily into the night? Had he served in the military? Or been in law enforcement?

The way he'd questioned her earlier gave the impression he might've been. Hadn't he said that he and his father shared similar professions? She wanted to know how it was even possible that her father had met the man. For reasons she couldn't explain and didn't want to analyze, she wanted to know more about Holden.

Another swish of the door and she realized she'd been holding her breath.

"It's all good," Holden said, reclaiming the duffel. He had a second helmet and she figured he must've left it at Rose's on a prior visit.

Ella followed him out the door, surprised at the stabbing pain in her chest at leaving. She'd lost so much already and Rose had managed to wiggle her way into Ella's heart in the short time she'd known her. Rose's eyes belied her smile. There was emptiness there, a hollowness that Ella couldn't ignore.

"I'd like to check on her when I get my life back," she said to Holden. "We have our annual fall festival coming up in a few weeks. Maybe she'd like to come."

"When this is over, you can do anything you want," he said. He wasn't arguing against the idea but he came off like he didn't care either way. Was he reminding her that they'd go on to live their separate lives by then? She couldn't see his face with his helmet on.

Leaving Rose was harder than Ella expected it to be. Her heart broke a little as she climbed onto the back of Holden's motorcycle. She was glad that he didn't notice the tears welling in her eyes at the thought of leaving Rose by herself.

The highway was long and empty when they first

started out. Traffic thickened as they headed east and neared major cities. After riding on the back of Holden's motorcycle so long Ella's arms felt like they were being dragged down by hundred-pound weights, they exited the highway.

Holden located a dirt path about a mile off the highway and Ella lost count of how many minutes they'd been on it until he finally stopped.

After Ella climbed off the back of the bike, Holden threw his leg over and hopped off.

"I thought we'd camp for a few days. I have camping gear in my duffel," he said. With his helmet on, visor down, she couldn't read his eyes.

Ella balked. "Seriously? Out here?"

"Sure. Why not?" He removed his helmet to reveal concerned, pinched eyebrows.

"Mosquitoes for one. They'll eat me alive. Showers for another. You won't want to be anywhere near me without one." She was getting nowhere and could tell by his tense expression.

And then his face broke into a wide smile, revealing near-perfect white teeth.

"You think this is funny?" She really was working herself up now and it seemed to amuse him all the more.

"Actually, I do." He turned and walked to a clearing where one of those tiny houses stood. He was jiggling what sounded like keys.

Ella blew out a frustrated breath as she watched him unlock the door.

"Coming?" he asked, and there was a contrite quality to his voice. "Or do you plan to stand out here and become mosquito bait?"

"Think you're funny?" she shot back with a look meant to freeze boiling water.

"I used to," he said under his breath.

And that made her laugh as she walked past him. She couldn't help herself. It was most likely the stress of the past few days and how out of control her life had become, but she laughed.

"I don't know what shocks me more. The fact that you made me laugh or used to think you were funny," she said as he opened the door.

A laugh rumbled from Holden's chest and it was sexy. Ella wanted to shut off her attraction to him. But it felt impossible at the moment. No matter how much she tried to hold it back, she couldn't. So she gave in and it was probably the stress that they'd been under more than anything else, but both of them laughed until she had to sit down.

"That felt good," she said, ignoring the feeling like champagne bubbling up her throat as she wiped tears from her eyes.

"It did." Holden stood at the door, leaning against the jamb, arms folded. "Life used to be...more funny."

"How long did you say you've been living like this?" she asked.

"Twenty-five months." His smile faded.

"That's a long time." She stood.

He nodded and she thought he said, "Too long."

"What about Rose? Will she be safe now that we're gone?" she asked.

"That's the idea. But if they figure out her connection to me…" He stopped as though he couldn't finish the thought let alone the sentence.

"Would she be safer at my family's ranch?" Ella asked. "I could have someone pick her up. No one would have to know."

"She's stubborn." He was already shaking his head. "There's no way she would leave her precious garden for more than a few days."

"What if I talked to her? Maybe she'd listen to me if I came up with a good argument."

"You'd be wasting your breath," he responded.

"It'd be worth a try," she argued.

"You really think you can change people, don't you?" Holden asked, and the question took her off guard.

"Why do you make it sound like a bad thing?" Her defenses flared.

"It's good." He shrugged. "Probably naive. You do realize that you can't save every stray."

"Maybe." She probably shouldn't speak her mind to the one person who seemed intent on helping her. Especially when she was about to send out a zinger. "But at least I don't quit."

That brought an amused smile to Holden's face. "And that's what you think I did?"

"Obviously. You got into trouble and you've been hiding ever since," she surmised.

"I'm sure it looks that simple from the outside." He picked up the duffel and brought it over to one of the chairs. The living room of the place was too small for a couch, but there were two reasonably sized, comfortable-looking chairs with a small table in between. The kitchen was more like a kitchenette with a microwave and a hot plate. Ella's dorm room in college had been bigger, and yet she was never happier to be in a space. There was a full-size bed on the back wall. It would be way too small for a man like Holden Crawford. And a closed door that she assumed led to an equally small bathroom, which was fine because this was so much better than being out there in the elements, exposed.

"How'd you know about this place?" His comments still stung, which meant there was a tiny bit of truth. Ella didn't believe in lost causes. Everyone could be saved. *Except those who refuse help*, a little voice reminded.

"Belongs to a friend of mine." He pulled out the makings for coffee.

She must've balked because he got a defensive look on his face.

"I have friends," he said, defensive.

She wasn't touching that statement. "Are you tired after that long ride?"

"Not really. Riding helps clear out the clutter in my head." He moved to the kitchen and held up a mug.

"Yes, please," Ella said.

"Our conversation is churning through my mind." He heated water on the small stove before filtering the grinds.

"Anything stick out?"

"I just got to thinking about your life, your activities and who might benefit from your death."

"No one, really. The ranch would continue to run.

Dad had a trust set up years ago in order to protect jobs in the event something happened to his kids. It's part of the reason his employees were always loyal to him. He looked out for them," she said. "Ed Staples, the family attorney, would oversee it and then he'd name a successor. There are a lot of controls built in so no one can override the document or successfully challenge it in court. I wish I'd paid more attention to that part but I honestly never thought I'd need to know. My dad was such a presence. I just never believed anything bad would happen to him."

Holden paused long enough to make eye contact before continuing. The look seemed meant to be reassuring.

"But we have no suspects and we're no closer to figuring out what happened than we were after the first rock to my head," she said, frustrated.

Holden handed over a mug of fresh steaming brew.

Ella took a sip and mewled with pleasure. "I will never tire of the taste of your coffee."

Her response netted another smile and she liked the way his lips curved.

"You figure out how to make do with what you have in your environment," he said.

"Where are we, by the way?" she asked, realizing it hadn't occurred to ask before now. She'd been too busy laughing and her stomach still hurt.

"We're in Texas," he said.

"I figured that much out," she quipped before taking another sip.

"A couple of hours from Cattle Barge," he said. "I

keep rounding back to the fact that we need to be near here in order to track down leads. We might be able to clear this whole thing up if you could talk to people."

"Agreed."

"Don't get any ideas because you can't go back home," he said. "It's too risky and we have to give the sheriff time to do his job. He has more evidence to work with now."

Ella got quiet for a long time. If she could stay alive, Sheriff Sawmill should be able to find the person after her, especially after that last attempt. "I know you make an amazing cup of coffee, and I mean pretty much anywhere with whatever's around. But I don't know much else about you."

Holden's gaze narrowed and his lips thinned, and for a long moment she didn't think he was going to respond. "I told you that I was set up for murder before. Doesn't that make you a little scared to be around me?"

"Why should it? You're innocent." She didn't hesitate.

"I am. But how do you know?" An emotion passed behind his eyes. Hope?

"I've been around bad men before. I'm not as naive as you believe. Dad taught me how to tell the difference a long time ago. Said he was protecting me. When a man's truly evil he has a dead quality to his eyes. A darkness that no light can fill. A man capable of murder, even if it was a passion killing, would have those eyes," she said.

"I was out jogging that morning when it happened,"

he said after a thoughtful pause. "Came back and found her stabbed to death."

There was an almost-audible thud in Ella's chest at the tight-clipped pain in his voice—pain that he'd held inside for too long. "What happened?"

"As in details? You don't want to know."

"Maybe that's true on some level. You haven't spoken to anyone in more than two years and I think it's time you got this off your chest," she said quietly.

Holden blew out a sharp breath, and for a minute she thought he'd change the subject. There was so much pain behind those pale blue eyes—eyes that had spoken so much to her when she'd first seen them while the rest of his face was buried underneath that beard.

He took in a sharp breath. "Her name was Karen. Blood was everywhere. I bolted over so fast that I didn't even look to see if anyone else was around. Everything moved in beats after that. One beat and I'm standing in the doorway in shock. In the next, I'm beside the bed. My field training told me that pulling the knife out of her chest would make everything worse. Her eyes were already fixed, open…blank."

Ella didn't speak, even when Holden looked like he might not continue. She just sat there, still, patient. Wishing there was something she could do to help ease his heartache.

"Another beat and I'm trying to stem the bleeding, performing CPR. None of my years in the corps mattered because I couldn't bring her back." He clenched his back teeth. "A few beats later, cops are there. Looking back, that part was strange because I never called them. Guess I just assumed one of my neighbors had heard her screaming. Another beat and EMTs arrived. The whole place was chaos by then. A few more beats and I'm in the back of a squad car being taken in to give my statement, and that should've been my first clue that something was off. Looking back, why wouldn't the cops have had a witness ride in front? And then the cop pulls off on this back road. I had blood all over me, my hands, Karen's blood. I was in shock so it took a minute to register that the cop wasn't heading toward the station anymore. I was in a fog. He orders me out of the back and pulls out his service weapon. Throws a cord at me and tells me to wrap it around my neck."

Holden paused. Ella touched his arm for reassurance. She was listening. She cared about the truth.

"Cop gave me two options. Wrap the cord around my neck or be shot. I told him he forgot my third choice." Holden looked high and away from her like he could see the past there. "Run."

"How did he react?" she asked.

"I dropped down and caught his leg as he tried to shoot me. He went over backward, landed pretty hard and started calling for help on his radio," he said.

"And that's when you got away," she finished.

"My father was tortured and killed a few days later and that's when I knew something big was going on. I still don't fully understand why I was set up to look like a murderer in the first place. I'd only been dating Karen for a few months when the whole thing went down. And, yeah, it was my blade, but I wasn't even in the house when it happened." Holden stared at a spot on the wall for a long moment and she could only imagine the horrors of what he'd witnessed.

"Wouldn't the evidence have cleared you?" she asked.

"If the officers in charge of the investigation had followed it, I would've been fine. They didn't. The officer who took me in supposedly to give my statement never intended for me to live long enough to say what really happened," he said.

Ella gasped.

"Within days of my disappearance reports started showing up about me suffering from PTSD, going berserk and killing my girlfriend and then my father." He made a disgusted face and grunted. "They were so off base and I was angry. But someone important was pulling the strings. Had to be, and I realized how far they would go the minute they killed Pop."

"I'm so sorry," she whispered.

Silence sat between them for a long moment.

"What did you do?" she finally asked.

"At first, I'll be honest. I thought I'd bide my time and then creep back into the shadows. Figure out who committed these crimes. Make them pay with their own lives. The thought of revenge kept me moving forward when I wanted to die," he admitted.

"And now?"

"I remembered a promise that I made to Pop once about looking after Rose if anything ever happened to him. We were fishing and I guess he was getting older. Started thinking about the day he might not be around any longer. She was his only friend when he lost his parents and had to live with a relative in New Mexico. He was kicked around from place to place after that, to whoever would take him. But he and Rose managed to get back in touch," he continued. "She was his North Star and helped him get his life together when it was falling apart. They kept their friendship a secret so none of his relatives knew where to look for him. He'd show up at her parents' place when life got too real and they'd take him in. I guess it never occurred to them to go public with their friendship once they were adults. When I was born and my mom took off, Rose urged him to join the military to straighten himself out. He did. We moved around a lot before settling in Virginia, where my father established a moving company, but we had each other and we had Rose. Pop might not have been perfect, but he did the best he could, and I respect that in a man."

Ella could relate to those feelings. She and Holden weren't so different no matter how much he wanted to be a man stranded on an island. At least he was talking to her, revealing something about his past and why he was in this predicament. She couldn't imagine walking in to find someone she loved—that word pained her to think about when it came to Holden and another woman—murdered. She shuddered at the thought. And then to find out that your father had been tortured and killed and you'd been blamed. The worst part was that she could see why Holden would hold himself responsible for all of it even though something else had to be going on. Would it really be any different for her?

There was a storm brewing behind Holden's blue

eyes as he spoke. He'd lost two people he cared about in a very short time and he held the blame for both. Two long years. So much pain.

"Were the two of you in love?" Ella surprised herself with the question.

"I thought I might have been at the time," he said.

"What changed?" She didn't look at him and scarcely registered that she was holding her breath, waiting for his response.

"My definition."

"How so?" she asked, still not able to look him in the eyes.

"I met you."

Chapter Eleven

Light peeked through before Holden seemed to quash it by turning away from Ella. When he looked at her again, he was all business.

Ella had no idea how to process what he'd just said, but she couldn't ignore how his words made her feel. Before she could gather her thoughts to speak, he said, "Tell me more about what kinds of projects you were working on leading up to the attack at Devil's Lid."

Ella stretched out sore legs and pressed her fingers to her temples, trying to make her head stop pounding. Refocusing might give her a chance to get a handle on her runaway emotions. "I'm on a committee that was formed to clean up the creek along Slider's Rock. Another to raise funds to build a bigger playground at the elementary school in town. Both of those met recently. And then there's our recycling program. We're always trying to drum up support and raise awareness of the benefits of recycling in schools and at parks. Let's see. What else?" It was hard without having her schedule in front of her to work from. "We're working on raising awareness for elder abuse and neglect. So many in our community don't have enough money to run AC in the summer or have to resort to eating canned dog food when their Social Security check doesn't stretch far enough."

"And these projects have opposition?" he asked, a dark eyebrow rose.

A frustrated half laugh, half snort ripped from her throat. "Every single one."

"Who could argue against preventing elder abuse?" Disdain brought down the corners of his lips.

"You'd be surprised," she said. "Anytime you draw a line in the sand, you separate sides. People may not disagree about educating others about the needs in our community, but everyone will have a different opinion about how to get it done. And I mean everyone. From the mayor to someone's uncle to the town's barber."

"When you put it that way, I believe it." Holden took a sip of coffee. "We should make a timeline of events and include every meeting you attended recently, especially those with heated debates. Also, I'd like to get the names of everyone who is involved in the organization and any persons who might have something to lose based on outcomes of your decision or decisions you heavily influenced on paper."

He moved into the kitchen and opened the few drawers until he pulled out a pad of paper and a pen. "This'll help."

AN HOUR AND a half later, Holden stood in the kitchen reading the long list of Ella's activities. "You're one busy person."

"I already said I was involved in the community," she said, and that solicited a grunt from Holden.

"Involved? Is there anyone else in town doing anything?"

Ella laughed. "I'm sure that I'm forgetting something. Like I said, the days following Dad's death are a little hazy and my head hurts when I try to overthink."

"You mean there's more than this?" He held up the paper. "When do you have time to do anything else?"

"Like what?" she asked.

"Date, for one," he said.

Ella laughed. "It'd be crazy to empty my schedule and wait for Mr. Right to waltz in when there's so much to be done. Besides, I already told you about my personal life."

It looked like a small smile crossed his lips before he took another sip of coffee. "The person who tried to kill you wanted it to look like an accident at first. I'm guessing they were expecting a headline that read Grieving Socialite Falls into Canyon Days after Her Father's Murder."

"Right. But the second attempt was out in the open."

"He could've planned to kidnap you and then set the scene once you were secured. No one had seen you since you'd disappeared at Devil's Lid, so he might've figured that he could kill you and stage it to look like an accident."

"Wouldn't someone notice the bullet holes?" she asked.

"True. The assailant did shoot but that was most likely out of panic."

"Now that I think about it, he shot when I fought him off and ran." She sighed. "Pretty much every household in this part of Texas has a shotgun on property. If not to deter criminals then to shoot predators stalking their herds, so that doesn't help us."

Holden nodded again as he examined the list. "There are a lot of names on here. What about friends? Any arguments with the people in your circle?"

"When do I have time?" she quipped. "I do charity work, which I'm passionate about, and I help run the ranch. I barely have time to eat and sleep."

"That's a choice," he said with a look.

"You're a man on the run and I doubt you've made time for *friends* in the meantime," she quipped. Yeah, she was being defensive. There was something about detailing the boring nature of her private life to a ridiculously handsome man that put her on edge.

Holden held up a hand in surrender. "I make no claim about being perfect. But I have a good reason to stay solitary. Everyone I get close to ends up dead."

She started to argue but he'd made a good point. Had she been pushing people out of her life? Keeping everyone at a safe distance? The short answer? Yes. Never knowing her mother and growing up with an emotionally distant father wasn't exactly the recipe for letting people in. She was as close to her siblings as she could be, but Ella could admit that she'd taken on a mother-like role with them since she was the oldest. At least until the boys were old enough to do what they wanted, and that came early for the independent-minded Butler men. Even now while her life was in danger she was focused on protecting them. Maybe she and Holden had more in common than they wanted to admit.

"Anyone stand out on that list you're holding?" she asked, figuring she'd done enough self-examination for one day. Her brain hurt and that wasn't helping her figure out whatever was pressing against the back of her skull. Something was there but she couldn't reach it, and that was frustrating under the circumstances. The stakes were high and it wasn't like she was trying to remember her shopping list. Trying to force it didn't help, though.

"I'd have to dig around and figure out the impact these decisions could make to know anything for certain," he said.

"Impossible out here with no laptop or Wi-Fi," she explained. "You already said contacting people is out of the question."

"When my choices are to keep you safe or investigate, I'm always going to choose the first," he said, and there was an emotion present behind his eyes that stirred something primal inside her.

Ella ignored it. Sort of. Her body trilled with awareness.

"We could talk it through over lunch," she said, her stomach rumbling. Had they eaten breakfast?

"I'll head into town for supplies," he said. "I don't like leaving you here alone but it'll be safer for you if we split up."

Holden pulled his Sig Sauer out of his duffel and set it next to Ella.

She glanced at the weapon before locking onto his

gaze. "I guess I should've seen this coming. This is the first time I've seen you with a gun."

"I didn't need it before now," he said, and she figured he had a military background by way of his commitment to everything being on a need-to-know basis. "You know how to use it?"

"I have experience with shotguns mostly, but I'll figure it out if I have to," she said with sincerity.

He nodded and that should've been the end of it. He should've walked out the door and gone for supplies. But he stood there like he couldn't move his feet. It dawned on her why he'd respond that way.

"I'll be okay. Go ahead," she urged. "Nothing will happen to me while you're gone."

HOLDEN WAS SURPRISED at how easy it was to talk to Ella. He'd never had a problem closing up and keeping everything locked inside until her. He shocked himself with the amount he'd wanted to share. He'd been a regular Chatty Cathy back there. He reminded himself to tread lightly. It probably had more to do with the fact that he'd barely spoken to a soul in twenty-five months than the possibility that he could have real feelings developing for someone he'd only known a few days.

Granted, there was something about Ella Butler that gave the impression they'd known each other for years, a familiarity he'd never experienced with another person. She was different from the women he usually dated. But this wasn't the time to get inside his head about it. There were more important issues to think about, like who was trying to ensure she took her last breath. And the issue of him still being on the run after two years in hiding, getting nowhere.

Holden thought about what Rose had told him. The numbers 1-9-6-4 still meant nothing to him and he'd racked his brain during the ride to the small cabin trying to find a connection. He'd first thought it referred to a year and then an address. Nothing came to mind.

Immediately after the murders he'd gone over his last conversations in his head a hundred times, and his thoughts became an endless loop. Looking back from a fresh lens, he thought about his relationship with Pop. How quiet he'd become in those last few weeks before the murders. People talk about intuition all the time. Had Pop sensed something was coming?

Holden parked his motorbike around the side of the country store and purposely kept his sunglasses on to shield at least part of his face. At his height, it was difficult to move undetected and he still felt exposed without a beard. He'd covered his face with one for two years—years that had felt like they'd dragged on for twice that amount.

Ella's words haunted him. Had he given up?

Holden pushed open the glass door and heard a jingle. The chipper cashier looked up from a magazine and welcomed him. He nodded but kept his face turned away in case there was a camera. Seemed like there was one in every store no matter how remote the location. Technology made it more and more difficult to stay off the radar.

He picked up a basket and loaded it with grilling supplies. Normally, he saved steak for a special occasion. In this case, he wanted to feed Ella a decent meal. Based on her devotion to her causes, she seemed like a good person and deserved at least that much.

Her situation haunted him.

The logical answer was that someone had killed Maverick Mike and had now set his or her sights on Ella. The responsible party had clearly wanted to make a statement with Mike's death, but something had changed when the person went after Ella. What? His thoughts kept rounding back to the same thing. *The person.*

He let that thought sit while he approached the cash register.

"This all for you today, mister?" the short brunette cashier chirped. She looked to be in her midtwenties and wore a green shirt and khaki-colored pants.

"Yep." Holden nodded and quirked a smile. He'd found a small gesture like that put people at ease around him. It wasn't difficult to find a smile when he thought about the simple pleasure of grilling a good steak and feeding someone he cared about.

Damn.

Ella's words kept cycling through his thoughts. He'd convinced himself that keeping to himself and staying so far off the grid that he'd become half animal, half man was to keep himself alive until he figured out who was behind Karen's killing. Losing her had been a blow. His father being killed so soon after had knocked the wind out of Holden. It had only been him and Pop since his mother had disappeared not long after he'd been born. Sure, Pop had made mistakes but the two of them had grown up together and Holden could easily forgive the shortcomings. Hell, he was far from perfect himself. When his old man was killed, a piece of Holden had died. His anger had turned inward and he'd retreated to nature, where he'd been trained to survive.

The cashier chirped an amount and Holden paid with cash. He'd cashed out his savings when he went on the run and had kept a low profile, sleeping in vacant cabins and trapping and cooking most of his own food. He took his bags with a thank-you and forced a casual-looking smile.

The cashier beamed up at him. The twinkle in her eyes said she was flirting. Holden wasn't the least bit interested. Being with Ella made him realize how far he'd drifted away from the man he used to be before his life had been turned upside down. That needed to change.

Holden kept his head down as he exited the store. Out of the corner of his eye he saw a white sedan with blacked-out windows fly past and a bad feeling took seed deep in his gut.

He broke into a dead run toward his motorcycle as his pulse galloped. His chest clenched at the thought of anything happening to Ella while he was away. He'd left her with his Sig for protection, not really expecting her to need it. Could she even use it on another human being? A moment of truth like that only came when confronted with the situation. He muttered a few curses after quickly securing the grocery items. He released the clutch and gravel spewed from underneath his back tire.

Ella should never be faced with a kill-or-be-killed

situation. Holden should know. He'd had to when he was in the service. And taking someone's life, even an enemy, wasn't something a decent man took lightly.

With the agility of his motorcycle, he caught up to the sedan in no time. As he neared, he heard music blaring. Teenagers?

He whipped around the vehicle in order to get a look at the driver. A strong honk-like sound caused him to look up in time to realize he was about to go head-on with a semi.

Holden zipped around the white car. In his rear-view, he could see the driver clearly. He was male and too young to buy a real drink. Relief was short-lived. Holden needed to see Ella with his own eyes and know that she was fine. In the future, he'd figure out a way to take her with him when he left for supplies because being away from her, not knowing if she was safe, did bad things to his mind.

By the time he navigated up the drive, checking several times to ensure no one had followed him, his nerves were shot. She was waiting outside, sitting in the sun, when he parked behind the shack. Seeing her caused a jolt of need to strike him like stray voltage. Holden was done. Done biting down an urge so primal his bones ached. Done holding her back when she'd been so clear that she wanted the same thing. Done protecting her from him. She needed to know that she meant something to him. So he walked right over to her and hauled her against his chest. Her sweet body molded to his. Her fingers tunneled inside his hair as he pressed his forehead to hers. "We can't let this go any further, but I had to hold you."

This close, he could feel her body tremble and need welled inside him. The feel of her soft skin under his hands connected to a life he used to know only this somehow was better. Sexual chemistry crackled in the air around them. Sex couldn't happen but he was done fighting the need to be close to her.

She looked up at him with those cornflower blue eyes and he almost faltered. He reminded himself to keep a grip on his emotions.

"What happened?" she asked.

"There was a car…"

"And you thought it was coming for me," she finished when he paused.

"Yes." He closed his eyes to shut out the other possibilities, the ones that involved him not making it to her in time.

"Are you okay?" she asked, and there was so much concern in her voice.

"I am now," he said, and she didn't seem to need him to elaborate. She just leaned into him and wrapped her arms around his neck. The movement pressed her full breasts against his chest and for a half second he pictured them naked, tangled in the sheets in a place far away from here.

But that wasn't reality and Holden didn't do fairy tales.

He took in a sharp breath.

"I'll make lunch," he said.

Ella took a step back, away from him, seeming to

understand that he needed space. Damn, it was going to be difficult to leave her once this was all over.

For now, he needed to concentrate on giving her her life back. She had plans, meetings and causes to fight for.

What did he have?

A ghost of a life. No family to speak of. Yeah, his life couldn't be more opposite. Another in a long list of reasons he needed to maintain his distance. He would only bring her down.

He was cursed.

Chapter Twelve

Ella smiled as she took another bite of perfectly cooked steak. The potato with all the fixings was just as amazing. "I'm impressed with your cooking skills."

"Don't be. Coffee and steak are all I can do," he said with a crooked smile. She was grateful for the break in tension between them and even more so that her comment brought out a lighter side of him. He looked pleased with himself and like a different person than the one who'd arrived an hour ago. Ghost white with anger written all over his face, Ella could see beyond the mask to the absolute fear inside him.

And then he'd taken her in his arms.

Their sexual chemistry was off the charts and she figured mostly because it felt like death lurked around every corner. The thought that one of them could be gone in an instant when they'd grown to depend on each other solely for survival was odd considering that she hadn't even known the man existed a week ago. Yes, there'd been an instant attraction even before he'd shaved the beard. The feeling had intensified the more time they spent together. A small piece of her—a piece she didn't want to give too much consideration—needed to acknowledge that there was more to their attraction than proximity and circumstance. The rest of her realized that none of it mattered because he carried too much baggage from the past to let it go anywhere. And where would it go? He was wanted for murder and someone was trying to kill her.

When she thought about it in those terms—and really all she could do was laugh—they were quite a pair.

The feeling that something lurked in the far reaches of her mind that she couldn't access frustrated her. She told herself that was the only reason she was preoccupied with her feelings toward Holden.

"What?" he asked, breaking into her thoughts.

"Nothing." She shook her head.

"Whatever it is made you smile and then frown." He set his fork down on his plate. "You should smile more."

If only he knew that she'd been thinking about him.

"It's the food," she lied. "Even if you are a one-trick pony as you claim to be, it's a mighty fine trick."

That netted a genuine smile from Holden. He should do it more, too. She imagined a life before his world was turned upside down where he laughed easily, held cookouts in the backyard and perfected his coffee-making skills.

"What was your life like before...?" she asked.

He shrugged his massive shoulders. "The usual stuff. Opening-day baseball with Pop in the spring. No matter where we lived we always drove to Queens to watch the season opener."

"What was he like? Your father?" Ella figured

Holden would stop her if she touched on a subject he couldn't talk about.

"Quiet. Kept to himself mostly. He and my mother, if you can call her that, had me when they were young. Dear old Mom took off and Pop joined the military after Rose's urging. We moved around a lot, going from base to base. And he was gone for long stretches but the military was family and we managed to get by. Rose was like a mother to me."

"Did your father and Rose ever go out?" she asked.

He shook his head.

"Why not?" Ella toyed with the fork.

"Honestly? I don't know. Pop had feelings for her. I didn't realize that until I was grown, but it's obvious to me as a man." Holden glanced up. "Guess the timing was never right."

"Shame. He sounds like a wonderful man and Rose is amazing. Plus, you would've grown up eating her chalupas." Ella smiled even though her heart dropped when he'd made the comment about timing. It applied to them, too.

"Her cooking skills would've been a definite plus." Holden stood up and she figured that was his way of saying he was done sharing.

Ella had to admit she was surprised at the change in him since visiting Rose. He seemed calmer, more at peace. Rose would've made a great mother.

"Any chance we can go into Cattle Barge safely?" she asked as he offered to take her plate.

"It wouldn't be a good idea," he said as a hint of that earlier fear flashed in his eyes.

"This feels like a stalemate. How are we supposed to make progress if we can't ask people questions or poke around?" Ella followed him inside.

"I've been thinking a lot about that. We could head to San Antonio before sunrise. Do a little digging online at an internet café," he said. "I'd like to make a few calls, too. I might be able to get a little more information from your acquaintances."

"What makes you think that'll help?" she asked.

"I've been thinking about your charity work. We need to see if any of your projects could have had a negative impact on anyone," he said.

"Sounds like looking for a needle in a haystack," she stated.

"It is. But we have to start somewhere and talking about it might help you remember." Holden stretched his long muscular legs. "Have you thought more about those last few days before you went hiking?"

"Yes, but it doesn't seem to be helping. I end up with a headache." She frowned. "Will it be safe for you in San Antonio? It's a big city and people could be watching for you."

"We'll have to play it careful. The murders happened two years ago and in Virginia, so they shouldn't be top of mind anymore. I'd go back to Rose's but that would be too risky for her." He turned on the water in the small sink and hand washed the pair of dishes.

"I know a place we can go in San Antonio," she said. "It's small but has high-speed internet and everything we'd need."

"Any place familiar to you could put us in danger.

Whoever is tracking you might know about it," he said. "Since we don't have a clue who is behind your attacks, we don't truly know how close they are to you."

"I could call in a favor from a friend," she said. "I know people who would be loyal to me."

"That may be true under normal circumstances, but believe me when I say a persistent person can break down pretty much every barrier." He wiped water from the plates and stacked them. "Besides, you wouldn't want to put your friends in danger by giving them information that could lead to you."

"I hadn't thought about it like that," she said, realizing that was most likely all he'd thought about since being alone after his girlfriend and father had been killed. The past week had been hell for her being shut out from everything she cared about and disconnected from everyone she loved. She couldn't imagine living like this for two years and especially after losing two people he cared so much about. Other than Rose, they were all he had.

"There's something else," he said. "While we're there I thought it might be a good idea to do a little digging into my past. See what kinds of stories have been running about me since I disappeared. That might give me an idea of who's trying to find me and why. I never could figure out why local police were involved but enough time has passed now that it should be safe for me to surface and dig around."

"I think that's a great idea." Ella managed a smile. When she'd first met Holden, he seemed uninterested in trying to find the truth. His life had become about staying off the grid and surviving day to day. She saw this as progress, good progress toward him reclaiming life.

"We'll grab a motel room in San Antonio," he continued. "See what we can come up with on a computer. I have a few tricks up my sleeve and by the time anyone figures out the IP address, we'll be long gone."

Ella nodded. "When do we leave?"

"Now," he said.

"MIND IF I stretch my legs before we sit on that bike for a few hours?" Ella asked, those cornflower blue eyes breaking down his walls.

"Not as long as I can go with you. I can use a walk," he said. Food was done, dishes were handled and he'd wiped the place clean of fingerprints. He had no intention of letting her out of his sight again after the sedan incident.

"It feels like we're a long way from answers." Ella started toward the trees and he followed.

"Which is why we have to change our approach," he said. Part of him wanted to hunker down right where they were and take a minute to catch his breath. Their luck wouldn't last forever. Ella Butler was big news and it seemed like everyone had a camera and a social media account ready to post news in a few clicks. He couldn't leave her alone and taking her with him to get supplies was risky. In the late-August Texas heat she wouldn't survive for long, and if he took her completely off the grid, they wouldn't know when it was safe for her to come home. Unlike him, she had a life worth returning to. Was that the reason he felt especially drawn to her?

It had been so easy for him to disappear. There was no one counting on him, no one expecting him to come back. No one except Rose, Ella would argue. She'd be right, too. He hadn't realized what this was doing to Rose until he'd seen the worry lines etched in her face.

As for Ella, she deserved to get back to her ranch and the land she loved so much. She was doing important work whereas he'd felt like a drifter since returning to the United States from the action overseas. Time had provided perspective and, looking back, he could see that he'd kept everyone at arm's length. Maybe his and Karen's relationship could've gone somewhere if he'd let her in. But that only made the guilt worse. She'd died because she'd been in his home at the wrong time. Holden knew there'd been a cover-up, but why? Questions he hadn't allowed himself to ask in two years started surfacing.

"Where are you from originally? You don't have an accent, so I can't place you," Ella said, breaking into his heavy thoughts as they walked.

"I'm from everywhere," he supplied.

She shot him a look.

"Military brat," he said.

"I already know that. You had to have been born somewhere," she countered.

"Colorado Springs," he said.

She responded by cocking an eyebrow.

"It's the truth," he said, holding his hands up in the universal sign of surrender.

She increased her pace, moving farther from the tiny

house that had felt like a temporary home. A little voice said it felt like that because of Ella.

"What?" he asked. "Am I doing it again?"

"Doing what?"

"I already told you that it's been a while since I've had a real conversation with another human being. I also plainly stated that I'm no good at it to begin with—"

This time her hands came up to stop him.

"You're doing better than you think," she said. "I wouldn't even be alive right now if it wasn't for you. Thank you for everything you're doing for me. I can see that it's taking you out of your comfort zone and putting you in danger and I just want you to know that I appreciate it."

Holden stayed quiet for a long time. A thousand thoughts raced through his head. He finally settled on "You're welcome."

Ella swatted at a bug as she stomped ahead with a smile. "Did you spend much time in Colorado?"

"Not really. We moved every couple of years, so I never really got attached to one place," he continued.

"That must've been hard in high school." She glanced at him.

"I managed to get out with a diploma. Although I'm not sure how. I got into trouble. Guess you could say I was a brat." Holden grinned.

"I doubt it," she said, rewarding him with another small smile that was sweet and sexy at the same time. "At least this partly explains why you're so self-reliant."

"All my self-reliance can make me difficult to get

along with," he warned, and she immediately made a sound.

"I have noticed that you can be—"

"Stubborn."

"Determined," she corrected. "But your skills and knowledge have been useful in keeping me alive, so I'm not about to complain. Even if you can be a little blunt at times."

Holden grunted. "Say what you mean. I'm a jerk."

Ella stopped and turned to look at him. She fisted her right hand and rested it on her hip as she seemed to study his features.

"Are you always this hard on yourself?" She stared into his eyes when he didn't respond. "Never mind. I can already tell the answer to that question. Yes."

"We should get on the road," Holden said. Talking about himself, opening up to another person, was foreign. Especially since it was so easy to do with Ella.

"Okay," she responded. "But first you should know that you always change the subject when I try to talk about you."

"There really isn't much to tell," he said, and she made another one of those harrumph noises that sounded like it tore straight from her throat.

"I could probably write a book about your experiences," she said. "And I'm pretty sure the least exciting thing in your life would be more thrilling than anything I've ever done."

Holden caught her stare and intensified his gaze. "I could tell you everything about my past. But then I'd have to kill you."

Silence stretched on between them in a checkmate. Until Holden burst out laughing and then she did, too.

"You didn't believe that load of nonsense, did you?" he teased as she swatted his arm.

"Only because I know you were in the military and I assume most of what you did there is classified," she said.

She reached out to swat him again and he caught her hand in his, ignoring her delicate, silky skin.

"At least you know I have a sense of humor now," he said, figuring touching her had been another mistake. His were racking up. He hoped it wasn't a mistake to dig into the past, too. This was the first time in two years he could let himself hope to find answers and bring justice to the person behind the murders.

"You call that funny?" She withdrew her hand.

"I thought it was," he said.

"You really have been alone for a long time." She looked indignant right before her face broke into a wide smile. "See. I can do it, too."

Holden didn't hold back his laugh. "We should head back and then get on the road."

"Think I can check in with my family again?" she asked. "Might be able to fill in the gaps in my memory."

His first response would be *hell no*. But the sorrow mixed with hope in her eyes made him think twice.

"We'll look online first. If anything happened to one of your family members, it would be news," he said. "And then we'll play it by ear."

He wasn't exactly promising her contact but knowing everyone was okay would ease some of her stress. He wanted to give her that much.

She twined their fingers and he didn't stop her even though alarm bells sounded off at her touch.

The campsite wasn't more than twenty yards away. As they neared the clearing, Holden heard noises. He stopped and listened, squeezing Ella's hand to catch her attention. He motioned for her to crouch down and then bit back a curse.

Moving stealthily along the tree line, Holden kept diligent watch ahead. Had the teens been a cover, or had they alerted someone to his and Ella's presence? His friend who owned the place wasn't coming back. As they neared, he heard banging on the door.

"David?" an unfamiliar male voice said. "Are you home?"

Holden navigated him and Ella around the woods so that they could get a look at the front door. Branches snapped as Ella moved and that would give them away to a trained ear. No way was he separating the two of them no matter how much noise she made. As it was his heart pounded his rib cage and all his muscles chorded, thinking someone might've found them.

Moving through the underbrush, Holden positioned them so that they could see the front door. A male figure, thin, wearing dress slacks and a collared shirt with short sleeves stood there. He was holding something in his hands and had to reposition it, balancing the bundle against his arm and side in order to free his hand and knock.

The situation looked innocent enough but Holden

wasn't taking any chances when it came to Ella. He held her hand and watched for suspicious activity from the intruder.

After a few more rounds of knocking without an answer, the older man set down the bundle and reclaimed the driver's seat of his vintage Ford pickup. A minute later, there was only dust settling along the drive.

Holden waited just in case the old man returned.

When enough time had passed, he stood. "Stay right here until I give a signal."

"Who was that?" she whispered, her eyes wide.

"Probably a neighbor thinking that David had come home, but I need to check the contents of that package before you get anywhere near it." His tone was emphatic.

"What if something happens to you, Holden? Where does that leave me?" She made a good point. Without him, she had little chance of survival.

"Okay. Together." He linked their fingers and realized immediately that she was trembling. He never would've known she was scared based on her calm exterior. Ella Butler knew how to put on a brave face.

Holden picked up a branch and moved slowly toward the package, measuring his steps carefully. "We treat this like a ticking bomb, okay?"

"Got it," Ella replied. Her palm was sweaty, so he gave her hand a squeeze for reassurance.

"We'll be fine." He moved with precision toward the object. As he neared, he saw the small box filled with what looked like produce. Brightly colored apples, bananas and zucchinis peeked over the rim.

Holden maintained as safe a distance as he could. He didn't specialize in bombs but it didn't take a specialist to know being this close to one wasn't the smartest idea. He tossed a stick at the box.

Thankfully, nothing happened.

"We're good," he said. But they weren't. Just because they'd dodged a bullet this time didn't mean they would the next.

Holden needed to keep that thought close to his heart as they moved into a more densely populated area.

Nowhere was safe.

Chapter Thirteen

The motel not too far from State Highway 151 was sparse but had all the basics—two beds and a decent shower. The best part was that they could pay with cash and Holden seemed to have more than enough to cover the bill.

"I hope you'll let me repay you for all of this," Ella said, grateful for clean clothes, hard walls and a shower. With Holden, she never knew what to expect, and she could admit there was an excitement about that.

He shot her a look that said he wouldn't.

She started to argue but he brought his hand up.

"I haven't done much of anything for anyone for the past twenty-five months, so no arguments," he said with a tone that said it wouldn't do any good to protest.

And on some level, she understood. She would figure out a way to thank him because he'd gone above and beyond anything she could ever expect. It was a foreign feeling being on the other end of someone's kindness. Ella had always been the one taking charge and thinking of everyone else. Maybe she could take what she was learning back to the ranch with her and allow others to do more to pitch in. It had felt like the weight of the world rested on her shoulders her entire life.

"The guy at the front desk said there's an internet café a couple of miles from here open until 2:00 a.m.," he said.

"What kind of place is open that late?" she asked almost to herself as she pulled her hair off her face and into a ponytail. It was barely dark, so without looking at the clock Ella knew that it must be after eight o'clock.

"We'll see."

THE PLACE WAS actually a hookah lounge. The atmosphere was perfect for going unnoticed. It was dark inside and surprisingly not as smoky as she'd expected. There were small round tables with pillows on the floor. And the place was filled with what looked like college-aged kids who were chatting in between taking puffs off the hookahs positioned in the center of their tables. Ella had never been to one before but she knew others who frequented them in college. Come to think of it, Ella hadn't done much socializing in the four years she'd attended university, and she'd gone to a state school legendary for its parties. She'd never once thought about letting loose and having a good time. Her life had been filled with purpose and she'd always been an overachiever. A thought struck. Had she been trying to find her worth in being the perfect student? The perfect daughter? The perfect sister?

The revelation caught her off guard. She loved the ranch but had she thrown herself into her job so that she could win approval from her dad? The realization knocked her back a step mentally.

"How many?" the hostess said with a smile, interrupting Ella's thoughts. The young woman, maybe twenty, had beautiful dark hair and wore a jeweled dot on her forehead. She batted long dark lashes at Holden and Ella bristled.

"Just the two of us," he said, then added, "and we'll need access to a computer."

She smiled up at him, a mix of courtesy and flirting. Couldn't she see Ella standing right there? Technically, she and Holden weren't a couple, but this woman didn't know it by the looks of them. They *could* be a couple and this woman was being rude.

"Follow me," she said with a silky voice.

Ella rolled her eyes.

Holden laced their fingers and she noticed he was scanning the room as they walked, a sobering reminder of the danger they were in being out in public. Suddenly, she felt silly for being jealous of the hostess. Was that what she was? Jealous?

Ella sighed sharply.

It had been a long week. She was fatigued and sad and had had a personal revelation that still had her mind spinning. Honestly, she was scared no matter how much she didn't want to own up to it. The nightmare that had started with her father's murder and extended to her present situation wouldn't end and it felt like the stakes were growing with every passing day.

"How's this?" the hostess asked, beaming up at Holden.

"Fine." He barely seemed to notice that she was

standing right next to him inside his personal space. Most would consider that rude but Ella decided that it was a cultural thing and not meant to rile her.

"Can I get you anything to drink?" Her gaze dropped to their linked hands and her smile faded just a touch.

A satisfied smile crept across Ella's lips.

"Water for now," he said. "We'll order off the menu after she's had a chance to look over the options."

"Fine," the hostess said before giving Ella a quick acknowledgment and then disappearing.

Ella took a seat at the bar stool facing the wall. Holden glanced around and mumbled something. Best as she could tell, he didn't like the idea that their backs were to the door. He repositioned the chairs so that they could both easily see the screen. His was more to the side, positioned so that he could keep watch on the door.

Holden handed Ella a menu.

"An Americano sounds fantastic," she said, referring to a shot of espresso topped off with hot water.

"We should probably order something for that," he motioned toward the hookah.

Ella scanned the menu. "Sour apple sounds good."

The hostess returned with two glasses of water. Holden relayed their hookah and drink orders—his was strong black coffee—and then he waited for Ella to make a decision on food.

Everything on the menu looked amazing, or maybe Ella was just starving.

"Gyro sandwich," she finally decided.

Holden ordered the same.

The hostess nodded, gave a curt smile and scribbled down their orders on a small pad of paper.

"Do you remember having any arguments with anyone, specifically during any of your meetings?" he asked as soon as the hostess disappeared.

"I honestly can't say anything sticks out. I mean, people fight back all the time over personal gain. It feels like there's something right there—" she motioned toward her forehead "—but every time I think too hard, I get a headache."

"Effects from the blow you took. If I'd been there five minutes sooner I could've saved you all this," he said with a look of frustration. He might've been able to interrupt whoever did this to her but he would've exposed his presence and put himself in more danger, so she was glad that he hadn't in some respects.

"I've been thinking about the shotgun," he said. "Most people have one beside the bed."

"Which means it could've been anyone," she said.

"Exactly."

"Why is that a good thing?" she asked.

"Because it means we're not dealing with a professional. The guys after me would use a Glock or a weapon that is more precise. I would never see them coming because they wouldn't have to get close enough to hit the mark. They're skilled shooters whereas the person who shot at you couldn't hit you at close range," he surmised.

"Okay, but what about one of my father's exes?" she asked.

"I've been thinking about that," he admitted. "The

person who killed your father wanted to make a statement. That could indicate someone angry, vengeful. So, the person kills him and wants everyone to know how mad he or she is. Hurting you doesn't have the same impact because your father wouldn't be around to see it."

"Meaning if this was a revenge killing against my father, they'd save him for last?" she asked.

"Yes," he said. "The first attempt on your life was meant to look like an accident, like you fell and died."

"He goes back to find a body and doesn't. So he sets up and waits," she said. "But the second time around he doesn't care because he figures I'm going to turn him in."

"At that point, he just wants to get rid of you," he said. "He figures that he's got nothing to lose because if you make it to the sheriff, you turn him in. Think you can remember anything about the man in the mask? Height? Weight?" Holden's fingers went to work on the keyboard.

"If my brain will cooperate, I'll do my best." Ella stilled when the hostess returned.

"Do you have a sheet of paper and a pen?" Holden asked, pulling out his wad of money and peeling off a twenty.

"I'll find something in the manager's office," she said, taking the offering with a grateful smile. Ella was pretty certain the woman winked. Wasn't there a waiter in the place? Why did the hostess have to keep coming back? And she did return not two minutes later with a pad of paper and a pen. When she handed the offering to Holden, she brushed her fingers against his arm.

Ella was starting to see red.

"Excuse me," she said curtly. "Those are for me."

Holden gave her a bewildered look. Surely he hadn't been off the grid so long that he didn't recognize when a woman was practically throwing herself at him.

The hostess walked away with a frown.

"I can't believe how rude that woman is being," Ella said.

A quick glance at Holden burned in her belly because he must've caught on and now he was smirking.

"All I'm saying is that it's bad manners to be so obvious," she defended. "And we don't need the distraction with everything else we have going on."

"Are you jealous?" he asked. "Because I'm fairly certain the woman was trying to be nice."

Ella's gaze caught on the ten-digit number scribbled across the top of the page along with the woman's name. She held up the notepad. "And what do you think this is doing on here?"

A bemused Holden broke out into a smile. "Guess you were right."

"I'm not blind," she said. "And she was being so obvious."

The door opened behind her and Holden's smile disappeared. Ella followed his gaze and saw a lively group of college-aged kids walk inside. Holden's relief was almost palpable and this was a good reminder of the tension.

"I don't like putting all these kids in danger with our presence," he said, demonstrating once again that he put others first. Holden might see himself as selfish but she wished that he could see the real him, the man she saw.

"I don't either," she agreed.

"Let's speed things along so we can get out of here." Holden motioned toward the screen in front of them. His left thigh was positioned on the outside of her right, effectively providing a barrier between her and everyone else. The denim material of his jeans against her leg sent volts of electricity at the point of contact.

He did it without thinking, with such ease, yet the dark circles cradling his eyes told another story. He must be exhausted even if he'd never admit it.

Ella tried to ignore the sexual magnetism pulsing between them with contact. When the hostess returned with food she seemed to pick up on it, too. She shot an embarrassed look Ella's way.

At this point, she was too hungry and worried to stress over a little flirting. Holden was a gorgeous man, tall, built like a brick wall, but his body didn't feel like one. When her skin was pressed against his it was the feeling of silk over steel. He was sex appeal and masculinity and resourcefulness wrapped together in one seriously hot package.

A dangerous package.

HOLDEN DRUMMED HIS fingers on the keyboard and then hit Enter.

Maverick Mike's murder still pervaded the headlines.

"My brothers and sister seem to be safe." Ella sighed. "Nothing is going on at the ranch."

Holden entered a new search, using only her last name.

"What's this?" she asked, scanning the stories. "Two men have shown up in town claiming to be heirs."

"Looks like your long-lost brethren are giving interviews," Holden said, pulling up the site running the stories.

"He looks nothing like us," Ella said of the first person who popped onto the screen.

"The amount of money your father owns will bring out a lot of crazy," Holden said, watching as the man claimed Maverick Mike had had an affair with his mother that had produced a son, him. The journalist conceded that the accuser had declined a DNA test to confirm.

The second accuser agreed to a test, but only on his terms. He said he'd bring in his own, whatever that meant.

"I'm pretty sure these guys aren't being taken seriously," Holden said.

"Could either one of them have tried to kill me?" she asked.

"Anything's possible. Your father has enough money that even if it was divided between either or both of these yahoos there'd be more than enough to go around," he added. "I doubt they'd target each of you individually if they wanted to take it all. They'd most likely set a bomb and take all of you out at once. But then that would be too easy, as well."

Ella shuddered.

"Sorry. It must be strange for a civilian to hear someone talk about life and death so casually," he said. "We got used to it in the military. Doesn't lessen the effect of your actions. But I learned to compartmentalize the missions by becoming numb to the words."

"It's okay," she said but her voice was a little shaky. "I'm just still trying to wrap my thoughts around the fact that any of this is happening. Before my father died, my biggest concern was making sure that I secured funding for the new animal shelter being proposed and now death just rolls off my tongue."

"Do either of them match the size of the man who tried to shoot you?" Holden asked.

"This one is too big. I would've remembered someone who looked like he should be a defensive end on a football field."

Holden's dark brows drew together.

"What is it?" she asked.

"You didn't mention the animal shelter before," he said, turning toward the screen.

"I must've forgotten. I don't know if it's from the hit I took or just stress in general," she said.

Holden pulled up a map of Cattle Barge. "Can you tell me where the proposed site is?"

"Yeah, sure." Her look said she had no idea what he was getting at. She took over, zooming the map into a location east of downtown. "There. Right there."

"What's around it?" he asked. "Anything interesting?"

"Pilsner Lake isn't far." She pointed it out on the map. "We have a cleanup project going on there. People love to use the lake and the adjacent park but don't feel the need to clean up after themselves. We get a lot of debris on the beaches and animals are getting sick off the rusting cans tossed around."

"Whose property surrounds the proposed shelter site?" he asked.

"Mr. Suffolk," she said. "Why?"

"Is he against the building being so close to his property?" he asked.

"Not him so much but his son has been cranky about it. Says it'll be too noisy and bother his father," she supplied. "It won't. He's just being difficult. Old Man Suffolk's house is all the way over here."

Ella pointed to a spot on the west end of the property.

Holden leaned back in his chair and brought his index finger to his lips. "Wish we could talk to the old man."

"I guess that's out of the question given our current situation," she said. "Seems like he and my father butted heads from time to time. I might not be his favorite person but I doubt he'd want me dead."

He nodded.

"Are you the only one pushing this project?" he asked.

"Mainly, I guess. Without my support it wouldn't make it far but none of these initiatives would," she admitted. "There was talk of him selling his property a little while ago but I think that's off the table."

Holden needed to figure out a way to talk to the Suffolk family.

Ella tensed as someone approached from behind.

"Hour's almost up," the male voice said.

"Thanks for the heads-up," Holden said to the waiter.

Holden typed his name and a moment of hesitation struck as he wondered what would fill the screen when he hit Enter.

His mind hadn't strayed from the numbers Rose had given to him, 1-9-6-4. Talking about Pop had reminded Holden how much he loved fishing and camping. It was probably just a random thought but it was sticking in his mind for some reason. Maybe there'd be something to point him in the right direction out of the dozens of articles that had popped up in the search engine along with several pictures of him, most of which were in his battle fatigues. Where'd they come up with those pictures? He scanned the stories, noting the strong emphasis on him being ex-military and considered armed and dangerous. Stories like these would bring out all types of bounty hunters hungry for a reward. In his case, it was substantial. Two hundred and fifty thousand dollars were being offered for his safe return to Hampshire Police. That kind of cash would bring people with guns out of the woodwork to hunt him down. No wonder it had always felt like eyes were on him, like he was constantly being watched.

"That seems high," Ella said almost under her breath.

"It is," Holden agreed. He read other headlines. Ex-Marine/Killer Suffers Signs of PTSD.

If the news affected Ella, she hid it well.

"This is untrue," she said hotly. "I don't know that much about PTSD except that you've been around gunfire and I'm pretty sure you would've had some kind of reaction. You have no nightmares, which I've read are part of it. Plus, all the stress we've been under would've triggered something. You're the most calm and collected man I've ever known."

Her indignant tone brought a wave of relief. Holden didn't want her to believe the lies that had been spread about him. For some odd reason that mattered a great deal.

"I thought journalists had a responsibility to print the truth," she huffed.

He covered her hand with his and she looked at him. Those penetrating blue eyes, the ones capable of seeing past the facade to the real him, searched his face.

"Thank you." His throat dried and he had to resist the urge to lean toward her as her tongue darted across her lips. "Your confidence means a lot."

Her eyes darkened as she held his gaze.

"I've been around you long enough to know this is fiction," she said. "You're kind and giving and nothing like the picture painted with these articles."

Well, hell, those words did it. Holden dipped his head and kissed her moist mouth anyway. She'd just taken a drink of her Americano and tasted like coffee.

He caught someone walking toward them out of the corner of his eye. He put his arm around Ella and turned to acknowledge the figure moving their way. Relief washed over him when he saw that it was the hostess.

"Everything taste okay here?" she asked with a glance toward the hookah pipe.

Holden didn't acknowledge the irony there.

"Perfect." And he meant that about Ella. She was the most giving person he'd met. She'd grown up with every privilege but it didn't show. She was down-to-earth and put others' needs first.

The hostess smiled and told them to call for her if they needed anything else.

Holden picked up the mouthpiece as he thanked her. They didn't have to smoke but they did need to put on a better show. He touched it to his lips and then handed it to her. She did the same.

"We should eat," he said as soon as the hostess was out of earshot.

Ella's plate was cleaned and her mug was drained ten minutes later.

"Maybe I can call the sheriff and see if he found any evidence at the scene," she said.

"There should be shell casings," he agreed.

"Is it risky to call from here?" she asked.

"We'll pick up a throwaway phone at a convenience store tonight on our way out of San Antonio. That way you can call in the morning when we're on the road. We'll set out north, make the call and then double back south once you find out what else the sheriff knows," he said.

"He might've solved the case by now and we wouldn't know." Ella motioned toward the screen.

"Are you kidding? You and your family are news." His fingers pounded the keyboard and she saw that he was typing her name.

Socialite Believed to Be Dead read the headline. She stared at the screen. The article went on to say that a substantial amount of her blood had been found at the scene of a shooting and a blood trail ended in neighboring bushes. The suspect was still on the loose. The last line in the article read that her body had not been located and the sheriff's office wouldn't close the investigation until he found answers.

"I spoke to Sheriff Sawmill. There's no way a story like this should run. Why would he say something like this?"

Holden studied the screen. "The way this article reads, the journalist suggested you were dead and the sheriff didn't correct him or her. I'm sure he has reasons for allowing the public to buy into that nonsense."

"May must be worried sick. She reads the paper every day," Ella said. "I can't even imagine what the others in my family must be thinking, my friends."

"We'll get word to May. Let's hope the others aren't watching the news," he said.

"They probably aren't. They've been avoiding the media and I'm sure they won't want to read all the stories that will come out about our father." Ella's gaze narrowed. "I'll never believe another thing I read online again. I had no idea there were so many lies and untruths."

"Agreed. And I don't like seeing this any more than you do, but this is good news for us," Holden said. "The person responsible for the attempts on your life will most likely let his guard down now."

"What if he's smarter than that?" she asked. "What if he realizes that I'm alive and is waiting for me, biding his time?"

"This guy makes a lot of assumptions and mistakes," he stated.

"Truc." She seemed to catch on to what he was really saying, that if this guy was any smarter, she'd already be dead. "Think we can go back to Cattle Barge if I put on something to cover up my face?"

He remembered why fishing with Pop had stuck in his mind a few minutes ago. Rose had mentioned his father bringing up fishing. It might mean nothing but Holden wanted to explore it anyway. There was a place the two of them always returned to. Maybe something was there?

"There's something I need to do in Colorado first," he said. "We need to go there before we do anything else. I need to look through my father's personal items. My father gave Rose the message 1-9-6-4 for a reason, and we might find answers in his belongings. Are you good with that?"

"I'm all in, Holden."

Chapter Fourteen

"I think my arms are actually going to fall off." Ella gladly climbed off the back of the yellow-and-chrome motorcycle. She shook her hands and wiggled her arms, trying to get blood flowing again. They'd stopped off every few hours on the ride to Colorado for coffee and snacks but hadn't slept.

Holden took off his helmet and cracked a smile that didn't reach his eyes. "You didn't enjoy the open road?"

"I've been on the back of that bike more than I ever want to be on the back of anything ever again. I don't even think I could get on another ATV now." Ella bit back the urge to complain about the fact that they were in a remote area. Granted, it was beautiful. The landscape was filled with dogwood, birch and towering oak trees. She recognized the scent of Douglas firs and it made her think of Christmases back home with her dad. Her heart ached at the thought she would never get to spend another holiday with him. Sadness overwhelmed her and she had to move. Walking helped her refocus on what needed to be done instead of on the hole in her chest when she thought about her father.

The last road sign she'd read said they were in a town called Newburg. Holden had parked near a shed that looked like it could house a minivan. It was old and looked abandoned from outside appearances. She figured this was the perfect location for hiding valuables. The sun would dip below the mountains soon and darkness was imminent. The small shed didn't look to have any power running to it and there was no sign of a light bulb.

"How long do we have before we run out of daylight?" she asked.

"Not long. I'm hoping that the flashlight app on the throwaway I bought will suffice." He'd bought one of those pay-as-you-go cell phones at a gas station convenience store that couldn't be traced back to him.

"I'm guessing there are boxes or containers in there," she said.

"This is where we used to keep camping supplies." The hollow note to his voice reminded her that he hadn't allowed himself a chance to grieve. Work and staying busy were good for sorrow, but bottling up emotions was dangerous.

Ella couldn't imagine that going through his father's personal items was going to be easy for Holden. She couldn't even begin to fathom going through her father's. She and her siblings would have to face that task at some point and she dreaded it with everything inside her. "What are we looking for?"

"Good question." Holden pulled out a small satchel from underneath the seat of his motorcycle and retrieved a key from it. He unlocked the storage shed and opened the doors. The entire building could house a minivan and that was about it.

Boxes were stacked floor to ceiling with a little room for walking to the left. The two of them wouldn't fit inside, not with Holden's sizable build. The idea of climbing in there with spiders and possibly field mice made Ella shiver, so she would let Holden do the honors.

"You don't have to go in there." Holden stood there, looking like he wasn't quite ready to cross that threshold either.

"I'll be fine. In case you hadn't noticed, I grew up on a ranch." She wanted to spare him but knew there wasn't much she could do.

"Right. I did know that," he said. All humor was gone from his eyes and he looked like he was staring at a ghost.

"We don't have to do this today," she offered. "We could grab a room. I saw a town an hour ago. We could eat and you could have a cold drink."

"We're already here." There was a somber quality to his tone. "We might as well get started."

"Is it safe to be here?" she asked.

"If anyone knew about this place, the boxes would already be gone," he informed.

"I can get a box. Step aside," she cautioned as she moved past him. She was pretty sure something moved in the grass next to her and she almost chickened out until she took another look at his face; his eyes were so intent. Her legs felt like she was walking on rubber bands and her stomach clenched, but she forged ahead like nothing was wrong.

He hesitated for a second and then pulled out the first box. "It's light." He opened the top. "Clothes." He picked up a couple other boxes. "Same in here. I doubt we'll find what we're looking for in any of these."

"We can keep going until we find something. I'm sure 1-9-6-4 will make sense when we see it," she said, not sure what *it* was.

"Pop always talked about buying land and building a house in Colorado. He wanted to be closer to Rose so the two of them could keep each other company as they grew old." Holden opened another box. "Maybe he moved some of his valuables here to prepare. He never really talked about retiring but he'd never really talked much about his moving business."

"I'm guessing no one knows about this property," she said.

"Rose would've said something before if she had any idea." He lined up a few boxes on the ground.

Ella began with the one on the end and he moved to the other side.

Carefully, she examined the box for any creepy-crawly bugs that might be lurking inside and especially for anything that might be venomous now that her radar was up.

"We have no idea what we're looking for." Frustration edged his tone.

"We'll know it when we see it," she reassured.

Light had faded and it was hard to see inside the boxes. Ella didn't feel great about sticking her hand inside them in the dark.

"Hold this." Holden held out the throwaway phone.

Ella took it.

"Position it this way," he said, moving her hand.

He moved back to the box he'd been working on. He pulled out two heavy-duty bags by their handles. He set them down in between two tall fir trees.

"What are those?" Ella followed him, positioning the light so he could see what he was doing.

"You'll see." He didn't look up as he unzipped the first and pulled out a bundle.

"That a tent?" Ella had no plans to sleep in there. She hadn't done that since she was a little girl out with her brothers.

"Better. I have a pair of sleeping hammocks." He seemed pretty pleased with himself but they were losing light and her sense of humor was fading along with her energy.

Ella bit back a yawn. Exhaustion made her wish she had toothpicks to prop her eyes open with.

"How tired are you?" he asked.

"There's no end." Her arms had felt like dead weight hours ago on the bike and it would take days to recover.

"You can get some sleep as soon as I get these up." There was no sign of him making a joke.

"You're kidding, right?" She hoped.

"Why? They're still in good shape," he said.

"Because I'll be mosquito food," she stated. "Are there no motels in Colorado? I could've sworn we passed a couple on the highway before our exit."

"Don't worry. These have nets and we'll be safer if we stay away from major roads. No one knows about this place and I have power bars and water in my backpack to keep us from going hungry. They'll get us through the night and morning, when we can finish going through the boxes. We're about to lose light and we should probably save phone battery." He hooked a rope around one of the firs and then secured it with some Boy Scout maneuver she'd seen one of her brothers do when they were kids.

She couldn't argue with his logic. It would most likely be safe for them out here in what felt like the wilderness even if the place did give her the creeps. Living on a ranch was a different beast. Ella was used to wide-open skies after growing up at Hereford. Colorado was beautiful, but it also felt a little claustrophobic with the thick layers of tall trees.

"It'll be good. You'll see," he reassured when she didn't respond.

"I'm sure it will," she said without much conviction. "Want some help?"

He nodded.

Her vision was blurring and sleep, even out here, sounded better than a steak dinner about now.

"Hold here," he said and his fingers brushed hers. He moved next to her and she could feel his masculine presence.

Being out here with no one and nothing besides each other made her miss the ranch. She couldn't remember the last time she'd wanted to leave Hereford, but it had to have been college. She'd gone to state school to be close to home. *Home.* Ella wished she and Holden were there now.

But what was home to him?

She couldn't even imagine this being his life for the past two years. She thought about how alone he must've been feeling, must still feel, being away from everything and everyone he cared about for so long. Two years could seem like an eternity. So much could change.

Holden moved away from her and she immediately felt his absence.

"Thanks for everything you've done for me," she said. "I realize you have a lot going on with your father's case, and yet you're still helping me."

He waved her off like it was nothing. But it wasn't. And when this was all over she would figure out a way to show her appreciation.

After tying off the ropes and ensuring their hammocks were secure, Holden went to work building a fire. His movements were swift and there was a certain athletic grace to them, his muscles tensed and stretched against the cotton fabric of his sweatshirt.

Ella redirected her thoughts. No use going down that road again, the one that had her attracted to a man whose past would always haunt him.

Although the landscape looked completely different, being outdoors reminded her of home. She sat down in front of the campfire. Everything about Hereford reminded her of her father and, once again, she couldn't believe he was gone. Holding on to her knees, she rocked back and forth.

"EVERYTHING ALL RIGHT?" Holden dropped down beside Ella and handed her a power bar and bottle of water.

"I miss him," she said, and he could see tears streaming down her cheeks in the glow of the campfire. She hugged her legs even tighter. "Everything's been happening so fast that my brain hasn't had time to process the fact that when I go home he won't be there. He's never coming back."

"I'm sorry." Those were the only two words he could think to say and they fell short of what he wanted to communicate.

"He was larger than life. He was just this huge presence. You know? And now there'll be a gaping hole in his place at the ranch," she managed while fighting off sobs threatening to suck her under. "I can't imagine life on Hereford without him, and that's exactly what I'm going back to. A life where he doesn't exist. Going through your father's belongings made me realize that I'll be doing the same thing very soon."

"He sounds like he was a good man underneath it all. I have a lot of respect for him," Holden said. He knew firsthand what it was like to lose a father, and that meant he also knew there was nothing that he could say to take away the pain. Instead of issuing empty words, he put his arm around her and drew her close. She responded by leaning into him.

"He was," she said quietly.

To say the day had been difficult was a lot like saying bears had fur. Being around his father's things brought back all kinds of memories, most of them good. Hell, Pop's clothes still smelled like him.

Being here made Holden feel close to Pop, in a way. Holden remembered the first time his father had taken him fishing. He'd caught a large-mouth bass twice the size of his fist and they'd gone most every weekend until Holden reached the age hanging out with his old man on the weekends wasn't cool. Then they'd gone on holidays like Father's Day and Fourth of July. Forget barbecuing hamburgers—they'd clean the fish they caught and toss them around in batter. They'd fill up on fried catfish until neither could walk. There'd been hard times, too.

Growing up without a constant feminine presence, save for occasionally spending time with Rose, had brought its own set of challenges. Holden couldn't help but notice the similarities between his father and Ella's in that regard. The men were completely different but each did his best to bring up his family.

Despite any hardships, Ella had turned out all right. It couldn't have been easy for a girl to grow up without a mother. Nurses and caretakers only went so far. But she'd grown into a caring, intelligent, giving woman. *Beautiful woman*, a little voice felt the need to remind him. He wouldn't argue. She deserved better than this.

For tonight he was pleased that she had a soft hammock, warm covers and food in her stomach.

THE SOUND OF twigs breaking underneath shoes woke Holden with a start. He glanced around quickly, gaining his bearings. He didn't mention to Ella that black bears can be up to nine feet tall and weigh in at close to seven hundred pounds.

He closed his eyes and listened.

The twig snaps grew louder, indicating that the snapper was heading toward their campsite.

Holden moved into action, swiftly and quietly. He was at Ella's side in a heartbeat, gently shaking her.

Her eyes opened and he said, "Someone's coming. It's okay."

He deliberately said someone and not some*thing*. Startle her and she might panic, drawing unwanted attention toward them. "We need to move away from camp as fast as possible."

She nodded and bolted into action, throwing off the blanket he'd placed on her last night. He handed her her shoes and she put them on and laced them up in a snap.

The sounds were getting closer and this time he heard voices. It was a relief on some note because that meant they weren't about to encounter a bear. However, people often turned out to be far more dangerous than wildlife. Wildlife made sense. They simply followed the natural order and acted according to laws of nature and their DNA's programming. Humans were unpredictable.

"What is it?" Ella whispered, and the sound of her voice first thing in the morning stirred dormant places inside him that he couldn't afford to let wake. Not when everything in his life was uncertain.

"Hikers," he said. "I need to get a closer look to evaluate the threat. I'm not leaving you here alone."

"Okay." She yawned. "Let's go."

"Stay low and close," he said.

He led her into the woods, far beyond the hikers. He wanted to come up on them from a different angle, from behind. And especially so that he could draw them away from camp.

There were two males and a female. They were chatting easily and looked to be in their early twenties. They were dressed like L.L. Bean models and the female had a black bandana tied around her head. Their hiking boots were clean, which meant they'd just been bought or didn't get taken out much.

Holden looked at Ella and whispered, "Follow my lead."

She smiled her response.

He took her hand, stood up straight and said, "It's chillier this morning than I expected even at this altitude."

"I know, right?" She beamed at him as he made an effort to stomp through the underbrush toward a path. "Brrr."

"Oh, hey. Morning," Holden said to the trio as he and Ella approached.

"Morning," the female said as the guys nodded and smiled. She had dark hair in twin braids running halfway down her torso. Up close, the guys looked to be nineteen or twenty at the most. His estimate of the group being college coeds seemed to be spot-on.

"Been up here long?" he asked.

"Aiden had the bright idea to wake up at four this morning," one of the guys said. "I'm Patrick, by the way. And this is Keisha."

Holden shook hands with each of the guys and then Keisha offered her hand. The group exchanged perfunctory greetings before Holden laced his fingers with Ella's.

"We ran into a park ranger a mile or so back. He said to watch out for black bears. A big one was spotted heading south," Holden lied. He pointed almost directly toward camp.

Ella's hand tensed. She must not have considered the possibility of bears last night, and that was probably for the best. Holden had learned that being stressed about danger didn't make it go away. Stress was an unnecessary distraction on a mission. All a man needed was enough fear to keep him sharp and give him a clear mind and the confidence that he could handle whatever he faced.

Damn, it dawned on him that he'd strayed far from the one philosophy that had kept him alive through countless missions as a marine. As soon as he figured out what the men after him wanted and who was ultimately behind the murders, he had every intention of reclaiming his life.

"How big?" Keisha asked.

"Maybe eight feet tall and close to six hundred pounds," Holden stated.

"Thanks for the heads-up, man," Aiden said with wide eyes as he repositioned his body east. "We'll keep watch."

"The ranger said we should make a lot of noise," Holden added.

"Cool. Good idea." Patrick paused, his gaze landing on Ella. "Do I know you?"

"I doubt it," Ella said a little too quickly, giving away her nervous tension.

Patrick's eyebrow shot up as he studied her face. "I know I've seen you before."

Chapter Fifteen

Holden squeezed Ella's fingers for reassurance. All she had to do was breathe and she'd be fine.

"I'm not from around here," she clarified, and that seemed to satisfy the coeds for the time being.

They turned to face the same direction as Patrick.

"Wouldn't hurt to find a big stick and carry it with you just in case you run into that bear," Holden said, turning in the opposite direction, west.

"Thanks for the tips," Patrick said. His gaze was fixed on Ella. "I could swear that I've seen you before. Have you been on TV?"

"Me? TV?" She shook her head and laughed. "Nah."

Patrick seemed to accept the answer but the puzzled look stayed on his face. He was scanning his memory for where he'd seen her before and that wasn't good.

"Keep watch out for that bear," Holden reminded, trying to distract Patrick.

"You got it. You, too," Patrick said before shaking his head and refocusing on his group.

When the trio disappeared, Ella exhaled.

"That was close," she said. "I almost panicked."

"You were fine," Holden reassured her, wanting to give her confidence.

"I thought I almost blew our cover," she continued as he redirected their movement toward base camp.

"We deflected them for now but there could be more hikers, and since your face has been splashed all over the media we can't be too careful," he said.

"Right," she agreed.

"So, we find what we came for and get out of here before we run into anyone else." Holden located a walking path.

"I thought your dad owned this land," she said. "Why not just kick people off?"

"First of all, I didn't want to attract any more attention to us than we already had. And this land is very near a hiking trail, so it'd be easy to end up on Pop's property," he clarified.

Back at camp, he produced a couple of power bars and bottled water. Ella already had her own travel toothbrush that she used after breakfast. Holden made quick work of doing the same and then built a small fire. Ella was already through the first box when he produced two tin cups of coffee.

The idea of going through more of his father's personal effects sat hard on Holden's chest.

"I'll never figure out how you do this so well, but I will forever be grateful that you can," she said with a little mewl that made him think of the similar sound she'd made when the two of them were in bed at Rose's house.

"You learn to make do with what you have in the military."

"Thank you for your service, by the way. I meant to say that earlier," she said, and the reverence in her voice made his chest fill with pride.

"You're welcome." Holden drained his cup and joined her at the boxes.

The ones with clothes had already been stacked next to the storage shed, so he pulled out a few more. One by one they were working their way through them. Nothing stood out in the memorabilia, except the depressing note that the most important items in his father's entire life could fit into a ten-by-twelve-foot shed.

"I thought for sure we'd find something here," he said, doing his best to hide his frustration as he stared at the last couple of boxes. This was turning out to be another dead end and they needed to get on the move again before anyone else stumbled upon the place.

"We've checked everything in these." Ella motioned toward the line of opened containers. There were a couple dozen. "Unless you think there might be something in one of those clothing boxes."

Going through his father's personal effects caused a lump to form in Holden's throat. He could only imagine what it would be like to go through the old man's clothes. His trophies and metals were personal items, but garments were even more so.

"I guess it's worth a try," he agreed.

"We don't know what we're looking for, so how can it hurt?" she asked.

"True."

"This must bring back a lot of memories," she said and there was a sad note to her voice.

"It does," he admitted. "A lot of good memories."

She smiled.

"I just saw something move and I'm pretty sure it's a copperhead." The haughtiness in his voice should've warned her that he was goading her, but she hopped to her feet faster than he'd ever seen lightning strike.

"Where?" She froze, holding perfectly still as she searched the grass.

Hearing Holden's laugh rumble from his chest had her swatting his arm. She drew her hand back pretty fast, and that got him laughing more. It was probably the stress of the last few days that had him needing a break.

"If you want my help, you're going to have to quit giving me a hard time." The pout to her lips made him want to kiss her again.

"Fine. We'll call a truce." He offered a handshake. She took it.

"No more teasing," he said. "It's just nice to have a normal conversation for a change."

Ella nodded. She shot him a look that said she got it. They both could use a sense of normalcy after everything they'd been through and what they faced ahead.

She dropped onto her knees and opened another box. "Do these make you think about what happened?"

"Yes. At first, I was filled with so much rage. I wanted to track down the men responsible for his and Karen's deaths." Holden paused, fighting back the images of Karen on his bed with blood everywhere and where his imagination always went thinking about what they'd done to his father. Guilt tore into him at the memories.

"What changed your mind?" Ella asked.

"I realized that if anything happened to me, the men responsible would never be brought to justice. I wanted to wait so I could get revenge on my own terms," he said.

"Being angry must come with the territory," she said. "I feel that way now sometimes and I get frustrated. It doesn't change anything. Won't bring back my father."

"Don't be too hard on yourself. From where I sit, you have amazing strength," he stated.

"Maybe from the outside." She pointed to the center of her chest. "In here, I feel like a fragile mess."

"Believe me, you're not." Holden moved to her side and tucked a stray strand of wheat-colored hair behind her ear.

"I wish I was more like you," she stated and it caught him off guard. "You're strong." She glanced at his chest. "And resourceful."

"You think that you're not?" he asked, trying not to let his emotions get the best of him because they had him wanting to pull her close. There was always an undeniable draw toward Ella. Were his emotions getting the best of him being around his father's things?

"I'm nothing like you," she pointed out.

Holden broke into a smile. "That's probably a good thing. I'm stubborn and difficult."

"I was going to say focused and intelligent." It was a good thing she didn't look up at that moment. Holden fisted his hands to keep them from reaching for her.

"You said your dad was into baseball." She held up a card. Holden took a couple of strides toward her. The card was encased in plastic, a collector's edition Hank Aaron. "He was my father's all-time favorite player."

"He's a legend," she agreed.

"You know Hank Aaron?" Holden asked.

"Everybody knows him," she said matter-of-factly. And then she rewarded him with a smile. "Plus, I have brothers who were obsessed with baseball."

That made more sense.

"This is the only card in here. The only thing to do with sports at all." She held it up.

A flood of warm memories bombarded Holden as he took the offering. "I haven't even seen a game in years."

"Do you miss it?" Ella asked, and the question caught him off guard.

"I guess I haven't allowed myself to think about it. You get focused and shove everything else out of your mind in order to survive. All you think about is making it through each day."

"There's something perfectly simplistic sounding about that," she said. "No complications."

"Not much of anything. You can't let yourself focus on what isn't in your life." Holden looked at the card. "To do otherwise would ensure a slip."

"You didn't miss home?" she asked.

"Only one place remotely felt like home to me. Your ranch." He didn't look at her. Before he could get too caught up in nostalgia, he reminded himself the longer they hung around the more danger they were possibly in. They needed to stay on the move and they needed to get going.

"I'm glad you found me, Holden," Ella said.

"Yeah?" he asked.

She nodded. "Not just for the obvious reason that you saved my life. I mean that I'm glad it was you who found me."

He offered a smile. He was, too. He pocketed the card, hoping that keeping it with him would make him feel somehow closer to his father. The past two years had been about trying to forget. It was time to remember. Everything.

"I'd forgotten about how much Pop loved his favorite player," he said appreciatively.

"It was in there all by itself, so I thought it might be important to him." Ella went to work on another box.

Holden dug into the clothing box in front of him and his hand hit something hard. He felt around and realized it was metal. It was the size of a small cash box but sturdier. He pulled it out.

"What is that?" Ella stopped what she was doing and moved beside him.

Holden played with the heavy metal in his hands. "Some kind of lockbox."

He looked around for something he could use to break it open.

"I'm guessing you don't have the combination." She examined the strongbox along with him.

"All I need is a crowbar." He didn't have anything close on hand.

Ella disappeared inside the shed. "There's nothing in here."

Holden picked up a rock and Ella shivered when she got a good look at it.

He set the box down and dropped the rock. Nothing happened. Not even a dent. Holden dropped down to his knees and slammed the hard edge again and again against the box. Nothing.

"My dad has a few things like that at the ranch. He uses our birthdays as combinations." She pointed to the numbers on the side.

"Here goes." Holden entered his birthday.

More nothing.

Except voices. Holden listened. It was the trio from earlier and their voices were drifting up.

"Let's clear out," he said. "We'll take this with us and play around with it once we settle into a motel."

Side by side they took down the hammocks and replaced the moving boxes.

"Where are we going next?" She looked up at him with bright, trusting eyes after he closed and locked the doors.

"I plan to find a hot shower and a soft bed for our next stop," he said.

"That sounds like heaven." She clucked her tongue. "Actually, better than heaven. But I'm grateful that I got to brush my teeth this morning."

"Little things like that make a huge difference when you've lost everything," he agreed, securing the strongbox on the back of his motorcycle.

"They really do," she agreed. And then she took one look at the bike before shaking her head. "I don't think my body will allow me to get on the back of that thing again."

"It would take a lot longer to hike down the mountain, but we can if you want," he offered.

She eyed the motorbike and then the woods. "Were you kidding about black bears earlier?"

"Afraid not," he admitted. "We can do like I told the others and make a lot of noise on our way down. Believe it or not, those bears don't want to be around us any more than we want to run into them."

"As much as that may be true, we can't walk all the way back to Texas," she said on a sigh.

"I have a surprise waiting," he said. "If you can make it down the mountain."

"Then I'll get on the back of that thing again," she said, and he almost laughed at the sound of dread in her voice.

He handed over her helmet. At least it shielded her face. Especially when she put the visor down.

"If I end up with bugs in my teeth, I know who to blame," she said as she climbed on behind him.

"I'll take the hit for that one. Just don't smile," he quipped. Despite himself, Holden laughed and it was good to get a break from his somber mood. Going through Pop's things proved more difficult than Holden had expected, but having Ella there made it tolerable. He'd forgotten what it was like to have real companionship with someone he cared about, partly because he'd never connected with someone like he did with Ella. Yeah, he cared about her. He'd fallen down that rabbit hole. Couldn't say he was especially sorry either.

Talking to Ella was easy and he was starting to enjoy the way they bantered back and forth. This was real conversation and the closest he'd come to talking about something normal in two years. Before her, he didn't realize how much he missed it. Or course, he couldn't deny that he liked talking to her more than he'd ever liked talking in general. In fact, he didn't remember being all that into conversation before spending time with her. Few people made him laugh. Fewer got his sense of humor and laughed with him.

There was something special about Ella Butler.

ELLA LET OUT a yelp of excitement as she followed Holden into the standalone garage and stood in front of the sport-utility vehicle.

"This is our ride?" she asked. "Are you serious?"

"Belongs to a friend of mine who said I could take it anytime I needed to," Holden said. "I figured this was as good a time as any to take him up on it."

"Won't he miss it?" she asked.

"He would if he was in the country." Holden moved to the workbench in the detached garage. "As for now, he's a contractor for the US military and living in Jerusalem."

"You're sure he won't be upset?" She clapped. She couldn't contain her excitement any more than a kid could refuse an ice-cream cone on a hot summer day. This was just as good. It would have AC and doors and a real seat. The banana-like wedge on Holden's motorcycle had her bottom completely numb after an hour.

"Are you kidding? He'd insist." Holden felt along a wooden workbench before his hand stopped and he came up with a set of keys.

"We won't be putting him in danger, will we?" The last thing she wanted to do was involve anyone else in their problems.

"None that he wouldn't welcome if he were stateside," Holden said. He jangled the keys. "Ready?"

"Am I?" she said. "Are you kidding? I could kiss you."

Those last words hung in the air and had come out completely on impulse.

"I didn't mean," she started to say, but words were pretty useless. Her cheeks felt like they were on fire.

"Don't be embarrassed," he said. "I want you to feel like you can relax around me."

"I got a little too comfortable," she said along with an apology. "Because I wasn't joking."

"Don't be sorry," he countered.

"The problem is that I do want to kiss you, Holden. And that's not where we need to be right now," she said and walked to the passenger's side. She didn't exhale until the SUV blocked her view of him. It was true. She liked kissing him. And where would that get either one of them? They were on the run and their heightened emotions were running away with them. Realistically, Holden would move on as soon as she was out of danger. Sure, they had chemistry. That was obvious. But real feelings?

Ella couldn't even go there. Not with him. Not with anyone. Not until she sorted out her life and got a handle on the property. Once she was clear of this danger, she'd go back to her life on the ranch, her charity projects. That life made sense to her. This, being on the run with a magnetic roamer wouldn't last. He'd get bored and move on.

Besides, Holden was in love with a ghost and Ella couldn't compete with that. Not to mention the fact that neither had a future at the moment. She expected him to unlock the door but he didn't. Instead, he came up from around the back of the SUV.

"Where should we be?" he asked, and there was so much torment in his voice. Even so, his deep timbre washed over her, warming her.

"Probably inside this vehicle and on the road to Texas," she said, turning until her back was against the door. She couldn't look at him. Not right then. Because all her defenses would come crashing down around her feet and she couldn't be that vulnerable to him right now.

"Why not right here?" he asked, and his voice was husky as he trailed his finger along the line of her jaw. He dipped down and kissed her collarbone. A thousand volts shot through her as need welled up, low in her belly.

"Holden," she started but stopped.

"What about here?" He caught her stare for a few seconds and then dipped his head down again. This time, he kissed the spot where her pulse pounded at the base of her neck.

"We shouldn't…"

"Tell me to stop and I will," he said, holding her gaze. There was so much power and promise in that one look from him. This time, she knew better than to seek comfort in his arms. How many times had he pulled away from her every time they got close already?

She tried to form the words but couldn't. She wanted him to keep going until they were lost in each other, in complete bliss and a tangle of arms and legs.

So she looked him dead in the eyes.

"What if I can't?" she asked. "What if I want this?"

Holden swallowed, slicked his tongue across his lips and captured her mouth. He was warm and tasted like the coffee they'd had earlier. Awareness trilled through her at his nearness, at how fast his heart pounded. She brought her hand up to his chest and ran her fingers along the layers of muscle. She smoothed her hand over his masculine pecs.

He captured both of her hands in his, braiding their fingers, and lifted them over her head. Movement thrust her breasts forward and he groaned when the tips of her nipples brushed against him. They beaded and her breasts swelled, needing to be touched. He let go of her right hand and palmed her breast as she arched her back.

Ella opened her eyes and the world tilted when Holden did the same. A bolt of electricity shot through her and she immediately realized that she was in deep trouble.

"Can I keep going?" he asked.

"Yes," she responded without thinking—thinking would have her realize this wouldn't go anywhere. One night sounded amazing and great sex would dim some of the tension pinging between them...

All rational thinking stalled when he brushed his thumb across her nipple and her stomach quivered. Tension corded her muscles, needing relief that only Holden could give.

Ella leaned against the solid vehicle behind her and brought her hands up to Holden's shoulders. Her fingers dug into his shirt as he made her body hum with need by trailing his tongue across her collarbone. Not having sex had never felt so sexy.

His hands cupped her bottom and she wrapped her legs around his toned midsection after he lifted her off her feet. She tunneled her fingers in his hair and his tongue slid in her mouth as his erection pressed into her sex. A familiar force started building inside her body as her tongue roamed freely. She bit his bottom lip as ecstasy pulsed through her. All her senses heightened, her breath started coming out in quick bursts and she could feel that his was, too.

The fact that they were in a garage fully clothed took nothing away from the intimacy and heat of the moment.

"Holden," she managed to say against his mouth, breathless.

"I know." He nipped the conversation in the bud. "This can't go any further."

"Not right now," she said, trying to steady her rapid breathing.

He didn't immediately move and she was grateful.

"This, whatever's happening between us, is moving too fast," she said.

"I know." He surprised her with his response. "We need to take it slow."

"That would be smart," she said, even though her body begged for more.

"We have time to do this the right way," he continued.

A trill of awareness goose bumped her arms and her stomach free-fell. He feathered a kiss on her neck. And then another slow one against her lips. She loved the way he tasted.

"That's the only way I know how to do things," she said. There was so much craziness going on all around them, and yet this was the only thing that made sense to her. She'd never felt this strong of a pull toward another man and that excited and scared her at the same time.

"I could really like you," he said so quietly she almost didn't hear him.

Ella didn't respond. She just stood there with Holden for countless minutes, letting the world stop for just one moment. She wasn't grieving or running or scared. And the world had a strange sense of rightness that she'd never felt before.

Without analyzing it, she breathed in the calm feeling that came over her. Then she wrapped her arms around Holden's neck and looked him in the eye. He had that same hunger she felt deep in her stomach and she needed to let go with him. Life was crazy. Tomorrow wasn't guaranteed. They had *this* moment. Right now. Letting it slip through their fingers would be a costly mistake.

Ella pressed up onto her tiptoes and his mouth came crashing down on hers. No words were needed to move things forward. She could feel his body humming with the same awareness and desire rippling through her.

He brought his hand up and cradled her neck, tilting her head back a little as his tongue brushed against the tips of her teeth. She pushed him back long enough to help him out of his shirt and a few seconds later hers joined his on the floor.

Holden pressed his lips to hers as he cupped her breasts and groaned. "You're beautiful."

"So are you," she said against his mouth.

His hands wrapped around her back, unsnapped her bra and then it joined the shirts on the floor.

Her chest rose and fell quickly as tension heightened her nerves with anticipation. She brought her hands to the waistband of his jeans and tugged at the zipper. He helped her take his off and then her jogging shorts and panties flew to the floor.

She pulled his masculine body against her, her back against the SUV. His erection pulsed against her stomach and she wrapped her legs around his midsection as he lifted her. He eased her down on his full shaft, dipping the head inside and groaned with pleasure when he discovered that she was ready for him. She wiggled her hips until she could take in his full length.

"Holden," she whispered, tangling her fingers in his thick, wavy hair. The feeling of her naked skin against his brought on a wave of ecstasy and anticipation.

He drove himself inside her, his hands on either side of her hips as his mouth found hers.

She said his name again and he thrust deeper in response. Her entire body hummed with need as all her emotions heightened. She matched his thrust this time and then the next. Faster. Harder. Deeper. Until her entire body begged for release. His hands caressed her bottom as he drove inside her until she tipped over the edge of the precipice and free-fell as explosions filled her.

"Holden." She breathed his name as she felt him reach the peak. His muscles corded with tension as she ground her sex on his erection until he rocketed toward the same release.

She had no idea how long he stood holding her in the garage before he finally opened his eyes.

"Ella." Hearing her name spoken softly into her ear was the sweetest sound coming from him.

As her breathing returned to normal, Holden pressed his forehead to hers. He didn't immediately move away and she liked that he didn't. His hands cupped her neck and hers had dropped to his waist. It felt so right to stand there with him in the quiet.

Neither spoke as he eased her to her feet. Neither had to. The silence was comforting. He picked up her clothes first and she admired his glorious body for another few seconds before he dressed.

He gazed at her with a look of appreciation as she dressed and it felt like the most natural thing to be naked with Holden, another foreign feeling.

Once they were dressed, he palmed the keys. He clicked the button to unlock the door and then opened her side first.

Life was short and all her careful planning felt stifling now. Being with him made her feel alive. At first, she'd chalked it up to adrenaline rushes and danger. But it was Holden. What was so wrong with taking it a step further? Of completely letting go and being with this man in every sense of the words?

One word came to mind. *Love*.

Ella had fallen down that slope and risked her heart being shattered. Sure, she'd been with other men, but she'd never felt this deep of a connection during sex than she did with Holden. Mind-altering, heart-all-in sex.

And when he walked away, her heart would be shattered into a million tiny pieces and scattered across the ranch. She'd already lost her father. While this was no comparison, she couldn't risk losing anyone else. There wouldn't be enough pieces of her to pick up.

Their temporary shelter against the world was about to disappear. She knew full well that they couldn't stay there forever. And yet a piece of her heart wanted exactly that, to hide out with Holden until the rest of the world forgot about both of them, to stay in each other's arms, found instead of lost in the world.

"Ready?" he asked, turning the key in the ignition.

"As much as I'll ever be," she responded.

"Let's see what kind of trouble we can get ourselves into," he said with a wink and a smile that unleashed a thousand butterflies in her stomach.

Ella, who never let anyone break inside her walls, was in serious trouble.

Chapter Sixteen

The highway stretched on for miles. Ella had finally fallen asleep in the passenger seat. And Holden tried to ignore the ache in his chest. He'd stepped in where he had no business going earlier. Caring about her more wasn't going to help their…*situation*, for lack of a better word, one bit.

The physical attraction pinging between them was one thing. This was another. It was so much deeper than that. The air had changed between them after sex and he needed to protect her more than he needed to breathe. The problem was that nothing had changed. Being seen with him was still a death sentence. He had to figure out a way to give her back her life. He'd bring justice to the men who'd killed his loved ones. Holden was alive again for the first time in two years and his anger bubbled to the surface—anger that had been at a steady simmer since he'd walked inside his house and seen that lifeless body.

And he had a problem because his feelings for Ella were out of control. He needed to bring them back down to earth because they were dangerous for her. It didn't matter the pain it would cause him; he had to push her away for her own sake.

Could he, though?

Holden watched as cars zipped around him. Morning light was close and there was a motel off the highway where they could get a couple of hours of shut-eye. He grabbed a room key and walked her inside.

The place had two full-size beds and a decent shower, so they could clean up and get a nice meal not far from there. Holden had made this drive on his motorcycle more than once over the years. A piece of him felt contentment with Ella that he'd never experienced before. Leaving her was going to hurt like hell.

"You shower first," he said.

"Okay." She blinked her eyes up at him and he'd be damned but he kissed her.

Holden palmed his father's favorite baseball card as he waited for Ella to finish her shower. When this was all over, he would circle back to Rose. One way or another, this would end. Ella made him see that he'd stopped living, stopped caring. The only thing that had been keeping him alive was his promise to his father and the fact that Rose needed him.

He flipped the card around his fingers, frustrated that he was missing something. His father had been obsessed with Hank Aaron and then Rose had passed along the message 1-9-6-4, which could be a combination or address.

Holden studied the card.

"What are you thinking about so intensely?" Ella

asked, and he hadn't even realized she'd turned off the water.

"I'm missing something." He sighed sharply. "What does 1-9-6-4 mean?"

"A home address?" she asked.

"I thought about that, too. Seems like I would remember something and that could be anywhere." He held up the card and flipped it around his fingers. Staring at the back, he said, "1-9-6-4 could be 1964, as in the year."

Hank Aaron's batting average in 1964 was 340.

"What does 340 mean?" she asked.

He pulled the strongbox from his duffel and set it on the bed in between them. She looked up at him and it seemed to dawn on her.

"The combination." Holden punched in the numbers and the box cracked open. He thumbed through ledgers, pages and pages of documented illegal activity. His father was involved in illegal activity?

"Pop got himself into trouble," he said. From what Holden could tell, his father was being forced to use his interstate moving company to move other things. "And the Hampshire Police Chief is involved."

Ella touched his shoulder.

"They were after Pop all along," he said, and it was like a balloon in his chest had deflated when he exhaled.

"Why? Seems like he was cooperating." Ella studied the documents over his shoulder.

An envelope fell out of the papers with Holden's name on it.

He ripped it open. The note from his father read "If

you're reading this, things must've gotten bad. Chief Mallory approached me a year ago with an offer he said I couldn't refuse. He wasn't kidding and made it clear. I cooperated. At first, it was small stuff, a little bit of narcotics and weapons. It grew fast. Then one of my drivers disappeared with a shipment. Forgive me? Love, Pop."

"They must've tried to get to him through you," Ella said.

"All this time I thought it was my fault. I thought I did something to cause the deaths that followed me. I thought I was responsible for Pop being killed." Holden fisted the paper. A mix of sadness and anger and a little bit of hope that this could end filled him.

"I bet the people who showed up at your place that morning thought they would find you, wanting to use you against your father." Ella sat back on her knees. "Karen was in the wrong place at the wrong time."

"That cost her her life, which is something I take seriously."

Ella nodded. "The cop tried to kill you. The police chief must've believed you knew or were in on it somehow."

"And then I went into hiding and they couldn't track me. They tortured and killed Pop because they believed he was involved in that shipment disappearing," he said, anger filled him. "I wish I'd known what Pop had gotten involved in."

"Your dad must've realized how deadly this information could be," she said. "He was trying to protect you."

Holden no longer cared what happened to him. He

had to bring the chief to justice for his father and Karen's sakes. Otherwise, their deaths meant nothing. "There was a young attorney general who'd been trying to make a case against the chief for something. I can't remember what exactly. I don't even know if he's still after the chief, but I need to turn this information over to him."

"First, we'll call. Make sure he knows this is coming from you and that you are in no way involved," she said. "And then we'll FedEx the documents. This is all the proof he'll need to bring the chief to justice."

"I don't want to wait. We can stop off on the way to Cattle Barge to send these," he said.

"We'll make a copy. Just in case," she said.

"Let's get out of here." Holden dared to imagine a normal life again. Friday night date nights and a cold beer while watching a game. It had been out of reach for so long that it seemed foreign now. Like all that was a lifetime ago, similar to when he'd returned from overseas after three tours.

And it was still at arm's length. Because he was still wanted for murder.

THE MOTEL ROOM was wiped down and empty inside of twenty minutes. Tension radiated from Holden as he took the wheel of the SUV.

"It's going to work out," Ella reassured, noticing the white-knuckle grip Holden had on the steering wheel.

"What if they've gotten to the attorney general?" He started the engine and navigated out of the pay-by-the-night motel parking lot. "He may want to strike a deal instead of clearing my name."

"He won't," she reassured. "We have definitive proof that you weren't involved and if the attorney general doesn't want to do the right thing, we'll go to the media."

Holden nodded and she was satisfied that he believed her.

"I wish Pop would've told me before. I could've prevented his death." He pulled onto the highway.

"And involve you even more?" she asked. "He loved you too much for that. You would've taken this up for him and he knew it. You would've ended up dead and he wouldn't have been able to live with himself."

"I had a chance. I could've gotten to him sooner," he said, and she could see the torment he was putting himself through.

"You have to accept the fact that even though you're a grown man capable of defending yourself and everyone else around you, your father is still your father. If he's anything like you, and I'm guessing the apple didn't fall far from the tree, then he would rather trade his life if it meant saving yours. Besides, he probably blamed himself for not figuring a way out of this sooner."

Holden paused thoughtfully. He focused on the patch of road ahead with a nod.

"I just wish he hadn't been so stubborn," he said. "I could've kept him alive."

"I'm sorry, Holden. I really am. Fathers are hardwired to protect their children no matter how old we are. Yours sounds like a good man, an honest man until his back was against the wall. He didn't deserve what happened to him. And neither did you." She twirled a pen in between her fingers.

Holden gave her a look of appreciation.

"There was no way I could've hurt Karen. I hope the attorney general will be able to see it. I wasn't even there when it happened," he said.

"The attorney general won't overlook that fact," she reassured.

"I hope you're right because you know what the implication is if you're wrong," he said.

She did know. It meant that they were about to turn over the only true evidence in the case, the only evidence that could clear Holden. "We'll make a copy and keep the original. We'll threaten to use the media if he doesn't cooperate. It'll work out."

"I wish I had your optimism."

Morning traffic was thickening as the sun rose.

Ella sipped the coffee that he'd bought from the mini-mart. It tasted burned in comparison to the stuff Holden made over nothing but a few fire logs, but the caffeine would do the trick. "This attorney general person, is he legitimate?"

"I believe so," he said.

"First impressions are usually right." Even when he had a beard covering his face and hadn't spoken to a person in almost two years, Ella had known that there was something still good about Holden. She was intuitive enough to realize that he was holding something in, too.

His demeanor had changed like it did every time their defenses started tumbling down. It never lasted long and she could see that he was still holding on to the past. He'd never be able to move into the future—a future that she was beginning to hope that the two of them could spend getting to know each other better— if he couldn't let go of the past.

"I guess." He shrugged, keeping his focus on the stretch of highway in front of them. "We'll stop off along Interstate 40 to give the impression we're heading west. It'll add time to our trip but it'll be worth it. In case."

Holden didn't finish. The rest of that sentence involved what would happen if the attorney general didn't believe him. And they both knew what that meant. She could eventually go home but he would have to disappear. Again.

THE CALL WITH the attorney general, Calvin Edwards, had gone better than expected. Holden had tilted the phone so that Ella could hear. He'd said he wanted her perspective. She'd had a good feeling when they ended the conversation.

An hour later, they stopped off at a mailing center.

"This will give Edwards everything he needs to go after them," Holden said to Ella under his breath at the copy company's business center. He placed the package inside the small mailing box and sealed it at the self-check counter. "If it makes it."

"It will," she urged. "Make sure to get a signature."

"And receive confirmation where?" he asked.

She thought about it for a moment. "My email should be fine."

"No way," he said.

"Why not?" she asked. "It's perfect. You don't have one and no one involved would connect me to your father's case."

Holden conceded. He punched in the mix of letters and numbers as she spoke. He printed the mailing label and placed it on the small box before taking to the cashier.

"Two years is a long time." Holden leaned down and brushed a kiss on her lips after taking a deep breath.

"The timing of this is perfect," she said. "Everyone involved has moved on. No one is expecting evidence to show up now. It'll come out of the blue. You stay under the radar a few more weeks, like Edwards said, and the key players will already be in jail."

As they walked out, Holden fished his cell out of his pocket and held it flat on his palm. "Your turn."

"Sheriff Sawmill, this is Ella Butler," Ella said into the phone after dialing a number.

"I have good news for you, Miss Ella," Sheriff Sawmill said. "We have Suffolk's son in custody."

"Why? What happened?" She tilted the phone so that Holden could hear.

"The shell casings on his father's shotgun matched those at the crime scene. When we hauled his father in, he did the right thing and stepped forward," he said. "Suffolk's gun wasn't stolen and his son took it right from inside the back door."

Ella looked at Holden, searching for something that she wasn't sure could exist so early in their relationship.

"It's over, Miss Ella. We got him. Handcuffed him this morning," he said. "It's safe for you to come home."

"He's responsible for both attacks? For the rock at Devil's Lid?" she asked. Tears brimmed at that last word because without her father she wondered if Hereford would still feel like home. What would it be now? An odd feeling settled in her chest. Nothing felt the same anymore, nor had it since her father's death, and she doubted it ever would again. And she had to wonder how much the man standing next to her influenced that.

"We believe so," Sawmill supplied.

"Thank you, Sheriff," Ella said.

"I didn't want to release a statement to the media until I delivered the message to you personally," he said. "They're outside now."

It would be all over the news soon.

"I appreciate it," she said. "Can you give me five minutes to tell my family that I'm okay?"

"You bet," Sheriff Sawmill said.

The two exchanged goodbyes and she made a quick call to May, who promised to let the others know immediately.

"Everyone's fine, other than my sister having the flu. It's over. And I should feel more relieved," Ella said to Holden.

"Do you think they have the wrong guy?" he asked.

"I wouldn't say that exactly. I'm not sure what's wrong." She couldn't pinpoint what was going on in her mind. "It's probably just me. I'm off. This whole experience has been surreal and it's just hard to believe that it's all over. Everything feels different about the ranch now. The second I start to feel relief about going home

I realize that my dad's not going to be there. Suddenly, Hereford doesn't feel as much like home as it used to."

Holden took her in his arms and she buried her face in his strong chest. Those strong arms of his wrapped around her and she couldn't deny that this felt like home.

"Will you come back with me?" She blinked away tears and looked up at him.

"I should check on Rose," he said before pressing a kiss to her forehead.

"We could send for her. She hasn't been away in a while and she might enjoy being on the ranch for a few days." Ella wasn't sure if she'd convinced him but Rose was always welcome at Hereford.

Holden stood there for a long moment. Ella pressed up to her tiptoes and placed her hands on his shoulders. She looked into his eyes before kissing him. There was no hesitation in his reaction, his lips pressed to her and his tongue tasting her.

Ella pulled back first and looked into his intense blue eyes. "Can you give me a few more days?"

His face broke into a smile as he trailed his finger along her cheek. "You can be convincing when you set your mind to something, can't you?"

"Only when it's the right thing to do," she countered, matching his smile. "Does that mean you'll stay?"

"Yes."

She wrapped her arms around his neck and rewarded him with another kiss. Happiness lifted the weight from her shoulders. They were going home. Even if Hereford was a temporary stop for Holden.

Chapter Seventeen

Being back in Cattle Barge reminded Ella of what a media circus the town had become. A hot shower, May's cooking and Holden nearby would go a long way toward making her feel like she could deal with it all again.

Of course, she would feel better if she could access the memory buzzing around in the back of her thoughts. Trying to force it threatened to split her head open. "Remind me to take a couple of ibuprofen the minute we get to Hereford."

Even with the pain, her excitement was building.

"We have some." Holden kept one hand firmly on the wheel and the other reached around and retrieved the duffel.

"I forgot all about these," she said. They'd been on the road twelve hours steady aside from a pair of bathroom breaks since leaving the motel. Ten was pretty much her limit. Even in the comfortable SUV, the ride dragged on and it was probably because she missed being home so much.

"Are you hungry?" Holden asked.

"I can make it. Another forty minutes and we're

there." She was already thinking about May's cooking, the kitchen. The place was an old-world farmhouse with the oversize single sink, and had white cabinets and granite countertops. There was a hand-carved wooden table in the kitchen that stretched almost end to end. One side was used for food prep and the rest of the table was used for eating. She couldn't wait to show Holden around the main house.

To avoid traffic, she'd directed Holden to a back road. There was no way she wanted to face the media. Not now. All she wanted to do was get home and call her brothers. She wanted to check on her younger sister, Cadence, to see if she was recovering from the flu she'd caught as everything was going down about their father. Cadence rarely ever got sick and stress had most likely weakened her immune system.

"Feeling better?" Holden asked a few minutes later.

"They're starting to kick in." Thank the stars for pain relievers.

"Are you worried about being home again?"

"Not as much as I thought I would be," she admitted, and it had everything to do with the man sitting next to her. The feeling of missing her dad wasn't going away anytime soon, but she felt ready to face the fact that he was gone, and that was a huge step for her.

Ella leaned her head back. A comfortable silence sat between them as Holden navigated the country road and she waited for the last of her headache to ease. She checked the time. They were ten minutes from home now and Ella's excitement only increased now that she was so close to Hereford.

Out of nowhere, the sound of a bullet split the air and the SUV spun a hard right. Ella gasped as the vehicle rammed into a tree. Airbags deployed. The next thing she knew she heard a door open and saw Holden being dragged out of the driver's seat.

It took a second to register that he wasn't fighting back. Was he conscious?

Ella tried to work her seat belt but it wouldn't budge and her fingers were so shaky. Panic seized her lungs as she tried to climb out anyway. How had the man gotten Holden out so quickly? She craned her neck to the left and then to the right but couldn't find him. "Holden."

The fact that there was no response chilled her to the bone.

"Holden," she shouted, louder this time.

A hand wrapped around her mouth. She tried to bite the fingers. Failed.

"You just won't die," the masculine voice said. And she absolutely knew that this man was there for her. Because that memory she'd been trying to reach came crashing down around her at the sound of his voice. He'd shouted for her to stop when she'd taken off running. He was the man who was trying to kill her, Troy Alderant. He was the developer who'd tried to buy Suffolk's land.

Old Man Suffolk's son was in jail. He'd confessed. Why would an innocent man confess to a crime he didn't commit? All the details of the conversation she'd had with the sheriff jammed in her brain. Nothing made sense. Except from somewhere deep down she knew this was the man Sheriff Sawmill should be looking for.

She was jerked out of the passenger seat and then

thrown onto the unforgiving dirt. Her hands were rammed behind her back and tied. She struggled, kicking and screaming.

But Alderant was strong. Too strong.

"Holden," she shouted out of panic and desperation.

She rolled over in time to see a leering face coming toward her. "Why are you doing this?"

"You and your little pet projects. You couldn't leave well enough alone, could you?" he mumbled. "You don't have my vision for Cattle Barge and that's your problem. Donating more land for animals instead of taking advantage of the lake as a destination is beyond me."

What was he talking about? He'd been around the past year or so, trying to get involved in local politics. Was he trying to develop the land for something? He must've had his eye on Suffolk's land and the surrounding area.

And she'd accidently gotten in his way.

"We were coming to terms until you ruined it," Alderant said, dragging her by her feet behind the SUV.

If he'd put his plans out in the public too early, residents would've denied it. People had been trying to develop the lake for as long as Ella could remember. Proposals were always being shot down in town hall meetings. This guy must've figured if he bought up enough of the land, he'd have more voting rights. Once he hit the tipping point he could make his plans known and no one would be able to block him.

Ella gasped. Could he be responsible for her father's murder? "Why'd you kill my father? Did he find out about your plans?"

A strangled noise tore from his throat. "I didn't. Your father's death was the best thing that ever happened to me. He was always in Suffolk's ear and the old man wouldn't have sold his land without Butler's approval. I wish I'd thought of killing him. I seized the moment, figuring if I got rid of you I'd be set. Your siblings don't share your passion for animals. No one would've been left to block me. I'd followed you for days when you took that walk on Devil's Lid. I saw my chance to make this go away, to make *you* go away and to keep my name out of it. Everyone would assume your father's killer had set his sights on you."

Ella kicked harder as she realized the other end of the line that tied her hands together was being secured around the back of the SUV.

"But there was a confession," she said.

"To keep his old man out of jail, I presume." The icy voice sent chills down her spine. "You can fight all you want. This time, you die."

A figure launched toward Alderant. Holden?

The two went down in a tangle of fists.

"Grab the phone, call 9-1-1 and get out of here," Holden shouted to Ella.

She used the SUV as balance to get to her feet. Her hands were still tied together behind her back and she needed something to cut the tie. Her pulse raced as she moved toward the open door of the SUV and raked the corner between her hands. Her wrists hurt like hell but adrenaline dulled the pain.

It felt like it took forever to break free from her bindings. She immediately located the cell and called 9-1-

1, as instructed, keeping one eye on the fight going on a few yards away from her. The two were on their feet now as she relayed details of their location to the dispatcher.

Holden slammed his fist into Alderant's face. His head snapped backward. The two struggled for something. *A weapon?* And she watched in horror as a metal blade was driven into Holden.

Ella screamed and Alderant glanced toward her, giving Holden the second he needed to regain the upper hand. Holden took the knife, tossed it far away and landed a punch so hard Alderant fell backward.

In a beat, Holden was straddled over Alderant, pounding him until he went still. And then Holden dropped, too.

"Holden." Panicked, Ella ran to him as he lay splayed out on his back. He looked like a doll someone had tossed onto the floor in a hurry and then left behind. His legs were bent and twisted at odd angles. There was blood everywhere, soaking his shirt and jeans. She couldn't even allow herself to think that anything had happened to him as she dropped down beside him. Her lungs felt like they would collapse and her throat closed up. Her chest seized as she saw him there, helpless. He'd taken that knife for her.

Ella folded forward next to his ear. His eyes were closed and he didn't move. Was he breathing? Panic squeezed her chest, making it almost impossible to take in air as she heard the faint sounds of sirens in the night air.

"Breathe," she said in his ear, fighting against the

wall of emotions threatening to break down and come crashing around her. She searched for a pulse on his wrist, any sign to tell her that he was still alive.

And then his eyes blinked open. Those gorgeous blue eyes of his. Tears streaked her cheeks.

"I love you," she whispered into his ear. "Stay with me. Please."

His eyes closed as the cavalry arrived.

"Help us, please," she said to the first officer on the scene. "That man caused us to wreck and stabbed my boyfriend."

Alderant was still knocked out cold as he was cuffed. He was going to jail for the rest of his life.

At least for Ella, justice would be served. As for her father, she was resolved to help the sheriff find the person responsible.

THE RIDE TO the hospital in the sheriff's SUV seemed to take forever. Once there, the coffee tasted watered-down but she was grateful for the caffeine boost after she'd downed several cups. There never was much else to do in a hospital while waiting on a loved one than drink cup after cup. She'd paced the halls the entire night even though the doctor had visited with her hours ago and said that Holden would be okay. She'd asked to see him but the doctor asked her to wait until Holden woke. That was four hours ago.

"Ma'am?" a female voice said, startling Ella out of her thoughts.

"Yes."

"You can go in now," the nurse wearing the name tag Roberta said.

"Thank you." Ella didn't waste time turning down the hall and rushing past the nurses' station. She already knew Holden was in room 132. She pushed open the door, scared of what condition she might find him in.

"Finally, the view is worth looking at in here," he said with a smile that reminded her of the fact he was on pretty good pain medication.

"Holden." She rushed to his side and took his hand. "How do you feel?"

"Better now."

She eased onto the side of the bed, afraid she'd hurt him if she moved too fast.

"You can't hurt me," he said with the smile that was so good at breaking down her walls.

"Doctor says you're going to be fine." She looked into those blue eyes of his. Those gorgeous blue eyes.

"He'll let me out later today if everything goes well," he said.

"Is that a good idea?" Panic gripped her.

"Yeah. I want to be with you."

"I'll stay here," she offered.

"It's not a bad injury. I'll be fine by dinner. And there's something I need to say that can't wait."

Ella tensed, afraid he was about to drop the bomb that it was time the two of them parted ways. Her heart would shred but she forced a game face.

"Life without you isn't living, Ella. I'm all in. I'm in love with you and I'd be the happiest man on earth if you would do me the honor of marrying me. I know it's early and we haven't had a long time to get to know each other. But I feel like I've known you all my life. I've made a lot of mistakes but this is a choice I feel good about. The choice I'm making is *you*."

Ella dared to hope this could be real because she felt it just as strongly. "Are you sure this isn't the medication talking?"

"Not a chance. I want to spend the rest of my life with you, but I'll wait until you're sure."

"I don't need time. I need you. Yes, I'll be your wife." Ella wiped away joyful tears streaming down her cheeks. "I fell in love with you the second I looked into your eyes and saw what kind of man you really are, the one I want to spend the rest of my life getting to know even better."

"I love you, Ella," Holden said as he looked up at her. There was so much love in those blue eyes. "I'm done drifting. You're my home."

A WAVE OF gratitude washed over Ella as she woke from a good night's sleep in her own bed for the second time since Aldcrant's arrest. The other side was empty, so Holden must already be up. The doctor wouldn't be thrilled but she had a feeling that Holden had a good handle on what was best for him while he recovered.

Besides, knowing him, he was probably making a cup of coffee for May. Lucky her. Ella was more than pleased that two of the most important people in her life got along so well. Her brothers would most likely be more critical, protective instinct being what it was, but Holden was exactly the kind of guy they'd hang out with. And soon the two of them would be married. Her brothers would never argue against a man who made her this happy.

Ella stretched and pushed off the covers. She could use caffeine and a pair of pain relievers.

The news had broken last night about the scandal involving the chief of police. Apparently, the attorney general had wanted to act fast before word leaked of the kind of evidence in his possession. The internet couldn't get enough of replaying a police chief in handcuffs. Holden would finally see justice served for his father and Karen. And when he'd gone to bed last night, it was as if a weight had been lifted.

Ella moved to the dresser to find a pair of jogging pants to throw on so she could find her fiancé. Rose would be flying in later today and Ella couldn't wait for her to see Hereford.

A folded piece of paper caused Ella to freeze. She'd forgotten about the note her father had left there before his death. She picked it up, thinking that his hands had touched the same places not so long ago. Ella pressed the paper to her chest and forced back the tears threatening.

She opened the paper and read the words.

You haven't hiked Devil's Lid since you were little. A trip there might just help you find where you belong.
—D

Ella's heart fisted and tears streamed down her cheeks as she realized that her father had been trying to lead her to Holden. That, even now, she felt like her father was looking out for her.

And even though he was gone, she knew in her heart that he would always watch over her.

* * * * *

LET'S TALK
Romance

For exclusive extracts, competitions
and special offers, find us online:

Or get in touch on 0844 844 1351*

For all the latest titles coming soon, visit
millsandboon.co.uk/nextmonth

*Calls cost 7p per minute plus your phone company's price per minute access charge